"Madeline Hunter . . .

embodies the best of the genre."
—*Publishers Weekly* (starred review)

SHAMELESS

He slowly crossed the few feet that separated them. Her heart pounded so hard it intruded on her breath.

He gazed into her eyes as if she held no secrets from him. "So very delicate, like perfect porcelain." His fingertips lightly touched her face, and his gaze followed their path down her cheek.

A glorious tremor of pleasure thrilled down to her toes. She groped to keep some hold on herself, but that touch defeated her.

His firm hand cupped her chin and gently tilted her head. Warm lips brushed hers.

That felt so good. It had been so long, so achingly long since she had been touched and kissed. Her body reveled in the arousal streaming through her.

She shamelessly waited for more.

Praise for *The Romantic*

"Every woman dreams of being the object of some man's secret passion, and readers will be swept away by Hunter's hero and her latest captivating romance." —*Booklist*

Praise for *The Sinner*

"Packed with sensuality and foreboding undertones, this book boasts rich historical details and characters possessing unusual depth and vitality, traits that propel it beyond the standard historical romance fare." —*Publishers Weekly*

"Sensual, intriguing, and absorbing, prolific Hunter scores again." —*Booklist*

"There are books you finish with a sigh because they are so rich, so tender, so near to the heart that they will stay with you for a long time. Madeline Hunter's historical romance *The Sinner* is such a book." —*Oakland Press*

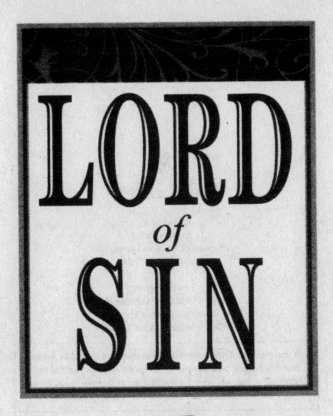

LORD *of* SIN

Madeline Hunter

BANTAM BOOKS

LORD OF SIN
A Bantam Book / May 2005

Published by
Bantam Dell
A Division of Random House, Inc.
New York, New York

Bantam Books and the rooster colophon are registered trademarks of
Random House, Inc.

ISBN 0-553-58730-7

Printed in the United States of America
Published simultaneously in Canada

www.bantamdell.com

OPM 10 9 8 7

This book is dedicated to all teachers who light fires of imagination, hope, and curiosity in their students. The good ones guide young minds, and the great ones inspire new dreams.

LORD
of
SIN

CHAPTER ONE

~

The Earl of Lyndale was dying.

Again.

He lay shriveled and frail in his bed, cheeks sunken and skin wan. His right hand rested over his heart as if he waited to feel its last pulse. He presented a pitiable image of an old man facing the end.

Ewan McLean was not impressed. His uncle Duncan pretended to lie at death's door at least once a year. Each imminent departure from the earthly realm summoned his sons and nephew so they could ease his passing. While on his deathbed he issued demands and extracted promises of outrageous presumption. Then he would "recover" and use those promises like a whip to get all the cattle lined up in the direction he had decided they should go.

"I fear the end will come tonight." The earl spoke it like a line in a stage drama. Which, for all intents and purposes, it was. "I need to set matters in order before I go."

He held out a trembling hand.

Ewan took it and smiled indulgently. He had been here for four days, waiting for the earl to decide when to finish the game.

"Since Hamish is not here, I must confide in you," the earl said, referring to his heir.

Ewan was all too aware that Hamish was not here. Right now Hamish and his younger brother were enjoying fresh air and sunshine on the Continent and not sitting in this drafty old castle in a room hung with heavy green drapes. The same faded fabric framed the earl's body on the big bed, falling in languid swags like stage curtains.

The interruption of Ewan's visit to London by the summons had been irritating enough, but the discovery that his cousins, the earl's own sons, had escaped the call by going abroad, really annoyed him.

"I will confess that I am glad it is you, my boy. Hamish would not have understood the matter that weighs on me. You know how he is."

"I certainly do." All too well. Hamish had grown into one of those purse-lipped, morality-spewing, judgmental Scots. When the earl eventually died, which Ewan expected would not happen for another decade or so, Ewan anticipated that Hamish would try to reform his cousin by threatening the allowance that augmented Ewan's income from his modest property.

His uncle had never been so intrusive in his private life, but then, his uncle had a history that did not permit umbrage over bad behavior without considerable hypocrisy. The current Earl of Lyndale had been a rake in his youth and a roué in his maturity. Ewan suspected that the fair-haired woman floating about the castle today was the current mistress.

In short, the earl had more in common with his nephew than with his sons. If he chose to play at dying when only Ewan was available, that meant his demands for promises this time probably had to do with matters that only another rake would take in stride.

"There is a letter that explains it all." The earl pointed his trembling hand toward a writing table. Ewan watched the arm and finger stretch out while the earl rose on one shaky arm. His pose imitated that of a dying father in a painting by Greuze. An engraving that reproduced the painting was in Uncle Duncan's extensive fine-print collection, its theatrical sentimentality obviously appreciated often by its current owner.

"You must give the letter to Hamish. You must swear that you will see that he carries out my wishes that are contained in it."

"I will be in no position to do so. He will be the earl. I will remain a dependent relative and can demand nothing of him."

"Tell him you are bound by your promise to me."

"That will be of no account to him. You are asking that I harass a man for the rest of my life. That I pound my head against a stone wall. It isn't fair to make demands that I cannot fulfill."

"You can make him see that it must be done, if you put your mind to it. You are far more clever than he is."

Ewan was losing his patience. Being blackmailed into his own promises was one thing. Being forced to ensure that others acted in compliance with Uncle Duncan's whims was another.

"What is this vitally important matter, Uncle?" Attending the next sheepshearing? Escorting some cast-off mistress to a ball? The earl's demands were never dreadful, just damned inconvenient and often boring.

"I did a grievous offense to a man in my youth. The next earl must right this wrong."

"What kind of wrong?" Most likely his uncle had bedded a friend's wife. For all of his envy of the last century's ribald behavior, seducing a friend's wife was something Ewan himself would never do. Once, when he and Uncle Duncan had gotten foxed together, he had tried to explain to the old goat how that was dishonorable. Uncle had simply been unable to grasp the nuances.

"I was vengeful and went too far. It has preyed on my conscience ever since. I had intended to right matters, but now . . ." His hand went to his heart again.

"Well, if it is something that the Earl of Lyndale should do, then you can still make it right yourself. When you are better."

"I will never be better. I tell you, I am dying." Uncle Duncan spoke emphatically, with powerful strength of voice. His dark eyes glared out from under his bed cap's edge and his color rose to a nice, healthy pink.

Ewan experienced profound annoyance. This entire drama had been so unnecessary. There had been no reason for Uncle Duncan to pretend he was dying. There had been no justification in dragging Ewan from London and from the delicious pursuit of pretty Mrs. Norton.

"Swear it," the earl demanded. He sat upright, looking fit and hale and ready to ride for twenty miles. "Would you allow me to go to my grave with this unfinished, with no assurance that this sin will be mitigated? Ungrateful wretch! I will make a codicil to my will at once and cut you out without a penny. I will—"

Here it came, the blackmail. The threats. Really, Uncle Duncan should hire a writer to devise a new set of lines.

"—leave a letter for Hamish, telling him to cut off your allowance. I will—"

"Fine, I swear," Ewan snapped. "I swear that I will do all within my power to see that the next earl fixes the problem that you created but never bothered to fix yourself."

It was a toothless promise to make. There would not be a "next earl" for quite some time. Swearing to do all within his own power meant little since he would have no power at all.

Uncle Duncan did not see the huge holes. His ire receded. He sank back into his pillow. He arranged for his body to go limp and for his cheeks to appear gray.

The earl vaguely waved Ewan away. Still annoyed, but also amused by the theatrics, Ewan played his role to the end. He got up, leaned over, and kissed Uncle Duncan's head affectionately before leaving.

That night the earl surprised everyone by actually dying. He passed quietly in his sleep.

Ewan was stunned by the unexpected turn of events, but he suspected his amazement was more than matched by that of the earl himself.

Two weeks later Ewan lay on a sofa in his chambers in London.

If life were fair he would not be reclining alone. Mrs. Norton would be here with him, receiving the lesson in love that he had long anticipated giving her. Right now he would be plucking at the laces of her stays, preparing to unveil her abundantly luscious beauty.

Instead, he'd had to beg off on their assignation. He could not move, let alone seduce a woman tonight. He could barely think.

He lifted a limp arm and raised the letter. He read the first line again. It was unbelievable. Incomprehensible. Just a month ago he was happy and innocent and going about his business, which was easy to do because he made sure his business only dealt with pleasure, and now—

His manservant entered, carrying a fresh bottle of wine to replace the one that Ewan had just finished. Swigged, to tell the truth. Gulped down as if it were rum and he were a sailor.

Another man came in, too. Ewan glanced up from beneath the arm draped over his forehead to see Dante Duclairc gazing down at him. Dante's limpid brown eyes showed more amusement than concern and a smile wanted to break out on his angelically handsome face.

"Duclairc. Good of you to come."

His friend's presence touched him, and a pang of nostalgia sounded in his heart. Dante Duclairc had not been in these chambers since he married Fleur Monley last spring. The parties that occurred in this apartment were a lot less fun now that Dante had been domesticated. Only a calamity such as had visited Ewan today would get Duclairc here now.

"Your message seemed desperate. Are you unwell? You look like someone in a bad Greuze painting."

"Disaster has struck. Complete and total catastrophe. Once you learn of it, you will understand why it has laid me low." He lifted the letter.

Duclairc took it and sat down on another sofa to read. He did not even notice the little bronze statue on the table beside his seat. The latest addition to Ewan's renowned collection of fine-art erotica, it was a Renaissance work displaying a nymph servicing Pan. Ewan had been proud of the acquisition yesterday, but his friend's indifference seemed appropriate to today's solemnity.

"Jesus," Dante said after peering at the letter for a few minutes.

"I knew you would appreciate how outrageous this is."

"It is certainly unexpected. And amazing. I do not know whether to congratulate you or help you to mourn."

"I'll be damned if I'm going to mourn. It was very inconsiderate of them. Hugely so. There should have been a law against both of them putting themselves in danger at the same time. Where was Hamish's sense? If he wants to climb a damned mountain and die in a damned avalanche, let him go I say, but to drag his younger brother on the adventure and risk their both dying in the same damned avalanche—" He closed his eyes. It was all too much.

"Pity that they both dallied in marrying."

"'Pity'? 'Pity'? Irresponsible! Look where their negligence has left me."

"It appears that it has left you the Earl of Lyndale." Indeed it had.

Hell.

Ewan swung his legs and sat up. "Make yourself comfortable. I plan to get drunk and need company. I trust you told your pretty wife that you will not be home soon."

"Fleur assumed you were in horrible trouble after reading the dramatic message you sent me. She insisted I come. She had no idea that the terrible news was that you have inherited a title and a significant fortune."

"Do not get sardonic on me, Duclairc. A man has a right to some warning on such a thing. There I was, assuming there were two strapping men between the title and me . . . What were the odds they would both die before one produced a son? Negligible. Damned near impossible, or at least reassuringly unlikely. And now . . ." He waved the letter that had come from Switzerland, then let it drop to the floor.

He looked down at it. Something nibbled at his dazed mind. Something just as unpleasant as that letter had been. He tried not to acknowledge its intrusion, but it nudged and poked until it had his stomach sinking.

"Oh, hell."

"Your shock is understandable, McLean, but you will be a fine earl. You will rise to the position. It will not disrupt your life as much as you think."

"Yes it will, but this 'oh, hell' was about something else." He got up, walked around the assortment of sofas and chaise longues that dotted the chamber, ducked past the swing hanging from the ceiling, and went to a writing table in a dark corner.

"I promised Uncle Duncan to give Hamish a letter should Uncle Duncan die, which I never expected him to do. I brought it here so that I could fulfill his final wish by handing it over to Hamish as soon as he returned to England." He pawed through a drawer for the infernal letter.

He brought it back to the sofa and stared at its seal. He gulped down another glass of wine.

I swear that I will do all within my power to see that the next earl fixes the problem that you created but never bothered to fix yourself.

"Duclairc, let me pose a philosophical question to you. Suppose a dying man extracted a promise from you, but you did not really believe he was a dying man, nor for that matter did he. Let us say further that both of you thought the ultimate responsibility would fall to someone else, but that a freakish coincidence caused it to fall to you. With all those peculiarities, wouldn't you say that—"

"No."

Ewan looked up to see Dante regarding him severely.

"Yes. Of course. You are right."

Well, hell and damnation.

"Perhaps you should read it. Maybe it is something very minor."

Sighing, he broke the seal.

"Well?" Dante asked.

"It appears that my uncle wronged a man named Cameron many years ago. Ruined him. He wants me to see that this Cameron and his family are cared for, that they do not want for anything. That is deucedly ambiguous. What if they want a coach and four? What if they want twenty thousand a year?"

"I think you would be safe to use your own judgment of what is adequate to ensure they are suitably cared for. I do not think your uncle means you have to hand them whatever their hearts desire."

"Good point. I knew having you here would be helpful. That is why I called for you and not one of the other lads. Marriage has made you so . . . sensible."

"There is no need to get insulting."

"My apologies." Ewan peered at the letter. "It seems this Angus Cameron lives all the way north, on the eastern border of Strathnaver. I get to pack myself back up to Scotland and brave the cold of the Highlands."

"*Angus* Cameron? My father knew an Angus Cameron. Spoke of him on occasion. They held a lively correspondence."

"Do you remember anything that was said about him? Uncle claimed this letter explained all, but he neglected to include just how he wronged this man."

"I only remember my father referring to Cameron as eccentric."

"That is not encouraging, Duclairc. Your father was more than a tad eccentric himself. If *he* used that word to describe Cameron, I could be facing a lunatic."

"I do not think it is as bad as that. I vaguely remember Father speaking of Cameron's erudition on ancient Celtic culture. Druids and whatnot. Unlike my father, who merely had an historical interest in such things, Cameron became more involved. There were some odd doings, but the fellow was only colorful, not mad."

"You are not making me feel better." Ewan

poured more wine. "I should have started with whisky. It would have done the job quicker. You must stay. I promise no women are coming. This entire matter has left me cold for such pleasures."

"You are indeed distraught enough to need my company if that is your condition. I never thought I would hear such words from you."

Hell, yes, he was distraught. In shock, and barely controlling his temper. He did not want to be the earl, and this business with Cameron was only one example of why. Everywhere he turned now people would probably be using boring words like "duty" and "responsibility" and "obligations."

"You probably should attend on that responsibility soon," Dante said, gesturing to the letter about Cameron, which had joined the other papers on the floor. "The duty will only get more onerous if you put it off. With winter coming, a journey to the Highlands should be made at once. After you fulfill your obligations at court, of course."

Ewan wanted to punch Duclairc in the nose.

It was all too much.

CHAPTER
TWO

~

"That should be it down there," Ewan said to Michael, his manservant.

"Lord be praised."

Ewan and Michael sat on their horses at the top of the hill and gazed into the glen where the home of Angus Cameron sat.

Highland vistas like this, with the treeless rolling hills and valley, with a sky so blue it blinded your eyes and air so crisp and clean it hurt your chest, inspired poetry.

The mutterings moving through Ewan's mind were not pretty verses, however.

After a hellish journey, most of it on horseback through icy rain and bitter fog and more than enough mud to fill this glen, here he finally was.

I hope that you are enjoying this, Uncle Duncan.

"Do not praise Providence yet, Michael. I do not expect the conclusion of this journey to improve our lot. Angus Cameron probably has six burly, red-haired sons who wear tartan kilts and hurl tree trunks for fun. No doubt the evening meal will be haggis."

"You do not have very kind words for your country-men, sir."

"I may be a Scot, but I am not fond of High-landers. Highlanders assume they are purer Scots than anyone else. They imply with their cocky grins that a Scot from the south is more English than Scot, in blood as well as loyalty. There are many Scots who never reconciled to the Grand Union into Great Britain, and lots of them live in godforsaken glens like this, on the edge of the world, being whipped by brutal weather that any sane person would flee."

He led Michael down into the valley, anticipating little welcome when he intruded. He had not written or contacted Cameron because that would give the man a chance to rebuff him. The last thing Ewan wanted was a recalcitrant victim prolonging the "making right" that needed doing.

Duty. Duty. He had been practicing that chant for two weeks now, ever since the ceremony at the House of Lords. Nothing like donning a coronet to carve the desolate message in stone. He was no longer Ewan McLean, man about town, gambler and drinker, lover extraordinaire and host of some of London's finest orgies.

Now he was a peer, a member of the House of Lords, and paterfamilias to a passel of relatives whose names he had made it a point never to know.

Worse, what had recently been an unremarkable life had now become notorious. Society had long ago ceased to notice his behavior, but suddenly it was grist for the rumor mill again. He had heard that already some unimaginative wag had dubbed him the "Lord of Sindale."

What a ludicrous development it had all been. The only good thing about this journey, and it was small consolation, was that it removed him from London, where several mothers of eligible daughters had sent him invitations to parties at houses that had never before received him.

He might be notorious, but now he was a notorious *earl*. Ladies who should know better apparently had no qualms about throwing their virginal daughters in the Lord of Sindale's path.

"I thought you said it would be a hovel. A dark, drafty, ancient cottage." Michael's blond head turned and he glanced back with resentment at the packhorse he had been dragging. "You made me bring good linens and soap, but it looks to be a house that will have its own."

It did look to be such a house. Uncle Duncan had said he ruined Cameron, but this house was the nicest one they had passed in many miles. It was not some thatched, wattle-and-daub cottage huddled in a township of others like it. This house was situated on its own and built of stone with two levels. It had attractive plantings all around it. A large stable stood to the north and a carriage waited out in front.

Perhaps the family hung on to their pride through

the property. Maybe they were one of those families that eats nothing but soup in order to keep up appearances.

"I say, sir, what is happening down there? Those people upstream?"

Ewan looked past the house to the congregation of dots about two hundred yards behind it. He hoped to heaven that he had not arrived on some festival day, or in the middle of a party or celebration. He really was not in the mood.

Since it appeared the household was busy by the stream, he and Michael passed the house and headed for the dots. They took on forms as they neared. A little group was watching something transpiring among three men.

Two of the men began walking away in opposite directions. Ewan was impressed by the determined expression of the blond-haired one heading his way. Then he noticed the pistols.

It was a duel.

The man coming toward him was much too young to be Angus Cameron. He looked to be no more than about eighteen. Ewan examined the other figure, the one heading in the other direction.

Cameron was dressed bizarrely, like someone in a Restoration costume drama. Boots, pantaloons, and a red doublet covered his body. He was tall and wiry, and his spry step implied the years had not taken much toll.

He wore a flamboyant brown hat with a broad brim and big red plume. It appeared this old man wore his ancestor's garments and had never purchased any of his own. Definitely *eccentric,* as Duclairc's father had said. Or too poor to hire a tailor. Well, it could have been worse. He could have been wearing Druid robes.

The pacing stopped. The red plume swished the air as Cameron turned. Ewan saw the face under the upturned right brim of the hat.

This was definitely not Angus Cameron.

It was a woman. Her steely expression made her appear hard and wise, but the face itself was fairly young.

The blond man turned, too. Pistols rose.

Jesus.

Ewan kicked his horse and galloped forward. Women in the little group cried out as he sped past. His thundering approach made the duelists pause long enough for him to pull up his horse between them.

He glared at the young man. "Good God, that is a woman over there. What are you thinking?"

"Ah'm thinkin' to shoot her 'fore she kills me."

"The hell you will. Stand down."

"Who are ye to interfere, mon?" The crisp, feminine demand bit into Ewan's ear.

He turned. The doublet and pantaloons hung loosely, but not so much that her curves were totally obscured. Wisps of curly red hair escaped the hat into which she had stuffed her locks. Her face was very lovely, with skin showing the translucent whiteness that marks a true Scottish beauty. Her bowed raspberry mouth and her delicately boned oval face competed with her jade eyes for his attention.

"I am Lyndale." It was the first time he had used the title to presume rights to do things that were none of his business.

"I hae ne'er heard o'ye. Now, move the horse so we can be done with this." She waved her pistol toward the southern hills, to emphasize just how far away he should go.

"You will not be done with this while I am here."

"Then leave. Gae on to where ye were headed."

"Since this glen is on the road to nowhere, it should be obvious that I was headed right here. Put down that gun, woman."

"Nae. Jamie MacKay has dishonored my sister." The plume angled toward a young girl in a brown cape with big, frightened eyes. "She is too young and stupid to ken the ways of men. He has been after her for months, and talked her into meeting him last night. Now, move yer horse so I can kill him."

Ewan eyed Jamie MacKay.

"Did you have her, boy?"

Jamie shook his head emphatically. Ewan shot a look at the girl in question. She shook her head, too.

He returned his attention to the older sister. "I said to put the gun down."

"The hell I will. Move yer horse's arse."

He dismounted and patted the horse's arse so it would indeed move. He walked toward the pointing gun. "Your sister says it did not go too far. You should believe her. Put down the pistol or shoot me, because I will not move out of the way."

Her green eyes sparked with tiny lightning bolts. For a moment he thought she might actually shoot. Deciding not to take the gamble that she was only half crazy but basically sane, Ewan flashed out his hand, gripped her wrist, and raised her arm up high. He pried the gun from her grasp with his other hand.

"Who are ye to stick yer nose into this? Mind yer own—"

He ignored her ravings and walked back to Jamie MacKay. The boy was looking far too relieved. A touch of smugness was inching on to his face.

Ewan only had two rules where women were concerned. No friends' wives, and no innocents. If the dishonor of the latter's seductions was obvious to him, of all men, he assumed it was abundantly clear to others.

"You did not have her, but you intended to," Ewan said quietly with a man-to-man smile.

Jamie could not entirely suppress a roguish grin.

Ewan swung his right fist. It landed in the young man's stomach with a satisfying *thud*. Breath *whoosh*ed out. The little group gasped in unison and Jamie fell to his knees. Ewan swung again, connecting with the pale face. Jamie fell back.

"Are you his second?" Ewan asked another young man who rushed over.

"His brother. Our father sent me lookin' for him when he didna come home last night. I got here just as she was bringing him out for this duel. Good thing he isna dead. That would take some explaining, what with the challenger being a woman."

"Yes, I expect that would be hard for the family to live down. Get him out of here before she finds another pistol."

"Get him oot o' here," a voice echoed at his shoulder. "Put him in yer father's fancy carriage and take him home and make sure he and all the others like him ken that the Cameron sisters arna their sluts for the takin'."

Ewan glanced at the plume and hat. She was very tall. Evidently she was also one of those irritating women who had to have the last word.

He ignored the feminine fury beside him and waved the boys away. Jamie staggered under his brother's arm toward the house. A bevy of cloaks strolled after them, subtly opening to absorb Michael and the horses. Ewan fell into step at the back of the procession.

Boots suddenly paced next to his. "Where are *ye* goin'?"

He kept walking and did not look at her. If he did they would get into a row, with her accusing him of interfering, which he had done, and his calling her a lunatic, which evidence indicated she was. He did note, however, how the legs that moved the boots looked quite slender from the knee up, despite the pantaloons.

Long legs. He had a lot of practice in imagining women without any clothes, and his mind's eye now saw the knees and thighs of this one, snowy white and naked.

He resisted the temptation to picture the rest of her. "I am going to this house to call on Mr. Angus Cameron. Would he be your grandfather?"

"My faither. What dae ye want with him?"

"I have important business to conduct with him. I have journeyed all the way from London to attend to it."

"That is a lang journey to accomplish nae mair than saving the sorry hide of Jamie MacKay. Ye should o' written. I could o' let ye know that Angus Cameron is dead. Has been these five years noo."

Ewan stopped walking. Wonderful. Just like Uncle Duncan to give him a mission, to provide directions, to demand action, but to forget to check whether the victim of the great sin was even still alive. It was a wonder he had not arrived in the glen to find the homestead in decay and the whole Cameron family living in Brazil.

On the other hand, the promise had not been about Angus alone. This news of Angus's death hardly relieved him of the obligation.

"I am sorry to hear that your father has passed. I will speak with your mother or brother, then."

"If I had a brother, do ye think I'd be fighting duels that he could fight?"

"Well, you appeared to be enjoying it so much."

"Listen, Mr. . . . um . . ."

"I am Ewan, *Earl* of Lyndale." He had considered never demanding use of his title from anyone.

However, right now, with this particular anyone, he enjoyed demanding it enormously.

"Well, Lord Lyndale, I didna enjoy it. It was necessary, however. There's those like Jamie who think my sisters are without protection, that no one will stop them if they try something, or call them out. Now I've reminded them all that isna so. I expect we will have a lot less trouble with such things for some months to come."

He barely heard her. His concentration had been distracted by how changeable her eyes were. Right now they appeared like emeralds, full of lively facets and sparks. And her skin was really very beautiful, quite fragile-looking, like the finest japon paper. She was not a girl, but probably in her latter twenties, and that made her beauty even more appealing.

"Are you saying there is no male relative here to protect your sisters? No cousin or husband?"

"Nae. It falls to me."

Ewan looked toward the house and the disappearing cloaks. It suddenly struck him that all the spectators had been women. "No male servant whom you could trust to guard the gate, so to speak?"

She chuckled, low and velvety. She shook her head, as if she had never met such a stupid man. "Well, now, that is like inviting a fox to guard the henhouse. Nae, sir, I am the best protection they have, such as it is. If ye came all this way to conduct business, ye are stuck with me for that, too. I am the head of this family now."

Ewan inwardly sighed. Somehow he did not

think that last pronouncement would be good news for his mission. He would much rather deal with an eccentric old man than a crazy young woman.

Duty called nonetheless. He'd deal with this responsibility forthwith. With luck, he would be on his way back to London in the morning.

Bride put Lord Lyndale in the library, sent his manservant to the stables with the horses, then hurried up to her chamber to change. As she tried to tame her hair into something that might have been fashionable at some point in history, Mary slipped into the room.

Bride looked in the mirror at Mary's downcast eyes. The morning's episode had been all Mary's doing, and Bride was not convinced that her youngest sister was nearly as contrite as she now appeared.

"Were ye really going to kill him?"

"Nae. I was only going to scare him good."

"I told ye nothing happened. That Lord Lyndale was right and ye should have listened to me."

Bride stuck some combs in her hair to hold the hopeless mass of long curls back from her face. "Dinna tell me nothing happened. I am the one who found ye, remember? He had yer dress half off and his mouth where only a wee bairn's or a husband's should ever be." She turned and wagged her brush at Mary. "Ye have nae fortune and nae dowry. Nae MacKay son is going to marry ye. He will take what he can get and then disappear into the mist, and there is no father or brother to make him do what is right by ye."

Mary nodded her blond head while her lips folded in with chagrin. Bride was not reassured. She had given this lecture to Mary before. The plain fact was, Mary was too pretty, and at sixteen years of age, already too appreciative of a man's touch and smile.

Well, nothing new there. It ran in the family.

"When ye go down, tell Jilly that I think Lord Lyndale intends to stay for dinner. With luck, I'll have him gone before the evening meal, however."

"Do ye think he has come from the duchess?"

"Nae." When she first saw the fine horse and the expensive coat, that was exactly what she had thought, however. She had come close to turning her pistol on him.

Only, the Duchess of Sutherland did not send lords to do her dirty work. Nor did she send her factors to explain her actions in advance. They arrived unexpectedly, sometimes in the middle of the night, to clear tenants off her lands so she could give the farms over to the sheep herds that made her rich.

For years she and her husband had been doing that to the south and west in Sutherland. "Agricultural improvements," they called it. Now they had bought this county, too, and were seeking to "improve" it, as well.

The death last summer of the Duke of Sutherland had not stopped the clearances. Two townships had been burned out in an eastern glen last month. Bride and her sisters had watched the displaced families straggle toward the poverty waiting on the coast. A woman who had given birth on the road was buried with her bairn in the nearby town's churchyard.

She prayed that this farm would be spared. She hoped that if the duchess's men came to clear them out, she could convince them to allow her and her sisters to stay in the house, even if the land was taken.

Mary took over with the combs and managed to make some progress. "Lord Lyndale is very handsome. Dinna ye think so?"

Bride definitely thought so. She already had a long list of the man's faults, and his looks were at the top of it. A face like that usually meant a man assumed he could have whatever he wanted in the world. Combine that with a title and you had nothing but condescension and arrogance.

"It was very thrilling how he just took command," Mary said.

"I am thinking that I need to marry ye off soon, dove. I'll find ye a handsome, masterful man whom ye can admire for two months before ye grow up and understand what that means for a wife. Then for the rest of yer days ye can serve his every whim and cry yer eyes out when he goes to his other women."

Mary mumbled something. Bride's ears burned. It had sounded like "a lot ye ken about it."

Bride let the mumble pass. Mary was alluding to Bride's own questionable judgment with men. The mutter caused a pang of worry and nostalgia in her heart, even as it made her sigh over Mary's willfulness.

Raising Mary had been the biggest responsibility among the many she shouldered. It was a miracle Mary had even been born, however, and that meant she had indulged her as a child and was paying for the laxity now. Angus had been old when Bride came, and very old at Mary's birth. Their mother's health could not bear the strain of the last lying in, and at twelve years of age, Bride had been left with three wee sisters and an elderly father to care for.

Jumping now, moving fast, she pulled on a dress and turned for Mary to fasten it.

"I canna take the time to scold ye further, Mary. I have to hurry downstairs. Lyndale didna come from Sutherland, but he could be here for more dangerous reasons. He said he was from London, which could mean trouble. He might even be here for the government."

Mary's eyes widened. "You doona think that—"

"What other business could he think to have with our dead father?"

She thought about that man sitting in the library. She wondered if he was so bold as to poke around in the writing table there. Or, worse, wander through the house.

"Go down and thank his lordship for saving Jamie's life. Distract him for a few minutes. I had better do something before I join him. And, Mary, tell the others there is to be no Gaelic or Scots spoken in the earl's presence. We will speak book En-

glish like he does, so he daesna think we are ignorant or easily guiled."

Bride slipped down the stairs and into the drawing
room across from the library.

She had not put Lord Lyndale here because this
room was not used for entertaining. Long tables
lined the northern wall beneath the windows. Four
chairs were set at intervals, and each place held im-
plements. Not eating utensils, but burins and awls
and metal rockers.

Only one place was being used this morning. Her
sister Anne sat near the window with the best light.
She held no burin, but a quill pen. Her head was bent
over a square sheet of paper.

"What in heaven are you doing?" Bride demanded.

Anne lifted her auburn head and blinked, as if
waking from a daze. "You said you needed them.
You said you were riding to town today and—" Anne
spoke in Gaelic, as they usually did among themselves. Only Mary resisted using it. As the youngest,
Mary had experienced the least of their father's influence, and she wanted to be modern.

"There is a stranger in the house, Anne, and Lord
only knows why he is here. This will have to wait.
Use some common sense, dear."

Anne watched with befuddlement as Bride
scooped up the paper and the stack of others nearby.
Anne often had a bewildered expression. The next

oldest after Bride, Anne was dreamy and distracted most of the time. Father had been sure she was a bit fey, and spent years trying to prove that Anne held some extraordinary sense or gift like talking to spirits.

Bride knew the explanation was much simpler. Anne merely had none of the common sense that Bride kept imploring her to use. She was not stupid, just vague. Anne never understood that one and one always, irrevocably, equals two. If presented with that truth she was apt to suggest that, given a certain perspective, it could be otherwise, and that two could well mean something other than one plus one if you only thought about it long enough.

Bride tucked the papers into a box in a drawer. She then hurried to the far corner of the room where the printing press stood.

She made very sure that nothing untoward had been left out after yesterday's project. Reassured that all was in order, she took several deep breaths to calm herself.

"Where is Joan?" she asked.

"She went to help that other man with his horses."

The other man had been as pressed and elegant as his master, and handsome enough in a young, fair way. Bride did not think a city servant would find Joan appealing, but— "Go and tell her Jilly will need some hare for dinner. Then she is to get back here quickly to clean up. Tell her she must wear a dress for meals today, and that if she does not change her boots I will make her do all the darning for the next month."

Deciding that all was in order, that her sisters were accounted for and ready to march to their instructions, Bride approached the library. She took two more deep breaths, called forth her "book English," and prepared herself to deal with the pain-in-the-arse intrusion of Lord Lyndale.

Yes, he was handsome. Lethally so.

That was the first thought that entered her head as she closed the library door behind her.

He had removed his fur-collared redingote. He stood near the fireplace, perusing a book he had removed from a high shelf. With his height, Bride judged he had not needed the ladder to reach it.

The cut of his black riding coat showed an athletic and broad-shouldered build. Fawn doeskin and high boots encased his legs. Bride wanted to think that his masculinity, so rare to behold in this house, did not affect her. Being an honest woman, she admitted it did. His presence had so totally taken over the small library that she felt as if she were the one intruding.

He looked over at her entrance. Thick, dark hair framed his face. His dark eyes, large beneath the perfect curves of his eyebrows, gazed at her long and hard. His wide mouth made a small smile that was not kind. His whole expression was one of barely contained annoyance.

The effect was to put her off her game immediately. She stood by the door like a mute.

"Thank you for your hospitality," he said dryly.

She had left him here too long, he was letting her know.

"My apologies, sir. You were not expected."

"Yes. Of course."

He appeared to be waiting for something. When she did not move, he gestured to the sofa with some exasperation. "Perhaps if you sit, I can, too, and we can discuss why I am here."

She walked over and sat, feeling stupid and awkward.

He settled himself in a nearby chair. Boots stretched out and body relaxed, he lounged like a man accustomed to taking his ease anywhere he chose. He propped his elbow on the chair's arm, rested his chin in his hand and regarded her.

He did not speak, and she found that she could not. His masculine presence assaulted her like a challenge she did not know how to meet. The way he looked at her made her want to check that her petticoat's torn edge was not showing and that her face was not dirty. She tried to find something authoritative to say, but instead she just kept swallowing, even though it was hard to do.

He flashed a much friendlier smile. A very charming one. She felt herself flushing. The room became hazy, except around the chair where he sat.

"You are much prettier in a dress."

That snapped her back to her senses. She eyed him cautiously.

He wanted something.

"Do you often dress, um . . ." he made a gesture that implied the pantaloons and doublet.

"Only when I am going to kill someone."

"Not often, then."

"Not too often."

He laughed lightly, as if she had made a little joke. She didn't, so he might wonder if it had not been a joke at all.

"You spoke of your sisters. How many are there?"

"There are four of us."

"And you are the eldest, if you are now head of the family. Might I know your name, Miss Cameron?"

"Bride."

"And have you been someone's bride?"

She felt a sneer of distaste starting to form. Her name, a form of Bridget, had given rise to some very tired jokes in recent years.

"I am not a widow, if that is what you mean."

"Are all of your sisters unmarried, as well? May I ask their names?"

"My sisters are Anne and Joan, and then Mary. All are unmarried."

"Do you often have to load a pistol to protect them?"

"Not more than once a year or so. Is there some reason why you are so curious about the matter, sir?"

"Indeed there is, and it would be best to explain.

Did the name Lyndale mean nothing to you? Did your father never mention the Earl of Lyndale?"

"I cannot say that he did. Did you know my father?"

"Not me. The late earl, my uncle, knew your father many years ago. Before you were born, I suspect."

"Well, the name has no significance to me. I am sorry."

Lord Lyndale frowned while he thought about that. "Here is my situation, Miss Cameron. I have come here to investigate your family."

Her heart got thick and heavy. Her stomach churned. It was as she feared. He had come all the way from London to investigate them. Perhaps if she feigned ignorance he would assume that four women could not possibly, on their own, have—

"You see, I promised my uncle before his death that I would search out the family of Angus Cameron and make sure that they were well cared for. That is why I am here."

It was an unexpected and peculiar thing to hear. Bride was so relieved, however, that she almost burst out laughing. "Truly? That is the reason you are here?"

"Yes. What reason did you think?"

"Oh, nothing. Nothing at all. I was just curious, as you might imagine. It was quite a mystery to me. However, as I said, you should have written. I would have assured you that we are fine here and contented

and well cared for. You can return to London knowing that you fulfilled your duty."

"Actually, I cannot. I am not at all convinced that
you are fine and well cared for."

"Excuse me?"

"Consider what I have seen thus far. A household
of women living in isolation in a Highland glen,
with no source of income from what I can tell, and
with one of them wearing pantaloons and brandish-
ing pistols to try and offer some security."

"My father left us a legacy. We are hardly destitute."

"Indeed? Did he have employment? My uncle, I
will tell you, confessed to me that he ruined your father. That is the reason for my deathbed promise. So
I will be surprised to hear that there was an estate of
any amount on his death."

Bride suddenly knew who the last Earl of Lyndale had been. She was heartily grateful that the current Earl of Lyndale was ignorant about all that.

"My father left us a legacy, sir. Your concern for
our welfare is admirable, but I assure you that—"

"How much? He has been dead five years, you
say. Is there enough left to keep you in the years to
come? Despite being isolated here, there is some
chance your younger sisters may marry, but it is unlikely that you ever will. Unless there are funds with
an income of at least several hundred a year, I would
hardly say that you are well cared for. . . ."

He went on and on. Bride stopped hearing him

after the second sentence. *Your younger sisters may marry, but it is unlikely that you ever will.*

This arrogant, tactless man had her whole future wrapped up in his mind. He assumed she would lead a spinster's existence on the edge of the world, her life dragging on through the years as one by one her sisters left until she dwelled alone in this house in lonely poverty.

It did not help that she had on occasion glimpsed the same future for herself the last year. She resented this man stating it so baldly and so casually, as if she should not mind his unkind words.

". . . therefore, Miss Cameron, I think I should ascertain for myself if my obligations to my uncle's wishes require any settlement."

The statement broke through her boiling thoughts.

"You want to make a settlement on us?"

"Possibly."

"Free and clear? No conditions?"

"Well, I think that you should move from here. I will arrange a home for you where your sisters might meet suitable husbands and where you will not have to protect their virtue with duels at dawn."

It was just as she expected. No one ever gave you money without conditions. Accepting money always incurred a debt of one kind or another.

If this lord helped them in any way, he would be sticking his nose into their lives all the time. They could badly use the money, but they dared not give a member of the government cause to notice them, let alone interfere.

"We are not moving from this glen, sir. If that is the price of your settlement, we decline."

"I am speaking of a better life. I will set you up in Edinburgh, if you like."

"We will remain right here. We do not need your money, or your care. In fact, after dinner I will prove it. You see, Lord Lyndale, my father not only left us with a legacy, he also gave us the means to support ourselves."

CHAPTER THREE

~⌒~

Dinner was not a formal affair in the Cameron household.

Ewan found himself at table not only with Bride and her sisters Mary and Anne, but with an old woman they called Jilly, who took the chair beside his. Since Jilly directed the arrival of the food, Ewan assumed she was the cook.

They were speaking Gaelic when he arrived, but immediately switched to English when they noticed him. Their English was not laden with the dialect used by the stream earlier, either, but was instead a slow and deliberate proper English. Bride had adopted the same careful tongue when they conversed in the library, now that he thought about it.

He wondered if he should tell them the effort was unnecessary. He could haesna and daesna along with the best of them if he chose, and understood enough Gaelic to follow a person's thoughts.

As they settled in, the sister named Joan arrived. She entered the room, adjusting her dress as if its fit irritated her, and managed to trip twice on the hem as she crossed the chamber.

Ewan had not met Joan yet. Her appearance and manner impressed him, despite the stumbles. Dark-haired, gray-eyed and handsome, she showed more self-possession than the other two. Where Mary was silly and Anne was dreamy, Joan seemed more like Bride in her presence.

After introductions, Joan walked back to the door and gestured. A man entered and she sat him in the empty chair next to hers.

She had invited Michael to dine with them.

Ewan gave Michael a scowl. Michael looked pointedly toward Jilly, then ignored the glare of disapproval. He turned his youthful, blond charm on the young ladies and acted as if sitting at table with his master was a common occurrence.

Which it was, but not in public and not for meals. Michael sat at other tables besides those designated for dining. Card tables.

It was part of their unusual arrangement, proposed by Michael four years ago when Ewan was in financial straits. His manservant had departed and Michael applied for the position. Barely twenty-one at the time, he had only asked for a chamber, board, and the chance to relieve gentlemen of bundles of money by being included in the card games frequently held in Ewan's chambers. Michael's dream was to make a fortune at gambling, then open his own gaming hall.

"Your horses are very impressive, Lord Lyndale," Joan said.

"Joan has a great love of animals," Michael said. "She delights in taking care of them."

"Are you saying that the young lady, not you, groomed my horses?"

"She insisted. Didn't you, Joan?"

"You have no need to worry, Lord Lyndale. I know what I am about. I have been tending to our horse for years."

"She did a fine job, sir. I stayed to keep an eye on things." He bestowed on Joan the special smile that had won him feminine favors when some of Ewan's parties had taken certain directions. Experimenting with a servant was unaccountably seen as a new adventure by some ladies.

Ewan watched Michael ooze the appeal of a bad angel, and noted Joan's wide-grinned reaction.

Both had been out of sight for hours. It would not have taken much time to deal with the horses. . . .

He glared at Michael again.

Out of the corner of his eye, he noticed Bride glaring, too.

"Fine weather you have here. Not nearly as cold as I expected," Ewan said in his most jovial, divert-the-pistol-toting-harridan tone.

"Better if it snowed," Bride said. "Fewer intruders in the glens, then."

Now that was uncalled for. The woman had

clearly decided to be obstreperous instead of grateful, but that did not mean she had to be rude.

"She didna—that is, *did not*—mean you, Lord Lyndale," Mary hastened to add. A tiny smirk on Bride's mouth said her sister was too optimistic about Bride's manners. "By 'intruders' she means the duchess's factors and their men. That is who we thought you were at first. Bad weather slows them down."

"They were just east of Shenwell last week," Anne said in an ethereal voice. "Three townships got burned out."

Bride's attention sharpened. "Where did you learn that? I have heard nothing of it."

"Roger MacKay told me this morning, while he was waiting for you to kill Jamie."

"I wish you had told me this, Anne."

"Why?" Anne asked, puzzled. "You canna change or stop it. Nothing much you can do except—"

She stopped talking in midsentence. Ewan was sure he heard a collective inhale from the other women at the table.

Anne smiled nervously and began to shovel soup into her mouth.

Joan deliberately engaged Michael in a spirited exchange about horses he had known in bygone years. It did not seem to dampen her enthusiasm that Michael waxed most eloquent over the ones who had helped him win big wagers.

Their chatter tried to banish the quaking silence,

but it was still there, hanging in the room, pushing the conversation to one side.

Bride did nothing to dispel it. Nothing to make her guest at ease.

Well, what did he expect. He *was* an intruder. It wasn't her fault that he had this duty.

Then again, it wasn't his fault, either, and her pointed lack of welcome was annoying.

He could understand that his arrival and intentions caught her by surprise. He was sympathetic if she had been too startled in the library to comprehend her good fortune. However, she needed to use some sense now, and see that if she would set pride aside, she and her sisters would be better off for it.

He would explain all that to her before sundown.

He turned to Jilly, who ate silently by his side.

"Do I have you to thank for the excellent food?"

"They help me. Too much for me to dae alone noo, especially when we hae nobility to feed."

Her tone was just shy of resentful. Ewan surveyed the various dishes on the table. It would hardly impress the ton of London, but he suspected it was a feast for them.

He glanced around the dining room's furnishings. Like the ones in the library, they were presentable but worn, and the type of objects a prosperous merchant would have bought a generation ago. The drapes at the windows had faded with time. A platter in front of his plate showed a few chips. The pewter in his hand wore the patina of age.

The whole room spoke of better days gone bad. It

was the kind of room in which genteel poverty dined. The sisters' dresses, at least a decade out of style, displayed bits of careful mending. Considering they entertained a guest, these were probably their best clothes, but their dated, middling elegance was all too fitting for the environment.

Mary passed down a platter of rabbit. Jilly had cooked it in a pleasant sauce, and Ewan thought it was the best dish in the meal.

He told the cook that as he helped himself to half of what he normally would take. He did not want to eat them out of a month's provisions in one day.

"Joan got it," the old woman said. "She's good at that."

Got it?

Ewan looked at the rabbit, then over at Joan who was blushing under Michael's attention.

Ewan pictured the map he had followed to this glen. He seemed to remember a hunting preserve nearby.

He looked down the table at Bride. She returned a level gaze of utter indifference.

His mind was making a long list of things to discuss with this woman, and the means by which Joan had "got" this rabbit would definitely be among them.

"If Roger MacKay is correct, we need to finish the last batch and be ready," Joan said.

"I know that."

Normally Bride was grateful for Joan's practicality. Joan possessed the common sense and sobriety that Anne and Mary sorely lacked, and served as Bride's right hand. Bride did not understand Joan's love of horses or enjoyment of physical work, but they still had much in common.

Right now, however, she did not appreciate someone echoing her thoughts. "We cannot finish until Lord Lyndale leaves."

"Then you had better find a way to make him go. Michael said that the earl assumed it would take a few days to settle matters. He was asking what chamber he should prepare."

"They can use the stable."

"Now, Bride, you know they can't."

Bride gazed around her bedroom. The privacy of this chamber was one of the few benefits of being the eldest, and it was small compensation for all the worry and responsibility that came with the privilege.

"Lord Lyndale can use this room. I will move in with you and Jilly."

"And Michael?"

Bride did not miss the familiar way Joan referred to Lyndale's servant. Her sister had blushed more at dinner than she had in five years combined.

That was not like Joan at all, although Bride could understand the appeal.

Michael was handsome and charming enough, although there was a subtle air to him that suggested he was far less angelic than his countenance implied. He reminded Bride of the kind of person who flattered you silly while picking your pocket.

"Michael can share this room with Lord Lyndale, or sleep in the stable. There is no place else to put him, and I won't have him underfoot in the kitchen or library."

Bride began collecting some garments and belongings for her move to the other bedroom. "Help me do this quickly, then go and get a cot. And, Joan, about Michael—I saw how he flirted with you at dinner. It is bad enough I have to watch Mary every time high boots walk this property. I really do not need the vexation of worrying about you, too. You are too sensible to be taken in by such a man and should know better."

"Well, you would know all about knowing better, now, wouldn't you."

Bride halted her work. This was the second time today one of her sisters had all but said she had no business giving such advice. There had been allusions before, but rarely anything this blatant.

She lifted her stack of clothes and shoved them into Joan's arms. Without another word, Joan left the room.

Bride made sure that her trunk was securely locked. She checked that the wardrobe had enough space for Lord Lyndale's coats, then went to work clearing a drawer in her chest for his use.

She stuffed its garments into other drawers, then dealt with the private treasures that had lain beneath them. She tucked the miniatures of her father and mother into her writing table. She lifted a tiny leather booklet. She paused with it in her hand.

She had not opened this memento in close to a year.

She remembered distinctly the night when she had decided to no longer depend on the promises this object symbolized. She had left her bed in the dark and carried it over to the moonlit window and held it for at least an hour, wanting badly to look at the image inside. Her soul had argued not to, however. Her essence knew that there would be pain, not comfort, in gazing at that face.

Would she still react the same way now?

Testing herself, she opened the little cover and looked at the drawing that showed the portrait of a young man.

She had made this herself. She had lovingly crafted the leather-covered boards to hold this small piece of paper. She had neither the skill nor the materials to make a miniature, but she could catch a likeness with lines, and she had labored to make this one perfect and to mount it so it had an elegant home.

She tried to remember if this portrait was very accurate. Had his sandy hair been that wild? Was that warmth truly in his eyes, or had she imagined it?

The man pictured on this paper would never have abandoned her. He would never have left her worried and vulnerable.

He would not have claimed he was going away so

he could help her when in fact he was merely running from her arms.

The man in this drawing would have returned or written months ago, unless something bad had happened to him.

Then again, perhaps the likeness was not accurate at all. Maybe her heart had distorted her vision and she had not seen the truth. Mary and Joan had clearly decided so.

She had half decided so herself.

She closed the leather cover and put it with the miniatures in her desk. It still saddened her to see that face. It brought back nostalgic memories of joy and laughing pleasure.

It also provoked her two worst fears. One was that he had come to harm while trying to protect her.

The other was that he was hale and fit and living in some distant town, caressing another woman's body.

When Bride joined Lord Lyndale in the library that evening, he was paging through one of her father's notebooks.

She barely suppressed a hiss of annoyance. The room was stuffed with books. How did he light upon that in this sea of bindings?

"Your father's intellectual interests were far ranging," he said. "It appears he collected all the information he could find about the Celtic culture north of Hadrian's Wall."

"He was by nature a thoughtful and curious man."

"Educated, too, it appears."

"He did not attend university. But then, many do and remain ignorant, so that accounts for nothing, don't you think?"

Lord Lyndale's cocked eyebrow said he suspected she included him among those who had studied but accounted for nothing.

He looked to the shelves across the room. "There are schoolbooks there. Yours?"

"My parents educated me. I helped my father teach my sisters. This library is well used by us all."

"That explains your manner and speech. I admit this household is not what I expected, in many ways." His attention returned to the notebook in his hands. "He describes rituals here. Did he ever recreate them?"

She knew where this was going. Shortly he would be thinking her father had been eccentric at best and a madman at worst. "He did so, as experiments. There was no other way to know if they had any merit."

"Did they have merit?"

"He thought they had some. His study and research were not intended to promote a new paganism, Lord Lyndale. He wanted the Scots to know and take pride in their ancient roots. He loved this country."

He set aside the notebook. "I assume he was a Jacobite."

"Isn't every true Scot?"

He pierced her with a suspicious gaze. "Was your

father radical on the matter? There are those who still think Scotland should secede from the Grand Union."

"If you have read those notebooks for very long, you know his views on the issue." More than radical ones. Her father had toyed with strategies and theorized plots and written them down in those notebooks. "If you are other than a complete fool, you no doubt realized they were the private musings of a creative mind, and never true threats."

"Others might disagree. I suspect my uncle did. I think whatever occurred between the last earl and your father can be blamed on those creative musings."

She was more than happy to let him think so, and did not disagree.

"And you, Miss Cameron. Do your views match your father's?"

"What a peculiar question, sir. You ask it as if it matters what a woman has as a view."

"In other words, they do match his."

"When you said you had come here to investigate my family, you claimed it revolved around our care and well-being, not our private political views." She picked up her father's notebook and returned it to its shelf. "Your interest piques my own curiosity, however. I am half inclined to ask where your ancestors were at Culloden, or even Bannockburn, for that matter."

A flush blotched Lord Lyndale's cheeks.

It was as she expected. This earl may have

Scottish names and a Scottish title, but his family had been tools of the English for half a millennium.

Content that she had communicated the uncomfortable conversation that awaited in any further investigation of her loyalties, she strolled to the door.

"Enough of boring politics, Lord Lyndale. I said that I would show you my father's legacy this afternoon. If you are agreeable, I will do so now and you can conclude your mission quickly."

"Amazing."

Lord Lyndale paced around the drawing room, clearly impressed.

Bride beamed with pride. This room represented her life. Here she had continued her father's work. Here she and her sisters had supported themselves. They were very good at what they did, too. Among the best. She knew that, even if the world did not.

She led him to a place on the worktable where she had set up a little display.

"Here is a drawing I am reproducing. I place it so it is reflected in that mirror propped there, because the image has to be engraved in reverse in order to print in the correct view. Then we use this pointed instrument—it is called a burin—to make the lines and marks on the copper plate that will reproduce the drawing when the plate is printed. To print, the plate is inked, and the ink descends into the grooves we have made. The press will create pressure on the wet paper, and force the paper into those grooves to pick up the ink. That creates the image."

He lifted a rocker lined with fine teeth from the table. "You make mezzotints, too?"

"On occasion. Mezzotint plates fetch more money. There is a lot of work in them. Also, the publisher cannot print as many images from them, so their prints are more expensive for that reason, too."

"I know all about the costs, Miss Cameron. I buy the kind of engravings your plates provide. I inherited the interest from my uncle, and have an extensive collection of my own."

Bride's heart sank. This was not good news.

She had intended to drown him in talk of burins and scrapers.

She had expected to bore him quickly, while ensuring he believed this studio was an enormous success.

Instead, Lyndale appeared captivated. He looked to be a man who would want to poke around for hours, when she could not allow him to poke at all.

"Did your father teach you this craft?"

"Yes. And my sister Anne. She and I helped teach Joan and Mary."

"So your father was an engraver, and made plates for engravings that reproduced great paintings. How did he obtain the drawings on which to base his craft?"

"He had gone to Europe as a young man, and made his own."

Lyndale moved over to the press. "You check

your work with this, I assume. Print the plate at stages as you go, to see how it appears."

He seemed to know an awful lot about it. Too much.

His tour took him to the other side of the room, and the portfolio on a table there. He opened it and began flipping through the prints they had saved of their finished plates.

He pointed to one. "What is this here?"

She went over to see what he meant. "The blank border? That is where the publisher will add his name, date, and address to the plate, along with credit to us. Surely you are familiar with that. It is a common practice."

"Of course. How stupid of me." He flipped another sheet.

Which brought his arm and hand very close to her for a moment. He did not touch her, but she reacted as if he had. A liveliness woke her body like a beam of morning sunlight. Her physicality became very aware of how close he stood, and of the dominating aura he projected.

"Raphael's 'Alba Madonna,' " he said. "I think this is the best copy I have ever seen. Far better than the one in Lyndale's collection."

"Thank you." Her voice sounded small and unsteady.

His arm moved again, to turn another print. He might as well have brushed against her breast, she felt him so plainly. Her attention fixated on his hand, and how handsome and masculine it looked. She tried to control the sensual vitality transforming her, but it was too delicious to deny.

Lyndale appeared ignorant of her disadvantage. Except she wondered if he was. There was something in his eyes as he perused the prints—a contented, dangerous little spark—

"To which publishers do you sell your plates?"

"MacDonald in Edinburgh."

"I have visited that establishment. I never saw prints with the name Cameron."

The comment brought her back to her senses as quickly as a slap. She stepped away from him.

He did not look at her. He just turned another sheet. She could not shake the sense that he knew how she had reacted to his closeness, however. He had feigned ignorance about the border so he could call her over and test his power.

"Since buyers do not think much of a woman's skill in anything, least of all the arts, we use a different name," she said.

"Of course. A fictitious name. Most sensible." His gaze sharpened on the engraving in front of him. For a moment his concentration permitted no intrusion. "Would you happen to use the name Waterfield? I have a work by him, bought at MacDonald's, and the technique is similar."

She just stared at him.

"No?" he asked, glancing at her.

She found her voice despite the alarm buzzing in her head. "You have an expert's eye, Lord Lyndale. There are those who can make such attributions to *peintre-graveurs* who create engravings of their own original compositions. It is rare for someone to do so based on the technique used for reproductions."

"It was only a guess, but I have had a lot of practice."

Too much damned practice. He did not only collect. He was one of those collectors who counted the burin lines used to model an arm.

He was a connoisseur.

She needed to find a good excuse to end this. Fast.

"Tell me, Miss Cameron. If your father made drawings when a young man, and had been creating plates from them for years, how many drawings are left?"

"Enough."

"I doubt that."

"They can also be used more than once."

"Now, now, that is not true. Your publisher copyrights his printings and pays for the plate's exclusive use. If Mr. Waterfield makes another, it would be known." A subtle smile broke. A smug one. "I suppose that you could use yet another false name when you make the second plate. However, that would be illegal, so I am sure you do not do it."

He had her cornered. She wanted to kick herself. Or him.

"Under the circumstances, I would feel more confident about your future if I knew there were sufficient drawings left to sustain your industry and thus your keep. Why don't you show them to me."

"Certainly, Lord Lyndale. Please wait here and I will bring them to you."

She walked to two map drawers stacked on a table at the other end of the wall. As she did so, she saw a blond head peek through the doorway to the drawing room.

She gestured furtively to Mary, telling her to come in.

"Stay here," she whispered when Mary joined her. "Close the drawer when I am done. Then pretend to have work to prepare. When I have him distracted, remove the box from the other drawer and take it upstairs. He is going to stick his nose into everything and I cannot risk his becoming aware of it."

Mary nodded. Bride quickly opened the top drawer, removed another portfolio, and turned back to Lord Lyndale.

She caught him studying her much as he had been examining those engravings.

She halted in her tracks, portfolio in hand, blood coursing with alarm.

His focused eyes held the same objectivity. The same assessment. His gaze was in the process of judging value and worth along with the details of form and line. She could almost hear his mind working. *Is it good enough for my collection? Do I want to acquire this particular specimen?*

There were important differences, of course. This calculating inspection was that of a man observing a woman. It created an undeniably sexual atmosphere that descended on her with irritating effectiveness.

She looked him in the eyes with her best disdainful glare. She let him know that his behavior was crossing a line.

He ignored her. He finished his slow inspection like a man accustomed to following his own mind in such matters, as if the decisions were all his.

Finally, the demeanor of a polite guest reclaimed his countenance, except for a half smile that said they both knew what he had been thinking. The notion did not embarrass him at all.

He gestured to the portfolio. "You can bring it here. You do not have to be cautious with me."

Evidently the work of art titled "Bride Cameron" had been deemed lacking by this connoisseur.

She could not ignore that she had just been insulted at a basic, primitive level.

She set the portfolio on the table. She lifted the top board.

Mary began fussing on the other side of the room, setting up her tools.

"This holds the original drawings, and also my father's own collection of old master prints. You may find them interesting. Most are by *peintre-graveurs,* not reproductive. All are very rare."

As she expected, the word "rare" instantly captivated him. He flipped through the drawings so quickly she doubted he counted them. When the turn of the last revealed one of her father's prized possessions, he exhaled in awe.

"Dürer's 'Melancholia.' I have never seen a finer example," he muttered.

He set it aside so it would not be buried. The next sheet almost had him swooning.

"Rembrandt's 'The Three Crosses.' My God. Only one other example of this suite has been documented."

"Two, actually."

He glanced at her in question.

"There is one in Germany," she explained.

"Your expertise surpasses mine on the matter, I can see. I am impressed."

He returned his attention to the prints. He became a man absorbed and possessed. She helped him set them out one by one on the large table.

She gestured behind her back to Mary.

Lord Lyndale was too busy bending over the glories spread before him to notice Mary approach the map drawers.

"This is the legacy you referred to." His keen eyes roamed over the atmospheric flicks showering "The Judgment of Paris" by Bonasone. "They are now yours, I assume, as the eldest child."

"The legacy is in our craft, sir. These are family heirlooms."

Out of the corner of her eye, she saw Mary easing open the lower map drawer.

"Many would pay handsomely for any of them." He straightened and turned to her. "Would you consider selling some? I would pay whatever—"

His attention shifted past her. His gaze lit on Mary.

Bride tried to reclaim his concentration. "I had

never thought to sell them. However, perhaps I should. What would the Rembrandt be worth?"

He did not even hear her. The avarice gleam of acquisition beamed out toward the other table. "There are more, aren't there? I must see them."

He strode toward Mary, who jumped in alarm when she saw him coming.

Mind shrieking with panic, Bride hurried after him.

"What do you have there?" he asked. "Small, so they must be German Renaissance, is my guess."

Eyes wide, Mary clutched the wooden box she held close to her chest. She looked like a thief caught in the act.

Fortunately, Lyndale did not comprehend Mary's reaction. His thoughts appeared to be on nothing more than rare engravings, unknown states, special papers, and other erudite details.

Knowing all too well just how rare the engravings in that box were, Bride rushed past him and thrust herself between Lyndale and Mary.

There was only one way to distract him. She prayed it was not as risky as she feared it was.

"My sister has nothing of value in that box. She is still learning, and that is where she keeps the plates on which she practices, and the prints she pulls as she progresses. They are study pieces by an apprentice, nothing more." She quickly opened the bottom drawer. "However, there are a few more rarities here. Perhaps you can advise me on their value."

The promise of rarities succeeded in reclaiming his attention. Mary eased away while he opened the leather boards to see what was inside the portfolio that Bride handed him.

His eyes widened just enough for Bride to know Mary had ceased to exist for him.

Bride averted her gaze from the prints. "I do not know what Father was thinking in owning such things. I found them after his death, and was astonished. I put them away at once, of course. They have been in this drawer ever since."

"You were wise to do so. The subject matter is not appropriate for young ladies to see."

"I suppose I should burn them."

"*No!* That is, I do not believe that is the best course. Such engravings are not without collectors."

"Really? What sort of person would want such scandalous things? No one of good family or breeding, I am sure."

She kept her gaze on the wall. She sensed a subtle flexing in the man at her side.

"Miss Cameron, do you have any idea of what you have here?"

"Immoral images of an amorous nature."

"Yes, but very special ones. I think that you have the Caraglio addendum. Indeed, you may have the only good impressions of it known in the world."

She contrived an expression of surprise and curiosity. She turned to him, trying to appear confused. Lord Lyndale quickly closed the portfolio so her virtuous eyes would not be offended.

"Miss Cameron, you may have heard of the

massive catalog of old master prints compiled by Adam von Bartsch."

"Of course."

"You may not be aware that during the Renaissance, several Italian engravers did series of prints with subject matter that was of an . . . amorous nature, much like these."

"All that I know I learned from Father, and he never told me about those."

"Well, since you are a woman . . ." He looked at her sympathetically, as if that said it all. "Recently, a scholar has been expanding and completing Bartsch's catalog. He searches out other images by each old master and creates an addendum to Bartsch. His name is Johann Passavant, and he was in England last year. He told me then that one series of amorous engravings, that by Caraglio, is incomplete in Barstch. Passavant has seen six other images that belong to the series. They were in very poor and worn condition, but he is sure that the set originally contained these other prints."

She gestured to the portfolio on which his hand laid possessively. "And those are the images?"

"They conform to what was described to me. I would need to study them more closely, of course."

"Study such scandalous images? I cannot imagine that a decent man like yourself could bear to do so. I could never impose on you that way. No, it would be better to just burn them. If they are so rare, it is probably because others burned them in the past, and for good reason."

He shifted his weight. He scratched his head as he glanced to the floor.

"Miss Cameron, in the interests of truth, knowledge, and art, I am prepared to examine and investigate these engravings and ascertain if they are indeed the addendum to Caraglio's series. It would embarrass you to request another expert do this, I am sure, and I did come here to aid you."

"That is very generous of you, Lord Lyndale. Uncommonly so, since it will be such an unpleasant task."

"Think nothing of it."

"Perhaps you should take them with you."

He tucked the portfolio under his arm. "That is an excellent idea. I will bring them to the chamber I am using. I cannot study them here, where young innocents might come upon me."

She encouraged him toward the door. "I did not just mean today. I think that you should take them with you when you depart for London in the morning."

The collector's distraction disappeared. "In the morning?"

"I am sure you will want to be off as soon as possible. Your mission here is completed now. You have seen how we support ourselves."

His sharp gaze raked her, then did a quick survey of the drawing room. "My duty is hardly completed, Miss Cameron. The evidence of your industry only raises new questions and concerns for me. You and I still have much to discuss."

CHAPTER
FOUR

❦

"My, this is cozy," Michael said. He squeezed past the bed on which Ewan sat that night.

The accommodations gave physical form to how big an intrusion they were. With Michael's cot under the window, the chamber barely had enough room for them both to stand at the same time.

"This must be where the big red one sleeps." Michael pawed through valises for the night's necessities. "A regular Bodisha, that one is."

Ewan glanced up from his examination of the engravings that he had spread on the bed's wool blanket. "If you mean the Celtic warrior queen of the Iceni, her name was Boudicca, not Bodisha."

"She looks to be a woman quick to kick a man where it hurts, is what I meant."

"When you are less green you will appreciate such women more. My mother was taller than most men, and quite formidable, for example. She never lacked admirers."

"If you say so. Now Bodisha's sister Joan is jolly fun, although she likes horses more than I think any female should. She wears breeches, too, did you know that? Had them on under that cloak at the duel. Back at the stable, there she was, very familiar and friendly, talking horses, walking around and bending to her work in those breeches with her bottom just begging to be—"

"Michael, hear me plainly. Trust my words as your lord and master. No matter how much her bottom seems to be begging, you must beg off. If you touch any one of these young women, I will skin you alive."

"That is like forcing me to sit on a rock in the middle of a lake, all parched like, and telling me I can't drink the water."

"Since the lake is so pure, we must die of thirst rather than so much as sip."

With a laugh that was not reassuring, Michael laid a shirt on the writing desk so he could refold it.

Ewan returned his attention to the engravings. He tried to focus on their technique, but his concentration kept wandering to their content. He repeatedly saw the positions being depicted, only the god and goddess on the paper were replaced by himself and Miss Cameron.

It was a stupid speculation, of course, even though he had sensed the tremor in her while she stood beside him at that table. She was not very good at hiding such things.

That only spoke to her inexperience, however. Still, he had not merely considered sipping from the lake while with her in the drawing room. He had wanted to rip off his clothes and plunge in.

Duty. Duty.

Forbidden, of course. Not only was she an innocent, her welfare was his responsibility.

Although . . . perhaps she wasn't an innocent. He could reconsider the responsibility part if she wasn't.

She was in her late twenties. What were the chances that a woman with her face would reach that age without doing a bit of sipping herself?

His gaze lingered on an especially explicit view of a goddess posed to reveal her treasures. It came alive in his mind. The woman's Roman coiffure grew until it became a tumble of long, copper curls. The legs lengthened and turned creamy white, and her breasts' nipples protruded with a dark, rosy hue. The expression on her face softened to one of welcoming ecstasy.

Hell.

Of course she was an innocent. What else could she be, living in this isolated glen, caring for three younger sisters.

That did not stop his imagination, much as he tried to build a barrier against the fantasies. It did not help that he had concluded in the drawing room that Miss Cameron was more than ready for drinking, whether some of her cool water had previously been tasted or not.

"What do you have there?" Michael peered over to the engravings. "Say, there is no woman in that one there."

"That is the god Apollo, and the boy is Hyacinth, for whom he had a *tendre*."

"That is *disgusting*. The others are nice, though. Even nicer than those *'Modi'* pictures you have in London. Not as instructive, but fancier."

"I was just thinking the same thing. Although Raimondi's *'I Modi'* are refreshing in their lack of allusion to mythology. They are boldly and frankly what they are, which is why the artist was imprisoned by the pope. The Renaissance was quite free about such matters, but his *'I Modi'* went too far." Ewan gestured to the prints in front of him. "These by Caraglio are ostensibly the 'Loves of the Gods.' Less explicit, and ultimately more artistic."

Michael snorted. "Artistic, maybe, but they still show people swiving. Don't be looking too long, sir. No one here but me if you get ideas, and I'm no Hyacinth."

Ewan looked up at Michael's grinning face. "I do not know why I tolerate you. Your presumptuous familiarity and lack of manners are beyond the pale. I should have sent you packing years ago."

"You need someone to look after you when you are drunk, that is why. Also, I tolerate a good deal myself, things no respectable servant would, what with the doings in your chambers."

His duties completed, Michael shifted around the room, poking at drapes and pictures. Ewan returned to the prints and managed to force some analytical objectivity.

They looked right. The technique was appropriate to the early sixteenth century, before engravers began employing the swelling contour lines for shadows. The paper had been trimmed right to the plate edge's indentation, as was typical of the time.

The images were remarkably fresh, however. They looked as if they had been carefully preserved.

Considering their erotic subjects, it was entirely plausible they had been hidden away for centuries, of course.

"Look here," Michael said. "This must be their parents."

Ewan diverted his attention to where Michael sat at a well-nicked writing desk. He had two miniatures laid out on its scratched top. The desk's drawer stood open.

Ewan got up and walked the three steps to close the drawer. "The poor woman had to give up her own bed. You might spare her your disgraceful prying."

"Handsome man, her father was." Michael touched the miniature showing a red-haired man of striking countenance. "Mother was pretty enough, too."

The mother bore a resemblance to the second sister, Anne.

"This must be a brother." Michael's finger pressed open a little leather holder to show a drawing of a man's face.

Ewan picked it up.

Bride had drawn this. He just knew it. No objective artist would ever catch that expression on a young man's face. No male artist would even notice it.

"They have no brother."

Michael inched open the drawer again. "Must be Bodisha's lover, then."

Ewan watched Michael's blond head bend to peek inside the drawer. The last statement had not carried any speculative tone.

"What makes you assume it is a portrait of a lover?"

Michael slipped his hand in the drawer and felt around for something interesting. "Joan said something about it being a long time since there had been a man in the house. Not in over a year, since Walter left. Seems Walter was Miss Cameron's friend. All but lived here, from the way she spoke of it." He glanced up with a smile. "Not all the water in this lake is pure, is how it sounded to me."

Ewan examined the portrait.

Bride's "friend." Gone over a year now.

Well, well.

"We need to make some plans," Bride said.

She sat in Joan's bedroom, now cramped with her sisters and Jilly, all decked out in nightdresses, shawls, and caps. The box that Mary had secreted out of the drawing room rested on a nearby table.

She had just explained all her conversations with

Lord Lyndale. Her sisters were still absorbing how precarious their situation had become.

"I dodged him tonight, because I could not bear any more of his arrogance in one day. Tomorrow, however, I expect he will demand that I accept his grand scheme for easing his conscience and for allowing Duncan McLean's ghost to rest in peace."

"I knew he was trouble." Jilly shook her head. Her well-lined face folded into deep creases. "Soon as I saw him galloping up like he owned the place."

"We can be thankful he does not own the place," Bride said. "That is the one consolation. He has no connection to Sutherland, or even to the Highlands, for that matter. He is a lowlander through and through."

"I say we take his offer," Mary said. Her eyes sparked with excitement. "It would be splendid. We could go to Glasgow and live there in style. He would buy us gowns and bonnets. We might even get a carriage."

"Mary, should we agree to his offer, which we will not because it would be stupid for reasons everyone in this chamber except you immediately recognized, you would never ride in that carriage. Upon arriving in the city I would lock you in your bedroom until you convinced me you would not run off with the first lying wastrel who smiled your way."

Mary's expression turned resentful. Bride heard her thoughts. *You would know all about lying, smiling wastrels, wouldn't you?*

"You only want to stay here because you think he is coming back," she blurted. "It isn't fair."

"Do not be silly," Anne said, rousing herself from some daydream. "We need to stay here because we are safe in obscurity. We cannot do what we do in a city."

"If we live in a city, and Lord Lyndale pays our keep, we won't have to do what we do," Mary said.

"Stop being selfish," Joan said. "This is not only about us. If we leave to improve our own comfort, it would dishonor everything our father taught us."

"Of course, no matter where we live, we could be transported," Anne said. Her airy voice was not joining the argument, merely speaking a line of thoughts coincidentally connected to it.

Unfortunately, she had touched on Bride's biggest concern.

They had been safe in obscurity for years now. There were recent indications, however, that somewhere out in the world events were occurring that would land them all on a boat to New South Wales eventually.

Should those events start closing in around them, she did not want Lord Lyndale involved in their lives, no matter where they lived. She hated to admit it, but he appeared to be an intelligent man. He also possessed an expertise that might allow him to make certain connections that most other men would never see.

She opened the box and removed some papers. "Tomorrow I am going to invite Lord Lyndale to ride with me. I will ask to use his servant's horse and remove him from this house for several hours. While I am gone, Joan, I want you to take our horse and ride to town with these. Try and exchange them for that large banknote at Holland's inn. I intended to go today, but with Lyndale's arrival—"

"You think Mr. Holland will still have the note?"

"I doubt he has spent it by now. He would want to show it around first. He said it was used by a large hunting party to pay a steep bill. It is vital that we get hold of it, however. Also, see if you can learn where the party came from, but do not be obvious. Just get Holland talking. If he is curious why you want the exchange, say I am planning a journey and it is easier to hide one note instead of ten."

Joan took the papers. "These are the last, aren't they? Anne had better get busy."

Bride looked at Anne. "Can you work in this room tomorrow while Lord Lyndale is gone?"

Anne glanced at the window. "The morning light here should be enough, if the day is fair. I could get a few finished, I expect."

"What do I get to do?" Mary asked. "Everyone always has important things to do except me."

"You are going to do what you do best," Bride said. "While we are gone, you are going to charm that servant Michael into the kitchen to help Jilly fix the chimney, which is going to develop a blockage tonight. Jilly, once you get him there, do not let him leave. He is not to roam freely around this house."

"Joan should have the horses ready," Bride said. She pulled on her gloves as she joined Lord Lyndale in the library.

He looked very handsome this morning. His blue riding coat glowed expensively in the eastern window's light. His boots appeared to have been newly shined. No doubt Michael had been up before dawn, pressing and polishing.

Lyndale subjected her to a quick inspection, too. It was mild enough, but thorough.

"Do you intend to ride wearing that?" he asked. It was not a challenge. He almost sounded concerned.

"This will do. I do not own a riding dress."

"No? Then wouldn't you be more comfortable . . ." he used the same gesture he had made yesterday to indicate her pantaloons and doublet.

She had considered putting them on, but did not want to invite disapproval today. She needed him amenable to reason, not glancing askance at her garments.

"Should we meet someone, I do not want to embarrass you."

"My dear Miss Cameron, it is unlikely we will meet anyone. Nor would it embarrass me if we did. I am a man of the world. A woman in pantaloons does not shock me, and I do not care about the opinions of those whom it does." He smiled with kind understanding. "Please change, if you wish. I do not mind waiting."

Disarmed and grateful, she returned to the bedroom and pulled off the dress. Lord Lyndale was being much nicer today. Perhaps his journey had tired him yesterday. Maybe he just needed a good night's sleep.

She removed her petticoats and set them aside. They would not have done well on a saddle. She had anticipated a very awkward ride in that dress, with layers of garments hilling around her. Nor could the dress stand the damage that might come from the outing. It was very nice of Lord Lyndale to have surmised that.

She donned pantaloons, sleeveless doublet and shirt, and pulled on her half boots. She slipped on one of her father's old frock coats. It was too big, but it would not be clumsy.

Lord Lyndale did not even blink at her peculiar apparel when she rejoined him. Exuding gentle charm, he escorted her to the horses.

"It is very generous of you to allow me to ride one of yours," she said.

He helped her to mount a tall chestnut. "You are very sure he won't be too much for you? I would be grieved if you came to any harm."

She laughed. She turned the chestnut's head, dug her heels into his flanks, and flew away.

The rumble of the other horse's galloping hooves bore down on her soon. She did not rein in the chestnut until the house was a mere dot in the distance.

She kept her horse trotting west. When they approached a large stand of trees, she aimed north.

Lyndale looked at the forest flanking them on their left. "It is unusual to find such a woods here."

"It is a hunting preserve. It was Lord Reay's, but since Sutherland bought the whole county four years ago, I expect it belongs to the duchess now."

"Does her family ever come to hunt here?"

"Not that I've heard."

"So it just sits here, full of rabbits and deer. It must be tempting to poachers."

She slid a glance at him. There did not appear to be any suspicion in his expression.

He noticed her attention. He returned a friendly smile.

"How did your father come to learn his art if he lived in this glen, Miss Cameron?"

"He was not born or raised in these parts, but west of Glasgow. He learned engraving in that city, then traveled the Continent for a while as a journeyman. He worked in studios in Rome and Paris and other cities. When he returned to Scotland, he opened his own engraving studio and a print shop."

"Not here, surely."

She chose her words very carefully. "No. He returned here before I was born, however. He had met my mother, and her family was from this region. When they married, he moved his press here."

It was the truth. She hoped he would not pursue whether it was the entire story, however.

He did not. Today Lord Lyndale did not seem to have interrogation on his mind. He just trotted on, taking in the scenery.

"I think those prints are indeed the addendum to Caraglio's series, by the way. I took a good look at them last night."

"You truly think so? How extraordinary."

"Your father must have come upon them while traveling as a young man. He would not know what he had, of course."

"I am a little shocked he bought them, in any event."

"That is understandable. However, they are very well done. The compositions and the technique are superior. If you had studied them, which of course you did not, considering the subject matter, you would agree."

"I am in a quandary on what to do with them now." She tried hard to appear perplexed and embarrassed.

"I would like to bring them back to London with me, if you will permit it. I could consult with other experts. I also have the rest of the series and could do a comparison, side by side, to ascertain if—"

"*You* own a set of the series?"

"Yes. I inherited them from my uncle. Did I neglect to mention that?"

He certainly *had* forgotten to mention that.

He noticed her dismay. "I am afraid I have shocked you. The rest of the series is not as . . . inventive as these engravings. I have a theory that these were removed from most sets because they were more licentious than the others. My images are very, very mild in comparison. Couples embracing and such."

That was a blatant lie. She knew very well that the rest of the series, while milder, did not merely show embraces.

"As I was saying, if I took these back with me, I could compare—"

"I do not want to sell my father's collection, Lord Lyndale."

"You do not have to sell them to me. It would be a loan, so I can research them. You offered just such an idea yesterday."

Yesterday she did not know he owned the rest of the series. Yesterday she did not expect him to do a side-by-side comparison.

"I realize that I did. I apologize. My embarrassment over the content made me want to assure you I had no interest in them. However, on reflection, I have decided that, for good or ill, they are part of my father's legacy. Short of dire need, I do not want to part with any of it. Please understand that his collection is all that I have left of him."

"Certainly, Miss Cameron. I would never want to interfere with those memories or that sentiment. After all, if their authenticity remains unknown, what does it matter."

What a nice thing to say. If he was the kind of connoisseur she thought, not pursuing this chance to identify rare, lost prints would drive him half mad. Yet here he was, retreating without an argument, to spare her any distress.

He had sounded so sympathetic that she felt guilty for deceiving him. His manner this morning made it hard to remember that he was an irritating and potentially dangerous intrusion.

"Let us go up that hill," she suggested. "There is a wonderful prospect from the top."

She led the way up the high hill. At the top she slid off her horse. Lord Lyndale joined her and she showed him a spot from which one could look down on two glens.

It was a beautiful vista, even in early winter. Steep hills poured down to the valleys on either side. Far to the west, beyond the blunted tops of other hills, one could just make out the peaks of mountains.

"Isn't it remarkable?" She raised her head and inhaled the crystalline air.

"The view is so beautiful, it stirs my soul," he said. "It makes me wish I were a poet, and could capture the sensation in words."

What an astonishing thing for this man to say. His voice had been so quiet, too. So heartfelt.

She glanced over at him.

Her breath left her.

He was not gazing at the glens and hills. He was looking at her.

And what a look it was. Dangerous, but deliciously so. Her blood pulsed with caution and excitement. There was no doubting what this man was thinking, and the thoughts made his handsome face even more devastating.

It was not base lust reflected in those dark eyes, but a determined warmth that promised it was truly Bride Cameron he wanted, and not just any woman.

That mesmerized her. That and the invisible, misty fog suddenly wrapping her, isolating her from the world. His attention captured her so completely that suddenly nothing existed except the wind and sun and him and her.

"Exquisitely lovely," he said. "It is the kind of beauty that only Scotland can produce."

She felt herself flushing from the praise. An inner voice cried that she was an idiot, but her essence refused to listen. Lyndale's gaze had her heart swelling and her stomach tightening and her limbs shaking.

He slowly crossed the few feet that separated them. Her heart pounded so hard it intruded on her breath.

He gazed into her eyes as if she held no secrets from him. "So very delicate, like perfect porcelain." His fingertips lightly touched her face, and his gaze followed their path down her cheek.

A glorious tremor of pleasure thrilled down to her toes. She groped to keep some hold on herself, but that touch defeated her.

His firm hand cupped her chin and gently tilted her head. Warm lips brushed hers.

Her most womanly parts trembled alive.

That felt so good. It had been so long, so achingly long since she had been touched and kissed. Her body reveled in the arousal streaming through her. She shamelessly waited for more.

He embraced her and her senses swooned from the warmth and strength of his arms and chest.

He kissed her firmly and took control.

She had forgotten how delicious the pleasure was. Its sly rivulets kept multiplying and growing. His kisses got harder, bolder. More demanding. They bit down her neck to her pulse and fire joined the river awakening her.

Slowly, with excruciating deliberation, his kisses trailed back up to her lips. She focused on each inch of their progress with breathless, mindless anticipation. She vaguely heard her own deep sighs marking every blood-scathing seduction.

Warm breath and gentle teeth on her ear made her shiver. A soft kiss on her cheek demanded she turn her lips to him. The next kiss was invasive and ruthless, demolishing her sense of self completely.

Her senses swam, twirled, spun in a chaos of eager pleasure. Hungers began claiming her consciousness. Cravings escalated, driving her mad.

A firm press on her back made her arch against him. A shift in his embrace freed his right hand. A caress moved down her side, wonderfully. She wished no cloth protected her skin.

His hand slid beneath her coat and cupped her breast and she almost died. The slow movement of his hand had her gritting her teeth so she would not beg the way her dazed mind urged her to.

The long kiss stopped. Soft hair brushed her face. A new, intense pleasure shot through her body. She opened her eyes and watched his head bending to kiss and arouse her breast through the shirt's linen. The pleasure was almost unbearable.

She saw more than that dark head lowered for her pleasure, however. She also saw the ground and the sky and part of the distant glen. The bits of reality blinded her for a moment before collecting to become the world she knew.

His reality split through her daze, too. Who he was, and what was happening. Shock crashed against the seductive euphoria.

She pushed his shoulder, hard. She squirmed to escape his embrace.

He let her go instantly. She jumped away and stared at him.

He did not say anything. His expression remained annoyingly confident, however. The way he regarded her said he believed that if he reached for her again, she would not refuse.

That alone created another traitorous tremor. Shaky and appalled with herself, she strode to the horses.

She scrambled to get into her saddle. The chestnut was too high for her and she only made it halfway. She hovered there, right leg trying to swing over, desperate to get home. She knew she looked stupid, but she refused to hop back to the ground.

Lyndale grasped her bottom from behind. He just held her for a moment, cupping her fullness like that shocking touch was due him. Then he gave the push that allowed her to find her seat.

She yanked the reins to turn the horse. He grabbed the bridle and stopped her.

He captured her gaze in his own. His expression made caution prickle her neck. It made other reactions prickle other parts of her body.

Worse, she could tell he knew about all the prickles. He knew exactly what he was doing to her.

He grabbed her arm, pulled her down toward him, and kissed her hard. It was a possessive, dominating kiss.

She jerked back, out of his grasp.

"I think that you are a scoundrel, Lord Lyndale."

"And I think that you did not mind at all that I am, Miss Cameron."

She tried to think of a good response, but her muddled mind would not cooperate. Cursing herself for weakness and stupidity, she aimed down the hill so she could gallop to safety.

CHAPTER
FIVE

Bride tore down the glen as if a devil were chasing her.

The demon in question did not follow. He watched from the hill as her red hair and flying frock coat diminished with the distance.

She was running away, but not from his advances. That much he knew with certainty, despite her parting insult.

He had been a scoundrel with women often enough in his life, but not this time. He had given her plenty of opportunity to discourage him. Ample time to walk away.

Instead she had welcomed the pleasure long enough to drive him mad before deciding to act like an importuned innocent. She had opened the door to abandon, beckoned him to cross the threshold, then slammed it in his face.

His slowly easing frustration hurled a silent string of curses onto her fleeing head for that.

His better sense knew none of her reactions had been planned, however. She had yielded completely, but then something in her had been shocked.

Guilt, the great nemesis of pleasure, had reared its head.

It had to do with that portrait drawing. Probably thoughts of her "friend" had broken through her ecstasy.

He guessed that she had made all kinds of excuses for her old lover rather than face the humiliation of the truth. If given the chance, she would live here until she turned gray, awaiting the return of the man who had taken her passion and abandoned her.

Ewan had seen that often enough with women, and it was a criminal waste. It was related to the peculiar illusions women constructed around lovemaking. Most women felt obliged to convince themselves that physical pleasure had to be something other than what it was in order to be enjoyed.

It would help enormously if the poets would stop using the language of religious transcendence when they spoke of passion. There were actually people who took all that seriously, and what a disaster it always created.

Bride became little more than a speck moving toward the distant house. Ewan mounted his horse. He would ride awhile before returning himself. When he did, he would explain to her how there was no need to run from passion.

He would instruct her on the one great truth he knew—that sexual pleasure kept one excited to be alive. It made existence extraordinary instead of drab. He would reveal to her that lovemaking slowed the march of time, and created tiny eternities of complete perfection if one embraced the sensations openly and freely.

If his visit here succeeded in nothing else, he would make sure that this exceptional young woman did not ruin her life and bury her womanhood while she pined for her worthless friend.

She had not run away from him. She had fled from herself.

When Bride left the horse at the stable, she saw their white mare there. Joan was back.

She entered the house through the kitchen to find her sisters and Jilly gathered around the chimney. Michael had removed his shirt, and all the females were intent on watching the taut muscles of his naked back as he jammed a stick up the flue.

Just as Bride closed the door behind her, a shower of cinder fell on Michael's head and shoulders. A huge wad of black straw rolled down his back.

Covered in soot, he turned to glare at the straw. "How in blazes did that get up there?"

"It must be a nest," Mary said.

"Yes," Joan said. "Some big bird must have

built one atop the chimney and yesterday the wind blew it in."

"Doesn't look like a nest to me."

"Oh, we have birds up here that make those kind," Anne said. "They are very unusual, with blue wings and silver tails."

"Silver tails?"

"They have some red feathers, too, and are the size of—"

"Joan, our guest looks to need some water to wash," Bride interrupted. Given any more time, Anne's imagination would grow horns on the bird, and turn it into a prince under a spell. "Thank you for helping with the chimney, Michael. We would have been without hot food for days otherwise."

Joan led a blackened Michael outside. Bride caught his eye as he passed. "The chestnut needs tending. I require my sister's company, so you will have to deal with it."

Jilly took the brooms out to clean up the straw. "Took a good, long time to get it out. You did a fine job with the straw, Bride."

"Anne, help Mary and Jilly, then please join me upstairs when that is done," Bride said.

She hurried up the stairs to the bedroom she was using, to seek a few minutes of privacy before her sisters arrived.

Arms folded over her shirt to hold her emotions steady, she tried to calm the chaotic thoughts that had filled her head as she rode home.

She had been an idiot today. A ridiculous, silly fool.

Lyndale had not even had to try hard to start that seduction. A few deep gazes, a few weak flatteries, and she had all but torn off her clothes and jumped on him.

The memories of her behavior were so embarrassing that she wanted to die.

Only, the excitement had been so . . . enlivening. The thrills so delicious. The pleasure so . . . unearthly.

It had felt so damned good.

She had forgotten how wonderful those sensations could be. Their resurrection had disarmed her, caught her off guard. They had made her weak and indifferent to costs and consequences and just plainly, bluntly, and shamelessly hungry.

Lyndale had reminded her of what she had lost when Walter left. Whatever had happened with Walter, whatever it had meant or not meant, she could not deny she had thoroughly enjoyed making love with him.

He may have betrayed her. He might have run away after feeding her lies. She could not pretend that he had used her badly in bed, however. She had welcomed all of it, whether it had been in love or lust.

She walked into Mary and Anne's little bedroom and peered out the window to the west. She could not see Lord Lyndale approaching, but he would eventually.

She did not know how she could face him now. Maybe he would pretend nothing had happened. She had been late to stop him, but she still had done so. He had not liked that, but he had accepted it.

"Why are you in here?"

Bride startled. She turned to see Anne's expression of curiosity.

"I was looking to see if Joan was coming," she lied.

"She will be here soon, I am sure. Come and look at what I finished."

Bride followed Anne into the other bedroom. Ten squares of paper were laid out on the writing table.

"You just left them out like this?" Bride admired Anne's skills, and loved her sister, but sometimes . . .

"The servant was busy downstairs. I do not think he would be so bold as to enter our chambers, anyway."

Bride was not so sure. She lifted one paper and angled it for the best light. "Perfect, Anne. Just right, as always."

Anne blushed. "Once Lord Lyndale leaves, we will have to make more. If Roger was right about the clearances, we will need a lot this winter, after all."

That was true. Which meant that Bride would have to journey to Edinburgh and back before the bad weather really set in. She had thought she was done until spring, but it seemed not.

Joan's boots sounded on the stairs. She entered the bedroom, snug breeches moving to her long strides, and closed the door. She fished under her waistcoat.

Bride appraised the way her sister wore those garments, and noted how quickly Joan had changed into them upon returning from town.

Both she and Joan had turned to the old trunk of men's clothes in order to spare the household's few, aging dresses from hard wear. Joan, however, had decided she actually preferred the freedom of men's attire.

Since Joan cared for the horse and animals, and did most of the gardening, Bride was hard-pressed to give good reasons why a dress should be worn.

"Here it is." Joan handed over a banknote. "Holland did not want to part with it, even though he knew it would be hard to change, short of going to a city. I barely convinced him to let me buy it. It was becoming his prized possession."

"He probably has never seen one before. Most people haven't." Bride unfolded the fifty pound note. She handed it to Anne.

Anne peered at the signature at the bottom. "Oh, dear. I fear you are right, Bride."

Bride took the note and set it on the dressing table. The three of them stared at it, shaking their heads.

"You can imagine my shock when Holland waved this in front of me last week, so proud and all," Bride said.

"Such careless work is inexcusable. Have they no pride?" Anne asked.

"It isn't even close," Joan mumbled. "Any fool who has seen the banknotes from that time can tell the cashier's signature is a forgery."

"Most notes from thirty years ago are gone," Bride said. She wanted to believe this one did not herald the disaster she feared.

Joan's finger traced the signature. "Since it will not be returned to the Bank of England for silver now, maybe no one will—"

"I doubt this is the only one. Eventually one *will* be turned in for the silver," Bride said.

"It isn't even well aged," Anne said, still clucking her tongue over the shoddy craftsmanship, and completely missing the bigger implications. She held the paper up to the light. "The watermarks are fairly decent, however. The laid lines from the screen are very close to correct."

They stood silently together, sharing the weight of this discovery.

Joan finally asked the question Bride loathed answering. "Is it from Father's plate?"

"Only one way to know for certain." Bride opened the box Mary had snuck out of the studio under Lyndale's nose.

She fingered to the bottom and extracted several notes bearing the inscription of the Bank of England. She flipped through them until she came to one for fifty pounds. It only bore the parts of a banknote that were printed from an engraved plate. Like a new note awaiting issuance, the handwritten parts were blank.

She placed it next to the note Joan had bought at Holland's inn.

Her sisters' heads lowered with hers and they all did a side-by-side comparison of the engraving technique.

"Oh, dear," Anne cried.

"We are doomed," Joan muttered.

"Damnation," Bride whispered.

Ewan paced his horse north toward the coast. He took his time, crossing another glen and climbing a higher hill. The clear air invigorated him.

Actually, when experienced on a day like this, with the sun shining and a dry bed waiting, the Highlands were quite magnificent.

He would have to investigate Lyndale's various properties when he returned to London. Perhaps a Highland manor was among them. A hunting lodge would be welcome. It might be pleasant to come here for sport, not duty and obligation.

He crested the hill and headed toward lower ground. He had not seen a soul since Bride left, but a long string of people moved down the road snaking in front of him.

As he neared, he noticed the cattle and pigs accompanying them. Some mules pulled large wagons laden with furniture and objects.

The crowd saw him. Arms rose in enthusiastic greeting. Children jumped with excitement. Several women called out to him.

He had intended to merely cross the road, but their reaction piqued his curiosity. He trotted toward them.

As he got closer, the voices drifted away. The interest in him abruptly vanished. He waited by the side of the road as the troop trudged on. A few women looked his way resentfully.

A young man at the back of the line gave him a smile and shrug as he passed. Ewan moved his horse alongside the fellow.

"Your friends appeared disappointed once they got a good look at me."

"Thought ye wus someone else, they did. Stupid galoots."

"This is a large group. Where are you all going?"

The man shrugged again. "The coast for most. I'm thinking I'll gae tae Nova Scotia, though, if the passage is offerit. I figure I'd gey be poor there instead of tucked agin the sea here, trying to be a fisherman when I'm a crofter. If it gets bad, I cud always eat a tree if I'm in Canada."

Ewan surveyed the people walking ahead of him. These must be some of the families thrown off the land by the recent clearances that had been mentioned at dinner yesterday.

In contrast to the others, his companion showed remarkable spirits. The tired postures and silence of the parade indicated most of the rest had little optimism.

"Who did they think I was?"

"The faerie. The *sidhe*." He chortled and shook

his head. "Last night a group of the wifies held vigil, waitin'. I cuda told them no faerie was comin', but figured if it helped for a night to hope and wait, no harm done."

"They think a faerie will come and restore their homes?"

"Nah. Just come and give 'em some money to make it easier. There's been such nonsense stories in the hills for years now. How when some townships get burned out, a faerie comes at night and gives money so's the people have something to get them started again."

"This faerie must be very rich, to be resettling whole townships."

The young man did not pick up the sardonic cue. "He daesna give much, but enough to buy the tools and pay the leases and such, so they dinna begin with debts to those waiting to skin them. It's all just rumors, coming from someone's dream." He looked up and grinned. "I cuda told them the rider they saw wasn't him. You arna faerie, and it isna night."

Ewan heartily wished he were a faerie. The progress of this sad troop was slow, and it would take many days to reach their destinations. The government had tried to alleviate the suffering of the clearances by establishing work on the coast, but as this young men said, what industry waiting would leave them in poverty and debt.

He fished in his waistcoat pocket, and cursed that only a few coins met his fingers.

"You seem an honest fellow," he said. "I regret

this is all I have. Take it, however. It should pay for some food for them to share."

The young man accepted the coins and nodded his thanks. Ewan turned his horse toward the hills.

"If ye see that faerie, ye send him this way," the young man called. "I cud be wrong and the wifies cud be right."

Bride kept staring at the fifty pound note.

"We could be in bad trouble, couldn't we?" Joan asked. Anne had left to help Jilly with dinner, but Joan had stayed to commiserate.

"Yes." Bride sighed out her worry and frustration. "I had so prayed that whoever stole the plates had melted them down. The copper had value in itself."

She remembered all too well the day they had all left with Walter to attend a festival in the town. Her heart had sunk when they returned and saw evidence of an intruder.

The loss of some money and her mother's necklace had been the least of it. Days later, when checking the trunk where some of her father's plates were stored, she had found the lock picked and the trunk half empty.

Not just any plates had been stolen. That trunk had contained very special copper plates that her father had worked before she was born. They bore engravings that displayed the heights of his unsurpassed skill. Unfortunately, they were also plates that revealed his pride and weakness.

The special plates buried in that trunk had all been forgeries.

Some of them copied famous old master engravings. Several invented compositions that could be passed off as new discoveries by famous Renaissance artists. A few recreated prints lost to time but known to history.

The Caraglio prints that so excited Lord Lyndale and been printed off some of those plates. They were not originals, created by Caraglio's burin in the sixteenth century. They were impressions of engravings made by her father, forgeries intended to expand the Caraglio series showing the "Loves of the Gods." No doubt her father had seen the same old, tattered images of the addendum that Lyndale's expert, Johann Passavant, had seen.

It was not the theft of the plates that forged artistic compositions that concerned her, however. The danger they represented was small compared to the one that worried her now.

Not only old master forgeries had resided in that trunk.

Her father had also expertly engraved counterfeit banknote plates.

And unlike the old masters, he had printed and used the banknotes.

So had Bride.

They had both used them sparingly, carefully, as

well they might. The penalty for such forgery had been execution, until very recently.

That forgers now faced transportation to New South Wales, and not death, did little to console her.

"Whoever stole the plates realized what they had," she said. "Either they are printing them or they sold them to someone who can. It would take a long time to set it up, so it may have just started. They would need the press, and forging the paper would be difficult. They would need to find someone to do the signature."

"Looks to me they got impatient on the last part," Joan said. "The signature is not good at all."

No, it wasn't. Eventually that would be noticed.

"They may just keep circulating," Joan said hopefully.

"Small notes circulate forever, until they are faded and in tatters. The problem with large denomination notes is that people *do* turn them in for silver at the bank. You know the bank will check the number and the signature and the paper, Joan, and even have a record of the person to whom the note with that number was originally issued."

"Maybe these forgers were careful enough to copy another, good note from that year," Joan said. "Maybe they duplicated the number, so if one is returned, the bank would think it was good."

"Any forger who is careless with the signature is unlikely to get all the details right. If the person doing this is caught, the source of those plates will be learned." Bride forced herself to spell out the danger. "Those thieves have no reason to shield us. It will be assumed we are accomplices."

"Maybe they only printed a few."

Bride grabbed at that possibility. Maybe they *had* only printed a few. Perhaps the risks had been learned when they passed the first ones. And even the boldest forger would only dare pass one or two fifty pound notes a month, unless he was stupid. She had never dared pass a single one herself.

Unfortunately, criminals often *were* stupid, which was why they got caught. If these forgers got caught, they could point their fingers right at this house.

Joan began putting all the papers back in the box. "It appears Walter did not find them."

Bride's heart sickened. Walter had left to track the thieves, to ensure this day would never come. He had sworn he would get the plates back, or see them destroyed.

Joan's tone indicated she did not think he had even tried.

Bride feared he had. If he had confronted men who saw a way to make fortunes for themselves, he had put himself in great danger.

She prayed that he had lied and abandoned her. She hoped he had not discovered those thieves and those plates.

Joan stacked the papers Anne had finished. "What about these? Do we dare use them now?"

Bride held out her hand for them. She gazed at the top one.

It was not a fifty pound note, but a five pound one. Not a sloppy signature, but a perfect one, as only Anne could forge. Not a rare specimen of money that an inn owner would show all his friends and patrons, but a very common one that merchants and grocers and coachmen saw all the time.

All her father's banknote plates were perfect. Superb. No one could handle a burin the way he had. The five and ten pound note plates had not been stolen because they had been in the studio.

"If we are ever caught, it will not be because of these," she said. "We have used that plate for years, and no one has ever questioned the notes. We will proceed as before. I will take them to Edinburgh to pass, as I have always done. As for that," she gestured to the fifty pound forgery, "we do not even know where it was received by that hunting party Holland served. We will have to pray that no more are circulating, that the thieves realized the folly of such an enterprise."

Joan took the notes and stuffed them in the box. "I wonder if they have a lot of horses in New South Wales."

CHAPTER SIX

⸻

"A faerie?" Michael greeted Ewan's tale at dinner with a laugh.

"A faerie," Ewan said. "The poor people are reduced to putting their hope in folklore fantasies."

"How peculiar," Bride said.

She looked only at Michael. Ewan had noticed that she had completely managed to avoid looking at *him* since his return. Her expression had assumed a stonelike blandness, too.

That was fine. He could wait. She would most definitely be looking at him, and giving him all her attention, soon enough. The stone would melt, too.

He had thought of little else besides making love to her since he saw her again. She anticipated it, too. She pretended to ignore him, but they were as starkly conscious of each other as if they still embraced on the hilltop. The mutual awareness tantalized him like a constant feathery touch.

"A faerie! I cannot imagine what gave rise to such a silly notion," Joan said, rolling her eyes.

Anne turned a perplexed frown on her sister. "It is not a silly notion, and you know it."

"We know no such thing, Anne," Bride said pointedly. "We do not want *Lord Lyndale* to think we are superstitious, do we, dear? Please excuse my sister, gentlemen. She is inclined to believe such fantasies herself if one does not watch her."

"Of course there are faeries. Everyone knows that," Anne insisted.

"Everyone in Scotland," Ewan explained to Michael.

"Father thought Anne was part faerie," Mary piped in. "He thought Mother had—"

"That is enough, Mary," Bride interrupted. "Father thought nothing of the kind."

"He did *too.* He said she—"

"Jilly, please pass Lord Lyndale the sneeps," Bride said.

"Faeries," Michael said, shaking his head. "If someone tried to burn me out of my home, I'd not be waiting for some faerie to make it better once the embers died. Better they should be waiting for Sutherland's men with knives and pitchforks, if you ask me."

"That would only get them hanged," Ewan said.

"Some things are worth getting hanged for, then."

"One's own rights, perhaps. But they have none. They are tenants. Neither the land nor the homes are theirs, no matter how long their families have lived there."

Suddenly Bride's attention was on him. A thousand golden lights sparked in her emerald eyes. "Some that you saw today will die because of this. The old and the weak. Some have even died in the fires in years past, and no law punished the men who let them burn, because those men worked for those with power. Do not speak of rights to me, sir. No one has the right to cause such suffering as I have seen."

"Father always taught us that there are laws higher than man's and that one must do what one can to help the poor and weak, no matter what the risks," Anne said. "He said—"

Bride's hand came to rest on Anne's. A firm squeeze stopped the sentence.

All the sisters began passing platters. Joan muttered something about the weather.

Michael's face had flushed. "No need to be telling me who owns what in this world, sir. I know all about the rights of those who do these things. I took a long walk like those people did, when I was six. Not just Scotland where these things happen. There's times the law does not handle things fairly, and then it is time to fight."

The outburst astonished Ewan. He knew that Michael had been little more than a street urchin as a boy. He was aware that what polish Michael possessed had been learned through careful study of the clientele while he worked in elite gaming halls as a youth.

He had never known, however, that his manservant had been part of a farming family displaced by the enclosures sweeping England.

Nor had he suspected that Michael harbored some revolutionary beliefs. Or any beliefs, for that matter.

Bride's stone had cracked. She looked at Michael and a sweet softness claimed her expression. "Jilly, I think we should have a cake for this evening."

"Sugar cone is aboot gone," Jilly said.

"Then use what is there. I think we should celebrate our good fortune in having such an intelligent and kindhearted guest."

Ewan did not miss the singularity of her favor. Michael brightened at the clear approval of his hostess.

Absolutely no such approval marked her expression when she again turned toward Ewan. "Lord Lyndale, perhaps this afternoon we should discuss your great mission here. I trust you have had time to do the investigating you thought was warranted."

"Certainly, Miss Cameron. I believe I have learned all that I require."

"Remember, do not say a word," Bride said as her sisters gathered in the library that afternoon. "I will speak for us."

She gave her sisters a quick inspection. They had dressed in their best garments for this meeting. Bride, however, wore an ugly pelisse robe of severe and relentlessly modest cut. It fastened up the front to her neck and no decoration relieved its brown wool fabric.

"Mary, if you encourage him in the least, it will be bread and water for you for a week."

Mary sank into a pout that claimed her whole body. Anne's attention drifted to the heavens. Joan fidgeted in the dress that Bride had forced her to stay in after dinner.

Lord Lyndale entered, looking as impressive and handsome and arrogant as ever. He paused a moment when he saw she was not alone.

"How good that you are all here," he said dryly. His attention focused completely on her. His expression implied he found her attempts to find protection charming.

Did the man think she was such an idiot she would meet with him in privacy?

He gave her a smoldering look that made her nape tingle. No, not an idiot. He thought she was an eager, starving, shameless woman.

She leveled an indifferent gaze at him in response. That appeared to amuse him.

He did not sit in the chair waiting. Instead he cocked one elbow on the mantel and relaxed into a pose that spoke assumptions of command.

"Here is how I see things, ladies. Bear with me while I share my thoughts."

"Take your time, sir. We are sure your judgments are considered and sober, and that you only have our welfare at heart." Bride made no effort to keep sarcasm from tingeing her tone.

"Your industry is impressive." He did not even pretend to be speaking to her sisters. He addressed only her. "However, conducting it here is very inconvenient. The closest publishers are in Edinburgh, after all."

"We manage that inconvenience, thank you."

"Knowing something of the income such plates might achieve, I calculate that it barely pays the lease, let alone keeps you in food and fuel."

"We are neither starving nor freezing."

"You are not starving because you are poaching Sutherland's game. I daresay you help yourself to fuel from that preserve, as well, so the lack of both starving and freezing involves criminal activity that must not continue. I must insist that you cease that at once."

Out of the corner of her eye, Bride saw Joan suck in her cheeks in amusement at Lyndale's assessment of the criminal ways that needed ceasing.

"At best your lives are precarious, Miss Cameron. You cannot afford new dresses, and resort to your father's and grandfather's old garments. The horse you use is at least ten years old—"

"Twelve," Anne corrected, displaying once again her regrettable tendency to pay attention only at the most unhelpful moments.

"You have land leased that you cannot work, and too few livestock to do more than barely keep poverty at bay. In short, this household is a tragedy in the making."

"Well, sir, if things get truly bad, I will sell off one of my sisters. No doubt there is some unscrupulous, aristocratic libertine who will take one on and pay well for her."

Silence fell. Lyndale just looked at her.

"I do not expect to need to, however," she added. "I am very sure that the faeries will see that our situation does not get that dire."

Joan swallowed a laugh too late. A deep snort snuck out.

Lyndale was not amused. "I sympathize with your desire to stay in your family's home. However, it is no longer safe or realistic to do so. I will buy you a house in Edinburgh and supplement your income so that you have a decent and secure life there. The allowance will permit you to dress appropriately, and begin moving in society. You will have friends, and a future. If you choose to continue the engraving, that is your decision. I will not insist you give it up."

Bride felt her neck tightening. "How generous of you."

"Now, we should accomplish this move at once. I will go to Edinburgh, find the house, and return for you within the month at the latest."

There it was. Just like that. The lord speaketh and the women accepteth.

The man's arrogance was not to be borne.

"Lord Lyndale, allow me now to explain how *I*

see this." Bride struggled to keep her voice calm despite the way blood heated her head. "Your promises to Duncan McLean are not our concern. We do not choose to have you take over our lives. We will not be moving to Edinburgh, or anywhere else. Our life and our work is here."

Anne decided to chime in again. "Yes, our work is right here, in these glens, doing what our father taught us to do. If we were to move, what would hap—"

Bride grasped Anne's arm again. Hard. "Furthermore, Lord Lyndale, we do not want you buying us new dresses and bonnets and food."

"I do," Mary whispered.

"I will, however, agree to a suggestion you made the day that you came," Bride said. "If you choose to make settlements on my sisters so that they have some security, and better chances of marrying, I will not interfere."

Mary began weeping with happiness. Joan regarded Bride with shock. Anne cocked her head, confused.

Lord Lyndale's gaze captured Bride's. His attention became invasive, as if he worked at deciphering her mind.

"Your sisters, you say. And you, Miss Cameron. What of your future?"

"I have my father's legacy. If need be, I can sell his collection, too, one print at a time. Should my skill in engraving ever fail me, that is. I assure you, my future is more secure than you can ever imagine."

It was not clear that he heard her. He just kept

looking at her in a way that had her feeling too much like an injured bird in a hawk's sights.

"It would be best if I speak with your sister alone regarding these settlements, ladies. Would you be kind enough to leave us." He walked over to the door and opened it.

All three of her sisters jumped to their feet in obedience.

"No," Bride cried. "That is, this concerns them all and they should be here."

"Miss Cameron, it would be indelicate to discuss the particulars in their presence."

He bestowed a magnanimous smile on them and crooked his finger to beckon them to the door.

Bride caught Joan's skirt. "Do *not* leave this room," she hissed.

"Bride, it really would be best if you alone settled the rest with him," Joan whispered. "Mary will be so glad for anything that she will make a scene that renders negotiation on the sum impossible. And Anne, well, who knows what disaster she will make. She has already come close to blurting everything twice today." She extricated her skirt from Bride's desperate grip. "We trust you to do your best by us. You have managed him brilliantly thus far."

Bride watched in horror as her sisters filed out past Lord Lyndale.

When the last skirt hem crossed the threshold, he closed the door.

And locked it.

CHAPTER SEVEN

"What are you doing?" Bride demanded. She intended her voice to be stern. Unfortunately, the question came out as a squeak.

"I am making sure that we are not disturbed."

A rising panic said that being disturbed would be a very good idea. Vitally important. "I insist that you unlock that door."

"Miss Cameron, if given the chance, your youngest sister will poke her nose in as she did yesterday in your studio. We must attend to matters without such interruption."

Bride's gaze darted from Lord Lyndale to the lock and back again.

"You do not have to look like a cornered rabbit," he said, strolling toward her. "I never force myself on women, as you already know very well."

She did not want him even alluding to that, let alone implying he knew she had been agreeable.

He sat down on the sofa. "Now, let us talk about these settlements. I am pleased you agree to them. It will make the discharge of my duty much easier."

He was not right next to her on the sofa, but he was still too close. His proximity provoked a physical hum all through her. She felt very much like the cornered rabbit he spoke of.

She jumped up and moved to a nice, separate, safe chair.

His reaction was a vague, patient smile.

"Shall we say I settle five thousand on each of them, invested in the funds? That will produce an income of approximately two-fifty a year apiece."

The high amount stunned her. She did not know what to say.

He waited for her response. When none came, he continued. "That should be enough for any of them to live independently. If they continue to live together, it will keep them handsomely. It is also sufficient to attract husbands of respectable means and intentions."

All that was true. She could not deny it.

"It is also sufficient to maintain the household in Edinburgh, or some other city," he added.

"No."

His gaze sharpened. "You are not being rational. Since you impress me as an intelligent woman, I cannot help but wonder why you are so resistant to this move."

She did not need him wondering about that, or

anything else. She just needed him to leave this house and this glen.

She rose from her chair. "Call it sentimentality. Perhaps I worry that such incomes will attract men for the wrong reasons if they live in a city. Your offer is generous, however, and I thank you. It is more than sufficient to discharge your obligations. Our business is therefore completed. Now, I must see to household matters, and you will want to prepare for your journey back to London."

She marched to the door. She fumbled at the lock.

A hand came to rest against the door's boards. Another closed over hers on the latch. A masculine scent and aura encompassed her.

"Our business is hardly completed, Bride, and you know it."

His voice was right near her ear. Each word felt like a tiny caress.

She battled to freeze out the traitorous chills shimmering down her neck.

She faced the door, refusing to look at him. "It is very completed, such as it will ever be."

"Hardly." He gently pried her hand off the latch. "Also, there is the matter of your future. I cannot leave that insecure, and fulfill my oath."

Also?

"I have the leg—"

"Even if you sell every print, it will not ensure your keep forever."

She sensed a warmth on her head. A tingling. He

was touching her hair. Her essence sighed and
started a wonderful melting, despite her best efforts
to turn to granite.

"You are refusing the income because of what
happened this morning, Bride. That is not necessary.
That is a thing apart from this settlement. I require
no more of you than I do of your sisters."

She groped for self-possession. "You are both
presumptuous and too familiar, sir. I did not give
you permission to address me as Bride."

He shifted until he leaned one shoulder against
the door. She could see him now, even without looking right at him. Her heart began pounding.

His hand cupped her chin and turned her face to
his. "I am inclined to presume the right to be very
familiar with a woman after she has let me kiss her
breast."

"I *did not* allow—"

"Yes, sweet lady, you definitely did. You are not a
girl, Bride. It is normal for a woman to welcome
pleasure. That is the great prize of maturity for females—the ability and right to enjoy pleasure without guilt."

As if to prove what he meant, he kissed her. Gently. Deliberately. Seductively.

She tried to believe she had not seen that kiss
coming, but a part of her, too much, had been waiting for it.

She fought to remain impassive, but her lips
throbbed under his skillful assault. The sensation
slid down in maddening streams.

She struggled to be strong and rigid, but her legs turned to water and a spinning daze made her dizzy.

His arm moved to embrace and support her. His fingers still rested on her face. He gazed down at her.

"You will accept the settlement, and you will all move to Edinburgh. The house and money will be yours free and clear. You will owe me nothing, least of all your favors."

She wanted to damn his arrogance. Her mind was incapable of forming the words because most of her attention was on his face and eyes. The settlements became a foggy memory within her mesmerized senses.

He pulled her closer, into a claiming embrace that held her tightly against his warmth. "Now, that is out of the way. Which means that we can finish this."

Her conscience shrieked a scold to stop this madness.

Her body just laughed at the shrill voice until it faded.

After that she heard nothing. Saw nothing. She dwelled in a mist of pleasure, where she was young and beautiful.

Ewan had forgotten how much he enjoyed a challenge.

It had been so long since he had met a woman who posed one, that the heady anticipation of victory felt new and potent.

It sharpened his senses and made him very aware of the woman he was kissing. He noticed things he never cared about anymore. How her height fit so nicely against his body. How her fading resistance slowly made her soft and pliable. How the gentle music of her sighs rose and fell depending on how he caressed her.

He kissed her hard, to defeat any remaining nonsense about guilt. His tongue stroked the warm, soft cave of her mouth. She stiffened for a moment, trying to control the deep tremors he felt in her. Then she yielded with a willowy, beautiful, fluid softening.

Her freed passion was as intoxicating as her resistance had been. She boldly captured his tongue, then used her own aggressively.

She touched his face and ended the long kiss with a deep gasp. She looked up at him with moist, dreamy eyes, the image of a woman lost to sensation.

"As seducing scoundrels go, you are superb, Lord Lyndale."

He took the opportunity to gently bite down her neck. "Thank you. It is my most prized accomplishment." His mouth closed on her pulse.

She angled her head so he could have a better purchase. "Did you have to study and practice hard to achieve greatness in your chosen area of endeavor?"

"Night and day for years. A man's life must stand for something, however, so it was worth it."

Her throaty, low laugh warmed his ear. He looked up to see a spark of intelligence brightening her gaze.

That would never do. The last thing he wanted was her thinking about this. Or anything. Who knew where that might lead? Probably to her running away again. If she stopped now, he would want to kill himself.

He used his hands to ensure that would not happen. He caressed her through the ugly dress, pressing her lithe form so she felt his hands. She flexed subtly, deliciously. Her responses spoke her pleasure, and encouraged more. Finally her arms rose so she embraced him, clinging to his shoulders as her body completely surrendered.

In a blur of savage response, he claimed her lips and neck and chest with his mouth and her body with his hands. He could not get enough of her. He came close to pushing her against the door and lifting her skirt so he could take her now, at once.

With another woman he might have. A spot of sense remained within that rough hunger, however. The awareness of who she was did not get consumed by the heat.

Forcing control, he caressed her breasts. Astonishment sounded on her sighs. Lovely, joyful wonder. He stroked their fullness while he kissed her, and the melody changed as her breath shortened. Her fingers grasped his shoulders harder. Her back arched.

He stopped kissing her and looked down at the

soft swell under his hand. He trailed up to her neck
and released the top little hook of the dress.

He looked into her eyes. No objection shadowed
the pleasure reflected in them. No resistance threatened to stop him. She was a woman entranced.

He lifted her in his arms, carried her to the sofa,
settled her beside him, and kissed her senseless. He
drowned her in pleasure and began working on the
dress again.

She looked down at his fingers while they loosened the tiny hooks. "It did not help much. The
dress. It was supposed to make me ugly."

"The dress is truly ugly, but you never could be.
Also, this style is so convenient it is bound to encourage a man's imagination." He pushed the two
sides of the bodice aside, revealing just how convenient it was. Her breasts rose above simple stays,
sheathed in the filmy fabric of a threadbare chemise.

He glossed his fingertips slowly over the firm
swells of her breasts. His sense contracted to only
the exquisite feel of her and the sound of her stac-
cato breathing.

Her lids rose a fraction and she watched what he
was doing.

"Is it your intention to drive me mad first?"

"The more you want it, the more you will enjoy it."

"I do not think I need to want it any more." She
moved his hand so that his fingers touched her
nipple.

That made him pause. Was she *complaining*? In-
structing him in his technique? *Him?*

Why, the little . . .

"Forgive me, my dear. I stand admonished."

He threw careful consideration to the winds. She had just cast down a gauntlet at the foot of a champion.

He gave her what she wanted, and made sure she enjoyed it. Deftly, ruthlessly, he aroused her until her breaths carried low cries. While he teased at her tight, hard nipples, he pulled the shoulders of her dress down her arms to her elbows. That forced her to release her embrace of him.

She tried to reach for the right cuff with her left hand, to unfasten it. The dress imprisoned her upper arms, making that impossible. She raised her wrist for him to help.

"No. I want you just like that, Bride."

That made *her* pause. She took in her situation with a quick, cautious glance. He lowered the chemise straps so her breasts were naked.

She blushed. She shifted, trying to release her arms from the dress. "I think—"

"You are not supposed to be thinking at all. I can see I still have work to do."

He caressed her breasts and her breath caught. He molded his hand around their warmth and softness. There was a small rebellion against the way the dress inhibited her movements, but she did not demand freedom. He wondered if she understood that the vulnerability increased the pleasure.

Tremors slid through her. He could feel their

echoes in his touch. She bit her lip against the faint sounds escaping her.

She looked stunning. Beautiful and wild and erotic. Her breasts were so lovely, full and high. And her skin—that of her face had astonished him from the start, but the skin of her shoulders and breasts beckoned his lips.

He indulged, kissing along the top of her shoulder. She jumped with surprise, letting him know he had found one of her special sensitivities. He moved down her chest and her breaths deepened. She tried once more to move her arms, but gave up. She surrendered to captivity.

He licked one erect, dark rose nipple. He lightly caressed the other. He felt the sensation overwhelm her. She fought it. He used his tongue and fingers to win. With a melodic, breathy moan, she gave in.

Her arousal turned wild. Her cries of sensual torment made his own control waver. His mind filled with images of what he would do and wanted to do and could not do. In all of it she was crying for him as she did now.

He shrugged off his coat. He laid her down and settled himself above her. She parted her legs so he nestled between her thighs. That had his mind clouding. Hard hungers drove out what was left of his sense.

Mad now, determined and impatient, he caressed up her leg, lifting her skirt and petticoat.

He rose enough so that his hand could reach her thigh. His fingers touched slickness and her scent filled his head. He kept laving her breasts while his hand caressed higher. Her cries grew frantic and frustrated. Her hips rocked as she begged for relief. He touched the unearthly softness of her curls and mound, and gritted his teeth against the primitive urge to go down and kiss and suck the sweetness waiting there.

He slid his finger into her cleft. She was hot and wet and unbearably soft. He looked at her face as he pleasured her. She had gone mad, completely crazed. She was ravishing in her passion. Perfect and free.

He wanted her badly. More than he had wanted a woman in years. Maybe more than ever before. It made no sense, but he could not deny it was true. The awareness that he would soon possess her appealed to something ferocious and rare in him.

Mind splitting, body howling, he began releasing his trousers. He would take her and it would be perfect. She would belong to him and never wear ugly dresses, and he would teach her all about pleasure and give her jewels and—

A ray of light poked through the roaring storm, making him stop.

No, he would not be doing any of those things, no matter how perfect this might be.

He looked at her face, so transformed and welcoming. Her cries and breaths said she was as impatient as he was.

He inhaled deeply. He moved his hand until it

rested on her hip. A battle clashed inside him and he did not even know who the opponents were.

Her lids rose. Realization slowly dawned in her eyes. With it came an awareness on her part of how insane they had both become.

He inhaled deeply again. His body comprehended what was happening and began punishing him.

Finally he admitted the truth.

He could not do this. He did not know why, and he hated that he couldn't. It infuriated him. All the same, he could not shake the intrusive idea that it would be . . . wrong.

That was such an absurd notion that it almost had him laughing. All the same, he sat up, and lifted her as well. He smoothed down her skirt and pulled up her chemise.

To say she was startled did not do justice to her reaction. Her expression changed from perplexed to stunned, to blank, to cold.

"It was going too far," he mumbled. He helped her fix her dress.

She shrugged off his hands and began fastening the front. "It appears you aren't nearly as good a seducing scoundrel as we thought."

He wanted to throttle her. No, he really wanted to rip off that ugly dress so she was spread out naked under him as he thrust into her so long and hard that she had one of those transcendent climaxes the stupid poets alluded to.

Instead he rose and walked to the door.

Here he had acted honorably for the first time in

his life, for reasons he did not even begin to know, and the harridan didn't even appreciate it.

Lyndale strode outside, badly in need of cool air. His body was giving him hell. He wondered if that was why his countrymen heaved tree trunks. Maybe the sport had started as a way to relieve untimely erections.

He wandered into the stable, thinking throwing around some hay would help just as well.

He heard Michael's muffled laugh. Following the sound, he climbed up to the hayloft. Michael stood at the wide door, coats removed and lying at his feet, looking down outside.

"You had better move. I don't want to fall on you," Michael called. He was so intent on the view that he did not hear Ewan come up behind him.

Ewan peered over Michael's shoulder. Joan lay laughing in a high mound of hay. Presumably she had jumped, and now Michael planned to join her for a little frolicking.

"If you jump down there, your neck will break," Ewan said.

Michael froze, then swung around. A cautious smile played at his mouth. "Oh, it ain't all that far."

"It will not be the fall that kills you."

Michael blanched. "It is just a game, sir."

"I know the game. I am a master at it. Remember?" Ewan stuck his head out and looked down at Joan. She saw him and her face went red.

"Get inside the house," he ordered. "And put on a damned dress. Don't the women in your family know better than to walk around showing the shape of their legs and whatever else in those breeches?"

Joan rolled off the hay and ran to the house. Ewan turned to Michael. Hurling a tree trunk was a poor substitute for thrashing someone.

Michael backed up. He raised two cautious and appeasing hands. "Now, sir, there was no harm done and none intended."

"*Do not* treat me like I am a fool. I tolerate you, and even enjoy your company, but when I say do not touch, I mean *do not touch.*"

Michael had never shown proper deference, and it was clear he was too callow to start now. "There was no touching, I swear." He sniffed. "You are just out of sorts because you did not get what you wanted with the big red one."

"*Excuse me?*"

"The others might not know what you were up to in that library, but I guessed. Saw you eyeing Bodisha all during dinner. I even distracted Joan here, to help you out. She's the only one smart enough to suspect." He assumed a hurt expression, as if all he ever got for his selfless loyalty was complaints. "I *told* you she was a woman quick to kick men where it hurts."

"She did not kick."

"No?" A frown claimed Michael's face as he pondered that. Suddenly it cleared. "Oohh, you mean . . . no wonder you are . . . I hear it happens to everyone, sir, if that makes you feel better. Especially once a man starts getting old."

"Old?"

"Well, you are past thirty. Even prized stallions can't go on forever."

"You are in grave danger of having me kill you. She did not kick, and I did not . . . what you imply. And none of this is your concern."

"Forgive me, just from your ill humor I thought that things went awry in that library, and I figured those are the only reasons why they might."

Yes, only two reasons Michael could understand. Only two that Ewan could, too. That was the damnable part of it. He had stopped and he did not even know why.

Maybe it had to do with this responsibility nonsense.

Yes, that was it.

He had never been responsible for anyone before, even slightly. Now he did not know how to quash the inconvenient notion that he was supposed to take care of this woman, not seduce her.

A livid fury joined his frustration. This was exactly what he had feared would happen when he inherited that damned title. Here he was, debating whether he was allowed to make love to a mature and experienced woman whom he wanted and who was willing.

It was absurd. It was *unnatural.*

Michael chose that moment to flash one of his

cocky grins. "I could sleep in the library tonight if you want to try again."

Ewan grabbed him by the collar and trousers and hurled him out the door. Michael flew through the air and landed in a sprawl in the hay.

Ewan stormed out of the stable.

This inheritance threatened to ruin him. He had suspected it could, and now he had the proof.

Well, he'd be damned before he turned into one of those saintly dullards who walked on a narrow path between two thick, high walls.

Those walls were named "duty" and "responsibility."

Bride did not sleep that night. She tossed in the bed she shared with Joan, hoping Lyndale would leave soon, and also hoping he would not.

The "would not" just kept intruding, never bidden. It was an irritating fantasy that kept sneaking out of her heart, accompanied by memories of luscious pleasure and the wistful illusion that she had mattered, if only for an hour. It was the silly reaction of that part of her that was still a girl.

Time would solve that quickly, however. In a day or so the childish excitement would fade. She would not humiliate herself further by building illusions on what had occurred. If ever a man had been honest about seeking only momentary pleasure, it was Lord Lyndale.

She mentally worked through the duties waiting

once he quit this house. The responsibilities pressed on her, already making her weary. The sense of being owned by dull drudgery was a familiar feeling of late, and one that had mercifully disappeared the last few days. Lyndale was an intrusion, but she had to admit life had been more exciting with him here.

She planned the trip to Edinburgh, and the work before and after. She thought hard about that fifty pound note. Was it safe to wait, or should she do something to discover how dangerous that was to them?

And Walter—she had told herself that he merely abandoned her, but what if he had come to harm, or was imprisoned by the forgers? Did she not owe him as much as she had wanted to believe he owed her? In the least, shouldn't she try to discover what had become of him?

Before dawn, she heard noise in the house. Muffled movement penetrated the wall that separated her chamber from the one Lyndale was using. Steps sounded on the stairs.

She rose from the bed and draped a knit shawl around her. She peeked out the door.

Lyndale stood atop the stairs, watching Michael descend with two valises in his hands. Lyndale held his hat and riding crop, and his redingote was slung over his arm.

She slipped out of the chamber and shut the door behind her.

He noticed her. The lamp glow from his room offered little light, so she could not see his expression when he turned to her. Just as well. She had avoided him last evening, and had tried to ignore his presence when they found themselves in the same room.

She did not understand everything that had happened in the library. All she knew for certain was that she had embarrassed herself again with that quick capitulation. She had acted like the lonely, forlorn, aging spinster he thought she was.

"I am grateful to see you, Miss Cameron. I was debating if there was some way to wake you so that I could express my gratitude for your hospitality."

"You are leaving?"

"We have imposed too long. The day promises to be fair and we should make good progress on our journey." He sounded very smooth, very confident. There was the smallest note, however, that suggested he found her presence as awkward as she did his.

"I will arrange for the house in Edinburgh at once, and send for all of you when it is established," he said.

He would no longer come himself, as he had first intended. He was distancing himself. Stewards and servants would deal with them now. Bride suspected that, barring a major problem, they would never see him again.

Unfortunately, major problems loomed and they could not risk he would interfere even then.

"No, Lord Lyndale, you will not find that house. We are not going to Edinburgh. If you at some point thought I agreed to that, I can only say that when you sought to settle the matter, I was at a disadvantage."

He turned his hat in his hands. She could not fathom his expression.

"Yes, you were. My apologies for that. I am left with no choice but to honor your preferences on the matter, or else appear to have dishonorable motives. The settlements, however, you still agree to those?"

"For my sisters. I would never have accepted for myself, so it is not your motives that I question."

"I will establish the necessary trusts as soon as I return to London. The papers should be posted to you soon."

Michael's head appeared halfway up the steps. He gestured to Lyndale, then turned and went back down.

"We will go now," Lyndale said. "Miss Cameron, you must promise me that you will let me know if you are ever in need of my assistance. Neither of us asked to have this obligation on my part bind us, but it does all the same. My fortune and my protection are available to you and your sisters, should either be needed."

She had to smile at the tactless word "obligation." Lord Lyndale did not bother with pretty turns of phrases. "I promise that I will never forget that your assistance is there if we need it, sir."

He turned to go, but stopped. He faced her again, his head cocked as if a thought had just occurred to him.

"Duncan McLean," he said. "Yesterday in the library you referred to my uncle, the last earl, by his given name."

"Did I?"

"I am sure you did. How did you know his name?"

"I have no idea. You must have mentioned it, or perhaps Michael did to Joan and she used it."

She sensed him thinking that over.

"Yes, that must be it." He made a small bow. "Please give your sisters my regards, Miss Cameron."

He took his leave.

She watched his broad shoulders descend into the shadows, disappearing from her life forever.

CHAPTER
EIGHT

~~

Ewan slid his arms into the dinner coat that Michael held. "I confess that I am a little nostalgic. This is the last time that I will dress for the night in this chamber."

"The new dressing room is big enough for a ball. I expect you will get used to the luxury soon enough. I will."

Michael fussed with the garments with a newly attentive precision. Out in the other chambers, crates waited for the move to Belgrave Square in the morning.

Ewan had settled on the house in December, soon after returning from Scotland. Now, with the new year, he was ready to take possession of the Earl of Lyndale's new home.

"You have seen to the servants?"

"They will be awaiting your lordship's arrival. All men, as you demanded, though it was not easy to find ones willing to do the women's work. Had to offer more than the going amount."

"Money well spent. I cannot have a bevy of female servants there. What a horror. Even with my collection in the second drawing room, they would complain. And the parties—" He did not even want to think about the reaction of female servants to that.

"These will know what to expect. I picked them carefully."

"You have been an enormous help. I could not have faced the ordeal without you."

Michael swiped a brush over the coat. "I am honored that you are pleased, my lord."

Ewan cocked an eyebrow at the deferential tone. The last few days, Michael had been acting like a servant who knew his place. That was suspicious.

"Since you are pleased, perhaps we could discuss my situation here," Michael said, as he laid out Ewan's watch and fobs.

"You are unhappy with your situation?"

"Things are changing. That big house and all those servants. I won't be doing all that I have. It is not clear what I will be."

He had a point. Up until now, Michael had served as everything. He was valet, coachman, groom, butler, and housekeeper. That the serious housekeeping was done by women hired by the day, only meant that he managed the hiring and paying of them.

"You will be my valet. The steward will handle the rest. You probably will have to take a more formal air when others see us, of course. The familiarity should not be copied by the new servants."

Michael appeared to think that an acceptable solution. "The steward will arrange the parties, then?"

"It may be best if certain parties are managed by you."

"He won't like that, my lord."

"He will have to accept it. I'll be damned if I am going to have servants commanding me in my home."

"There is one more thing, if I may mention it, my lord."

All these "my lords" had Ewan wondering just what Michael was plotting. "What would that be?"

"I thought that, with all these changes in your situation, we might discuss my wages."

Ewan took his hat and gloves. "You have no wages."

"Doesn't seem fitting for an earl's valet to have no wages, is what I meant. It isn't proper. It will affect your reputation if it is known. It could be badly misunderstood."

"Michael, are you blackmailing me?"

"Just explaining how I see it, is all."

"It also isn't proper for an earl to have a manservant whom he allows to play cards with his friends."

"Well, now, I don't see as how—"

"No, no. You are correct. It is time I reform my household in a manner appropriate to my station. Henceforth, I will pay you the going wage for your services. You, in turn, will perform as a normal valet. That means no more sitting at my tables to gamble. Since you have done very nicely these last few years, I am sure that you have more than enough under your mattress to open that gaming hall you dream of."

Michael's mouth formed a tight line.

"Yes, no more easy pickings at cards. No more scooping up the easier favors of certain ladies who—"

"Now, sir, no need to rush into things. I was only mentioning how it might be awkward, is all."

Michael turned to cleaning and straightening the dressing room. Ewan paused at the door and watched the young man tend to the mess.

He had a fondness for Michael, and admired his initiative and boldness. It had taken real brass to show up that day and propose this arrangement. God only knew where he had learned to be a valet, too. Ewan suspected Michael had just guessed what to do, and learned on his own that first year. It had helped that Ewan was not too demanding, nor in a position to replace a servant who cost almost nothing to keep.

It was an odd relationship, and one that might add to the tattle of the town once they moved to Belgrave Square. Ewan did not care what people said. He intended to give them plenty to gossip about, should they want to, but Michael was not an earl. There were hidden dreams and plans in that shrewd blond head, and it would not do to have them thwarted by a minor matter like this.

"Beginning tomorrow, you will receive the

wages common for your position," he said. "A bit more, I think. I will be depending upon you to keep one eye on that steward and the others. I do not want them robbing me blind."

"Tell me, Lady M., when do you intend to end the mourning for your late husband?"

The handsome woman beside Ewan at dinner leveled a dangerous gaze on him. "I dropped the mourning years ago, sir."

"You dropped the symbols only."

A tight smile of forbearance greeted that observation. Lady Charlotte Mardenford did not care for this conversation. "Why do you think I am still in mourning?"

"Because you never accept invitations to my parties."

"Ah, I see. A widow is in mourning because she declines to romp naked on your divans and sofas with heaven knows who, in full view of others."

He tilted his head toward her. "There need not be any others around to view the romping. It could be a party of two."

She laughed. "I can see the new Earl of Lyndale is as naughty as the old Ewan McLean. Be reassured, sir, that my lack of romping with you does not mean that I do not romp at all."

His flirtation was an old joke and an old game between them. However, Ewan suspected that despite her pose to the contrary, no romping had transpired since the baron died. He also knew that, should she ever truly drop the mourning, she would never seek out one of his sofas.

"I can see that the title has not reformed you at all," she said. "It is a good thing that Sophia had no illusions on that count. She knew what she was getting in inviting you tonight."

Indeed she had. Which begged the question of just why the Duchess of Everdon had extended the invitation to this dinner. Unlike some hostesses, the duchess did not engage in the contest of snagging the most recent sensation to her gatherings. Nor had she in the past included Ewan McLean at any of them.

He gazed down the table. It was a small dinner party, quite intimate. He was friends with most of the guests, as if the list had been devised for his comfort. Had the duchess decided to ease his way back into good society?

There was no other reason for the gesture that Ewan could imagine. Whatever the cause, it was proving to be a pleasant night surrounded by friends.

Dante Duclairc was here, along with his wife, Fleur. Adrian Burchard, the duchess's husband and consort, sat on Fleur's other side.

Down the table, Adrian's brother Colin could be found. Colin, like Dante, was a member of Ewan's set. The contrast of Adrian's dark, Mediterranean appearance with Colin's blond, thoroughly English one pointed up the open secret that they did not share the same father. Colin was the Earl of Dincaster's son, in truth, but Adrian was the by-blow of a liaison between the earl's wife and a foreign dignitary.

All in all, it was a delightful assemblage of people Ewan knew well, and most of whom had various connections. Lady Mardenford, for example, was Dante's sister, and one of the duchess's closest friends.

The only exception was Viscount Althorp and his wife. Althorp was Chancellor of the Exchequer, and Ewan's contact with him had been of the most formal sort. Nor had he surmised a friendship between Althorp and the others at the table.

"Where are you putting the infamous swing in that new house of yours?" Lady M. asked.

"In the second drawing room. You must visit and try it out."

She laughed and blushed. "You are really very bad, McLean."

"I look forward to the day when you are very bad, too, madame, even though I grieve it will not be with me."

An image entered his head of that swing, and the bad things one could do on it. The woman joining him as it swayed was not the baroness, however. The hair flowing over his face and shoulders was long and red and tight with curls. The breast in his mouth was full and firm and rosy-tipped. The naked legs straddling his hips were long, lithe, and milky white.

He wondered about Bride Cameron several times a day, and unaccountably did so now.

Was all going well up in that glen? They should

be receiving the trust papers soon. He hoped they would manage until the income on the funds was paid. If not, they would probably starve. Bride would never eat her pride and ask for his help.

The duchess rose. The other ladies followed suit. Rich, wide skirts swished around the table as the women retired to the drawing room.

Footmen passed port and brandy and cigars to the men, then left the room.

Now that was odd. Servants normally waited to attend to future needs.

Even odder was the peculiar silence that claimed the chamber.

The way that all the others looked in his direction was damned alarming.

Colin smiled apologetically. "There is an important matter that requires attention, McLean. Adrian arranged this party so that Althorp could ask you for aid."

"And here I thought that the duchess had a sudden yearning for my witty conversation."

"She was delighted you accepted," Adrian said. "As was I, just for a different reason."

"It is hoped that you will be of assistance out of a sense of responsibility. You are a member of Parliament now," Dante said.

"There are duties that go with the position," Adrian said.

"The obligations of privilege, so to speak," Colin added. "Not that you are truly under obligation to act, unless you so choose."

Ewan glared at the traitorous Dante and Colin, who dared throw his least favorite words at him. They were here to cajole him into something he did not want to do. Adrian Burchard knew it would be harder to reject whatever was being plotted if good friends joined in the request.

"Of course he is under obligation to act," Althorp said. "All loyal citizens are, but especially the nobility. It is the discharge of our obligations that allows us to govern. If we are negligent, no one can blame the people if they demand our heads."

"I cannot imagine how I can aid anyone with any act of significance. I have made it a point never to acquire skills or knowledge that would be called useful."

"As it happens, those skills which you *have* acquired are needed by the government right now," Adrian said.

"The government has some woman whom they want seduced? Your brother Colin here can accommodate you as well as I."

They all laughed. Except Althorp. He reached in his coat and extracted two papers. "Not that skill, sir. A more esoteric one."

He passed down the papers. Colin moved a candelabra close to Ewan's place.

Ewan unfolded the small, square papers. They were two fifty pound notes, issued by the Bank of England in 1803. With one glance, his instincts sounded a tiny warning.

That made him check the handwritten portions.

"This signature on the right one looks bad. It copies the signature on the left one, but is too tight and tense. Too careful."

"Yes," Althorp said.

Interested now, Ewan's gaze sharpened on the printed sections in each. He pointed to the one on the left. "If you are sure that this one is good, then even the engraved work on the right one is forged. It is a very good counterfeit. Astonishing. If the paper were not so clean, it would be missed. The only flaws that I can see are a few burin lines on the allegorical figure's drapery that are not as thick as they should be. Of course, if I studied it in a better light and with a glass, I might find more."

Extra candles instantly flanked his place. A magnifying glass appeared out of nowhere.

Ewan looked up to see four men standing, leaning forward, craning to watch him examine the notes.

"Is the paper right?" Ewan asked.

"Damned close," Adrian said. "Too close. That and the engraving is expert. The signature is not, and the number does not match the bank's records."

"Are there more?"

Althorp hesitated. He glanced to Adrian, who nodded. "That is the second to come to light in the last month. The first looked well used, so it was assumed it was an old forgery that had been circulating for years. That one, however, is quite fresh."

Ewan held the glass and checked the engraved work closely. "Gentlemen, this is an interesting exercise and not without its fascination to me, but since you already know you have a forger at work, you did not need me to say so."

"It may surprise you to know that the bank's experts were divided on the matter," Althorp said. "Two agreed with you, but there were two who insisted that the actual note was printed off the bank's plate, years ago, and stolen prior to its use by the bank. In 1803 a second cashier, Robert Aslett, was dismissed from the bank for embezzlement, and convicted. Who knows what else he got up to."

"It wasn't stolen or embezzled. The note on the right was pulled off a different plate." He set down the glass. "I am glad I could be of service in breaking the tie. Now, shall we talk about horses or boxing or some other thing. Politics, anyone?"

Colin's hand came to rest on his shoulder. There was something consoling and regretful about that firm touch. It reminded Ewan of the gesture the nicer schoolmasters would make, right before bending one over for a caning.

"These forgers must be found," Adrian said.

"Of course," Ewan agreed.

"Quickly and silently," Althorp said. "If confidence in the money is lost, well . . ."

"Should any forged notes come to my attention, I will be sure to immediately—"

"You must help, McLean. You are in a better position to do so than anyone," Dante said.

Ewan glared at him. Duclairc had become a lot less fun since he wed Fleur Monley, there was no denying it.

"The Bank of England surely has men to do this. The city has police. I cannot imagine how I can help."

Colin tapped the notes. "They are the same thing you collect, the same materials and the same techniques, only used to different purposes."

"It is our thought that your position as a collector might enable you to move in the world of engravers and paper suppliers and hear things, see things, that a formal investigation would never discover," Althorp said.

"You do frequent the publishers and print shops," Dante said. "You could ask discreet questions at the ones you trust."

"Such investigations can be very interesting," Adrian said.

"Great fun, I would think," Colin said.

"There could be panic if this is widespread and becomes known," Althorp said. "The solvency of the realm is at stake. You must do your duty."

Ewan held up a hand to stop the assault. He looked Althorp in the eyes. "I *must* not do anything unless I choose to."

The chamber went silent. Four men waited his decision.

He looked down at the forgery. "It was made by an expert engraver. One of the best. That narrows it down."

No one spoke.

"You assume this is happening in London?" he asked.

"Both bad notes were used in the city," Althorp said.

"Will you do it?" Colin asked.

Ewan looked at the note again.

Duty. Duty.

Well, hell.

"I will do what I can, but I promise no success. However, if the financial stability of Britain is shamelessly being thrown in my face, I suppose I have no choice but to try."

Bride trotted her horse up the hill, anxious to see her home. The journey to Edinburgh had transpired without incident, but riding back had tired her. An icy wind bit her skin and she felt the damp all through her clothes.

Not only the days in the saddle made these treks wearisome. Protecting the heavy bag hanging near her leg, next to the pistol, meant she had to stay alert every minute.

Early dusk was falling when she crested the hill and gazed down on the glen. Several miles to the east she could barely make out the tiny, shadowy roofs of the town of Doreri. To the north, dark clouds were moving.

Her gaze sharpened. No, not clouds. Smoke.

Sutherland's men had been busy while she was gone. She instinctively touched the bag. Its contents would be timely. Nor would she be allowed to drop into her bed tonight, the way she ached to. She would be riding again, into the night, to distribute the coin she had brought back.

She kicked the mare, and began down the hill. Her gaze fixed on the house that would offer some comfort for a few hours at least.

A movement made her stop. Someone had just walked from the house to the stable. The world had become a palette of obscuring grays, but it had not looked like Anne.

She shook her head in exasperation and moved forward. Jamie MacKay must have come visiting while she was gone. If he had gotten what he wanted, she would turn that rooster into a hen.

A lot of light came from the house as she approached. Too much. Normally they did not light the candles until night fell. Even then they used them sparingly.

No doubt Mary had decided to mend or decorate a dress this evening, and was wasting candles so she could sew. Mary often broke the rules of frugality when Bride went to Edinburgh. It was her way of pouting about not being taken to the city herself.

At the base of the hill, the mare stopped on her own. The horse's ears flicked up. Bride felt caution tense the animal beneath her.

Just then the house's door opened and Joan walked out. Joan paced out several yards, stopped, and looked to the hill. The mare snorted, as if answering a question. Bride doubted Joan had seen them, but it appeared her sister had sensed their approach.

That did not surprise Bride.

Something else did, however.

Joan was wearing a dress.

Bride gritted her teeth. It was not Jamie who had visited. Lyndale must have returned. The man refused to have his grand design thwarted, it seemed. He had bought that house in Edinburgh, after all. It was mere luck she had not bumped into him on the city streets.

She jumped off the horse, pawed through her valise, and pulled out the dress she had worn her two days in Edinburgh. She quickly peeled off her pantaloons and shirt, climbed into the dress, and threw her cloak back on. Transformed into a woman at least half respectable, she remounted the mare and trotted to the house.

Joan had gone back inside when she arrived. Bride tied the horse by the door. She debated whether to bring in the valise and bag. If Lyndale was inside, she did not want to draw attention to either.

She left them on the horse. She would send Joan out to take care of the animal, and Joan would know what to do with the baggage.

All too conscious that the journey had taken its toll, knowing she appeared windblown, ruddy, and tired, she walked into the house to cross swords once again with Lord Lyndale. She tried mightily to ignore both the stupid excitement building in her, and the sad regret she would appear so poorly.

The excitement transformed the instant she

looked in the library. It changed from silly, bubbling pleasure to foreboding fear.

Her sisters were all there, and even Jilly. So was a man. It was not Lyndale, however.

This man was a stranger. His garments and manner spoke authority and wealth. Not a lordly wealth, but contented comfort.

He rose politely, then looked her over less politely. He turned to Joan. "It appears you were correct about your sister's imminent return. Forgive me for doubting you."

Joan gave Bride a look of pointed warning. "This is Mr. Young, Bride. He is chief factor to the—"

"I know who Mr. Young is. His name is well-known in these parts." Bride entered the library and sat. "I assume we can thank you for the smoke I saw to the north as I rode in."

Mr. Young smiled like a man who knew he was hated, but did not care. "Not me directly."

"Only those whom you direct."

"I see you are a clever woman, with good wits. That is heartening. It will make this easier that you are smart enough to understand matters."

Her heart was already so sick she could not move. "What matters be those, sir?"

He sat down and tried to appear sympathetic. The result was theatrical. His face assumed the right expression, but one could tell it was not sincere. "I regret to tell you that I have been instructed to terminate your lease on this property."

Bride managed to swallow her reaction. Thankfully, her sisters did not display emotions either. But then, they had been sitting here, waiting for this announcement for hours, and she had known what was coming as soon as she saw Mr. Young.

She tried to find the composure to think straight. "Then take the land. We only ask that the house and garden remain for us. We have no need to farm the rest. What you saw being used as you arrived is all we require."

"That will not be possible."

"The house was built by my father. The lease on *this* land beneath it is by a separate indenture, and good for many years to come."

"The duchess's solicitors say the indenture is flawed, and unenforceable by you. You are free to challenge that decision, of course."

The glint in his eyes made him look smug. He knew that challenge would be nigh impossible, and very expensive.

Bride wished she had brought the pistol in with her.

"Leaving us this house will hardly inconvenience Sutherland's sheep," she said. "It is a small thing, and the income we pay will be in addition to whatever comes from the land itself."

"The house has other uses, however. It is of good size, and suitable for the family of the man who will be steward of the husbandry in these glens."

"In other words, the duchess is too miserly to build a new house, so you will throw us out of this one."

"That is one way to say it, although it is well she

cannot hear your disrespect. If she did, or if I got angry on her behalf, I might be inclined to forgo the generosity I was intending to display in her name."

"What generosity would that be?"

"I am authorized to pay you for the house and stable so that you can resettle. I will require your signature, giving up any claims through that old lease. It would not do to hand you such a handsome sum only to have you use it to petition the courts."

"How handsome a sum?"

"One hundred pounds."

The mood of doom instantly lifted. Her sisters' long faces relaxed.

Bride's humor improved, too. At least they would not be destitute. With that amount, they could buy a house elsewhere, with a freehold that Sutherland could never violate. They could still live there and continue their work.

Seeing she was amenable, Mr. Young reached in his coat and removed some money. He handed Bride the banknote.

"This is a very large note, sir."

He laughed. "Never seen one for a hundred, eh?"

"We would prefer silver, or even smaller notes. Fives and tens."

"I don't carry sackfuls of notes with me, Miss Cameron, nor the silver to pay such an amount. You just take that to any bank, even a Scottish one. You can get your silver there."

Bride handed the note to Joan. Joan glanced at it and blanched.

"One wonders why the duchess does not use Scottish banks, Mr. Young. Their notes are as good as the Bank of England's."

"The business affairs are handled in London, not in the Highlands. You ever get out of these hills, you will understand how the world works. Money is money. No reason to be a Jacobite about it."

Joan's eyes widened with mock innocence. She held up the note as if admiring it. "Oh, my, this came all the way from London?"

"Of course. You don't think notes that big are blowing in the air up here, do you?" Mr. Young took great mirth in their ignorance and his own worldliness.

Joan looked at Bride helplessly. Bride felt limp from her head to her knees. She tried to hold herself together as their lives fell to pieces in the silence.

"It is getting dark," Mr. Young observed. "I need to be going. You take that money and get yourself to somewhere else. My man will bring the paper for you to sign in the morning. I will expect you out in two days."

Bride rose so *he* would get *himself* to "somewhere else" at once. She had the urge to cry, and would be damned before she allowed this lackey of Sutherland's to see it.

She escorted him to the door and watched him stride to the stable. Another man waited on its eastern side, with two horses. The rising cloud of smoke could still be seen against the darkening sky.

She closed the door and returned to the library.

From Mary's tears and Anne's expression, she could tell that Joan had given them the bad news.

She took the note from Joan. Through brimming eyes, she looked down at a worthless forgery that she dared never hand to a bank.

Worse yet, it had been pulled from another one of her father's stolen plates, and had been passed all the way south in London.

CHAPTER NINE

D on't you agree that she is being very rude?"
Ewan asked.

Colin rubbed a towel through his wet, golden hair as they washed in the dressing room of the boxing club. "Well, it sounds like you did not actually request that she inform you when the papers arrived."

"Is that what the world is coming to? We now need to demand acknowledgment of settlements worth fifteen thousand pounds?"

Colin smiled in the damnably private way he had, as if he was smiling to himself alone. "Is there any particular reason why she would not want to communicate with you, McLean?"

Ewan decided his cravat needed retying. He peered in the looking glass and dealt with it.

"From your avoidance of my question, I assume you seduced her," Colin said. "That was not entirely honorable of you."

"I did not seduce her." And he had not, at least not entirely. "However, if I had, it would not have been entirely dishonorable, either."

It seemed to him that his "not entirely," when taken together, reduced the potential dishonor to zero.

Colin buttoned his waistcoat. "You are responsible for her, so it is murky, at best."

"She made it very clear that I am *not* responsible for her. Not in the least. She even refused a settlement for herself. She is one of those irritating women who thinks the slightest attempts of a man to help her are suspect, and who would prefer to live in a garret and eat moldy cheese before accepting assistance. She has not written because she likes to be stubborn."

"You are making a disaster with the cravat."

"To hell with it, then." Ewan pulled on his coat and aimed for the street, with Colin in tow.

"Perhaps *you* should write to *her,* if you are concerned," Colin suggested as they waited for their horses.

"I'll be damned if I will. Nor am I concerned. I merely said I find it rude that she has not written."

"You are surprisingly vexed about the matter. If I did not know better, I would say you had developed a *tendre* for her."

"If I were going to develop a *tendre* for a woman, which I never will, it would not be this female. She is just shy of being a shrew. Now, come to the house with me. It is almost finished and you must see it."

As they rode through Mayfair, Colin casually broached another matter. "How is that investigation progressing?"

"Did your brother set you to spy on me?"

"Not at all. The situation is very serious, however. I am interested, just as anyone would be."

"I have begun to make discreet inquiries. You may tell Adrian that thus far they have produced nothing of use."

"Truly, my brother has not—"

"Oh, tosh. Of course he has. However, I have added a strategy to my plan and you can help me. I will be conducting as much business as possible using notes, especially in the gaming halls. That way I can inspect the notes circulating, to see if there are more forgeries. If you did the same, it would give me more specimens."

"If it will aid you, I will begin at once."

They arrived at the expansive houses of Belgrave Square. When they reached Ewan's, a groom appeared at once to take their mounts.

Colin gazed up at the restrained classicism of the house's facade. "Do you get lost in it?"

"Every day. However, the world would cease its rotation if earls did not live in ostentatious luxury. It is doubly my duty to spend my inheritance, since my uncle rarely parted with a guinea except for prints. He left an obscenely large fortune for me to squander."

"Save some of it for the future. You will have a

wife soon who will want to do some squandering herself."

Ewan entered the house. It still tickled him to realize it was his. He had thoroughly enjoyed the spree of choosing the furnishings without asking their price. He had been able to obtain the best, when in the past he would have gladly settled for merely tasteful.

"I will ignore your reference to marriage, Burchard. I cannot go out in society without every conversation turning to likely brides for me. I do not need your hounding me into my own castle with the harping."

Colin handed his hat to the waiting servant, then followed Ewan up the stairs. "My apologies. It is just that Mrs. Norton has intimated—"

"I am sure she has. She has been intimating little else to *me* for weeks." Ewan climbed the stairs with determination. "I am done with her, by the way. It will be all around town in a day or so."

"Bit harsh, don't you think? You cannot blame her for being hopeful."

Ewan did not blame Jasmine Norton for being hopeful. He did blame her for being greedy, however.

Last night, when she saw the necklace he had bought her, she could have at least pretended delight in the gift before commenting that she had hoped for a different one. He might have overlooked her escalating avarice, then, even though she had boldly set her heart on a necklace that cost over a thousand pounds.

Instead she had pouted and sulked like a child, and even insinuated that if she did not get what she wanted, he should not get what he wanted.

It was moments like that which made Ewan wistful for the bygone days when he was too poor to buy necklaces. Women accepted him for what he was then, and came to him for pleasure and fun, not jewels. That innocence was hopelessly gone. Whether ladies of the court or courtesans of the night, women would be trying to use their favors in an unseemly game of blackmail now.

He put thoughts of Mrs. Norton, and the scene that had ensued when he broke with her, out of his head. He led Colin into the drawing room. As he did, he heard a faint rumble coming from the other chambers on the floor. It seemed the unpacking had not been completed as quickly as Michael expected.

"This house has a very special lay of chambers, Burchard. The ballroom is over there, but look, on this side here is the main drawing room. This is where I will entertain the Earl of Lyndale's boring acquaintances."

"Very stately," Colin said, surveying the Aubusson rugs and damask upholstery. "Not nearly as welcoming as your apartment, but that cannot be avoided, I expect."

"I know what you are thinking. You are trying to picture the party here, the one a fortnight hence that I am planning. Have no fear, good friend. Follow me."

Ewan paced down the room to large double doors at the end. He swung them open. "Here, in the house's corner, is the library."

"Your own library is respectable, but there must be a thousand volumes here."

"Those fellows who design interiors buy them by the weight, much like plaster and moldings. I will rebind the ones I want to keep, and replace those I don't." He walked to a side door and beckoned Colin. "The second drawing room is right behind this door. Not so large, but big enough."

"What are those sounds?"

"That is Michael unpacking my collection, and preparing a special surprise for you."

"You mean—"

"Yes, I will have a salon just for my prized possessions. All the sofas and chaise longues are in there, too, just like my old chambers. I can hold the boring, obligatory functions in the big drawing room, while I lock off this other one. Or I can have parties with my old friends in this second drawing room and we can spill out to the library and even the big chamber if we choose."

"It sounds perfect. What is my surprise?"

"Something just for you, my good friend, who has the sense not to get domesticated, and who would never want me to change. A special little gift."

Ewan swung open the doors.

His gaze swept the room's interior.

He froze in shock.

Colin looked around. "Impressive, McLean, and I am touched by your generosity. However, the one on the swing looks a little young."

The one on the swing was indeed young. Young and blond and laughing as she made the swing sweep back and forth.

Ewan found his voice. "Good God."

"Does that mean they are not my surprise?"

"No, but they are certainly a surprise all the same."

A big surprise. An astonishing one.

The Cameron sisters had invaded his house.

Not only his house, but his private retreat. He did a desperate scan and noted that only a small part of the collection had been unpacked.

Too much, however. Anne sat on a sofa, her head tilted as she frowned at the little Renaissance bronze of the nymph and satyr that had been set on the table beside her spot.

Mary squealed on the swing, showing a lot of ankle while a handsome footman happily gave her little pushes.

The other two sisters were on a sofa in a corner, poring over a portfolio of engravings. Ewan noted gratefully that it was not one with erotic prints.

Michael sat on the arm of the sofa, hovering over Joan and being worthless.

Suddenly Bride noticed them. That made Michael notice, too. He jumped up and began collecting cups and dishes that displayed the remains of extensive refreshments.

"Mary, stop that at once and make yourself presentable. Lord Lyndale is here," Bride said. "Anne, stop peering at that odd statue. If you have not comprehended it by now, you never will."

Colin tipped his head close to Ewan's. "Would these be the sisters you were telling me about?"

"Yes."

"Would the formidable, severe one who is issuing commands be—"

"Yes."

"I think I will be leaving. You can give me my gift another time."

"*No.* Do not leave. That is not necessary."

"Scares you, does she?"

"Of course not. I could thrash her with one arm tied behind me."

"I am not so sure. If you survive, be sure to call on me and tell me all about it." Colin fled back into the library.

It entered Bride's mind that she was seeing Lord Lyndale as stunned and discomfitted as she ever would. That was poor compensation for having to eat her pride, but it was something at least.

The handsome blond man with Lyndale disappeared.

Michael called for the footman and shoved a large tray in his hands. Then Michael turned to his master.

"I did not know where else to put the ladies, my

lord. Leaving them below in the kitchen did not seem proper. The furniture hasn't arrived for the library yet, and Miss Cameron declared the main drawing room was too fine for eating and such. She found her way back here and declared this would do."

Lyndale finally entered the chamber. He glanced at the tray passing him on its way to the door. "Of course the ladies would require refreshments after their journey. You arrived in London this morning, Miss Cameron?"

"Yes, on the early mail coach."

"I am, of course, delighted to see all of you again. However, if you had written, I would have seen that you were met. For that matter, I would have sent a coach to Scotland for you."

She had not written because the entire way here she kept trying to devise a plan that would spare her from asking him for help.

There had been no choice, however. Their meager funds had been completely depleted. She currently had less than five pounds in her valise.

"To what do I owe the honor of this visit?"

Lyndale tried to look welcoming, but his eyes still reflected shock. As he spoke, he strolled over to the table beside Anne and casually lifted the little statue. Without missing a step, he beckoned Michael and placed the little bronze in his hands.

"We were thrown out of our home."

She proceeded to describe the visit from Mr. Young.

While Lyndale listened, he calmly moved across

the chamber, lifted a small painting off the wall and handed that to Michael, too. Although shadows had shrouded its subject, Bride had surmised it depicted Venus and Mars mutually admiring each other's amorous attributes.

"We barely had time to find wagons in which to pack our belongings and our studio," Bride concluded. "Left with no resources and no home, I decided we had no course except to come here, since you demanded we seek you out, should we require assistance."

"Certainly. Most sensible."

Lyndale's eyes lit on a stone relief hanging on another wall. Bride wondered how he would deal with that. It looked very heavy, and displayed a variety of couples enjoying one another's company with creative vigor.

She could see him assessing its weight and size. Finally, he merely walked over and took a position in front of it so his body blocked its view.

"Well, here you are," he said with forced joviality. "Now we must decide what to do with you."

"I have that all planned." She'd had plenty of time to think about it during that long journey. "If the trusts were established—"

"Of course they were. You may not have received the papers before you departed Scotland, but they were sent."

"I am sure they were. *Since* the trusts were established, we will have income once the funds pay. That will be some months, and the first dividend will not be significant, but it will still be enough. Until then, we will make do here. I will seek employment with an engraver, however, so we may be able to achieve independence more quickly."

His eyes blinked several times, as if her words were stirring him to life. "You do appear to have thought it through, which is admirable. However, bear with me while I make sure I comprehend the details. When you say *enough,* may I ask, enough for what?"

"To enable us to let a house that can hold both the studio and our living quarters."

"You intend to move the studio to London? You intend to live here permanently?"

"If we have to move somewhere, why not London? There are far more publishers here than in Edinburgh. The equipment is making its way here by wagons. That cost a pretty penny, but there was no choice."

He took that in and nodded slowly, as if his wits needed a moment to accept the logic of it. She had made sure it sounded very logical, however. She did not want him probing. It would never do for him to know the real reasons they had come to London.

"I am understanding now, Miss Cameron. Forgive me, the surprise of your arrival, while it gives me untold joy, has also dulled my mind slightly." He smiled blankly. "Just one more thing, if you will. A minor point. When you say *make do here,* what do you mean by *here*?"

"Here." She gestured to the room's ceiling and beyond.

"*Here* here?"

The poor man really was addled. "Hear, hear, sir. Yes, *here.*"

"*This* house?"

"I promise we will not be a big intrusion."

He snapped to the alertness she knew. He began to walk toward her, realized that revealed the scandalous stone relief, and with some vexation reclaimed his spot in front of it.

"Miss Cameron, while I would be honored to have all of you as guests, that simply—"

"We will use chambers up with the servants. Truly, you will not even know we are here."

"The servants are all male. I remind you of the fox and hen metaphor you used when first we met." He puffed with the arrogance she knew too well. "I will make arrangements at a hotel, or take a house for you until the funds pay."

"I cannot allow you to incur such an expense. However, I can see that I have been too bold. I did not realize that when you said you would assist us, you meant only if it did not inconvenience you. We will leave, and make do elsewhere."

She rose and turned to her sisters. "One of us will have to sell herself tonight, to earn the funds for lodging. Do I have a volunteer, or should we pull straws?"

"That will be enough of *that,* woman." The command barked out from the stone relief. "Sit down."

She did.

Lyndale was thoroughly awake now. "How dare you imply that my desire to set you up elsewhere is shirking my responsibility. It is my responsibility that moves me to suggest it, not my own convenience. This is a household of men. It would be highly improper for any of you to sleep even one night under this roof."

"I am mature enough to serve as chaperone, so that is not true."

"My reputation requires that *you* have a chaperone."

"Don't you mean that *my* reputation requires *I* have a chaperone? If so, I disagree, since, as I said, I am a mature—"

"I mean exactly what I said."

"You must be very particular about your reputation, then. However, Jilly is with us. She fell asleep in the kitchen when we first arrived and is still there. She can be my chaperone."

"She is a servant, and therefore in no position to lay down rules for you. She will not do."

"Actually, Jilly is not a servant. She is our aunt," Anne said.

That left Lyndale speechless. Bride rushed into the breach. "Jilly will chaperone me, and I will chaperone my sisters. Everyone's reputation will be safe. More so than if you keep us in a house that you let, or in a hotel, I daresay."

"Keep you?"

"Someone may see it that way. Even if they did

not, I could not allow you to lay out funds in that way. I am even of two minds about accepting your hospitality, but see no alternative."

He looked like he wanted to throttle her.

Then his gaze altered. Not much, but enough. In an instant she knew that she had lost the upper hand. Suddenly Lyndale the Seducing Scoundrel was again eyeing a rabbit.

"Very well, Miss Cameron. I have done my best to offer arrangements that would protect all of you. Have it your way. I wash my hands of any damage to your reputation. Your aunt Jilly can be your chaperone, for as much good as it will do."

CHAPTER
TEN

⁓

E wan retreated to the library, called for the steward, and gave instructions that the guests were to
be accommodated.

Cockburn, the steward, was a prim, pinch-faced
man of middle years, average height, and thin pale
hair. His eyes vaguely revealed his distaste for the
notion that these barely presentable young women
would be guests of an earl, but he kept his face impassive.

"There are the chambers on the fourth floor," he
said, intimating with the distant location that hous-
ing them close to the servants would be appropriate.
"Three have been furnished already."

"The aunt will share with the youngest one."
Ewan expected trouble with Mary.

Actually, he expected nothing but trouble with all
of them. This invasion was going to disrupt what had
promised to be a wonderful home. Worse, he was al-

ready contemplating the delicious temptation of having Bride nearby and available.

He tried to feel guilty about that, but without much success.

He would have to find a way to remove them quickly. He would visit his solicitor tomorrow and determine if the funds could be made to pay more quickly. If not, he would offer to loan Bride an advance amount against the income.

"If the aunt and the youngest share, and two others do not, that leaves one to be accommodated elsewhere, my lord. There is the red suite on the second floor. It is already presentable."

Ewan thought about that. The red suite was tucked around the corner from his own chambers.

"We could put the aunt there," Cockburn suggested. "Then Miss Cameron could either share with the youngest, or another sister could."

Ewan gazed at the wall of mottled bindings awaiting replacement. Yes, Jilly should use the red suite. The Earl of Lyndale knew that was the way to do it.

However, Ewan McLean pictured Bride in that red suite, lying on the bed with her garments half off, her eyes moist with pleasure. Desire slashed through him, obliterating the earl's existence in a second.

"I think, Cockburn, that it makes the most sense to put Miss Cameron in the red suite. The aunt has never been in a city, and will want the company of her nieces. As the eldest, and a mature woman, Miss

Cameron is the most likely be comfortable away from the others."

"As you wish, my lord."

They returned to the drawing room together.

"Ladies, Cockburn will show you your rooms. There are no women here to settle you in, I am afraid. We will see about finding maids soon."

"That will not be necessary," Bride said. "We will do for one another, as we always have."

Cockburn was so shocked he all but swooned. He led the way out.

As the Cameron sisters filed out of the drawing room, Bride favored Ewan with a smile that had him imagining those deep pink lips doing wonderful, scandalous things to him.

"I promise that you will not even know we are here," she said, pausing as the parade moved on. "I daresay you will not even see us."

"I daresay I will. The steward will inform you when meals are served, and the other routines of the household. I am not always present at dinner, but on occasion I expect I will be."

"We will take our meals in our rooms. Truly, there is no reason for—"

"You thought to use my home as an inn? It will not work quite that way, Bride. If I am to play the welcoming host, you will play the gracious guest."

She flushed. A spark of caution entered her eyes. Evidently, she had actually expected him to allow her to live here, but remain invisible.

"The state rooms are closed off except when I entertain, but the other rooms are always yours to use," he said. "I ask, however, that this private drawing room not be frequented by your sisters."

She glanced past him to the stone relief. "I assure you we will never enter again."

"Only your sisters are prohibited. You may visit anytime you choose."

"I am sure I will never so choose."

"Pity. I will keep my art collection here. There are many items you would find interesting."

"If you think so, you misunderstand my character."

"Not all are of an amorous nature. My collection of etchings and engravings is one of the best in Britain. As for your character, I have only the highest estimation of it. I am not a man who thinks badly of a woman because she is passionate. Quite the opposite."

She pulled herself into a tower of indignation. "It is inappropriate for you to speak of that with me. Considering your late but ultimate restraint in Scotland, I assumed that I would be spared any further advances. If your honor checked you there, I expect you to be doubly honorable toward a guest in your home."

"Then you miscalculated badly, my dear."

Assuming the crisp chill of an iceberg, she turned and floated out of the room.

Ewan examined the Roman relief. As he gave a corner a nudge to straighten it, he pictured Bride catching up with Cockburn and learning that her chambers were separate from the others, and wonderfully convenient to his.

He wondered if she would present much of a challenge this time. A part of him counted on quick capitulation, but another part rather hoped the game would be more interesting.

It had been a stupid interlude of confusion that stopped him in Scotland, not false notions of honor. Now, here she was again, a gift from the gods. Or a temptation from the devil.

"They will be needing new wardrobes," Michael said. He was busy at a crate, unrolling a statue of Priapus from its shroud of cloth.

Ewan ignored him. He eyed the wall in front of him, deciding where to hang his framed engraved print by Agostino Veneziano that depicted Mars and Venus busy on a bed.

"It will reflect badly on you if they go about town in those old dresses," Michael said.

"I hear you, damn it. I will attend to it shortly." As soon as he figured out how to attend to it. Even if they soon lived elsewhere, the Cameron sisters would be associated with him and required presentable garments. He needed to impose on a woman to dress them, he supposed.

The problem was, he did not have female friends who owed him favors of that sort. Most of his married friends had wives who barely tolerated his presence in their husbands' lives. None of those ladies would look kindly on his request for aid.

"Should we be canceling the party you are planning?"

"Absolutely not. If they are still in residence, which I hope they are not, I will tell the Cameron sisters that they are to retire after dinner and not show their faces until morning."

"But their reputations—"

"I warned Miss Cameron about that. She would not listen. Besides, everyone will learn soon enough that my house guests will not be present at the party."

Michael heaved the statue up and placed it on its pedestal near the window drapes. He gazed down at the erect lower member of the armless figure. "Maybe we should wait with these. What if one of the sisters—"

"I gave instructions they are not to enter this room. Proceed, and stop trying to turn me into a boring guardian. I am not ignorant of my responsibilities to the Cameron sisters, but I will not be ruled by overwrought delicacy."

With a shrug, Michael started prying open the other crate.

Ewan set about placing his portfolios in the new cabinet he had procured. Michael's harping about the sisters' reputations played in his mind, provoking concerns quite different from Michael's.

He caught his manservant's eye. "You have spoken with the others?"

"As you instructed. Every man here knows that if he touches one of them, you will call him out and kill him. But first you will cut off his balls and feed them to pigs and then carve out his heart and—"

"You repeated me literally?"

"I could not improve on your eloquence. That young one will be disappointed that all the smiles are gone when she comes down for dinner."

Reference to Mary and how much she liked men's smiles dampened Ewan's mood. He would have to have a chat with Bride and alert her about the young men of London. He might even have to warn a few off, just to emphasize that his guests were not to be trifled with. Hell, if Mary was not watched closely, he could really be calling men out.

His enjoyment in setting out the collection disappeared in a snap. He was going to have to turn into a boring guardian after all, or face a disaster.

Michael approached with a hammer. Ewan handed him the Veneziano and pointed to a spot where direct sunlight would not damage it. Then he went to his writing table, sat down, and wrote a brief letter.

"These chambers are perfectly charming, Cockburn." Bride stood in the center of a beautifully appointed bedroom, admiring the fresh hangings and drapes in rose toile. She noted the unblemished nature of the furniture. Everything looked completely unused.

Michael had explained that the unfinished state of the house resulted from a recent move, and indeed, their hackney driver had first taken them to an address some distance away.

Bride had not expected a hovel, but the size and grandeur of this house awed her. The crisp, expensive elegance of the furnishings only made it more impressive.

Cockburn stood aside as baggage was carried in by two servants.

Mary trailed behind them. "I do not see why I have to share with Jilly when Anne gets her own room."

"You are the youngest, that is one reason why," Bride said. A long look in Mary's direction from one of the servants provided the other reason. "Also, Joan and I will be sharing, too, and our room is not even as large as yours, so you have no cause for complaint."

Cockburn raised one gray-gloved hand. "Actually, Miss Cameron, a separate chamber awaits you. If your sisters can manage, I will take you there now."

"That is not necessary. I will be fine here."

"My lord gave instructions. As your host, he took the liberty to assure your comfort."

Bride followed the steward down the corridor. To her surprise, he led her down the main stairs, down another corridor, around a corner, and to double doors near the end of the building. He opened the doors to reveal a cozy sitting room, then showed her to a spacious bedroom and dressing room beyond.

The luxury of the chambers made the expensive appointments in her sisters' rooms appear quaint. A princess would be at home here.

"There is a back stairs nearby that will take you to your sisters more quickly than the main ones," Cockburn explained as he checked the fireplace. "You can use either, of course, as you prefer."

She should find a way to refuse this arrangement. It did not seem quite right that she should sleep here, or be surrounded by such comforts. She also suspected that Lyndale's own chambers were not far away, and their last conversation had her worried.

Since he had aborted his seduction in Scotland, she had assumed there would be no repetition of such behavior. Furthermore, common decency demanded that he not importune a guest. Her deliberations and conclusions regarding all of that had allayed gnawing concerns about asking for his help.

Now she worried that she had indeed miscalculated.

"I would prefer to stay with my sister."

"The earl would prefer that you make your home here."

"I see. Yes. Well, it is his house, so I suppose he gets to decide."

"I think so, yes." Cockburn walked toward the door. "Your belongings will be up shortly. Someone will alert you an hour in advance of dinner. Now, if you will excuse me, the household is still unsettled and I should attend to some matters."

After he left, Bride ventured a closer inspection

of the little palace she would use. The bed was high
and wide and draped in a luscious jewel-red
jacquard duvet. Patterns of deep blue and red covered the heavily upholstered chairs. Lovely restrained carvings decorated the mahogany furniture.

The sitting room contained a sapphire chaise
longue and more chairs. The dressing room was
larger than the sitting room. Two huge wardrobes
covered one of its walls.

She opened one and pictured her paltry wardrobe
in it. She had never felt poor before, but right now, in
this house and in these chambers, she did.

It affected how she saw everything, especially
Lyndale's advances. In Scotland she could pretend
they had not been insulting. Here there could be no
illusions.

A man who lived like this saw women like her as
playthings to be used until a newer one caught his
eye. Undoubtedly, a city like London was full of
pretty toys.

Abandoning the rooms, she found the back stairs
and hurried up to her sisters. They were all in Mary's
room, admiring the view of a garden to the rear of
the house.

"I do not think I will mind sharing with Jilly after
all," Mary said. "This is the nicest chamber by far.
Why, it is almost as large as our dining room at
home."

An awkward silence fell. So did Joan and Anne's
faces. There was no longer a dining room at home.
They had no home. Nor could this be their new one.

"Where will you be sleeping, Bride?" Mary asked.

"Below. Well, we are here. Now we must make good on our plan."

"Can't we enjoy the city first?" Mary said. "I want to see the things we read about in the newspapers. The theaters and the zoo and such."

"You may do so if it can be arranged. I, however, must start seeking a position with an engraver at once, in order to establish an income. The sooner we leave this house, the better."

"I do not see why we cannot stay, if Lord Lyndale has permitted it. We could never afford such nice rooms on the earnings of engraving."

"Mary, we do not want to be beholden to this man. We dare not risk his involvement in our lives. Nor does he truly welcome us. He wanted to pack us off immediately. Enjoy playing the lady for a few days, but expect the visit to be brief."

"I will accompany you to the engravers'," Joan said. "I may be able to find employment, too."

"You are also better at dissembling than I am. You can help me try to find out about Walter."

Mary turned away as she rolled her eyes. Jilly's face folded into creases. Joan tried not to look sympathetic.

"Of course we must look for him. If he came here trying to help us, we must discover what happened to him," Anne said.

Bride was determined to do just that. She was also going to find those stolen plates before the forgers were caught and they implicated the Cameron sisters.

Should she fail, should disaster engulf them, she had another plan that none of her sisters knew about. One that would save the others, she hoped, even if it did not save her.

"We must keep our eyes and ears open," she said. "We must visit the establishments that sell prints, and the publishers, and the engraving studios. We did not come to London to live off Lyndale's charity. We are here to try and find those forgers and those plates, and to discover if Walter came to harm."

Everyone nodded.

"I expect that it will take some time, though," Mary said, looking around her room possessively. "We could end up living here for weeks. Months."

Not if I can help it, Bride thought.

CHAPTER
ELEVEN

〜

Beginning tomorrow, Charlotte, widow of the last Baron Mardenford, will require your attendance." Lord Lyndale made the unexpected announcement that day at the end of dinner.

It had been an awkward meal, full of long silences broken only by footmen pacing and cutlery clinking. The luxury of the dining room, with its rich hangings and abundant silver and huge candelabras, had thoroughly cowed Bride.

It vexed her to be at such a disadvantage, and she blamed Lyndale for the insistence that they all eat here. Joan and Anne also seemed subdued, which meant they were just as uncomfortable as she was.

Only Mary appeared at ease. She had peppered Lyndale with questions about London. She kept inviting him to offer to spend the next weeks showing them around the city. He had adroitly sidestepped her efforts to corner him.

Now he had indicated he had made other arrangements for their entertainment. Bride wished he had not.

"What could a baroness want with us?" Anne asked.

"She will be taking you to buy new wardrobes."

Mary squealed and clapped her hands.

"We cannot accept such beneficence," Bride said.

"Oh, *Briiide,*" Mary whined.

"As my guests, you reflect on me. You cannot walk about London and enter my home dressed as you are. You will present yourselves to Lady Mardenford at her convenience. I will see that the coach is made ready accordingly."

"My sisters are welcome to the new clothes, but I do not need them. I will stay here with Jilly," Bride said.

"Jilly will be going, as well. She is your aunt and chaperone, and must look like one."

Jilly's face went so slack with shock that all the lines disappeared.

"You are going, too, Miss Cameron. If I am going to have women in my home, they at least are going to be dressed attractively."

"I do not think we should be forced to—"

"If I say you are to spend the next week buying dresses, then by Zeus you are. The evidence indicates that it is necessary."

He looked down the table at her sisters, one by one.

They had all done their best with what they had.

They had curled and pinched and laced more the last two hours than the last two years combined.

It had not helped much. Bride saw her sisters as Lyndale did. Their garments had not seemed so poor in Scotland, but here, even in the candlelight, one could not ignore the truth.

Finally, those dark eyes came to rest on her.

His pointed examination made her squirm. The long expanse of the table and the distant placements of the diners left her adrift and vulnerable to his attention, out of reach of support to keep her afloat. Lyndale's gaze isolated her further.

His inspection lingered, slowly sliding from her hair to her face, then down shoulders, neck, and bosom. He wore a very different expression from when he had noted her sisters' poor attire. Possessive severity hardened his face. Male calculation warmed his eyes.

He did not appear to be taking inventory of her garments. In fact, she felt as though he was seeing her without anything on at all.

"Such beauty should not be shrouded in old, unfashionable clothes," he said. "It will give me great pleasure to see you free of them."

Bride darted quick glances around the table. No one seemed to realize he only spoke to her. Nor did they notice the double entendre. She felt her face going red. That escaped their detection as well, along with the rigidity she assumed in order to conquer the stupid shivers his concentration provoked.

The man was shameless. She *had* miscalculated badly, and it was imperative to rectify the mistake.

"Bride, it is apparent that Lord Lyndale *wants* to do this, because he is so good and kind," Mary said. "I think it would be *rude* to refuse."

Lyndale's gaze slid to Mary, then back to Bride. *See?* his smug little smile said.

"I think Lord Lyndale is being *too* kind and generous, Mary. It is clear that our presence has created obligations for him that I failed to anticipate. I am concluding that it would be better if we removed ourselves from his home."

Mary began pouting. Lyndale's gaze turned hooded. He examined Bride again, thoughtfully.

"I must insist that you explain where you will go and how you will live if you intend to leave," he said. "Perhaps the ladies should retire to the morning room while we discuss that."

"I think *we* should have some say in it," Mary said.

"*You* have no say in anything, young woman," Lyndale replied. "If I am satisfied, your sister can consult with your aunt and older sisters."

Verging on tears, Mary rose and hurried from the room. Joan followed, casting Bride a frown. Even Jilly managed to express with a sigh that she thought Bride had become strangely unpredictable.

When they were all gone, Lyndale gestured to a footman. A box and decanter appeared, then the servants departed.

Lyndale opened the box. "Cigar? Port? Now that the ladies have retired, we can indulge."

"That is insulting."

"I intended it as a compliment to your formidable skills of logic, organization, and persuasion."

He settled in with his lit cigar and glass of port. "Move closer, Miss Cameron. We will not have to shout then."

She did not budge.

"Are you afraid of me, Bride?"

She did not answer.

"There is no reason to be. I promise to be very good tonight."

With a sigh, she moved a little closer.

"Now, if you quit this house, where will you go?"

"I have decided it would be best to accept your offer of a leased house. We would pay you back once the funds came through. That way you will not actually be keeping us or giving us charity."

He rested his chin in his hand and looked at her. "As always, you have it all worked out. I considered such a solution myself, I will let you know. I even consulted my solicitor today, to find out how best to arrange such a loan."

"Then you are agreeable." She began rising. "I am glad we could come to an understanding so quickly. Now, I will rejoin my sisters and—"

"I decided, however, that doing that does not suit me."

"Excuse me?"

"It does not suit me."

She sat back down. "Why does it not suit you?"

"I do not know." He shrugged and appeared genuinely perplexed. "At first I thought it brilliant. It would restore my peace and satisfy your pride about being kept and whatnot. By late afternoon, however, it no longer suited me."

"Lord Lyndale, you created a home devoid of females. You cannot want us to stay."

"I will admit that I do not welcome the invasion. However, as the day wore on, I kept seeing more trouble if I put all of you elsewhere. I would still be responsible for you, but—"

"You would in no way be responsible for us."

"Of course I would be, only I would have no way to protect you. Mary, for example, is certain to do something rash if given half the chance. If she is here, men will know to think twice. If she is off alone with you, they will do their worst and I will be the one pacing off at dawn, not you. Your other sisters would be just as vulnerable. So, I concluded that until your situation is more settled, and until I am convinced that you all understand city ways, you should remain here. I assure you that my decision astonished me."

No more than it astonished her. He had seemed so eager to be rid of them this morning.

She thought about her chambers above, and his insinuations when they arrived.

"Lord Lyndale, are you very sure it was only concern for our well-being that led you to this change of heart?"

He sat back in his chair. He tapped some ash off his cigar. "Not entirely."

She felt her eyes narrowing. "You are the worst scoundrel. If you think that having me stay in this house means that I am going to be agreeable to—"

"It was the dress," he said. "Lady Mardenford was wearing a dress that was very lovely. Raw silk, I think, in a color like sea foam."

He made no sense. She began mentally counting the glasses of wine he had drunk at dinner.

"There I was, talking about her brothers and sister and whatnot, and I kept seeing you in that dress instead of her." He shrugged again, as if that said it all.

"I do not understand how her sea-foam dress factors into any of this."

"I realized I would very much like to see you in such a dress, Bride. If you leave, you will never allow me to buy you one. If you remain here, and I am purchasing wardrobes for all of you out of duty, you will."

"You are going to have five guests in your house for weeks or months, because you thought in passing that you would like to see me in a new green dress?"

"It appears so."

"Are you mad?"

A charming smile greeted her exasperation. "Possibly. However, I should probably explain that after I imagined you in that dress, I then imagined you taking it off. Very slowly."

She stood abruptly. "That will only happen in your mind. It is scandalous of you to insist we stay because of any such intentions."

"You are absolutely correct."

"I am?"

"Certainly. I cannot deny that scandalous intentions may be diluting my altruistic impulses." He leaned forward, exuding solicitous concern. "However, here is what I think we should do. You speak with your sisters and Jilly. If they agree with you that you should remove yourselves from this house, I will do it as you wish. We will find a nice little place where they can wear their old dresses and cook their own food and clean their own floors. After all, it is their money you intend to spend, so they should have a say."

She had not expected such quick capitulation, but she grabbed it. "I will consult with them at once. You should anticipate our departure as soon as the other house can be let."

Bride stood near the table in the morning room, with her sisters arrayed on chairs around her. She explained her new plan to them. "Since we will pay him back, it would not be charity, nor would we be giving him rights to interfere."

Everyone looked very thoughtful. Even Anne seemed to be paying attention.

"I vote we stay," Mary said. "I want to live here, not in some drafty old house among strangers."

"We are among strangers here, too," Bride said. "We are out of place. This is not our world."

"It seems to me we do not have a world anymore," Mary said, sinking into a sulk. "Lord Lyndale isn't a stranger, either. Nor is Michael. And if you would stop being so proud, soon a lady would be our friend."

"I am not sure I understand your decision, Bride," Anne said. "We are safe here, and protected."

Bride had not expected Anne to object.

"We are not going," a voice said from the corner behind Bride.

Bride pivoted. Jilly had risen to her feet and crossed her arms over her breast.

"We are not going," Jilly repeated. "No reason to take on debt for a house if this house welcomes us. Until we can support ourselves, or until the press arrives, this will do fine."

Bride did not know what surprised her more: that Jilly had an opinion or that she now voiced it with such authority.

"Jilly, I truly believe—"

"I am the chaperone, you said. Well, I say they stay here."

"It probably would be best, Bride," Joan said. "I also confess that the notion of having some new dresses is alluring."

"You never wear dresses unless forced to."

"Maybe I would if they fit properly and looked pretty."

"You are going to go against me because of a new wardrobe?"

Joan smiled sheepishly.

Bride threw up her hands. "I am very disappointed in all of you if your loyalty can be bought with a few yards of fabric."

"Be disappointed if you like, but we are staying," Jilly said.

"I expected more sense from you, Jilly."

"Well, I expected more from you. Normally you are measured in your decisions." Jilly eased herself back down in the chair and reassumed her diminished, gray appearance. "Besides, it has been twenty years since I had a decent new dress, and I'll be damned if I will let your pride interfere with my getting one now."

CHAPTER
TWELVE

⟨⟩

"I do not think any of these will do," Ewan said.

He sat at Nichols' stationery on The Strand, examining the shop's wares. Samples of ivory and cream papers and cards had been meticulously placed on a velvet cloth as if they were so many large, flat jewels.

Nichols' was not the most fashionable shop for stationery, and the arrival of nobility had initiated a flurry of hopeful activity. Mr. Nichols' eagerness to snag this patron had his eyes glinting more than was seemly.

"The prime minister uses this one." Mr. Nichols pointed to a heavy laid cream sheet. He allowed the insinuation to stand that the prime minister purchased said stock from this very store.

"That does not surprise me," Ewan said. "Lord Grey is rather dull."

Mr. Nichols remained deferential. "We *are* discussing formal stationery, are we not, my lord?"

"Indeed. However, I hoped to find something more distinctive. By coming to a different shop, I had hoped to find different choices. Something that says 'Lyndale' on immediate view."

"We could engrave the coat of arms, of course."

Ewan lifted one of the samples and held it toward the light. "The watermark. Now if *that* were my coat of arms, or something unusual related to me alone, then I might be happier."

"Are you saying that you wish to commission private stock?"

"It is sometimes done, is it not?"

Nichols pressed the gloved tips of his fingers together. The little chapel in front of his mouth failed to hide his glee. "I would be happy to arrange it for you."

"You are sure the papermaker could handle the insignia? I think it would be complicated to get all that detail into the wire screen used to lay down the pulp."

That made Nichols pause. "It will require inordinate skill and artistry. This will take some investigation. It has been some time since such a commission was requested. When I was much younger, we used Blake or Twickenham for such things, but Blake has been deceased these ten years now."

"And Twickenham?"

Nichols lowered his voice confidentially. "He makes inferior paper now, I regret to say. On a machine, no less. A wastrel of a son near ruined him, and he has been forced to resort to wares for shops that cater to the trade for their accounts and such. I hear the young man got in dun up to his eyeballs and it cost Twickenham a fortune."

"How sad."

Nichols began stacking the paper. "I will look into the matter of your watermark, if you will permit it. I am sure that we can find a satisfactory solution. It may take some time. Perhaps, until then, you would like to order something for current use."

Ewan had already procured what he came for, but he gave Nichols a small order all the same.

Pleased with the day's success in obtaining an unwitting ally for his investigation, he decided to push fate. After leaving Nichols' shop, he made his way to Aldersgate Street and the print shop of Mr. Strickland.

It was a large establishment, and surprisingly busy this day. Patrons flipped through engravings set up in vertical bins. Others perused folios laid down on tables or displayed in a square arrangement of tables with glass-cased tops. Strickland oversaw it all, with the help of his brother.

Strickland was a young man of modern, artistic appearance. His brown hair waved to his shoulders, and he sported a paisley waistcoat beneath his pinch-waisted black frock coat. Educated and elegant, he conveyed that his expertise meant he was not a typical shopkeeper. The art that he sold elevated him to something higher than a servant to his patrons, in his mind at least.

Mostly Strickland sold the kind of city scenes, reproductions, and maps that merchants would buy, but several trips per year to the Continent enhanced his offerings. He occasionally obtained rare and handsome old masters.

He came over to greet Ewan. "I never suspected that when next we met, I would be addressing you as Lord Lyndale."

"It is a hell of a thing, isn't it? Any new acquisitions here?"

"Quite a few, but not of your standard."

Pity. Ewan had hoped to lay down a tidy sum, then get Strickland in the back with some wine, as was usually offered after a significant purchase. "Let me see your *veduti* of ancient sites. I have cause to educate several young minds."

"Egypt? Rome? Athens?"

"Rome, I suppose."

He followed Strickland to a library table. Several bound volumes of prints showing the sites of Rome appeared. Ewan began flipping through them.

Since luring Strickland to inebriated indiscretion would not work today, he tried a different tack.

"I will confess that I also came for another reason," he said, as pages of ancient ruins flowed by. "I have reason to think that I purchased some forgeries. Not from you, so do not swoon on me."

"They must be very good ones if they got by you."

"Excellent ones, needless to say." He did not like letting anyone think he could be duped, least of all a purveyor of prints. But duty called and all that. "I suspect they were made here in England."

Strickland stepped closer and spoke in a whisper. "Who sold them? You must tell me. I cannot risk—"

"I do not even know if I am correct, and will not impugn another man's reputation until I am. However, I intend to get to the bottom of it. I thought you might help."

"I will do whatever I can. Such a scandal will affect all of us."

Ewan left the volume open to a view of the Pantheon. "Let us assume that my prints are superb forgeries. Expertly copied from original old masters. Who here in England could do work like that? So perfect, so accurate, that it left me merely wondering instead of certain?"

As Strickland thought about that, his gaze surveyed his shop, keeping an eye on things. "Damned few. It has crossed my mind that both Leighton and Jameson have the skill. Not that I would ever suggest—"

"Of course not. That goes without saying." Strickland was right. The engravings from both of those studios were of the highest quality.

"Of course, it need not be a reproductive engraver. Many a *peintre-graveur* could do it, if he put his mind to it," Strickland said.

"Only if he could resist improving on the original. Real artists almost never can."

"My father once told me that there were several sudden discoveries a few decades ago that he found suspicious. The men involved were dead or inactive at the time he confided, however, so that is not useful now."

"Do you remember their names?"

"I am sorry, no. If anything comes back to me, I will let you know, however."

"Please try to remember. An inactive forger may have turned his hand to it again." Ewan closed the volume. "Send this folio to me, if you will."

Strickland's gaze was still deep into his shop. Ewan glanced over his shoulder to see what captivated his attention, but nothing appeared untoward.

"Did you hear me? I said send this volume to me."

"My apologies. Of course, we will see to it."

"What has you so distracted?"

"I am not sure. Possibly a thief. She has been at it for some time and appears to know what she is looking for."

Ewan turned and tried to see the woman Strickland referred to.

"There, at the bin in the corner," Strickland said. "The big red one."

Ewan jolted alert. His gaze lit on her. The simple cap did not completely obscure the coppery curls.

What was Bride doing here? She was supposed to be spending his inheritance at modistes with Lady Mardenford today.

"She came in and asked some odd questions, and has been checking the prints for an hour now," Strickland said. "She knows what she is looking at. We can always tell the serious collector from the person wanting mere wall decoration. Her appearance does not indicate she can pay for the quality she studies, however."

Bride moved to another V-shaped bin and methodically began turning the large sheets of paper. She lifted one and held it to better light.

"What odd questions did she ask?"

"She wanted to know if a young man had been here the last year, asking about the best studios and printers and such."

Ewan experienced a sharp irritation. Bride had come to London to search for her "friend." She was still hoping for a miraculous reunion with her worthless former lover. Evidently, Walter was an engraver, too.

"Had there been a young man here, asking such questions?"

"I would not remember. A lot of questions get asked in the course of a year."

Ewan noted that Strickland's attention had not wavered from Bride. "It appears that you will remember her questions, however."

Strickland grinned. "Quite likely, but only because she is lovely."

Ewan did not care for that grin. Now that he thought about it, Strickland was a rather silly man, given to airs and posing. His whole romantic persona was overdone.

"I should tell you that I know the woman. She is not a thief."

"I am glad to hear it. Can I impose on you to make a social introduction?"

"I think not. Please remember to send the volume along."

Bride lifted a large sheet bearing a reproduction of Raphael's "The School of Athens." She examined the burin work carefully, then put it back in the bin.

It had been a most successful visit. In her head she had created two lists. A short one noted the names and addresses of the best London studios, those that employed superior engravers.

The other list consisted of studios that produced mediocre prints and might be amenable to giving work to a woman who surpassed their own employees in skill.

Her only regret was that her inquiries about Walter had yielded nothing. If he had come to London tracing those stolen plates, he would have called on shops such as this to obtain information with which to trace the forgers. It was possible that Mr. Strickland did not remember Walter and his questions, however. It could have been as long as a year ago.

She wondered how many more shops there were like this. London was very big, much larger than Edinburgh. It had taken a long time to walk to this shop. She had only learned its address from perusing Lord Lyndale's portfolio yesterday, while sitting with Joan in that scandalous salon.

As she flipped through the rest of the prints in the bin, she considered all the duties facing her in the days ahead. She would have to seek out other such shops, and start visiting engravers. And papermakers. Yes, the key might be the source of the paper. Forging the special paper used in banknotes would be as hard as forging plates.

She also needed to find a way to be shown any rarities these sellers had tucked away for special patrons. Not only the banknote plates had been stolen from her trunk. If another of her father's plates had been printed and made available for sale, that could give her a good clue as to who had the entire cache.

"The tonalities in that one are very weak, don't you agree?"

The voice at her shoulder startled her.

London might be very big, but it appeared it was not big enough.

She pasted a smile on her face and turned to the towering presence at her side. "Lord Lyndale, what an unexpected pleasure."

"The pleasure is yours alone, although this is certainly unexpected. What are you doing here? I gave instructions that you were to accompany Lady Mardenford today."

"Given a choice between garments and art, I decided I would prefer art."

"I do not remember giving you a choice."

"You did not really expect me to forgo the rich artistic culture of London in favor of being measured and pinned, I am sure."

"What I expected appears to be of no account to you." He gestured to the bin. "Are you finished here? If so, I will give you an escort. My carriage is nearby."

She was not really finished, but she did not want Lyndale hovering while she completed her investigation. Deciding she had accomplished enough for her first day, and not relishing the long walk back to Belgrave Square, she accepted his offer.

He handed her into a little carriage.

"If you had done as you were told, you would be traveling in style today," he said as he took the ribbons. "I have had this cabriolet for years, and should probably replace it."

"It is like the furniture in that second drawing room, you mean? That is the only chamber where everything is not new. It is understandable that you would be sentimental about some possessions and want to keep them."

He moved the horse into the flow of carriages. "I am not sentimental. I am a man, and we never are, unless we are among the young, silly, poetic types one trips over all the time now. Like Strickland back there."

"Mr. Strickland did not appear silly. I thought he was very dignified. Handsome, too."

"You are too generous. I would describe him as nice-looking, at best."

"Well, I think he is handsome. He is also quite elegant."

"Only someone who has been in London only one day would say so."

He was being very prickly. She assumed it was because she had not done as he commanded about the visits to modistes. "Are there many shops like that?"

"At least six worth visiting. There are others that only have prints of the most popular sort. Booksellers and such. On occasion, however, something of interest can be found in them."

"I look forward to visiting every one."

His brow knit. Not in disapproval, but thought. "Would you like to visit a few now?"

"With you?"

"You do not have to look so shocked at the invitation."

"You seemed very determined to avoid such obligations when Mary was trying to corner you."

"I have no interest in escorting a child about London, nor seeing sights and amusements I have visited often before. However, I frequent the print shops and enjoy them myself."

She would not be able to learn anything she needed from those shops with Lyndale by her side, but she agreed to accompany him. At least she would learn their locations, and see what they sold.

They spent the next two hours perusing the holdings of two large print shops. They debated quality and argued authenticity. They mutually admired great artistry or craftsmanship. They agreed as one mind or bickered like children when at odds in their judgments.

Lyndale's command brought forth the most valuable rarities for their consideration. At Ackerman's Repository of the Arts, however, the clerk resisted laying out his copy of Caraglio's "Loves of the Gods" when Lyndale requested it.

"My lord, the lady . . ."

Lyndale sighed with exasperation. "She is a mature woman and the images are barely risqué. There are paintings by Titian on display for all to view that are more explicit. Furthermore, she is schooled in the arts and knows visual metaphors when she sees them. Now, let us see the engravings."

They were produced. Lyndale set two side by side on the table. "These are copies, not originals," he said. "There were many copies down through the centuries. I have personally seen four separate examples, and there is no addendum in any of them. The extra six are missing. They appear to have been excised from the series very early."

Head-to-head they pored over the images, with Lyndale pointing out the signs that heralded a copy. He had Bride so thoroughly engrossed that she did not initially notice an unusually long pause that developed while her nose was stuck to the paper.

Eventually the silence penetrated her awareness. It carried a tremor that woke her womanly instincts. She turned her head to find Lyndale's attention on her, not the prints.

He did not appear predatory, even though it was a man's consideration that he gave her. His expression hinted that he found her peculiar and confusing.

She straightened and turned away from the prints. "It is getting late in the afternoon."

"So it is. We should be on our way."

He escorted her to his carriage. When they were moving down the street again, he raised a subject she had hoped he would forget.

"Did you bring them with you? Your father's collection, including the extra Caraglio prints?"

Of course she had. She had brought all of the legacy with her.

She had enjoyed the last hours sharing their common interest. Now she needed to rebuild the barrier that kept this man ignorant of her activities and history and problems.

She definitely could not allow Lyndale to see those Caraglio prints again, either. If he did, if he compared them to the originals in the suite he owned, he might identify them as forgeries, just as he had the ones at Ackerman's.

"They are deep in a trunk that I have not unpacked."

"If you retrieve them, I could conduct the study I mentioned in Scotland. Then you would know what you have."

She already knew what she had.

He did not press her, but she could tell he wanted to see those prints again. Silence fell as he drove through the city streets. She wondered if she thought her avoidance of the topic was suspicious.

"Thank you for inviting me to visit those shops. I

enjoyed it very much, and will feel more at ease entering such establishments in the future."

He moved the carriage around a corner, onto a long, wide street filled with coaches and people. "You cannot do so dressed as you are today. The combination of your obvious expertise and poor appearance led Strickland to think you were a thief."

"A thief!"

"It did not help that you were a stranger. The proprietors know the clientele."

"I am already known at three shops, and will be at others soon. My appearance should not be questioned by any of them in a week or so."

"I agree. For one thing, you will be presentable by then." He angled the horse to the side of the street and stopped behind a large coach. He threw the ribbons to a footman tending the other carriage, and hopped down.

Bride looked around in confusion. "I thought we were returning to Belgrave Square."

"I never said so. That is my coach there. In front of it is Lady Mardenford's. That indicates Lady M. and your sisters are abovestairs with the modiste who occupies this building." He offered his hand. "It is late in the day, but I expect that something can still be done for you."

CHAPTER THIRTEEN

~

"This one here, but in this color." Lyndale's arm intruded between Bride and Lady Mardenford. His finger pointed at two plates. The design he favored featured a mantle trimmed in fur. It would cost a small fortune.

Lady M., as Lyndale often addressed her, stifled a sigh. "How many carriage ensembles do you think she needs, Lyndale? She just chose one."

"It was very plain and boring. I think this one is more elegant."

Bride propped her elbows on the table and rested her head in her hands.

She had expected Lyndale to bring her up here, introduce her to Lady Mardenford, and leave. Instead he had poked around the modiste's salon, picked through lace, intruded on every decision, and turned the excursion into a trial.

She glanced to the woman lending aid to the im-

possible task of making Bride Cameron presentable.
Lady Mardenford was all elegance and grace, with a
delicate, pretty face and dark hair styled in the fat
ringlets and curls worn by women of society.

Upon meeting her, Bride had been cowed into co-
operating on this mission. Lady M. made her feel so
clumsy and rustic, so big and antique, that thoughts
of resistance instantly disappeared.

Lady Mardenford gave a strained smile to the
man peering over her shoulder. "There really is no
further need for you to delay your day's plans. I have
things well in hand here."

"I do not mind helping." His hand darted again
and reached for another stack of plates.

Lady Mardenford smacked his wrist. "If you insist on favoring us with your opinion, sit. Right
there. If you continue to buzz like a fly we will never
finish."

Lyndale took the indicated seat on the other side
of Lady Mardenford. Bride stifled a yawn. This had
been fun the first hour, but she was growing weary.
Her sisters had long ago finished and now sat in exhausted stupors on the other side of the room. Jilly
had fallen asleep in her chair.

Oblivious to his lack of welcome, Lyndale began
perusing the plates his last foray had grabbed.

"What are you looking for?" Lady Mardenford
said.

"A dress like yours. The greenish one you were
wearing yesterday."

"I bought that months ago. I doubt the design is still offered."

"I will be very disappointed if that is true."

"Perhaps I should give Miss Cameron mine, since you favor the style so much."

"If she were not far too big for your dresses, I would accept the offer."

Silence fell. Lyndale did not notice. He examined the plates much as he did his collection.

"Lyndale," Lady Mardenford admonished.

He looked up, confused by her tone. Her piercing glare provoked comprehension. "Ah, let me rephrase. If she were not so stately, so statuesque, I would accept."

"If you decide to kill him, Miss Cameron, I promise not to lay down information."

"I am not offended. I do not apologize for my height. I had no choice on the matter, and it has been useful on occasion."

"See?" said Lyndale. "She is not some vain woman who requires false flattery. She takes pride in that which makes her unique. She is not a slave to fashions of beauty, nor does she seek to be predictable. She is well aware that she is magnificent just as she is."

Magnificent?

Lyndale gestured for the modiste. "More plates, madame." He beamed boyish delight at Lady M. "I had no idea how diverting this is. No wonder women spend so much time at it."

"And so much money. You will clean your pistol

when you get the bills, but it will be your fault, so
aim for your own head, not mine."

With a reptilian smile, the modiste thrust a stack
of plates displaying luxurious evening gowns under
Lyndale's nose.

Lady M. gave the modiste a scolding glance. The
modiste chose to ignore it.

Lyndale discarded ten plates in rapid succession,
creating a blur of richly decorated bouffant skirts
and bulbous sleeves. Suddenly he stopped.

"This one. Just like this. Same color, everything."

Lady M. angled her head to see it. "You are being
reckless now. Where will she wear such a gown?"

"She will wear it for me."

Lady M.'s eyebrows rose. She gazed critically at
Lyndale as he happily admired his choice.

The modiste gave Bride a heavy-lidded glance
that combined disdain and admiration.

Lady Mardenford rose from her chair. "Lord
Lyndale, may I speak with you? Privately? Over
there?" She pointed to a corner of the salon.

Ewan obligingly followed Lady Mardenford to the
corner.

The woman waiting for him did not appear
friendly. She looked up at him with eyes as hard and
bright as crystals.

"Lyndale, were you so bold as to ask me to dress
your most recent conquest? Is that woman your mistress?"

"Good heavens, no. She is not. I swear."

Charlotte was the image of a suspicious harpy. "Are your intentions toward her honorable?"

Where the deuce had this interrogation come from? He had been an almost perfect gentleman since Bride had arrived and he had not so much as flirted all afternoon.

"Well?"

"Madame, I am thinking. I want my answer to be precise. I find that my intentions are inexplicably changeable these days. Also, exactly how does one define 'honorable' in a situation such as this? If you think about it, since she is mature—"

Charlotte stuck her face closer to his. "Listen to me, sir. You cannot take these four young women into your home and then seduce them. It would be the scandal of the year."

"I would never seduce all four of them. What do you take me for?"

"I know exactly what to take you for."

"That was the old me. Now I have duties. Obligations. Responsibilities."

"Stop smiling like that. I am most serious. Do you swear that you have no designs on Miss Cameron?"

"My dear Lady Mardenford, the woman is older than you. Furthermore, she is well schooled in using a pistol. It is comical for you to upbraid me and demand oaths. Miss Cameron is more than capable of guarding her own virtue."

Charlotte retreated a bit at his rebuke. Her pretty face still reflected displeasure.

"Does she know about you?"

"I daresay she knows enough."

"Let us be sure about that."

She pivoted on her heel and aimed for the table. "Miss Cameron, I think we are well done for the day. I would be pleased if you would ride back to Belgrave Square in my carriage. I welcome the opportunity to further my acquaintance with you."

"He hosted a most infamous party three years ago," Lady Mardenford continued. Her carriage was taking a long time to get to Belgrave Square.

Bride suspected the coachman had been instructed to tour the city so this litany of Lyndale's sins could be shared. The frank description of indiscretions had been both astonishing and fascinating.

"For several days, it was noted that flowers kept arriving at McLean's chambers. A parade of deliveries disappeared into the building. Word has it that when the guests arrived, the entire floor of his sitting room was packed a foot deep in petals and the scent was intoxicating. The sofas were not used that night, I have heard."

Bride tried to imagine making love on a bed of flowers a foot deep. Actually, the notion had some appeal. She would not want there to be others around, of course.

"His creativity was much admired," Lady Mardenford said. "The democratic quality of his guest list was, too, by some. Others think that is the worst scandal. He invites anyone whom he favors, no matter what their station. Even his manservant has been known to participate."

"The highborn need not accept the invitation if they do not care to mingle with such people," Bride said, thinking "mingle" a most inadequate verb.

"McLean's visits to London were greeted with joy by a certain set. My brother Dante is among his closest friends, and indulged in these diversions before he married. As for the ladies, many decline, or at least claim they do. Others go, but are usually masked. That only tells everyone they are ladies of high birth, of course."

Bride tried to picture that second drawing room filled with naked men and women, coupling in the candlelight. Her mind thoroughly failed her except in one small detail. She could imagine Lyndale's face gazing down in its severe, mesmerizing expression of passion, as rose petals blew over her body.

"He has had more mistresses than can be counted," Lady Mardenford said. "Actresses, singers, aristocrats, widows—the man is brazen. It is rare for any of them to hold his attention more than a month. His pursuits are reputed to be direct and bold, and he ends it without sentiment or regret." She trapped Bride's attention with a very direct gaze. "Only the most sophisticated woman could survive such an affair unscathed. Only a woman as indifferent as he to the emotional context of passion should indulge in such a liaison."

"You appear to be describing a man without honor."

"He does not leave ruined innocents in his wake. Nor has he ever been accused of seducing a friend's wife or relative. There are men who claim far better morals, who cannot profess that point of honor."

"Is that why you are his friend? Because he retains some sense of honor?"

"I am his friend because he amuses me, and represents no danger at all to me. As for his reputation, I decided long ago to ignore a person's carnal preferences in forming my judgment of him. I had reasons to believe this was the path of wisdom."

"This has been most illuminating, Lady Mardenford."

"I only speak so openly because of your dependence on him. I trust you will not think badly of me for alerting you to his history."

"Not at all. Even not knowing his reputation, I thought it best to remove my sisters from his house. Now I fear that their reputations will never survive our association with the earl."

Lady Mardenford gave her a long, deep look. "Since his standards are as well-known as his seductions, I think your sisters' reputations will remain intact. The world assumes they are innocents, so they will be safe both from him and from scandal."

"That is reassuring, since after today's indulgence in luxury I do not think I can convince them to leave."

"Miss Cameron, I fear that you are missing the

reason for my bluntness. It is not your sisters that concern me. Lyndale is not dangerous to them. He *is* dangerous to *you*. I fear that he has concluded, for some reason, possibly your age, that you are, shall we say, fair game."

Bride swallowed hard. She tried to look shocked. She did not know how Lyndale had surmised she was not an innocent, but her behavior had done nothing to tell him he was wrong.

"I did not intend to worry you," Lady Mardenford said more gently. "When I said he was dangerous, I did not mean he would importune you."

"That is very good to know."

"Certainly you suspected. After all, there is that collection. I hear he does not hide it."

"I will admit there were some works of art that startled me."

"If you were only 'startled,' he must keep the worst of it out of view." Lady Mardenford leaned toward her, as if someone might overhear. "Much of it is antique, and some is from the Renaissance. A few items are from exotic or primitive cultures, and I hear they are the most explicit. Of course, the *'Modi'* probably give them good competition."

Bride almost jumped out of her seat. *"Modi?"*

"That is Italian. *'I Modi'* translates to 'the positions.' Need I say more?"

Indeed not. Bride was speechless.

"It is a famous Renaissance series of prints thought lost," Lady Mardenford explained. "Lyndale owns the only known surviving copy, recently dis-

covered. Vasari wrote about them in the sixteenth
century. The engraver was Marcantonio Raimondi,
but the drawings came from Giulio Romano,
Raphael's student. The great Aretino provided poems. I have heard, however, that the images are not
very artistic at all, considering their pedigree, and
remarkably frank in subject."

Bride barely heard the historical litany. Her head
was splitting from a rush of panic.

Lord Lyndale had recently acquired a newly discovered set of *"I Modi."* Those extremely scandalous prints were currently residing in the same
house as she and her sisters.

Of all the tidbits of gossip Lady Mardenford had
just shared, this was the most appalling.

CHAPTER
FOURTEEN

꩜

It is a nice dress, though not as lovely as the ones the modistes are making. However, no one will ever know that Mrs. Thornapple added the flounce." Mary sat on Bride's bed, assessing the sapphire-blue dress she had just fastened.

It was one of several that had arrived the day before from the seamstress who kept garments partly made in anticipation of emergencies such as the Cameron sisters presented.

Mrs. Thornapple had not blinked an eye when she assessed the challenge Bride's height presented. A full, laced flounce had immediately been pinned to the hem that only reached Bride's shins.

Bride tucked a filmy fichu around her low neckline, ignoring Mary's objections to the attempt at modesty. She eyed Mary's own deep scarlet dress. It was restrained enough, but the color enhanced

Mary's beauty and made her lips very dark. Her sister looked like a strawberry ripe for tasting.

Bride looked down at the bodice of her own dress. It fit snugly, forming around her breasts. All the undergarments, bought yesterday in a grand assault on London's best warehouses, felt wonderfully soft and pretty.

The daily regimen of measuring and fitting and choosing was finally over. Bride had been unable to avoid Lady Mardenford's snare after the first day, which meant her own plans had been forced to wait. Beginning tomorrow, however, her days were her own again.

There were a host of things that she needed to do. One in particular demanded immediate attention. She had not been able to sleep well, because each night she fretted over her inability to deal with the matter.

Mary lifted her skirt to admire her new silk stockings and shoes. "You may think it good for one's soul to live in coarse wool, but I say if someone wants to give you silk, there is no sin in accepting it."

Bride decided to forgo a lecture on how there was no sin in accepting silk, provided one was not required to give one's soul in return.

She sat down at the dressing table and examined herself in the looking glass. From the neck down she appeared almost fashionable. No matter what she did with her hair, however, it always looked the same—lots of copper curls bound to her crown.

"I wonder if Lord Lyndale will be at dinner

tonight," Mary said. "It would be fun for him to see us turned out properly."

"He has not dined at home since that first day. I expect we will rarely see him at table."

His lack of hospitality had reassured her. If he saw her as fair game, surely the hunting would be more rigorous. Either his attention had already been diverted elsewhere, or he had been teasing her that first day, nothing more. It had probably been his way of punishing her for intruding on his castle.

"He must have a wonderful life." Mary gave a dreamy sigh. "Out on the town most of the night. Sleeping in most of the day. Calling on dukes and princes. Of course, he spends some time tending to his great fortune and doing important things for the government, but not enough to make his life dull."

Bride peered at her sister's reflection in the glass. "How do you know so much about his habits?"

"Joan told me."

"Which means Michael told Joan. What did he say about Lyndale's government duties?"

"He explained to Joan how we might hear scandalous gossip about the earl, spread by those who are envious, but in fact, his lord is an important man who is consulted by the highest government ministers. Michael scolded Joan about this just yesterday, when Joan made an impolite observation about Lord Lyndale never exerting himself for more than pleasure."

Mary came over and considered Bride's reflection. She removed two combs and tried to coerce them to be more effective. "I think you should cut your hair. Otherwise, there is not much hope."

Walter had loved her hair. She knew she should at least shorten it a little, but for the last year the idea of doing so had always seemed a betrayal of him. Or a surrender to the idea he would never want to wrap his hands in her long tresses again.

"I must go out with Joan today, Mary. However, I would be very curious whether Lyndale will remain abroad in the city most of the night."

"Are you asking me to spy on him, Bride? That seems ungracious, since we are guests."

"I am merely saying that should you learn whether he has left the house for a night about town, I would not mind being told."

"Jilly and I on occasion go below to the kitchen. The servants know everything, so I am sure I can learn what is happening in the house."

Bride swallowed her inclination to ask what Mary was doing with the servants. She decided not to wonder about the handsome footman who had smiled so much at Mary that first day. Jilly was the chaperone, and could keep an eye on Mary.

Besides, Bride needed the information that Mary could obtain down below.

"Your craft is excellent, I cannot deny that." Mr. Downey peered at the prints Bride and Joan had carried to his establishment. "The detailing is meticulous and the tonalities very rich. I see you do not resort to the cruder economies of technique that some engravers employ, either. It must take you a month to complete a large plate."

The sheets that he admired were spread on a large table at the back of his establishment.

Three men sat at another long table nearby, plying their burins on copper plates. Each had a drawing reflected in a looking glass propped on a table easel. It was the reflection being copied, so the plate, when printed, would show the image in the correct direction.

Three other men worked a large intaglio press near the front of the room. Freshly printed engravings hung from lines like washed linens set out to dry.

The scent of ink and damp paper made Bride nostalgic for home.

"We have drawings of old master paintings from Paris and Rome," Bride said. "They have never been used, and are most accurate. They were made from direct study of the original works, not copied from other engravings."

Mr. Downey appeared interested. He also appeared regretful. The latter did not bode well for the day's excursion.

"I would not mind having plates of those works," he said. "I am sure that if they are executed with this quality, I could sell the prints to establishments in London and other cities. I am not in a position to give you employment, however."

Bride's heart fell. This was the second publisher on her list to turn them down.

Joan donned her most innocent expression. "Sir, if you admire the skill, and covet the images, why are you unable to make use of both?"

Mr. Downey gestured to the men bent over their plates. "They've families to feed. It would be wrong for me to release them, to employ others, especially women."

"I understand. We would never want others to be put out to make room for us."

Mr. Downey gazed down at the prints wistfully. "Should you decide to work independently, I would be happy to consider any plates you make. I would pay fairly for them."

"We have no press," Bride said. "No way to pull the working proofs to check our progress on the image."

"Of course. Yes, that would be a problem."

Joan gave Mr. Downey a charming smile. Mr. Downey began blushing.

Bride realized with a jolt that Joan was flirting. She looked at her sister and saw for the first time that Joan was a woman who might fluster a man. Her face was quite handsome, but just soft enough to imply a sweet temperament. Her gray eyes shimmered when she smiled, and her new lilac-and-purple ensemble fit her neatly, revealing a fine form.

Bride had seen Joan in loose men's garments for so long, and apparently indifferent to her appearance for years. Now, transformed by Lyndale's largesse, Joan shone like a newly polished jewel.

A silly smile broke on Mr. Downey's face. It stuck there during a dumb silence.

"Sir, it is forward of me to suggest this." Joan managed to sound contrite and confidential. "I was wondering, however, since we are badly in need of funds to support our sisters and aunt, if you would consider allowing us to come and pull our proofs here? We would do so when the press was not in use, at your convenience. We would bring our own paper and inks, and require nothing from you except the machine itself."

"It is a splendid solution," Mr. Downey rushed to say. "If you promise to sell me the plates when they are done, well, that would be recompense enough."

"You are too good."

Bride took advantage of the man's pliable state. "We will need to buy plates and paper, Joan. We do not even know where to go for such things in London."

Mr. Downey hastened to reassure her. "I will write down some names for you. Places where you can procure good-sized copper plates and paper." He hurried to a desk and picked up a quill.

Bride waited for the little list, then examined it. "Are any of these stationers apt to make their own paper? We are very particular about the quality used when we pull proofs."

The quill's feather dipped over the list. "These two will take special orders. However, the others have a large selection and should have anything you need."

Joan gave Mr. Downey another bedazzling smile. "You have been very generous. I fear that we have tested your kindness more than is right. To allow us the use of your press is a rare boon."

Mr. Downey smiled sheepishly. "Not so rare, I am bound to say. I have on occasion allowed others to hire time on my press."

"Truly? This is common, then?"

"Not common, but I am not alone in permitting it."

"Would you be present when we use the press? Is it normal for the proprietor to remain when time is hired on his equipment?"

Mr. Downey tried to look indifferent, but Bride did not miss a roguish glint in his eyes. "I would want to ensure the proper use of my studio, so I expect I would be here. That is customary. Our arrangement will only be unusual in that you will pay with other than coin."

Bride packed away the prints. "You have been a great help. It will be some time before we have need of the press, I expect. We will write to you then. I look forward to our arrangement, and trust it will benefit us both. Perhaps, when we visit again, we will have the pleasure of meeting Mrs. Downey."

She led Joan out of the shop. Mr. Downey followed them to the door, and even stepped outside to watch Joan walk away.

"It was a most useful visit, Joan, thanks to you. This list of stationers might lead us to papermakers. The forgers had to have their special paper made somewhere."

"And if we can hire time on a press, so can the forgers. Mr. Downey says he remains when his studio is used, but for a price I expect a proprietor will make himself scarce."

"I am beginning to see how they arranged this," Bride said. "It was not as hard as I supposed it would be, once they had the plates."

"It is unfortunate that the forgers were able to hire a press, but it may be useful that we can do so."

Bride looked over at her sister just as Joan looked at her. Their gazes locked.

Hiring a few hours on a press could be very useful. It opened all kinds of possibilities.

Ewan placed a big wager on the vingt-et-un table. He awaited the outcome with a discouraging level of ennui.

In the past such a sum would have made his heart race with excitement. Winning or losing would have affected his whole life for a year.

Such a bet would have been so completely rash, so outrageously wrong, that he would have been impressed by his own audacity. Tonight the bet barely gave his heart a tiny bump.

He won.

He almost sighed. No joy, either. No elation. Worse, he always seemed to win now. It was as if Providence had decreed that he should inherit good luck with the title, so that all the thrills in life would be dulled.

The gaming room's owner walked over.

"Another big win, Lord Lyndale. Notes will do, I trust."

Ewan accepted the thick stack of banknotes. He carried them over to a vacant card table in the corner and gave the fifties a cursory glance. They all appeared good, but he would need to study them more closely in better light.

He took a small piece of paper from his coat and examined the list of names on it. He had visited Leighton's engraving studio today. When he drew Leighton into a little argument about the best masters of the burin in Britain, this distilled list of highly skilled hands resulted.

He would have to begin learning about these engravers, and discover if any of them had reason to be suspected.

He took a small pencil from his pocket and crossed out one name. It was that of Thomas Waterfield, the name Bride and her sisters used on their plates. Leighton had proposed its inclusion, but of course it had no place here, despite their notable skill.

"Working your accounts, Lyndale?"

Ewan looked up to see Nathaniel Knightridge smiling down at him. Knightridge was a young lawyer who argued cases in the Court of Common Pleas. His fame derived from other defenses, however. Those of criminals in the Old Bailey.

The golden-haired, dark-eyed Adonis had a remarkable talent for exploiting the theatrics of criminal trials. Ewan had long ago decided that if he were ever accused of treason, he would want Knightridge speaking for him.

"Rumor has it that a certain lady has been spending your fortune for you," Knightridge said. "It is said the dowager Lady Mardenford aims to put you in the poor house."

"So she has threatened."

Charlotte's pique over Bride Cameron's ambiguous status had provoked her to spend very freely the last week. She had written to him today to warn about the huge bills due to arrive. The tone of the letter had carried a note of vengeance.

The situation was typical of his upside-down life now. For years he had sinned and paid no penance, and now he was being punished for something he had not even tried to do, much as he wanted to.

"There are those who say you are trying to seduce Lady Mardenford's affections," Knightridge said. "I am sure they are wrong, and that you would never insult a fine lady thus."

"The lady has suffered no insult, unless having carte blanche is an insult. Since she demanded it, I doubt her sensibilities are offended, even if yours are."

"Carte blanche? Are you saying—"

"She agreed to dress some young women for whom I find myself responsible. I had to promise to accept whatever bills came. I suspect, however, that giving a mistress carte blanche for a year would have cost less."

Knightridge sat in a chair at the table. "If the

young ladies are expensive, you should do what my cousin did when he found himself with two wards."

"What was that?"

"He married them off. He had them both engaged within three months. The settlements were a fraction of the cost of keeping them, so he counted himself lucky."

Ewan looked at Knightridge. What an inspired idea. This was exactly what he should be doing. He would marry off the Cameron sisters forthwith, and foist the responsibility on other men.

He called for some brandy to thank Knightridge for his brilliance. While they sipped, he turned over his piece of paper and made a new list.

Anne
Joan
Mary

"How much did your cousin settle on his wards? What amount would be tempting?"

"I think it was six thousand each. The income would be tempting enough, I suppose."

"Would that tempt you?"

"I suppose it might, if I could be tempted at all. Less than that would not tempt anyone but a tradesman, of course."

Ewan pondered that. He would increase the settlements to ten thousand. That would tempt even the untemptable.

Anne   Knightridge
Joan
Mary

"Here comes Burchard," Knightridge said. "He has Abernathy in tow. Since they are both smiling, they must be up for the night."

Ewan watched his two friends approach. Colin Burchard glowed with the well-being of a man who had enjoyed a good night at the tables. Abernathy always glowed, being a somewhat stupid person who did not understand that life was temporary.

Ewan did not much care for Abernathy, but he did not exactly dislike the young man, either. It would be cruel to hate someone merely for being born with a lack of wits and an excess of optimism.

On the other hand, Abernathy possessed a handsome face and trusting demeanor that would make some equally silly woman very happy.

Anne   Knightridge
Joan   Burchard?
Mary   Abernathy

"What do you have there?" Colin asked.

"I am making reminders of the *duties* I have over the next few days." He gave Colin a hooded look and stressed the word "duties."

Colin's reaction all but said "Ahh." He understood Ewan's only duties involved Ewan's secret investigations for the government.

"And here I thought you were making a list of potential brides," Colin said, by way of covering for them both.

"I must add that to this list. Tell me, gentlemen, what qualities do you think I should seek? Someone who shares my interests? Burchard, wouldn't you prefer to marry a woman who enjoys equestrian pursuits the same as you, for example?"

"I expect that would be pleasant."

"I think a wife should be practical and intelligent," Knightridge offered. "God spare me from one of these dreamy women who cannot manage themselves, let alone a household."

Ewan licked his pencil.

Anne   ~~Knightridge~~

"The thing is, should I ever marry, I doubt it will be for any reason one can put on a list," Colin said. "It will be a match like my brother's. Having seen that, I cannot settle for less."

"It helped enormously that Adrian's great love was one of the wealthiest women in England," Ewan said.

"If she had been one of the poorest, it would have made no difference."

Ewan grudgingly turned to his paper again.

Anne   ~~Knightridge~~
Joan   ~~Burchard~~
Mary   Abernathy

"Abernathy, what do you think I should seek in a bride?"

"Someone young and pretty and sweet, I would say. Not too clever—only trouble there. I think it would be best to marry a girl who is fresh and still malleable." Abernathy gravely gave his opinion as if it was original and not the list of requirements most men used.

Mary   ⟨Abernathy⟩

Ewan felt a warmth near his shoulder as Colin leaned over his arm to eye his list. Colin's realization that the list had nothing to do with forgers produced a frown. The presence of his own name beside some strange woman's may have added to his pique.

"I notice one of their names is not there, McLean," he muttered.

"She is too old," Ewan muttered back. "Besides, she has no fortune. She refused any settlement."

"Once you marry off the sisters, how is she to live if she is not some man's wife? Become someone's mistress?"

Ewan had not considered Bride's financial vulnerability if he succeeded in moving her sisters off the field. He had assumed he would take care of her.

Ewan tucked the paper away. "If I could think of any man who would suit Bride Cameron, I would throw her at him. Now let us play cards. I have a fortune to squander."

As the cards appeared, he considered Colin's accusation. He would never stand in the way of Bride's security and happiness. He had to admit, however, that he did not like the idea of her as some man's wife.

He very much liked the idea of her as some man's mistress, however. His. That idea had never been far from his thoughts during the last week of inexplicable, virtuous restraint.

Bride cracked her door ajar and listened. Silence met her ears. It was very late, and the household had mostly retired. Sticking her head out, she peered up and down the corridor to make sure no one was about.

Carrying a lamp, she slipped out. She did not aim for the main stairs, but for the back ones that she used to go up to see her sisters. This time she followed the stairway down a level, to the public rooms.

She should be able to complete this mission quickly and unobserved tonight. Mary had been good on her promise to learn about the earl's movements from the household staff. She had reported before dinner that tonight Lyndale had told Michael not to wait for his return, a sign that he would be out most of the night.

Curiosity simmered in her, regarding the diversions that would occupy him. Perhaps he was with one of his mistresses. Or he could be attending a party much like those he gave, and making love in some grand salon strewn with flowers or furs or something else exotic and sensual.

Clearly this man was far too worldly for her. It was just as well that whatever interest she once provoked in him had quickly waned.

Only her little lamp lit her way on the first floor. She hurried through the big drawing room and into the library. She eased open the door to Lyndale's private room.

Her lamp revealed that the unpacking was completed. The golden glow washed over sculptures and paintings, revealing images too artistic to be merely licentious. The skill of these artists could make the most base subject appear elevated and important.

She spied a cabinet and moved closer. Behind the glass doors she saw the leather-covered boards of folios. She set down her lamp and pulled the doors wide.

One by one, she removed the folios, knelt on the floor, and flipped through the prints they contained.

Lyndale's collection was superb. With prints, at least, his tastes ran to more than erotica. One folio held engravings of the early Renaissance, when artists like Mantegna first exploited copper plates to make works of art. She set it aside. Another day she would like to enjoy those at her leisure, but tonight she had other concerns.

She spied a leather binding to the back of one shelf. It seemed the right size. She lifted it, opened it, and knew she had found Raimondi's *"I Modi."* She moved her lamp to a little table near one sofa, and sat down to examine the treasure.

The engravings had been laid down on the pages. That meant the watermarks could not be examined, since the engravings could not be held to the light. The poems by Aretino had been separated from the images, and adhered to the pages facing the pictures.

Hoping her initial instincts betrayed her, praying she was wrong, she lifted a little quizzing glass attached to a cord around her neck. She held it to one engraving.

The black lines jumped into view, each as distinctive as a thick line of a pen. The contours and crosshatching formed patterns as unique as a signature. The technique announced this was produced by the famous Renaissance engraver Marcantonio Raimondi.

She saw more than those signs, however, because she was searching for them. She saw atmospheric stipples that were longer than Raimondi would use. She saw the rendition of background details that would not match other engravings by that master.

The man who had made these plates had concentrated on duplicating Raimondi's technique in the most significant portions of the image, but had gotten too independent in the subsidiary parts.

A good forger normally would not be so reckless. In this case, however, he could afford a bit of license. After all, there were no surviving examples that could be used for a side-by-side comparison with these engravings. This forger had re-created a series now lost to time, but known to history. He had provided the only known example of a great rarity, and done a masterful job at it.

And he had fooled the connoisseurs, including the current Earl of Lyndale.

Bride stared at the engraving on her lap, not seeing anything but the burin work. A wave a nausea rose, then fell, until it affected her body down to her toes.

She recognized the hand that had made these. She had learned her own craft from the same man. She had also seen the plates from which these engravings had been pulled.

They had once been hidden in a trunk in her room in Scotland, along with plates that forged banknotes.

As Ewan mounted the stairs in his house, he retrieved a thick stack of banknotes from his coat. They represented not only his winnings, but notes he had procured off Colin Burchard by means of trades. Tonight, after they left the gaming hall, they had conducted some very private business that involved sizable amounts of money.

It was only a little past two. Normally he would still be out and about, but this stack begged a close examination.

He headed for his private salon, anxious to give these notes a thorough study. He ruefully admitted that this inquiry had engaged him more than he expected. Adrian had been correct. Such things could be very compelling, and even great fun.

He did not go through the main drawing room and library. Instead he approached the chamber from the other side of the stairwell and opened the single door not far from the servants' stairs. As soon as he did, light poured over the threshold.

A lamp sat on a table near a sofa that faced away from his spot. Its glow formed golden highlights on amber curls rising above the sofa's back.

A glance to his right showed the open print cabinet. Some folios lay on the floor. Bride had spent the evening perusing his collection.

He never would have left if he had known she intended to do so. It would have been pleasant to spend time with her, discussing these sheets. He rarely had the opportunity to do that with anyone who was knowledgeable, and never with a woman. Their few hours in the print shops together had been among the most pleasant he had spent in years.

Deciding the banknotes could wait, he entered the chamber and slipped them into the writing desk tucked in the corner. Then he walked over to Bride.

She did not hear him approach. Her head remained bent over the volume on her lap. As Ewan neared, he saw what had her so entranced. She had discovered Raimondi's *"I Modi."*

He looked over her shoulder at the explicit sexual activity on the page she observed. He angled his head to see her face. No embarrassment there. No virtuous dismay or blushing shock. She did not flip past quickly, either. She studied the image as if she wanted to commit every detail to memory.

His gaze drifted over her abundant unruly curls and lovely profile and flawless skin. While she scrutinized the details of *"I Modi,"* he pored over the details of Bride Cameron, noting how fine her figure looked in the new blue dress, and how perfectly the bones in her face framed her eyes and mouth.

He had been avoiding her all week because the alternative was to seduce her. He would never be able to simply look and not touch, especially since he had touched already. Normally, when a woman inspired this hunger, he wasted no time in seeking to make her his mistress. This time he had retreated.

He had been an idiot again, just like in Scotland. There was no rational reason to be so restrained. He wanted her. He had wanted her since that first day in Scotland, and right now, watching her on that sofa, he wanted her with a savage determination.

If she was a woman who gave *"I Modi"* such cool and sophisticated regard, she would not be insulted by a man's frank and honest desire.

Now that he thought about it, she had seemed annoyed when he ended things so abruptly on that library sofa.

Still oblivious to his presence, Bride turned the page to the next print. Ewan stretched to see the new image. Bride lifted a quizzing glass and peered closely, thoroughly engrossed.

Ewan strolled around the room, locking the doors. Then he walked over to a cabinet where spirits were stored, and poured two glasses of sherry.

CHAPTER
FIFTEEN

❦

Bride frowned at the print while she moved her quizzing glass across it inch by inch. She kept hoping to find evidence this series had not come from her father's plates.

She wished she still had the plates. She cursed herself for never printing proofs of them. If she had, she could quickly find out for certain if this set had been pulled from them, too. Now she had to rely on her memory of the ghostly images made by the gouged lines on the copper, and on her knowledge of her father's technique.

Both of which said repeatedly that these were her father's forgeries.

Thoroughly disheartened, wondering how she could entice Lyndale to reveal where he found this series, she turned another page.

"That one is among the best of the series, in terms of artistry. I discovered that the physical reality of duplicating the composition in life was very clumsy, however."

She jumped with shock and slammed the volume closed.

She turned her head. Lord Lyndale stood behind the sofa, setting a tiny glass on the table beside her. His expression bore a touch of humor. It also possessed a tightness that had her thinking she had better leave.

"Is that sherry?" she asked, gesturing to the glass. "I have never had it, so I must decline."

"If you have never tried it, why must you decline? Think of it as a new experience. A little adventure of the senses." He half turned, drawing her attention to the print cabinet and the folios on the floor. "You appear to have been at it for some time."

"I am sorry. I will put them away now. I am sure it is very late. I really must retire."

"It would please me if you stayed. There are some matters I would like to talk about."

"Perhaps tomorrow."

"I would prefer tonight." He walked around the sofa. Every movement said he assumed she would stay because he demanded it. His invisible force of will all but pinned her in place.

He knelt on one knee and built a fire in the fireplace facing them. Then he lounged on the sofa, stretched out his legs, stripped off his cravat, and sipped his sherry.

His casual demeanor spoke of a man settling in for a chat with an old friend. She might have even been a sister. There wasn't the slightest thing threatening about his behavior.

His aura told a different story. It projected magnetism and danger. Her instincts thrummed. She became acutely conscious of how far, and how near, he sat. His masculinity loomed, dominating her.

He gestured to the volume still cradled on her lap. "You appeared captivated by the series."

She felt her face warming. "I do not think captivated is the correct word."

"Enthralled? Mesmerized? You were so taken with the images that you did not hear me enter and walk about the chamber."

"I was neither enthralled nor mesmerized. I was shocked."

"You were not at all shocked. I have seen courtesans view those engravings and none showed the equanimity that you displayed."

"Well, I have experience in such images. The Caraglio engravings, for example."

"There is no comparison. There are no allusions or illusions with these. No gods and goddesses doing a little groping. *'I Modi'* is a sexual manual, for all intents and purposes."

She sought a way to turn the conversation away from her lack of astonishment at the prints. "What shocked me was their presence in this house. I wonder why you own such things." She gestured to the paintings and statues, to the Roman relief and the ribald herm of Priapus.

"I own them to be defiant. I am making a point to

the ignorant social leaders who presume to dictate behavior by claiming a moral basis for historical developments."

"Goodness, how high-minded. I never guessed you bought erotic art out of a sense of civic duty."

"Smirk if you like. Ever since I was a boy, this country has increasingly become critical of pleasure. There is an idea being preached that the future of Britain depends upon the populace ignoring their human appetites. The greatest civilizations acknowledged the joy of carnal pleasure, and my collection proves it. Now, here we are, creating another great civilization, but treating passion as essentially sinful. It is dishonest, and it is unhealthy."

"So this collection is your broadside announcing that you refuse to conform and bow."

"Exactly."

"I had no idea your intentions were so noble. Stupid me, I thought that you collected them to provide inspiration and excitement."

He took another sip of his sherry. "Well, there is that, too. You are not alone in being aroused by them."

"I was not a— I was not looking at the images at all. I was examining the technique, for goodness' sake. I am an engraver."

"So, you did not even notice that the pages showed nude people coupling with athletic abandon and amazing invention?"

"I noticed, and fully intended to immediately put them aside. I only studied them when the technique caught my attention."

"Taste the sherry. You will like it. Why did the technique catch your attention?"

Her disadvantage had led to an indiscretion that he had spotted with an eagle's precision. To hide her vexation at her carelessness, she filled the long pause by giving the sherry a sip.

Its sultry scent clouded her head. Its thick, layered flavor caressed her mouth. Its warmth glowed down her body when she swallowed. The taste stunned her.

"It is one of the best," Lyndale said, watching her reaction to the amber liquid. "Mature, and only fit for discerning palettes. Having experienced it, you will never be satisfied by a lesser choice again."

His quiet tone carried no insinuation, but she knew he was not speaking of sherry. Her pulse sped while she quickly assessed their isolation.

He had not moved, yet he felt closer. It was his expression. A subtle alertness had entered his eyes.

Masculine power flowed with his attention, making her breathless and flustered. Her heart beat so loud she was sure that he could hear it in the silence that had descended on them.

A delicious silence, as if she waited tensely for some glorious, wonderful news.

Worried now, appalled by the flutters in her chest and the tingling in her breasts, she desperately tried to distract him. "I was attracted to the technique because it looked wrong to me. I do not think Raimondi's hand engraved those. I think they are later."

She expected the connoisseur to immediately shift all his fervor to a long interrogation, thus saving her from the thrilling fear he inflamed.

Lyndale reached for the volume. His fingers brushed her thigh as he lifted it from her lap. She felt the subtle touch despite her layers of garments. Her body responded with a shiver that roused her most womanly parts.

"They are good, trust me." He set the volume to his other side, out of sight and, the action connoted, out of discussion.

She made motions to rise. "I will retire now, with your leave."

"You do not have it. I would like your company for a while longer. As I said, we have things to discuss."

"I cannot imagine what."

His gaze drifted over her again. "That is a new dress. It is very pretty on you. It complements your handsome form."

He did not actually look at her breasts, but they began swelling anyway, straining the garments that complemented them all too well.

"Will the other dresses arrive soon?" he asked.

"They will be delivered during the next week."

"When the evening dress comes, I would like you to attend the theater with me."

She took another sip of sherry while she considered a good response. Its languid warmth slid through her.

"Surely you have other friends who could attend with you."

"I would like *you* to accompany me."

It was not clear if he was inviting her, or creating an obligation. "My dress may be by the finest modiste, but I will hardly be fashionable enough to be seen with an earl at the theater." Her hand instinctively sought the mound of hair on her crown.

Lyndale's gaze followed the gesture. "Is your hair criticized? I think it is lovely."

"Fishwives have more style. I am sure I must cut it, but am loath to do so."

He turned slightly, and his hand also sought the pile. "I would not want you to cut it, either." His fingers probed for a comb. "Let us see. Perhaps you could cut it some without doing much harm."

"I do not think . . ." She was too late. Huge locks and hanks of hair began falling. His fingertips poked and caressed her scalp as he searched out every pin. Those discreet touches did sinful things to her. Delectable tiny tremors spread from the contact. She wanted to close her eyes and purr.

The curls poured around her. Lyndale lifted one long strand. He assessed how the others covered her shoulders and ended on her lap.

"You can cut it, but only to here." He lowered the strand he held, with his fingers indicating the length. His hand came to rest just at her breast.

He was not quick to move his hand away. It rested there as if by accident, but she felt it as though he caressed her. Devastating sensations slid and swam, reminding her once again of the glorious pleasure a man could give.

She swallowed hard. The rich warmth of the sherry returned, now provoked by her body as much as the final sip she took. She gazed at her empty glass.

She knew what he was thinking. It was all there in his gaze, and in the power that he cast during the pulsing silence. Those prints had convinced him that she was indeed "fair game" as Lady Mardenford had said. His expression all but dared her to try and stop him.

"You will cut it to here, no more." He pressed again. "We will find a woman to dress it most fashionably, not because I care, but because you seem to. Then you will accompany me to the theater."

She found her voice. "If I do, it will be misunderstood."

"Nothing will be misunderstood."

"If I live in this house and you buy me gowns and maids and take me to the theater—"

"Nothing will be misunderstood, Bride."

He was closer now, she was very sure. His scent and attention engulfed her. His gaze, warm and masculine, reflected firm decision.

"Are you saying my situation would not be misunderstood because I, in fact, would be your mistress?"

His answer was in his eyes. And in his touch. His hand gently brushed her tresses back from her face, as if he gazed upon something he had the right to care for.

She forced her heart out of her throat. "I must go—"

"You will not run away, Bride. Not before I plead my case. If you had truly wanted to leave, you would have done so at once. If you did not want me, you would have never come to London and to this house, no matter what your situation."

She had no good response for that. How could she explain that excitement and loneliness had kept her here, even while common sense urged movement? How could she describe her desperate need to find those forgers and save her sisters and maybe a man she once held in love?

And how could she explain that she feared what Lyndale evoked in her, even if her body thrilled to it?

His hand continued its gentle touch, playing with her hair. It brushed her ear and neck as it moved. It created seductive, alluring tingles.

"You should not have pretended with me," he said. "You should not have played the shocked lass when you showed me the Caraglio addendum. If I had known you were fascinated, or even curious, it would have been different. I would not have been so careful with you."

"I was not . . . I *am not* fascinated. I told you, it is the technique of these prints that I study."

"Of course it is." He leaned across the small space separating them. His lips barely brushed her cheek. She had to grit her teeth to keep a tremble from shaking her whole body. "You were not at all curious about the content, however? Not even a little?"

His soft, subtle kisses moved down her neck,

then up to her ear. It felt so good. She wanted to drown in the sensuality lapping through her. She had to grope for the rational words to answer, but only half her mind cooperated.

"A little," she heard herself admitting. "However, they all looked too . . . ambitious to me. Novelty for its own sake."

His finger crooked under her chin. He turned her face toward him. "Do you fear I will expect too much? Having had my fill of novelty, I do not require it."

He kissed her lips. A lifetime of practice went into that kiss. Every press and nip, each invasive stroke, was intended to conquer indecision.

It produced exactly the effect he intended. A euphoria built in her with each artful lure.

She did not entirely miss the implications of what he had said, however. He had spoken as if they had an understanding.

She broke the kiss. "I have not agreed to your designs. A kiss is one thing, but you should not expect ambitions on my part for anything more."

"Certainly. Forgive me. I assumed too much." His words sounded sincere, but she saw something else in his expression. A vague amusement, as if he found her protests charming.

He slid his arm behind her and turned to embrace her more fully. "As I said, it is for me to plead my case." His other hand traced down her chin and neck. Its light touch lowered to the swell of her breast. "It is only fair for you to allow me to do so. I promise to neither take nor request any liberty not freely granted by you on your own."

Even through her garments, his caress aroused her. Her breasts craved more. Memories of the delicious pleasure in Scotland threatened to leave her helpless.

She tried to summon guilt because of Walter, to create a shield. Her heart would not heed her. *You are lying to yourself about him. He was not harmed while protecting you, because he never followed those thieves.*

"You are already taking a liberty not granted." Her breath only produced a whisper.

His hand smoothed over her breast more deliberately. "It was granted in Scotland. As I recall, you demanded it."

What was left of her mind knew she should stop him right now. It was too wonderful, however. Unearthly and perfect and sweet. The pleasure made her beautiful and happy, with no worries or cares. There was no past with its hurts and no future with its consequences and no doubts about loyalties.

As if he read her mind, his head dipped and he kissed her breast. "This is the best of what I offer, Bride. The sanctuary of pure sensation, where the world does not exist. No obligations. No time and no infirmity. This pleasure is nature's gift to us, so that the tedium and duties of life and time do not grind us down."

"But the world returns eventually, and extracts its price."

He kissed the other breast. His hand moved on her back. She startled when she felt her dress loosen. "The cost to you will be small. I have the fortune and the station to ensure that. I will take care of you while we are together, and see to your security afterward."

Afterward. She had lost sight of what was happening, but that word cleared her vision.

It did not diminish the pleasure. It did not return her strength of will. It merely dimmed the giddy confusion. Most of her essence embraced the intoxicating excitement and floated in a sensual wind, but one foot returned to the ground.

"I am not going to be your mistress, Lord Lyndale."

"Your stubborn independence restricts my attempts to deal with you fairly. Fine, if you insist on it, we will merely have an affair."

"We are not even going to have an affair."

"You were willing in Scotland." His hand still moved, urging her to be willing again.

"You were not. You should have taken advantage of me when you could. I was caught off guard then."

"And now your guard is awake at its post?"

"Awake and well armed. Lady Mardenford told me all about you. Any dalliance would be pure folly on my part, not that I had considered such a thing."

He began lowering her dress's bodice. As he did so, he kissed along the top edge of her bare shoulder. She gasped and half rose off the cushion.

She felt his smile against her skin. "I look forward to discovering the other places where you are so sensitive."

He plucked at the ribbon atop her chemise. Through lowered lids she watched his hand undress her, unable to conquer the breathless anticipation that stifled the last vestiges of her dissent.

He plucked at her stays' lacing enough to loosen the top. He slipped the chemise off her shoulders, peeling the fabric down. He pushed the stays until her breasts were bare.

He looked down and glossed his fingertips over her breasts. They swelled more at his touch, aching with fullness.

"I remember you just like this, Bride, with your beautiful breasts waiting and your face transformed and inviting. The image intrudes daily. As does the way you abandoned yourself to me. I hear your cries in my head. Your passion was astonishing."

"I was caught unawares, as I explained."

"You think that is why? I do not believe it. I think you feel this pleasure more than most people. Maybe as much as I do."

He caressed her breast more purposefully. Her whole body flexed as she tried to contain the exquisite titillation.

"I already know you enjoy this touch more than most women do. It is probably the same with your whole body." He bent and flicked his tongue over her nipple, and she had to stifle a moan. "Then again, maybe you are only like this when you are with me.

If so, it would be a crime not to discover how good it might be."

Her body was unnerved and her frustration building. She could think of little else except the pleasure he kept promising. The anticipation was excruciating.

"Do not claim special power over my passions. I have known great pleasure before, and with a man who was quicker to use his mouth for more than talking."

It was out before she knew it. As the last word left her lips, she knew it was a blunder.

He reacted with neither anger nor insult. Instead he looked into her eyes with a gaze that was dangerously confident and darkly amused.

"I will have to teach you how to enjoy the waiting. That is for another day, however. Considering what you have offered, I would be a fool to risk losing the special liberty by delaying."

Liberty?

Her confusion over the point was brief, as Lyndale began using his mouth for other than speech. Most effectively.

His kiss claimed her possessively. His arm restrained as much as embraced. His palm brushed her nipples again and again. The teasing arousal increased their sensitivity and produced a pleasure so luscious she kissed him back so he would know how much she liked it.

Drifting in that slow, almost delicate pleasure felt so blissful she did not want it to stop.

"You seem very contented," he said lowly.

She nodded, closing her eyes to savor the dreamy sensation. "I require nothing more."

"Ah, but I do. I require you so crazed with passion that you scream loud enough to shake the walls."

She smiled. "It is unlikely I will so thoroughly forget myself. Even in abandon, I do not go mad."

"You will for me." He gently squeezed a nipple, waking her out of the lulling delight with a jolt.

It startled more than hurt. It also changed the pleasure to a stimulation less careful, less polite, less . . . safe.

In the next few minutes, she lost all control over what was happening on the sofa. Lyndale commanded her passion and responses. It was different than it had been in Scotland. An engulfing sexual haze permitted little perception, but she sensed that he was not nearly as lost this time as she was.

His head lowered. His tongue laved at her nipples, then flicked tiny touches at flesh so sensitive that each new contact increased the shuddering tension between her hips.

His teeth nipped carefully. A savage pleasure shot through her. He sucked gently, then harder, and a feral wildness tinged her body's visceral response. When he used his mouth on one breast and his hand on the other, the combined intensity sent her to another world.

She heard sounds, her sounds, the notes of her cries and moans. They rose and fell on her breaths.

"It appears you were right," she whispered.

He covered one breast fully with his hand, in a gesture both protective and possessive. He kissed the other, then nuzzled up to the crook of her neck.

A deep, sensual sigh flowed into her ear. "I said screaming, Bride. So wild that you cannot control the sounds, nor even try to. So mad with pleasure that you never want me to stop."

She fought for a deep breath, to retrieve some composure. A new wickedness with his mouth defeated her. She struggled to keep the sanity to speak. "We will stop anyway. I have already said I want no affair."

"You are not acting like you want no affair."

No, she wasn't. She was permitting liberties she should not, and all but begging for more. She had no right to expect the slightest restraint from this man, and no reason to believe he would not use her as thoroughly as he pleased.

She clasped his wrist, stopping his caress. Her body hated her doing that. It rebelled so fiercely she almost gave in. Her primitive essence began offering a hundred reasons why making love would be a marvelous idea.

"You said no liberties unless granted," she whispered.

He twisted his wrist free, but not to touch her breast again. He looked into her eyes and caressed her face.

"You believed me, didn't you? You are still somewhat innocent if you trust any man, let alone me. I am flattered. I do not think a woman has trusted me since I was twelve."

A devilish gleam quickly replaced the surprise she glimpsed in his eyes. He caressed down her body, reminding her he was no angel.

"I will be good to my word. In return, let us strike a bargain. If you do scream, I am free to seduce you another time, properly and thoroughly. If you do not, I will retreat and be so proper in the future that the bishops will have hope of my redemption."

He slid away from her, and off the sofa.

"What are you doing?"

He knelt, facing her, almost out of her reach. She, however, was well within range of his caresses. He shed his frock coat, then his hands smoothed up her legs, under her petticoats.

"I am pleading my case on my knees. Any woman would be flattered."

The only touch was on her legs, but she felt terribly vulnerable. Her instincts warned he was luring her out of her depth. He stroked up and down while his gaze caressed the rest of her.

This game had gone too far. There were excellent reasons why she should not be doing this, no matter how wonderful it felt. Important reasons why she must remain completely separate from this man and give him no excuse to notice her, let alone pursue her.

Her mind, dazed by pleasure, refused to cooperate. She simply could not piece together the logic for refusing him. Doing so seemed unnecessary in light of the marvelous warmth and thrills his invisible hands created. Seeing him fully, lit by the fire and lamp, so handsome and male and attentive, did not help her feeble brain's vain efforts.

He caressed higher, his arms making her skirt rise and bunch. The heat and pulse of pleasure lowered in her body, urging her hips to rock to an inner rhythm of desire. His gaze captured hers so she could not hide what was happening to her.

He stroked higher. Boldly, shamelessly. His expression assumed the severity she remembered, and the confidence of a man who knew his effect. Her mouth went dry and her head swam in a growing delirium.

He pushed her skirt and petticoat high, then looked down at her stocking-clad legs. "They are as beautiful as I imagined." He glanced to the mound of fabric bunched on her lap. "This will never do."

Before she comprehended what he meant, he had her petticoats unfastened. Effortlessly, he lifted her bottom and swept them away.

Her dress sagged down her hips. He helped it along. "It will only get crushed."

Further objections became pointless, since he had the dress off in a blink.

He looked at her differently then. It frightened her a little. She glanced down at the path his gaze had moved. She knew half her clothes were off, but it still startled her to see the scandalous image she presented, covered by nothing but slack stays, stockings, and the short, thin skirt of her chemise.

He leaned forward and kissed down every shocking inch. Along her naked shoulders to the drooping tab of her chemise. Across her chest to the top swells of her bare breasts. Down each breast, where he paused to tease until she arched and cried.

Then lower, over her stays and stomach and slowly along her left hip until his lips found her naked thigh.

Each kiss initiated a river of fire flowing downward.

She watched, barely breathing, unable to keep her body still. The warmth of his breath on her thighs, so close to . . . she struggled to not embarrass herself.

He knelt tall and caressed her thighs slowly. "You are beautiful. I wish you could see how extraordinary you are with your hair flowing over your snowy skin and your breasts so perfect and high. Giving you pleasure is an honor."

She believed him. She would have accepted anything he said. His words made her as proud as a queen.

A queen that he commanded.

His hands gently pushed her knees apart. The new vulnerability aroused her more. His caresses moved to her inner thighs, his fingers venturing higher and higher until she wanted to cry with impatience.

His hands slid around her hips, cupped her bottom, and slid her forward. She found her back and head flat against the cushion. She watched with shock as he slid off her drawers, then lifted her legs to rest on his shoulders.

He was not looking at her face now. She angled her head up enough to confirm just how scandalously exposed she was to him.

She began to force herself up to object. A deliberate, gentle stroke on the flesh he saw instantly defeated her. She sank back with a groan as the intense pleasure of that touch tremored through her body.

She closed her eyes as wave after rising wave of pleasure tensed through her. That delicate spot just got more and more sensitive. Her mind closed to everything except the incredible feelings and the savage desire. He made her thrash and whimper and cry, but she was beyond restraint.

"You make it hard for me to keep my word, Bride."

She opened her eyes to find him looking at her face. She saw how their positions would make it very easy for him to violate his promise.

She wanted him to. Right now, she desperately hungered for whatever would end this torture. She had felt that way in Scotland and this was much worse. He had not been looking at her in Scotland, or touching her so precisely, making the sensations direct and focused and intense.

He bent and kissed her thigh. She gasped at the way it made her vulva pulse. He kissed the other thigh, farther up. She rose up on her elbows and stared as he kissed again, this time the tawny curls.

"What are you doing?"

"Making free with the liberties you granted me."

His hands stroked both her legs and eased them back until her knees crooked over his shoulders. That raised her hips. She lost her balance and fell back on the cushion.

"You bid me use my mouth for more than speech. Remember?" He kissed the curls again while he touched the secret flesh. The kiss lowered to where he touched and an unearthly pleasure shrieked through her.

"Do you want me to stop?"

Of course she did. This was wicked and shocking and unlike anything she had done or heard of. She never intended—

A new pleasure sent her head spinning. She almost swooned. A primitive ferocity colored her arousal.

She did not stop him. She could not. The pleasure just kept getting better and stronger and more maddening.

She lost control. Crying, insane with want, she moved her hips, urging more. She stretched her fingers through his hair to hold him to her. He kept making it wonderfully worse until she could not bear it.

She felt him pressing her thighs farther apart, opening her more. Warmth saturated one spot, then concentrated and intensified so much it hurt. It was a good hurt, but still she cried out. She heard his voice, quiet and ragged, telling her not to fight it.

She released her last hold on herself. A powerful sensation tensed higher and higher until she was screaming. Then it snapped and shattered and saturated her body with a vibrant sensation of bliss.

She was completely helpless afterward. Surprised and frightened and boneless. He moved her legs and sat her up and held her while the aftermath of her climax tremored through her. She buried her face in his waistcoat and did not speak. She barely moved.

He was not in much better condition himself, so he embraced her in the firelight while she found herself again.

With any other woman, they would pass this time holding subtle negotiations, while he regained his prowess. Then again, with any other woman, they would be up in bed.

With another woman, his body would have anticipated her doing for him after he did for her, as was the normal course of such things, and it would not have betrayed his control so thoroughly when her screams filled the night.

Just as well it had. It went without saying that Bride Cameron had never done that to a man, just as no man had done this to her.

Well, life was not predictable anymore. There was no reason why tonight should be any different.

He gazed down at her snowy shoulders, enjoying the way she was tucked against him. With any other woman, he would be annoyed with these games. Instead, he experienced a peculiar contentment and a solid resolve.

He wanted her. Already his body was reviving.

"That was not in the engravings," she muttered.

"Not in those by Raimondi or Caraglio. There are more recent depictions, however, in case you think I invented it."

She quietly laughed. The sound was lovely and welcome. He had some concern that she would accuse him of taking advantage of her. Which he had, if he wanted to be honest about it.

"If you know it is not included, you must have looked at them all," he pointed out.

"Truly, it was the technique that enthralled me."

"I trust mine enthralled you more."

She laughed again, and lifted her head. She did not look directly at him. He could tell she was embarrassed. That touched him.

His gaze and hand came to rest on the volume of *"I Modi"* that still lay on the sofa. "Why did you think they were forgeries?" He asked it to put her at ease by speaking of commonplace things.

She shrugged. "I am probably wrong. Your expertise far surpasses mine. Where did you get them?"

"At an auction. As for expertise, yours is considerable. Your father's legacy includes several fine Raimondis, so you know his technique. What about these seemed wrong to you?"

The discussion did not put her at ease in the least. She appeared quite uncomfortable. "Some minor details. Stippling and such. I am sure I am wrong. I only feigned confidence to convince you I was not viewing them for . . . well, for other reasons." She stretched to reach her dress. "I should go."

He helped her dress. When she was set right, except for her hair, he took her waist in his hands so she could not bolt the way she looked apt to.

"You should not be embarrassed, Bride." He lifted her chin with his hand and kissed her. "Do not expect me to pretend this did not happen. Do not expect me to believe you did not enjoy it."

Her lids lowered. "No, too much to hope for that."

"And you did scream, so I am allowed to try for more. I want you, Bride, and I will have you."

She stepped away, out of his reach. "As with any siege, I need only wait you out. You will probably pack up your arms and retreat in less than a month. I am told your interest in a woman rarely lasts even that long."

He grabbed her arm and swung her back, into his arms. He kissed her hard before releasing her again.

"Perhaps so, Bride. But what a month we will have."

CHAPTER
SIXTEEN

~~

She found her way through the dark house to her chambers, her senses dazed. Beneath her glorious euphoria, enough sense returned for her to know one thing very clearly.

She should have resisted Lyndale's seduction.

Instead of taking the opportunity to quash his interest in her, she had encouraged him. Now he would be paying attention again. Maybe he would interfere. Possibly he would realize what they were doing here in London, and learn of their crimes.

No lamp shone in her bedroom and she had left hers in the drawing room. All the same, she knew she was not alone as soon as she crossed the threshold. Someone sat in a chair near the window.

"It is I," Anne said. "Where were you?"

Bride was grateful it was not Joan or Mary. Even in the dark, either of them would sense how unsettled she was. Her other sisters would be suspicious about late-night ambling through this house.

"I went to the library to find something to read." She trusted Anne would not notice whether she had carried a volume back. "Why are you here, Anne? You sound troubled."

Her sister was barely visible, but she could tell when Anne rose. A drapery slid back, so they had a little light.

"Joan told me about your visit to the printer," she said. "I think that we should take advantage of his offer to use the press."

"I expect we will in time."

"I do not mean for reproductive plates, Bride." Anne moved past the window, then turned and strolled again, pacing. "We have the note plates, and you brought the paper that is left from Father's stock."

"It is too dangerous."

"It is our duty. Are we to live here in luxury while others suffer? Are we to abandon them? I felt guilty when I donned this new dress today."

Bride walked over and embraced her sister. "We are too far away to make use of the notes now. Who will pass them, and distribute the money?"

She did not say that both she and Joan had immediately realized that printing notes was possible. She did not want to encourage Anne's impracticality.

"We could find a way if we wanted to," Anne murmured. "You trusted Walter. We could find someone else to trust."

"It would be reckless to—"

"You said we would come to London to find the forgers, to protect ourselves. I think that we may not find them, or ever protect ourselves," Anne said. "I think we will be caught. If so, we should do what we can while we are able, before the ax falls."

Bride smoothed her hand over Anne's head, to soothe her. Anne might be dreamy and impractical, but she was pure of heart. Sometimes she saw the world most clearly, as she did now.

They probably would not find the forgers before the government did. They probably would be caught and sent to New South Wales along with the thieves who had stolen those plates.

Anne had put into words the reason why distance had to be reclaimed from Lord Lyndale. An affair with him could put all of them in jeopardy. It would also be wrong to betray him with such deceit, even if he was only a paramour.

She embraced Anne again, but the comfort was for herself. A deep sadness throbbed in her heart. It would be hard to never feel carefree and young again, as she had tonight. Nostalgia already mourned the warmth and friendship this man offered her, if only for a short while.

It would be very difficult to regard him as a stranger, because he no longer was and, she realized, she was very fond of him. The truth was that she wanted to be seduced by him.

"We will talk with the others, Anne. We will all decide together. However, if we are going to do this,

we must not do it in this house and betray Lord Lyndale's generosity. We must find a way to live elsewhere."

The next morning Bride met with her sisters and
Jilly in Joan's chamber. Everyone was dressed in
new ensembles from head to toe.

Anne's concerns pricked everyone's conscience.
It was as if her blunt assessment of the future wiped
away a dreamy haze. Even Mary picked at her new
skirt while her face fell with an expression of chagrin.

"I suppose we should do what we can while we
can," Joan said.

"We have to, in Father's memory," Anne said. "It
is also the right thing to do, no matter what the laws
say otherwise."

"Aye," Jilly weighed in.

"Then I must convince Lyndale to loan us the
money so that we can establish a separate household," Bride said. "We will make and sell some
plates to Mr. Downey, then hire a press for printing
the notes. We will find a way to get the money back
home."

No one disagreed.

"He be here today, up and around," Jilly reported.
"Not sleeping until three as most times. They said
down below that his lordship called for coffee in the
main drawing room an hour ago."

"I suppose he was not out on the town all night after all," Mary said.

Anne blinked. She frowned, as if that fact should matter, but she could not remember why.

"Perhaps you should address the matter with him right now," Joan said to Bride.

Bride had no enthusiasm for a conversation with Lyndale this morning. Her sleepless night had not been spent on Anne's rebuke, but on warm, wistful memories of a man driving her to delirium.

Her sisters looked at her, waiting.

Trying to appear the tower of strength that they expected her to be, she rose and left the chamber.

CHAPTER
SEVENTEEN

◦∾◦

Lyndale was in the main drawing room, just as Jilly had said. He stood at an eastern window in front of a pedestal table. The drapes had been pulled back and bright light flooded his face.

He gazed out the window, but his true vision was turned inward. He appeared more thoughtful than Bride had ever seen him. She realized how much his good humor transformed his face. Contemplation revealed its hard angles now, and hinted at whole worlds inside him that she did not know.

She silently approached over the carpet, wondering how to broach the subject of the day. She also worried about what she would see in those eyes when she beckoned his attention.

Triumph? She could counter that with pride.

Lewd expectation? She would dismiss that with rejection.

Indifference?

She admitted that was the only reaction she truly feared, the only one that would humiliate her.

His profile captivated her. So still he stood, so contained. What thoughts had distracted him?

His head turned as she neared. In the instant when he became aware of her, Bride saw two things. The first was the expression that entered his eyes.

Not triumphant and not lewd. Hardly indifferent. He looked at her with a warmth and welcome that touched her heart. It sent her mind into the clouds. Suddenly she was not walking on carpet, but floating in a mist.

She saw something else, just barely. It was a mere blur in the corner of her vision.

She saw his hand closing the boards of a folio atop the table.

The image of what she glimpsed during that gesture flashed in her mind again and again as she moved toward him. Even as her brain muddled under Lyndale's attention, even as she drifted to the arm he extended to her, she kept seeing that hand move and that board lower.

There had been two small papers atop the others in that folio. They had looked like engraved prints.

Actually, they had looked like two banknotes.

Alarm righted her senses in time. She did not allow him to enfold her in the embrace his arm implied. Instead she extended her own arm. He took her hand and kissed it.

"I am grateful that you chanced upon me," he said.

"I did not chance upon you. I sought you out."

"Then I am doubly grateful."

"You are up and about early this day. I am told you rarely rise until afternoon."

"I have been hoping to see you this morning. I have something to say to you."

She had something to say to him, too. Something important and vital that could not be delayed. If she had just seen what she thought, however, she was not sure it should be said now.

She glanced to the folio. Had there actually been two banknotes? Brought here, to the raking light? Had he been studying them? Doing a comparison? If he knew there were forgeries, or even suspected, she wanted to know.

She gestured to the thin leather-clad folio. "New acquisitions?"

He dismissed them with a glance. "Hardly. Those are my government papers for a meeting later today."

A different daze engulfed her. A light-headed, dizzying panic.

He *knew*.

He was taking those notes to someone in the government. He had spotted one of the bad notes.

Or maybe he had been sent some to assess. A connoisseur of engravings would be useful in such an investigation. His practiced eye had been the reason she wanted to maintain his distance from their lives.

Maybe he was even actively looking for the forgers.

"You appear unsettled, Bride. I told you last night that you should not feel embarrassed with me."

"Unsettled" did not begin to describe the sickening confusion raging in her.

If she made good on the plan to quit this house, she would not be able to determine what Lyndale knew and what he did about it.

If she stayed, he might one day discover that the women he harbored in his own home were the source of the forged plates.

"I am not embarrassed," she said. That was a lie. Memories of last night made her face warm. Considering this new catastrophe, however, her loss of control on that sofa seemed quite insignificant now.

"I am glad, because I want to ask your help in something."

He turned to the table. She watched, horrified, as his hand lit on the folio. He slid it aside, however, to reveal the volume containing *"I Modi."*

"I have been examining it," he said. "I think you may be correct. I believe it may not be original to the sixteenth century. I think a forger may have produced the plates quite recently."

She had never swooned in her life, but she almost did now. It required real effort to keep the world steady.

"You give me too much credit," she said. "You should not question your own judgment so quickly."

"The excitement of the hunt may have obscured my better judgment. When these became available last year, others wanted them. Winning them became the goal. I think now that all of us were blinded by the prize and did not question all that we should."

Last year. The thieves had used the art plates soon after the theft, then.

"I need to know for certain now. You know how collectors are."

"There may be no way to know for certain." She hoped not.

"Whoever forged these knew Vasari's description. He knew of the French copies of fragments of the series that can be found. Those are woodcuts, not engravings, but the compositions were preserved in them. And he knew Raimondi's technique. He is not a common engraver, but knowledgeable, skilled, and possibly educated. We will not be without clues in tracking him down."

"We?"

"You will help me, won't you? After all, it was your eye that spotted the flaws."

"I could be wrong. You could be wrong."

A bit of vexation entered her head and voice. If Lyndale had not come upon her last night and flustered her with those touches, she never would have blurted suspicions regarding the series in order to distract him.

Doing so had not even made him pause on that sofa, so it was most unfair of him to decide *now* to develop suspicions himself.

"They may be good. In fact, I am more than half convinced they are," she added.

"And I am now almost half convinced they are

not. I must find out one way or the other. As I see it, our first questions must be put to the auction house that sold them, don't you agree?"

She looked at the little volume. She looked at Lyndale. She glanced at the leather folio.

Maybe she had not seen banknotes atop those papers. Even if she had, he may have put them there for some benign reason, such as making a payment somewhere today. It appeared the only forgeries that concerned him were the erotic ones.

Unfortunately, the same forgers probably had all of her father's stolen plates, and an investigation of *"I Modi"* could lead to more dangerous information.

She had come to this drawing room to be done with this man. She could not afford to retreat from him completely now. She either needed to convince him his *"I Modi"* were genuine, or learn what he discovered as he tracked down the people who had printed them.

"Will you help?" he asked. "Together I am sure we can get to the bottom of it."

She wondered how she was going to explain to her sisters that she had changed her mind yet again, and that they dare not use the banknote plates that they still possessed.

"Are they leaving?"

Michael asked the question as he gave Ewan's boot a final buff.

Ewan set his one foot down and raised the other boot to the stool for attention. "It appears not."

"Makes one wonder what they were talking about in that bedroom, then, doesn't it? The door was locked and there was quite a Gaelic buzz."

Ewan suspected the sisters had indeed been discussing their departure. When he saw Bride approaching him in the drawing room, she had looked ready to express regrets and farewells. No doubt, after reflecting on last night, she had decided she needed to leave.

He had anticipated that. He had been ready. She would not leave now. The chance to uncover the mystery of his *"I Modi"* would be too compelling. In this they were alike, and he had known she could not resist.

He saw her again, crossing that large room. So formidable at first. But in an instant she had softened, beautifully. The woman who had extended her hand to his had been vulnerable and shy.

And the man who watched her approach had been so joyed to see her, so hungry for her presence, it had left him dumb.

He laughed at himself while he checked his pocket watch. He had told her she must learn the pleasure of waiting. He had forgotten about that himself, it appeared.

He turned his thoughts to that little volume of *"I Modi,"* now tucked back in its cabinet. Of course they were good. He did not really doubt that. But as he pretended to pursue information on them, he could learn what he needed for the real investigation.

And he would have Bride by his side. She had a sharp mind and sharper eyes, and she might notice things he missed.

She would also be conveniently available for other pursuits and other investigations.

He did not know what he would learn about forgers, but he intended to learn everything about Bride Cameron, every inch of her body and every nuance of her pleasure, in the days ahead.

"You have been receiving a lot of acceptances regarding the party," Michael said, interrupting his thoughts.

"Party?"

"Your 'grand night of decadence,' you called it. Remember? You told me two weeks ago to make the arrangements. You even gave me the guest list. As you put it, you will pick up the reins of your old life and announce to society that the title has not reformed you, et cetera, et cetera."

Ewan had completely forgotten his plans for that party. The invasion of the Cameron sisters, and his investigation, had distracted him from it.

"You made sure you indicated that the classical theme would be Roman, I hope. I do not want the men to think it will be Greek. I could not bear the disappointment a few men would have if that were misunderstood, nor the concerns it would raise for most others."

"From what you have told me about those Greeks,

I would not remain in your employ if your parties went that far. Where I come from—"

"Yes, yes. Have no fear; before you die, this whole country will be as strict as where you came from. A glorious era of pleasure is ending even as we speak, so we must make hell while we can."

Michael picked up the leather folio. "Will you be wanting this?"

Ewan tucked it under his arm. He had requested a meeting with Althorp today, and the contents of this folio would be its subject.

Last night after Bride left him, he had studied that stack of banknotes he had carried home from the gaming hall. He had found a forgery among them.

Not a fifty pound note, as it happened. This bad note had been for a hundred pounds.

Althorp would probably suffer an apoplexy when he learned of it.

Lyndale wanted to visit the auction house in the afternoon, and Bride could not think of a way to delay it. She prepared for an outing in his company.

She chose her most severe dress from her new wardrobe. The rose hue, while fashionable, did not especially flatter her.

She made no attempt to improve her hair, and covered it with her simplest new hat. She covered herself in a dark rose mantle that closed up to her chin and obscured her bodice and gigot sleeves in its voluminous drape.

Then she arranged to take the best armor she could find. She invited Anne to join her on the excursion.

Anne's displeasure with the delay in using their special plates had turned her dreamy and distracted in the worst way. She refused to don one of her new dresses, because she said they were all selling their souls.

"I still think we should go forward," Anne repeated yet again as they descended the stairs to meet Lyndale. "Even if the earl is looking for banknote forgers, even if the government is searching, I still say that right is right and duty is duty."

"Anne, it is one thing to dare fate, and another to hand our executioners a rope."

"I do not see how discovering what he knows will prevent their finding their own rope. If we are doomed, we are doomed. Let us make good use of the time we have left."

Anne's calm acceptance of inevitable capture unnerved Bride. "You may want to be a martyr, but I do not. If I know someone is preparing the rope, I intend to find a way to cut it."

She had no idea how to do that, but she had to try. In the least, she wanted to know when capture was imminent. Then maybe she could make arrangements to save her sisters by directing all the blame to herself.

The hard part would be discouraging Lyndale's

interest in her while she remained close enough to learn what he was doing.

Lyndale did not treat Anne's presence as at all displeasing. He handed them both into his coach and sat across from them.

"It appears that I will be hosting a party the night after next," he said abruptly. "I had forgotten about it."

"Will this be a big reception to welcome good society to your new home?" Bride asked.

"This party has a limited guest list. Very selective. It consists of my oldest friends, not new ones."

"Lord Lyndale, are you informing us of this party merely to point out we are not invited?"

"It is a point that requires some pointing," he said, pointedly. "Furthermore, you and your sisters are to retire immediately after the evening meal and not leave the upper floors until morning."

It was going to be one of *those* parties. Bride could not resist taunting him. "Is there a particular reason for these instructions?"

Lyndale turned his attention to removing his gloves and setting them aside. "The only reason is my preference, and the fact that some of these guests are not suitable friends for young ladies. I asked if Lady Mardenford would accept you all as her guests for the night, to avoid any awkwardness, but she is leaving town today for a fortnight. Therefore, these other arrangements will have to suffice." He speared her with a commanding look. "None of you are to set foot on the first floor."

"I understand."

"Good. See that your sisters do, too."

Satisfied that his command had been heard, his pose and face relaxed. "Allow me to explain my plans today. The prints were bought at Bonham's a little over a year ago. The seller was not named, unfortunately. Today we will visit the viewing currently being held, and I will cajole the proprietors to divulge the seller's identity."

"Perhaps the seller used a false name," Bride said.

"Bonham's has a reputation to ensure. For such a rarity, they required some assurance of authenticity. They would not take the word of a complete stranger who had no home or references."

Anne had retreated into her head almost upon entering the coach. She did not show any reaction to Lyndale's orders about the party, nor now to his explanation about the auction house.

He noticed, and nodded in her direction. "Does she even hear others when she gets like that?"

Anne's complete lack of acknowledgment proved she did not.

"My mother was the same way. It is quite normal." Bride wanted to thwart any concerns for Anne's mental stability, even if she had wondered about that on occasion herself.

"I am not implying otherwise. I have met men who are so absorbed in their thoughts that the world did not exist for them. I was merely curious if she is as lost to us as it appears." He angled his head to eye her more directly. "She looks very young when in that trance. Younger than Mary, who must be ten years her junior."

Bride gazed at her sister. Anne did look young for her twenty-six years. She never seemed to age. It was as if her dreams did not count against time. Right now, despite the light streaming onto her face through the window, she appeared girlish and delicate and a little unreal.

A warmth on Bride's hand demanded her attention. She looked down to see Lyndale leaning forward, holding her hand in his palm.

"My sister may be lost to us, but I am not sure we are lost to her," she said quietly.

"I am convinced we are." His thumb rubbed her hand through her glove. "I thought about you all night. I could not sleep at all. My mind barely attended to my meeting today with Lord Althorp."

His expression told her just what thoughts had preoccupied him. His piercing gaze insisted she remember, too.

She did, vividly. Not the acts, but the sensations. And the intimacy. There could be no true distance after what they had shared. This man was starkly real to her, as if their passion had made her more susceptible to his vitality.

His gaze fell to her glove. He turned her hand and carefully unfastened the row of buttons near her wrist. Each tiny release, each inch of freedom, drew another long breath out of her. He might have been unfastening her dress or stays.

He separated the kidskin and gazed at the flesh

the gap revealed. He bent and kissed her pulse, then raised his head until his face was inches from hers.

"Is there another man, Bride?"

The unexpected question astonished her.

"A man whom you love, I mean."

He so flustered her she could not think. She just looked at him helplessly.

He dipped and kissed her naked wrist again. "Is there a man to whom you feel obligated, because of what you shared with him?"

He spoke so quietly, so gently, as if he had guessed all about Walter and wanted to help.

She told herself it was just a seducer's ploy, but her chin quivered from the emotions racing through her. She felt horribly exposed, and all her doubts and worries about Walter swelled her heart.

She swallowed the tightness forming in her throat. She had not once cried about Walter. She could not imagine why she had the urge to do so now.

"There are some . . . obligations," she whispered.

He pressed warm lips to her skin again. "But not love?"

She had never answered that question. She had never asked it. Now she found herself looking into a corner of her heart where she had avoided searching for a long time.

It both relieved and saddened her to discover it was empty.

"No. Not love. Not any longer." She said it to herself, but heard the admission whisper in the air between them.

"I am glad."

He lowered his hand to her knee, so it rested there as he cradled her wrist. He kissed her wrist again, his head low to her lap, so close to where it had been the night before.

She watched him make love to that small line of flesh. She fought the impulse to stretch her fingers through his hair again and hold him to her just as she had shockingly done mere hours ago.

He was fueling a fire that had been kindling all night. She had not slept, either. She had drifted, half conscious, in a state of sensual warmth and arousal.

That had happened before in her life, but this had been different. Her physical reactions all night had been vivid and real, and the man in her half dream had been Lyndale, not Walter or a faceless force.

He straightened, but continued caressing her wrist with his thumb, stroking so effectively that her whole body trembled. He looked into her eyes and she could tell he knew how easily he aroused her. His expression silently repeated his declaration of last night. *I want you and I will have you.*

She glanced nervously at her sister. Anne's head was turned to the window now. She remained sightless, however. Oblivious.

Useless.

"I will have to bring Joan or Mary with me next time."

"You will bring no one with you next time. I forbid it. If I was duped on these prints, I do not want the world to know."

He kissed her pulse again, with stunning effect. Then he began closing the glove's buttons.

Art crammed the viewing room at Bonham's. Ewan explained how the lots were organized, and the duty of buyers to examine everything closely.

"Bonham's takes care not to handle forgeries or questionable goods, but the ultimate responsibility to assess authenticity still rests with those who bid."

Anne had returned to reality, and she gawked at the paintings covering the walls and the tables loaded with folios and books and objets d'art. "One could spend days here."

"I often do," Ewan said. "It is an ever-changing feast."

Some paintings caught Anne's eye and she wandered off. Bride made to follow her, but Ewan stopped her.

"Let her go. We have business to conduct."

He led Bride through the room and beckoned one of the auctioneers who kept watch.

The man knew him, as did everyone else at this establishment. Not merely because he frequently bid and bought. Bonham's hoped to handle the sale of any prints inherited from Uncle Duncan that Ewan did not want to keep. One of the auctioneers had been among the first to call when news of Uncle Duncan's death spread.

"Lord Lyndale, we are honored. How can we serve you?"

"I would like to speak with Mr. Dodd. It pertains to the series I purchased last year."

The man's face fell just enough to show Ewan's tone had communicated trouble. A glance at Bride indicated that the ambiguous reference to a series was appreciated. This particular series had been offered at a private auction, and had never been on view in this room.

"If you would follow me, I am sure that Mr. Dodd can be found."

Ewan trailed behind the man, with Bride in tow. Their escort found the lady's continued attendance disconcerting. Ewan ignored the contorted facial language requesting that her presence be shed.

Mr. Dodd was found at once. In an elegant office decorated with expensive art waiting its day on the block, Ewan explained his concerns.

"I find myself questioning the series, now that the excitement of the hunt has passed. It is no reflection on your establishment, of course. I merely want to pursue a few questions regarding provenance."

Mr. Dodd had been guarded when the topic was raised, but now he smiled. "The provenance was excellent, I assure you."

"But not announced, nor was the name of the seller."

"Anonymity was requested, in light of the content. I am sure you understand."

"Of course. However, I would now like to know where the series resided all these centuries."

Mr. Dodd shifted in his chair. "I am unable to satisfy you. Our patrons expect discretion from us. When your own collection is eventually sold, I am sure your heirs will want to know we will respect their desire for privacy."

"Sir, I have important questions regarding the series. I am sure you do not want my suspicions to be known at large. If you cannot help me ascertain the truth, I do not think my collection, or any of my uncle's, or any of my friends', will ever be sold here."

"Lord Lyndale, this is most irregular. You have me at a disadvantage."

That was where Ewan wanted him.

He let Mr. Dodd contemplate the two unappetizing plates thrust in front of him. When the mood had gotten very heavy, Ewan offered a little sweet to help his own meal get swallowed. "I do not require the exact name. Merely some reassurance."

Mr. Dodd brightened a bit. He bobbed his head while he thought that over. "I can tell you that the series came from the estate of a gentleman deceased two years at the time. A man of high standing, much like yourself. His family made use of an intermediary, in presenting the series to us."

"Are you sure that the intermediary actually represented that family? Could their name have been used as a lie?"

Mr. Dodd's face fell. A pink curtain began descending on it. "We knew that man who approached us. We were satisfied all was in order."

"I am sure you were. Should you see your way

clear to enlighten me as to this intermediary's name, I would appreciate it."

Ewan rose and offered Bride his hand. He intended by the gesture to let Mr. Dodd know that any communication of that name need not be done with witnesses. It could be sent discreetly.

Bride appeared very subdued as they left the office and returned to the viewing room.

"I had no idea it would be so easy to sell forgeries," she said. "Not that your *'I Modi'* are forgeries. The more I contemplate that, the more convinced I am that they are what they seem."

An hour ago, Ewan would have agreed. The meeting with Mr. Dodd, however, pricked his confidence. If he had interpreted Dodd's reaction correctly, there had been no proof the series actually came from the family in question.

Anne spied them from across the room and hurried over, looking more lively than Ewan had ever seen her.

"Oh, Bride, this is such fun. You will never guess what I found. One of Father's engravings. Over on that table, in a big lot. It is his river god. You remember, the one after the statue in Rome. Imagine my delight in—"

"That is not so surprising," Bride said, cutting off her sister's excited flow. "There must be hundreds of prints here."

She raised one hand to her head and grimaced. "This has been fascinating and most instructive, Lord Lyndale. Thank you for inviting me. I am sud-

denly a bit dizzy, however. Would you mind too
much if we returned to Belgrave Square?"

She did not appear dizzy to him. She looked like
an amateur actress pretending to feel faint.

She walked beside her sister, and managed to
pull some distance in front of him. As he trailed behind, he saw Bride's arm circle Anne's shoulders.
Her head dipped low so she could say something in
Anne's ear.

As soon as the coach left Bride and Anne at Belgrave Square, Ewan ordered it back from whence it
had come.

He strode into Bonham's and aimed for the tables
holding the large portfolios of prints. They were
mixed lots for the most part, and common reproductive work that would be sold to the trade.

Positioning himself at the tables, he methodically
worked his way through the sheets. He kept his eyes
peeled on the borders at the bottom, looking for the
name Angus Cameron.

He flipped the bottom of the sheets with his
thumb, and turned them five at a time. Other names
blurred by, not even registering in his head.

Bride had become distressed at Anne's mention
of their father's work. She had moved to quash her
sister and divert his attention. He found that curious,
and now he wanted to see that print.

An hour later he frowned down at the portfolios.
There had been no border with Cameron's name.

He began again, this time sheet by sheet, searching for an engraving of the river god.

Suddenly it was in front of him. He did not doubt Cameron had engraved it. The technique was very close to Bride's.

He read the border. The words had not penetrated his concentration while he flipped quickly, but they should have. He should not have missed it the first time through.

This plate had been printed and sold by an establishment in Edinburgh. It had been engraved by Thomas Waterfield.

That was the name Bride and her sisters used on their plates.

Only this one bore the date 1804, before Bride had even been born.

He gazed at that river god while various ideas rearranged themselves in his mind. They pointed to conclusions that could not be avoided.

The figure of the reclining god was engraved using the patterned, tiny lozenges typical in reproductive prints. The setting, however, displayed freer burin work. The buildings and sky, the foliage and stones, employed a technique similar to that found in original Renaissance works.

Those details captivated Ewan's eyes. The technique appeared familiar. He had studied similar flicks and lines recently. Very recently.

It looked like the same technique used in the subsidiary portions of his *"I Modi."*

He noted the lot's number. He would buy it when

the auction was held, so he could do a comparison of this river god and his Raimondi series. If that examination proved his suspicions correct, it would explain how and why Uncle Duncan had ruined Bride's father.

It had not been political reasons. Uncle Duncan probably neither knew nor cared about Cameron's extreme political views.

But if Duncan had discovered that Angus Cameron was forging Renaissance engravings, if Cameron had tried to sell Duncan bad prints, Duncan would have demanded that Cameron either give up his craft and his trade, or be exposed as a criminal.

CHAPTER EIGHTEEN

The Earl of Lyndale is hosting a party tonight. As might be expected, there has been considerable discretion regarding the guest list, although it is said his house guests will not attend.

Bride read the few lines in a scandal sheet, then handed it back to Joan.

"It certainly makes clear we are not among his guests," Joan said, sounding a little hurt. "His insistence we not even be seen tonight means you were right, Bride. We really are not welcome here. He wants everyone to know we are not fit for his friends."

They certainly were not, but not in the way Joan thought.

Bride wondered about the last words in the scandal sheet, and who had ensured they would be included. Lyndale himself, probably. It was considerate of him to hand out that tidbit to protect her sisters.

That party was taking place right now in a chamber almost directly below hers. The public rooms had been locked for two days while the household prepared. She wondered what creative touches Lyndale had given this scandalous night.

Her chamber did not face the street, but she had heard the carriages arrive. She had seen the servants in the back garden, heading for the mews. Strains of music and an almost inaudible buzz filtered to the upper floors from the activity below.

An unwarranted vexation kept pricking. It appeared the Earl of Lyndale wanted Bride Cameron, but until he succeeded in seducing her, he would occupy himself otherwise.

She welcomed the evidence of just who and what this man was. She was grateful that every time she softened toward him, he managed to remind her that she should not.

She turned her attention to a list on her writing table that she had just finished composing.

"The last two days have been very full, Joan. We are making some progress. Lyndale escorted me to several engravers and two more print shops yesterday. I have learned much about the industry here in London that will be useful when we have our own studio. Lyndale has collected a little list of engravers who, in the opinions of the experts we consulted, could forge old master prints very well."

She could not say more. Her sisters did not know about *"I Modi."* She had only warned them that Lyndale had bought prints printed off some of their father's missing forged plates.

"That does not help our investigation much," Joan said. "We already know Father made all the plates being sought by us and Lyndale."

That was true. Fortunately, while Bride and Lyndale rode about the city, Joan had been out and about, too, visiting shops that sold paper.

"What have you learned?"

Joan handed over a small piece of paper. "These are some men who manufacture paper the old-fashioned way, by hand and not machine, such as was used for the banknotes years ago. The last two are quite old and experienced and have suffered changes in fortune recently."

Bride studied the list. She would have to shed Lyndale for at least one day so she could speak with these men, and ascertain their characters.

She turned the sheet on her desk, and looked at its blank side. The vacancy depressed her. She had hoped to add a fact or two to this side, as well. Lyndale's company had meant she could not ask the necessary questions, however.

"Did you learn anything about Walter?" She did not look at Joan while she asked the question. She did not want to see her sister's reaction. Joan's moist-eyed sympathy would be too much to bear.

That would be true especially now, after Lyndale had forced her to look into her heart and see what remained of that old love. Nostalgia and sadness, to be sure. Worry and obligation, too. But the memories were growing dim, and the passion had died. Maybe her doubts had killed it. Or perhaps she was by nature inconstant.

With a touch on her arm, Joan demanded her attention. The moist sympathy was waiting for her, more intensely than ever before.

"I did learn of him, I think," Joan said. "It was not clear it was Walter spoken of, however."

"What was said?"

"When I asked one of the stationers about papermakers such as we sought, he mentioned there must be a new fashion developing for hand-laid sheets among the Scots. He commented that some months ago a young Scot had been requesting the same references."

Bride's heart sped. "Which of these papermakers did this stationer name to you, Joan?"

Joan's finger pointed to the name at the bottom of the list. "This one here. Twickenham."

"I must find where he is located and visit as soon as possible. I always suspected it would be the paper that would lead us to our goal, and it appears as if Walter thought the same thing."

"It might be dangerous, Bride."

It might be, but she would have to find a way to do it anyway—

The door to her bedroom suddenly opened. Jilly stood on the threshold and peered around.

She shrugged and turned to leave. "I wonder where she has got to," she muttered.

"Who?" Bride asked.

"Mary. She was fussing all day with bits of notions she has bought, and I thought she was still in our chamber while I kept Anne company, but—"

"Are you saying Mary has gone missing?"

"Maybe she is trying to sneak a look into the party," Joan said. "She has been pouting for two days about not even being allowed to see the decorations or watch the guests arrive."

Bride felt her mouth fall open.

Mary at Lyndale's party?

She bolted to her dressing room. "Jilly, find a servant and ask that he check the kitchen, just to be sure she is not down there. Joan, come and help me dress, *quickly.*"

"My ass is cold," Abernathy mumbled.

"Do not blame my home's chimneys. You were the one who chose to come in that flimsy tunic as the god Apollo," Ewan said.

"It is not flimsy. It is diaphanous, like the garment Apollo wears in Raphael's 'Parnassus.' "

"Diaphanous, hell. If your ass is cold, get up and raise your skirt to the fire."

Abernathy peered resentfully across the card table. "As a Scot, you would know all about skirts and how to deal with cold asses, I expect."

"Indeed I do. You do not hear me complaining, do you?"

He had not complained, but in truth, his ass was cold, too.

He should never have left it to Michael to choose his garments for this Roman party. The result was a centurion's rigid breastplate, a ridiculously brief tunic, and naked arms and legs. Despite the high blazes in the fireplaces, necessary to keep all the Romans warm, there was a definite draft down below.

He glanced with envy at Colin on his right. Burchard had the good sense to come as a Roman senator. The extensive drapery of his toga would provide some privacy, should Colin leave the library and venture into the salon where costumes were being loosened and shed on the sofas.

"You appear out of sorts," Colin said. "The party is a great success, but you do not appear to be enjoying yourself much."

"Perhaps that is because a certain lady is enjoying herself *too much*," Abernathy said.

Ewan let that pass, although he was indeed out of sorts. Enough to almost respond that Abernathy had taken sanctuary at the gaming tables because Knightridge had also come as Apollo, and Abernathy could not suffer the comparison.

He had neglected to strike Jasmine Norton's name from the guest list because the arrival of the Cameron sisters had driven plans for this party out of his mind. Now she was in the salon, giving herself to another man, no doubt expecting Ewan to sulk with jealousy.

He did not give a damn about that. If Abernathy and others wanted to think that was why he played with cards instead of women, however, that was fine with him.

The truth for his mood was much more serious and alarming than the tedious presence of Mrs. Norton.

He was bored.

This party would be the talk of the town, but he did not care. He had reclaimed his place as a prince of pleasure tonight, but the excitements so abundantly offered to others could not raise any enthusiasm in him.

He could not ignore the implications of his reactions.

The recent changes in his life had ruined him after all. He was becoming as dull as he feared he would. Worse, the doings in the second drawing room struck him as vaguely . . . unseemly.

He resented that impression. He fought it. But there it was, returning again and again, heralding the end of his carefree, outrageous, thoroughly enjoyable youth.

Hell, yes, he was out of sorts.

"Perhaps you are vexed because none of the ladies appeal to you," Colin said.

"One woman is much the same as another," Ewan snapped.

"Normally with you that is true. However, you have been numbing my mind the last fortnight with unceasing complaints about one in particular, and she is not here."

No, she wasn't. She was up above.

He suddenly realized he wished he were up there with her.

He tried to muster a witty retort to Colin's insinuation, but his mind would not cooperate.

He was very glad she was up above, and not here. He wanted her worse every day, but he did not want to take her on a sofa in a candlelit drawing room while others cavorted nearby.

He wanted to make love to her privately, for years on end, where no man's eyes but his could see her body, and no man's lust would dare dishonor her.

The cards blurred in front of him as he dwelled on the unexpected insight. He blinked himself alert, but that did not shake how stunned he was at the extraordinary ideas and possessive feelings blotting out all thoughts of the party.

Damnation, this was all her fault. *She* was the reason his life was ruined.

Suddenly a body warmed his shoulder. A blond head dipped down to his ear. "Best you come with me, my lord. We have a problem in the next chamber," Michael whispered.

Ewan threw in his cards. Probably Mrs. Norton was making a scene.

"The younger one tried to slip in a while ago," Michael muttered as they headed for the doors. "I caught her, though, and sent her away."

"Younger one. What are you talking about?"

"Mary tried to enter."

Jesus. "Where did she go?"

"Down below, toward the kitchen. I expect her to

try and get in again, but I'll stop it, do not worry. Unfortunately, while I followed to make sure she kept walking, this one slipped in through the side door."

This one?

Michael opened the drawing room door to reveal which one *this one* was. She wore a crudely cut ivory silk mask over her eyes, but it did nothing to obscure her beauty.

Bride stood in the middle of the chamber. Unlike its other denizens, she was completely clothed in respectable British garments.

She wore the evening dress he had bought her and its deep sea-foam color and wide skirt and sleeves gave her a regal appearance. She had tucked her curls into an evening headdress decked with one modest plume, but a few naughty curls dangled along her cheeks and brow. No jewelry decorated the perfect skin of her neck and deep, wide décolletage, but she looked like a queen.

He had to stop and just look at her. She was so lovely and perfect. And so still. Not a hair or limb moved. She gazed into a corner of the chamber, an exquisite statue frozen for his admiration.

"Should I ask her to leave?" Michael said.

"I will do it. See to the others, and continue guarding for Mary. If that child tries to enter again, tell her I will send her to a convent in France until she is thirty."

Ewan walked over to Bride.

She was oblivious to the male interest she garnered. She did not even notice *him*. Her attention remained fixed on the corner.

When he sidled up alongside, he saw what had mesmerized her.

A man and woman were entwined on a chaise longue in the shadows. Unlike the other couples dotting the drawing room's cushions, these two had removed most of their clothes and were well on their way to ecstasy. The woman was masked, but he recognized the man. A discarded tunic draping their hips hid their union.

"You should not be here," he said quietly.

She barely glanced at him. "I came to find Mary."

"She was discovered before entering. She has gone to the kitchen."

"She is not there. We looked."

"Then no doubt she is sulking in the morning room and plans to glimpse the guests as they leave."

"At least she did not see—"

"No."

But Bride was seeing. She was watching intently, with her head slightly cocked.

"They are beautiful," she said. "The lighting, their bodies— It is like a painting come to life. I thought it would be vulgar and shocking, not elegant."

He looked over. The scene *was* beautiful. But then, he knew it could be. He did not own his collection only to shock or titillate.

If he had any doubts about her, they disappeared as she stood gazing at that couple so honestly and openly. An insane notion had entered his head in the card room, but now it seemed the most logical decision in his life.

He took her hand. "Come with me."

He led her out the side door and up the back stairs. His grasp on her hand remained gentle but firm. It allowed no resistance.

Not that she could muster much. She was still absorbing what she had seen in that drawing room. Not debauchery and sin. There had been an innocence and joy filling the room when she entered. It had not been what she expected at all.

Her senses righted as he led her down the corridor. She had to smile at his garments. They did not appear nearly as silly as they should. He cut a fine figure as a centurion. His broad shoulders and taut, muscular legs fit the fantasy too well.

As they neared her bedroom door, she began angling toward it while she sought to remove her hand from his.

He just kept walking, yanking her back in line behind him. "Do not object, Bride. Do not dare. A woman who can view an orgy with the calm you just displayed, should not be shocked visiting a man's room."

"That would depend on the reason for doing so."

He all but dragged her the last few yards. "I must say something to you, and I do not want one of your sisters finding me in your bedroom as I do so."

He opened his door and pulled her inside with a sweeping swing. She retrieved her balance, removed her make-do mask, and looked around.

They were in a sitting room, much the size of her own. It was a man's chamber, however, and a little cluttered with some books on the floor and papers on the writing table. The chairs and rug were not new. After buying luxuries for the entire house, he had been spare with himself.

"Damned nuisance," he muttered.

She turned. He stood by the door, unbuckling the bronze breastplate. He lifted it off and let it drop to the floor with a *thud*.

That left him in a dark red, short-sleeved, thigh-length tunic belted at his waist. It revealed most of his body and hinted at the form of the rest. He looked indescribably wonderful. Strong and handsome and almost naked. And male. Very, very male.

Her mouth dried. A flush warmed her.

Still cursing his discomfort, he sat on a chair and began unlacing the high sandals on his legs.

"I think you and I should get married, Bride."

He did not even look up as he said it. He merely continued working on the long, crossing laces on his other shin.

She stared at him, dumbstruck.

A brittle silence formed while her stunned senses struggled to arrange themselves. When they finally did, she blurted the only sensible conclusion she could muster. "You are drunk."

"Not even half so."

"Then you are mocking me. Toying with me."

He cast aside the footwear and stood. "I would never take such a rash step solely to mock a woman. There are easier ways to do that. Why would you think such a thing?"

"Because I can find no other explanation for such an unexpected declaration."

"There are many. For one, I need a wife. The whole world is saying so."

"They are not saying you need a wife like *me*."

"To hell with that. I am not going to tie myself to one of the simpering, vain, greedy females they *do* say I need. You have never wanted a penny from me, and I admire that."

She still experienced a light-headed amazement, as if this were not happening. A very peculiar sensation spread inside her chest, however. It produced an aching fullness that she dared not allow to rise.

"With time, one of them will not be so greedy and vain. You will settle on a fine match."

"I have concluded that you are as fine as I will ever do." He grimaced as soon as it came out. "That did not sound as I intended. I meant that I will never find a finer match than you."

She tried to find some objectivity. She sought to see the humor in this proposal, with her in abundant evening attire and he in a red tunic that barely covered his body.

The situation was not only ridiculous, but bizarre. Despite his claim to the contrary, he had no doubt imbibed too much at his party. She tried to piece together a response that would return this man to his senses.

Instead, that fullness just swelled and swelled, tightening her throat. It caused an odd trembling below her jaw.

He came closer. He gazed at her with eyes lit with humor and . . . something else. Something deep and . . . vulnerable.

"You look about to swoon, but not with happiness."

She gripped the chair she stood beside. Hard. She would *not* swoon. Or cry. "I am flattered, of course—"

"I am no prize in this area, I know that. However, you and your sisters will never be in want. You will no longer spend your days and years scraping to feed and protect them. Also, we have much in common, Bride. I can tolerate your company far longer than I can most women's."

She almost laughed, but another emotion also wanted to surge through the break in her composure. "You are forgetting that you are not expected to marry for company, but for progeny. For the next earl."

"And you will give me one. You are certainly sturdy enough." He looked away, scowled, and muttered a curse. "That came out badly, too. I should have practiced, but the impulse was rather sudden and I thought I should— See, here. You are no girl, but you are hardly ancient. I do not doubt you will give me an heir. And you are a Scot. I have been thinking that I should marry one. My father did, and so did my uncle. There was probably a very good reason for that. I have decided to follow the tradition."

She looked at him. Her heart was aching, breaking, and fit to burst. His proposal touched her profoundly.

She would forever be grateful for this offer, even if she dared not accept it.

She would always remember that this astonishing man had thought enough of her to propose, even if it was a passing impulse that he would later be grateful she refused.

He took her hand in his. "Do you hesitate because of my reputation? I am sure Lady Mardenford filled your ears, and this night your eyes saw enough, too."

"No, it is not your reputation. Not entirely." Not the way he meant, although that might matter if she could allow herself to consider his offer seriously.

His thumb caressed the back of her hand, much as it had in the carriage the other day. He looked down at the slow strokes. "Is it because of him? Your old love? The obligations you said you feel to him?"

She gritted her teeth, but tears blurred her sight anyway. "In part." *And obligations to you, Lyndale.*

She could not marry this man, even if he were sober and serious and had weighed this offer for a month, which he had not. She could not repay his kindness with betrayal. She could not allow him to face the compromise to his honor if it were discovered his wife was the source of those plates.

He looked in her eyes, and she knew she would indeed have to say it. He would not retreat unless the words were spoken.

"I am honored, sir. So honored you will never know. I cannot accept, however."

He paced away, his body tense with exasperation. He stood with his back to her and with his arms crossed during a terrible silence.

Finally he turned to her, visibly angry. "I do not understand anything anymore. What is the world coming to when women do not want to marry earls?"

"I am grieved if I have hurt you, but I have no choice."

"You are honored, but you say no. You are grieved, but you say no. It makes no sense."

"I say no in part because you really do not want to do this."

"You believe that you know my mind better than I do?"

"You admit it was an impulse."

"Not an irrational one. I am decisive. Women are supposed to admire that in a man."

She had to smile. It felt good. So did the poignant warmth in her heart. The tears would come later, but they no longer threatened to pour out now.

"You do not want to marry me, Lyndale. You only want to have me in bed. Since you could not have what you desired through seduction, you proposed.

Maybe you thought I resisted you to encourage just such a development."

"Actually, that never entered my mind."

That was even more flattering than the proposal. She wished . . . well, it did not count what she wished. "When your desire passes, you will wonder why you acted so rashly."

His expression tightened. "I am not completely ruled by pleasure, woman. I am not made stupid by it."

"Can you deny it is desire that moves you?"

"Why should I deny it?" He strode back to her and stuck his face down at hers. "Nor were your own desire and passion removed from the decision. I am of the mind that desire between a husband and wife is a good thing. God save me from a marriage with a woman who thinks joining her husband in bed is an indelicate duty. If I marry one of the acceptable, fresh, witless young beauties being thrown in my path, that is what I may get. Where is it written that I have to be bored with my wife?"

"In a month, you would probably be as bored with me as with any woman. I doubt the enthusiasm that you expect of me would make a difference for long."

"So, it *is* my reputation that gives you cause to say no."

"I *said* it was, in part."

"Then give me the month and let us find out if my interest wanes, damn it. It is stupid of you to pass up a life of security on a guess."

She realized he had her in a very tight corner.

She also realized she did not mind being there.

If he had not softened her heart so much with this proposal, she might have found the strength to refuse once again. Only she did want him, badly, if only for a while. She could not deny that just standing here, so close, caused a thrilling liveliness in all her most sensitive places.

One kiss from him, one touch, and she would be helpless.

He just looked at her, waiting. His gaze and aura, his face and body, were seduction enough. She could not stop looking at him. An inescapable meeting of minds and desire occurred in their locked gazes.

There were good reasons to refuse.

She ceased caring about any reasons for anything except the ones making her tremble.

"Not here. Not now, while I live under your roof. My sisters and I will find a house and move there, and once we are gone, I will—"

"*Yes,* here. *Yes,* now. If you are willing, I'll be damned if I am going to wait."

Decision burned in his eyes. He firmly pulled her close and kissed her.

She offered no resistance. She met his hard kiss with an aggressive response and their small joining instantly became impatient and tempestuous.

He loosened their clutching embrace, swept her up in his arms, and carried her into the bedroom.

CHAPTER
NINETEEN

~

He had made love to her a hundred times in his imagination. In the most alluring fantasies the seduction had been slow and luscious and endless.

As he carried her to the bed, he knew it would not be like that. Eventually he would live that dream, but not this time. Desire raged so dangerously it was all he could do not to rip off her gown and ram himself into her.

She did nothing to calm matters. When he put her on the bed she rose to her knees and pulled him to her in a long, savage kiss.

Somehow they removed the gown and petticoats and headdress. The sight of her kneeling on his bed in stays and chemise awed him. Proud and tall, she watched as he thrust the billowing garments away. Her disheveled hair, still bound but loosened, looked like that of a woman who had already been well pleasured. Her expression welcomed more. Demanded it.

With a deliberation that hid the power ripping in him, he stood beside the bed and unlaced her stays. Her breaths shortened with every sly release. The garment finally fell away. Bold now, confident in her decision, she removed the chemise herself.

She was incredibly beautiful. Her breasts rose high, their tips hard and tight. Her eyes glistened. Her lips parted, inviting more kisses and anticipating the delirium to come.

He pushed her shoulders, and she fell back on the bed. As he stripped off her drawers and hose, she gazed into the canopy above.

"Oh, my." She moved so that she lay lengthwise on the bed, her shoulders propped on a mound of pillows. While he looked down at her naked body, she studied the canopy. "You really are bad, aren't you?"

He glanced above. A large looking glass hung beneath the drapery, held by strong wires. It reflected Bride in her majesty, naked and pale and awaiting the pleasure due her.

"Like a painting," he reminded her. He pulled down the duvet so she was on the sheet. "A moving painting."

"I never thought I would see myself in such a work of art."

He climbed onto the bed and knelt over her. "You will not see yourself much, but I will."

She eyed his tunic, and reached for the belt. She unbuckled it. "And I will see you."

He rose tall on his knees and pulled off his clothes. She looked him over very slowly, then glanced in the looking glass to see what it revealed.

Her attention returned to the physical view. She reached out and caressed the edge of his hip. His mind split in half.

Her hand slid down his thigh. He hardened even more, which he thought would be impossible. Fascinated, she moved her palm up his inner thigh, driving him insane. Her fingers and gaze moved to his erection.

Her touch tortured him, wonderfully. The recent oasis of control constricted. He leaned over her, his weight on his arms, and released some of his hunger in a hard kiss.

A wildness broke in them both. Her hands were everywhere on him, caressing and grasping. He used his mouth all over her perfect skin, unable to get enough.

Her sighs became gasps, then rose to begging cries. Darkness entered his head until only the quest for pleasure and completion existed. Licking her nipples, stroking her thighs, he forced her to mad passion until she was lifting her hips and parting her legs in her craving for relief.

Images entered his head of how much he wanted and how he would have her in the days ahead. They were too ambitious to act upon in his current impatience. They pushed the boundaries of that control, however, and created urges that howled in him.

He stroked into her cleft and caressed the sensi-

tive softness. Her hips rose to meet his touch. She
pulled his shoulders to her and pressed frantic kisses
to his face and neck.

"Could you—" the request dissolved into a moan
as his finger circled.

"Could I what?" He wanted to hear it. He wanted
her to learn to tell him what she needed.

"Do what you did . . . last time."

"You can have whatever you want."

He kissed down her body, savoring each taste,
slowing himself, leashing the savage drive.

He turned his body as he descended, and hers,
too. He lifted her knee to his shoulder and lost himself in the musky sweetness of primeval femininity.
He swept his tongue around the edges of that exquisite softness, until her initial tension ebbed. Then he
aroused her more directly and barely contained the
feral pleasure it incited.

A touch on his phallus sent new shards of hunger
through him. He glanced down his body to see her
caressing him.

She noticed he had paused, and that he was
watching. A question entered her eyes. He did not
doubt she saw the answer in his face. Her tongue
flicked tentatively. When a moan escaped him, she
grew more aggressive.

Somehow he found a place where he could ride
the waves of pleasure she gave and that he found
with his own mouth.

The urge to possess and claim, to enter and own,

became a flame in his body. Violent and ruthless, it finally exploded into a white blaze.

He swung his body and straddled her legs. He had deliberately not brought her to a climax with his mouth, and her wild eyes reflected the torture of her passion. He spread her legs, braced his body over hers, and entered.

Her moan in his ear matched the one in his heart. A moment of drenching peace restored an instant of lucidity. He kissed her, unable to hide the contentment and triumph permeating him.

The calm gave way to fury during that kiss. Senseless, furious passion took over. He thrust hard and slow, then savagely and fast, until her cries sang around them.

A lot could happen in a month.

Ewan gazed up at the looking glass. He could watch all of Bride in its reflection, not just the red curls pressing his shoulder and the ivory shoulders encircled by his arm.

The way he saw it, there were three possible conclusions to this affair.

He might indeed transfer his desire elsewhere, in which case she would be proven right.

Not about refusing him. That had been foolish, no matter how big a scoundrel he might be. Bride's pride might not like a husband's little infidelities, but such behavior did not create a disaster.

Lots of marriages existed nicely with their members pursuing other desires. His own parents both took lovers, and those paramours were accepted in his boyhood home with nary a scene. At each of their funerals there had been a contingent of mourners with very special memories.

All the same, if his desire waned and strayed, they would probably part. He would marry her anyway, but she would insist on ending things, being the stubborn lass she was.

History indicated the affair would take that path.

Something inside him, a newly born instinct, suggested it might not.

In the event it did not, he would have to ensure that by month's end he had conquered any other misgivings she had.

She stirred, and he studied her face in the reflection. He did not trust her to admit her misgivings, so how could he conquer them?

The obvious solution was to drown her in pleasure, and submerge the misgivings at the same time. He would make her so crazed, so thoroughly sated, that the idea of giving up the sensual fulfillment would be unthinkable.

There was a third possibility, of course. She might get with child.

The notion held surprising appeal.

She would be a wonderful mother.

All the more reason to enchain her with pleasure. No matter where his desire lay in a month's time, he would make sure she did not throw him over if she carried his child.

The ultimate conclusion of his deliberations was undeniable.

He was obligated to make love to her as often as possible in the weeks ahead.

Duty called.

Her long legs stretched in the looking glass. She roused herself out of the sleepy stupor into which she had lapsed.

"You appear quite thoughtful," she said.

"I promise the thinking is finished. Being the decisive sort, I did not need to strain my head long at all."

"What decisions did you make?"

"Nothing you would find interesting."

Her head rose and she looked to the jumble of her garments on the floor and chair. "I should dress."

"I forbid it."

"I cannot sleep here."

"Trust me, you will not be sleeping."

She laughed. He cupped her face with his hand and kissed her.

"You will be back in your chambers by sunrise. Nor will you need to dress to return to them. Consider the lay of the house, Bride. As it happens, our dressing rooms meet, and there is a passage between them."

Her brow puckered. He could see her lining up the rooms in her mind. "I did not stand a chance, did I?"

She had stood a better chance than any woman had in years. His inexplicable restraint had delayed this night far too long.

"As you can see, the arrangement of chambers is very convenient."

She nodded. "Too convenient."

"I do not think it is possible to be too convenient."

"I expect you do not. I, however, do not want to be kept quite this conveniently."

He flipped her on her back and pinned her down with his body. "And I want you where I can have you whenever I choose. If I only get a month, I demand full measure."

She laughed and shook her head. "I will not live in this house as your mistress, Lyndale. Have you ever before allowed your lover to live under your roof?"

No, but that was different. He could not name how it was different, but it was. It had nothing to do with propriety or scandal, either.

"I am not completely indifferent to my reputation. If I stay here, I will be thoroughly ruined and whispered about far and wide."

The whispers will become inaudible once we are wed. "So, you are going to move to another house, and I am going to have to arrange assignations, and we are going to have to be discreet, and I will wake wanting you and have to wait, and—"

"I am afraid so. I trust you know how to manage such things discreetly."

"I have almost no practice in discretion. However, for your sake, I will arrange everything with the secrecy worthy of a bishop."

She smiled so sweetly that he had to kiss her.
Which led him to want to do more. She sensed the
change in him, and a response instantly flexed
through her. They exchanged slow, long kisses with
their heating bodies pressed close.

"Even after I move away, I can still help you investigate the *'I Modi'* if you like," she muttered
while he tortured her ear.

Yes, she would want to do that.

"Certainly, Bride. I doubt I could manage it without you."

He had much to say to her about those prints, but
not now. Not until he was sure, and not tonight, in
any case. Before the month was up, however. She
might have refused his offer in part because of all
that, and he would have to remove her concerns.
That was one misgiving that pleasure might not be
able to drown.

He slid off her and rolled her onto her stomach.
He swept her tumble of hair aside so he could see her
whole body as he caressed it. He bent to kiss down
her lithe back while he smoothed his palm over her
thighs and bottom. He sensed every tremble that announced her arousal.

She tried to turn to him, but he kissed her shoulder before she could. "No. Stay like that." He took
her hands, and held them together near her head.

"Is this a novelty?" she asked.

"Hardly. Although if you ask, it must be for you."

She turned her head so it faced away from him.

He realized she was embarrassed.

He leaned over her until his mouth nuzzled her ear. "Do you think it matters to me what you have known or not known? I wanted you when I thought you were a virgin, and still wanted you after I decided you were not. If you had known every novelty with another man, I would not care, nor does it matter if you have experienced nary a one. You give passion more honestly than any woman I have known, and that is all that is important to me."

It was the truth, but he could not ignore that her lack of experience appealed to him. That he would be the first in many things with a woman would be a . . . novelty.

He made love to her back. He lost himself in her reactions as she accepted this new sensuality. The small of her back dipped and her bottom rose as he kissed her length. He caressed the firm swells of her bottom more firmly. The erotic vulnerability caused her hips to gently rock in the way that revealed her climbing arousal.

"Part your legs, darling."

A tension briefly claimed her, but she obeyed. He braced up on one arm and watched her as he used two fingers to trace the line of her cleft from the base of her spine to the moist heat at the end of its path.

Her hands clutched the pillow beneath her head as she tried to contain what he did to her then. He made sure she could not. He caressed slowly and deeply, learning every nuance of her reactions to that touch, learning what made her gasp.

When he knew she was impatient with need, he

eased atop her, covering her body fully with his, even her legs, so she would know what he was going to do. He held her like that, reeling from the intense impact on his primitive instincts that the domination produced.

She reacted with astonishment, and a fear as ancient and intuitive as his own sense of triumph. He soothed her little rebellion with kisses, luring her into submission.

"You are not truly afraid, Bride. You know I am not dangerous to you. I could never hurt you."

When she had accepted his benign restraint, he rose back on his knees. The sight of her, naked and beautiful and waiting, intoxicated him. He lifted her hips and slid a pillow beneath them, so her bottom rose erotically.

He caressed her shadowed, wet vulva, deliberately driving her to a delirium of desire. When she was clawing at the pillow, smothering her cries of need, lifting her bottom more, he gave her the relief that they both ached for.

Bracing his weight on his arms, he took her in a way that was not novel at all, but as old as humanity. Only this time his passion was tinged by an intense satisfaction in the ancient claiming of rights, and in his possession of her.

Lyndale opened a door, revealing a short corridor. Clutching her garments, Bride entered the little passage that connected Lyndale's dressing room to hers.

He caught her arm and turned her to a parting kiss. It deepened in a way she had learned to recognize during the night, and her body stirred as it had so many times already.

Day was breaking, however, and they could not indulge. She did not want Michael finding them here, naked. Nor would her sisters remain abed much longer.

She eased out of his embrace. He let her go. She felt his gaze on her until she closed her chamber's door behind her.

She leaned against its board and closed her eyes. The night had been astonishing. Her face warmed at some memories, but she felt no real embarrassment. There had been nothing wicked in that bed. She had known only joy and incredible pleasure.

Her senses were still dazed. While she pulled on some clothes and put away the gown, her brain was not really in the world. A cloud occupied her head, dulling her perceptions.

"I see you are awake."

The voice shocked her out of her stupor.

She turned. Jilly stood at the threshold to her bedroom.

Bride desperately calculated the odds that her aunt had just come down looking for her.

Jilly moved about the room, fixing the disorder from last night's hurried change. "When you did not come back, we wondered what became of you. You had left in such a state."

Bride tried to find a story that would explain her

extended disappearance. She suspected any she gave would not sound credible.

"Michael found Mary," Jilly said. "Caught her hiding in the reception hall. He brought her up."

"I am relieved. I knew she had not managed to enter the party, but—"

"You did, I expect." Jilly straightened some items on the dressing table. "That would explain why you did not return, wouldn't it?"

"I did dally for an hour." She prayed Jilly never learned about those parties. If so, she would have some explaining to do.

"I'm thinking you dallied well longer, and not at a party." Expression bland, Jilly headed for the door. "If you want to sleep, I'll keep the others away. You should call for a bath, too. You smell of him, Bride."

Jilly's calm assumption left Bride with nothing to say.

Her aunt gave her a long look before leaving the dressing room. "I'm trusting his lord is as worth dallying with as he appears."

Bride swallowed hard. "I would say so, yes."

"Then you'll not be hearing nay from me. I never scolded about the last one, and won't this time, either. I know you won't be stupid about him. You know better than to believe the lies men tell to get their pleasure."

CHAPTER TWENTY

J ust draw freely," Lyndale said.

Bride poised the crayon over the thick, flat stone, searching her mind for an image. She closed her eyes and saw the view of her Highland home from the hill to the south, with the glen stretched out under a summer sky.

She touched the oily crayon to the stone and drew a quick picture of the scene. It was just like drawing with charcoal on paper, quick and immediate, and very different from painstakingly gouging thin lines and tiny dots into a copper plate.

When she was finished, Mr. Vouet, the man who owned the lithography studio, called over his workers.

"Come and watch the magic," Lyndale said to her.

He guided her to the tubs where her stone had been carried.

"The stone will be treated so that the parts left blank by you are receptive to water. That is what they are doing now. Then, when the stone is rolled with ink, the oily ink will adhere to your oily lines, but not the other, wet places. In that way your drawing will be ready for the paper and the press."

She watched the whole process with fascination. She knew about lithography, and its increasing popularity. Mr. Vouet had already shown her some plates he was making, where the same paper had been printed over and over, each time with different colors for different sections. The result was a very vivid and very expensive image that imitated a painting.

"It is not a technique for reproductive work, but for original art and for illustrations," she observed.

"Engravers will not be replaced, if that is what you mean," Lyndale said. "They will not go the way of the weavers. Although, eventually I suppose a machine might be invented to reproduce images. Not soon, though."

Side by side they watched her stone through every step, until an hour later she stood with a lithographic print of her glen in her hands.

She gazed at the image and her heart swelled with nostalgia. It also filled with warmth toward the man admiring it with her. He had arranged this outing as a surprise for her, so she could experiment with this new technique. It had been very kind of him, and another example of how his thoughtfulness touched her.

He filled her days now, escorting her around town. Together they visited artists and print shops.

Lyndale made his queries regarding *"I Modi"* at the latter, quizzing the owners about engravers and new discoveries, subtly seeking information for his quest.

Bride listened to the answers for her own purposes, but her fear regarding the banknote plates had receded. That found little room in the lighthearted excitement that dazzled her heart and body. It became a distant problem waiting in another life for another day.

She rolled her lithograph so she could carry it easily. "I do not know how to thank you enough for this wonderful day, Lyndale."

"I expect we can find a way."

She looked at him, and caught him watching her much as he had that day in Ackerman's, as if she perplexed him.

When her gaze met his, however, a different expression entered his eyes. He could still make her feel like a rabbit caught in a hawk's sight, and it still took her breath away.

She could not suppress a naughty smile. "I think I know what way you mean," she whispered.

"I doubt it."

She giggled. "Oh, dear. Another novelty?"

He took her arm and guided her out of the studio. As they walked he angled his head so he could speak lowly to her. "Nae, Bride. Ah dinna mean that kind o' way. Ye daesna ken me at all."

Not only his tongue had turned to Scots, but his

brogue had thickened. She laughed at this new surprise.

"Nae, Ah'll ne'er ken ye fur aw, Ewan."

He tapped the rolled sheet she carried. "Some summer day, we will sit on that hill and look at that glen, Bride, and you can thank me then with one kiss, no more."

Lyndale's attention had been so unflagging since the party, and their visit to the lithographer so much fun, that it surprised Bride when he did not invite her to join him when he left the house the next day.

The sudden loss of his company cast her adrift in her own thoughts. She spent the afternoon trying to concentrate on her true purpose in coming to London, but anticipation of his return distracted her.

That night when he arrived at her dressing room door, he pulled her through the passage connecting their apartments as if they had been parted a month. His expression as he undressed her was serious, as if the day's appointments had provoked a thoughtfulness that affected how he saw her.

There were no novelties that night after he laid her down. No games and no laughter. Just scorching kisses and possessive caresses and, finally, the comforting weight and warmth of his body covering hers.

The reflections in the looking glass captivated her when they joined like this, and she kept glancing to them while he made love to her. Golden candlelight flowed in a liquid shimmer over the body of the man in her arms. The eroticism of his embrace and caress were heightened by the view of his body suspended above them.

The light sculpted his shoulders and back into alluring ridges and hard cords. It glowed down his tapered torso and slid over the hard swells of his buttocks. It illuminated his legs, showing their athletic beauty.

She could watch the tensing and flexing of his body, and see the signs that indicated what he would do before her body felt it. She anticipated every stretching fullness of every thrust.

He moved again. His hips flexed and he withdrew until they were barely joined. She gritted her teeth at the momentary loss, and watched for the dip in his lower back that would herald a new completion.

Instead a different tautness hardened his muscles. His shoulders rose as he braced his weight on extended arms. His new position blocked her view of the reflection. She could see only his face and chest hovering above her.

"The glass fascinates you," he said.

"Like a moving painting," she said, and smiled. She shifted her hips a little, to encourage him to continue. His ability to simply stop what they had been doing surprised her.

He remained immobile, driving her mad with that slight, tantalizing connection. "I am not a painting, Bride." His head dipped down and he kissed her gently. "I know all about that reflection, and how it distracts. How it makes your lover distant, and the pleasure safe."

"That is not true." Except it was, a little. It did provide a certain distance. It transformed the acts even as it intensified them.

"You watch me, too," she said, uncomfortable with the directness of his gaze and the way he filled her vision. His form dominated her world and her body now. His reality almost overwhelmed her.

"I almost never watch you, except at the beginning and afterwards. That glass does not exist most of the time for me anymore." Locking her gaze with his, he finally thrust and filled her. "I do not think I want you retreating into that painting either."

She reached to pull him close, but he did not come to her. Braced on his arms, he continued his slow withdrawals and entries. His gaze invaded as much as his body. His expression demanded that she not look away or close her eyes.

The intimacy deepened. It changed the pleasure and the warmth, the excitement and the thrills. Her soul reacted with joy, but also experienced tremors of fear. His slow, deliberate claims seemed to peel away layers until nothing remained between them except a vibrant connection. The closeness awed her, but the vulnerability made her tremble.

Only at the end did he return to her embrace. Even then he cupped her head with his forearms and faced her, their eyes and breath mere inches apart as their rapture bridged every other gap.

When Bride slipped from his bedroom the next morning, Ewan found himself floating in a very peculiar mood.

He had brought a bad humor back to Belgrave Square the prior evening. Spending the day with an estate agent, finding Bride and her sisters a new home, had left him angry. As he viewed the houses to let, a tumult of resentments had flickered, then burned, and finally begun seething.

He hated that propriety decreed she live elsewhere and that they pretend they were not lovers. He hated that she had refused his proposal when any sane woman would have grabbed it. He hated that he wanted her enough that her imminent departure from his home affected him like this.

Ultimately, he had resented like hell her fascination with that damned looking glass. He sensed that in watching that reflection, she was making love to his image and not him. Last night that suddenly mattered to him.

In a fit of annoyance, he had demanded it be he, totally and without compromise. However, he had never expected the result to be this hazy cloud on his consciousness that refused to disperse.

Nor had he expected that the most ordinary sexual position would one day be the most stirring. Yet he could not deny it was true, and his reactions dismayed him. Last night had moved him profoundly and he did not know what to do about it.

He was grateful, therefore, when Michael entered his bedroom, along with a servant bearing a coffee tray. He was glad to have Michael intrude into his daze with commonplace activity.

"It appears you received an anonymous letter," Michael said, after the servant left. He handed over the *Times* and the post.

"Have you been reading my mail?"

"Did not need to. The seal is plain, the paper ordinary, and the letters are blocked, not in script. Just how I'd do it, if I wanted to be a mystery."

Ewan slit the seal. The letter was indeed anonymous, and very brief. It only contained one sentence.

> *The intermediary was Mr. Ramsey of Newcastle.*

Dodd had sent this. Whether Ewan's questions had piqued the auctioneer's own suspicions, or whether he feared Bonham's losing future consignments, he had discreetly given Ewan what he requested.

Ewan recognized the intermediary's name. He had met Ramsey, several years ago. He had visited his print shop in Newcastle once. The offerings had been predictable and boring, and insufficient to provoke future visits, but there had been nothing to suggest Ramsey handled forgeries.

It was possible that Ramsey did not know the *"I Modi"* were forgeries, of course.

For that matter, Ewan was not sure that they were either.

It was time to clarify the matter.

"I will dress now, Michael."

"It is barely ten. Normally, after she leaves you—
that is, you usually return to bed after coffee, sir."

"I know the time. Nor can I imagine whom you
mean by 'she.' There is no 'she' here, nor has there
been. Correct?"

"Correct. I will be ready for you in the dressing
room in a few minutes."

As the sounds of Michael's preparations began in
the next chamber, Ewan read the rest of his morning
mail. A brief note from Mr. Nichols caught his attention. The stationer requested that Ewan call at his
shop, to discuss the special paper they would commission.

When Ewan entered Nichols' stationery shop that
afternoon, he carried a large, flat package under his
arm. In it was the river god print, engraved by
Thomas Waterfield.

Mr. Dodd had been happy to extract it from the
lot going up for auction at Bonham's. Ewan had paid
more for this one print than he normally would have
bid for the entire portfolio that contained it, but he
had decided he did not want to wait on the auction.

Later today he would compare it to his *"Modi."*
He was fairly sure that he would find the same technique in them all. Then he would have to decide
whether to ask Bride outright if her father had

forged that series, and if so how they came into Mr. Ramsey's hands a year ago.

He had decided he did not care if her father had forged them. Bride, however, might care a great deal, and be afraid of the discovery. It would probably be best to raise the matter and get it out of the way.

Mr. Nichols greeted him with a cat's smile of contentment. "Lord Lyndale, I am delighted you could accommodate my request for your attention. I have found our papermaker, I am pleased to say."

"Have you now? That is good to hear. You are convinced he can form the coat of arms for the watermark? I would not want anything crude."

"I will leave it to you to decide." Mr. Nichols led him to the table that they had used on Ewan's last visit. He removed a piece of white wove paper about three inches square from a drawer, and placed it with solemn ceremony on the velvet-covered board.

"I was having difficulty finding another to do it, so I visited him and asked if he would consider the commission," Mr. Nichols explained. "He refused at first, until I explained it was for a peer. I did not give your name, of course. I will confess that I intimated that should you be pleased, and others learned of the commission, there might be more orders from others of your station. That changed his view quickly."

Ewan examined the sheet and gently ran his fingertips over its surface. Wove paper was finer than laid. Laid paper showed the subtle ridges created by its larger screen wires, and possessed a texture that was evident to the touch. Wove paper made use of finer, densely placed wires on the screens used to support the layer of sodden rag pulp, and was processed for a softer, even surface.

"It is very good. Why is the sample so small?"

"Our man made this for another commission. He did not want me to see the watermark he put on it, so he cut off a corner for me to show you. It was part of a very important commission, I suspect, and one of the highest prestige if he demanded such secrecy. It appears he has continued his craft in order to serve a patron of the highest esteem."

Nichols' wide eyes and pursed lips insinuated that such demands for secrecy could only come from one place—the crown.

"If he cut off the portion with the watermark, how am I to be convinced he can do *my* watermark?"

"Look at the lines. Hold it to the light. I have never seen such skill. He makes the paper a work of art. If he can manipulate the screen's wires such as you see there, he can form them into a very detailed watermark depicting your coat of arms."

Ewan held the paper up toward the window. Light penetrated the paper from the back. A vague pattern showed through, revealing the impression of the lines from the wire screen that had supported the pulp while it dried into paper.

Not normal lines at all. Not the standard horizontal and vertical ones found in most paper. This piece displayed curving lines, fine and densely placed.

The paper appeared to have one huge watermark of swirls and waves that covered it completely.

"Is it not remarkable?" Mr. Nichols said. "I have never seen anything quite like it. I am sure he can do what you request. I had no idea he had continued his craft in this way, and become so innovative."

It *was* remarkable. However, Ewan *had* seen something quite like it. Those swirls and waves bore a resemblance to the lines found in old banknote paper.

"I agree that the skill is extraordinary," he said. "By Zeus, Mr. Nichols, we may begin a new fashion."

Mr. Nichols clearly hoped so. The potential profit had his eyes sparkling with excitement. "I did have to offer him a handsome sum, but for stock of such distinction it will be well worth it."

"Of course. However, since the sum is mine to pay, can I know this great artisan's name since I am to patronize him? I promise to be discreet. I will never breathe a word to other stationers. Should a new fashion develop, the source will remain your secret to employ."

"Did I not tell you? Forgive me, it was not concern for my own future profit—"

"I am sure not. His name?"

"Why, it is Twickenham, the man I told you we used years ago, the one whose son near ruined him. He indeed uses a machine for common wares, but as you can see, he still plies his craft the traditional way as well, for very special patrons."

Ewan joined Nichols' enthusiasm over their success for a few more minutes, then gave a very large order for the commissioned stock.

"He will not be able to begin your paper for another week or so," Nichols advised. "He must first finish the other one. I will approach him with the details in a fortnight."

"I do not mind waiting for the best, Mr. Nichols."

Ewan left the shop and told his coachman to take him to the City so he could settle on Bride's new home with the estate agent.

He looked down at the wrapped print on his lap. It appeared that both of his investigations would be finished soon. The one regarding *"I Modi"* might have started as a ruse to lure Bride into his company, but by evening he would know if it had revealed those prints were forgeries after all.

The other, more serious investigation might conclude soon, as well. He would have to find out just how special and secret Twickenham's recent commission was, since the man clearly possessed the skill to forge paper for banknotes.

And if Twickenham had made the bad notes' paper, then Twickenham could lead him to the engraver of the plates.

CHAPTER
TWENTY-ONE

Bride strolled through her new home with her sisters and Jilly.

It was a very fine house. Situated on a street near Portman Square, it held good-sized, airy chambers on the first two levels, and adequate bedrooms above.

"The addition to the carriage house would suit your press," Lyndale said.

They all went outside and stuck their heads into the large chamber jutting into the garden from the carriage house. A merchant had owned this house previously, and used this space to store some goods.

"It is perfect," Bride said. "It was kind of you to find it so fast."

Not all that fast. Lyndale had taken a week to settle the lease. A week in which their pleasure had been very convenient, indeed.

Not only in their linked chambers. Last night, knowing the convenience would end, they had spent most of the night in the private drawing room, first talking for hours entwined by the fire. Then Lyndale had told her to undress, and watched from the sofa as she did so, his gaze exciting her until she was breathless. When she was naked, he had stripped off his own clothes and led her to the swing. They had swayed forever, joined in the slowest, most elegant lovemaking she could imagine.

"The light is excellent," Joan said. "There are a lot of northern windows. No glare when we work, then."

While Bride had played, Joan had been busy. Her sister had found piecework employment with a publisher named John Murray on Albermarle Street. For the last three days, Joan had risen early and bent her body to the engravings that decorated the publishing house's books.

Joan said Mr. Murray was amenable to giving Bride work, too. If they were going to keep themselves in this house, they would need those wages.

They returned to the house and her sisters went above to inspect the bedrooms again.

As soon as the steps on the stairs faded, Lyndale drew Bride into his arms. "Will this do?"

"It is too big. The furnishings are too fine."

"I will not have you in a hovel."

"Half this house would be more than adequate, and no hovel. I think you are misleading me on the cost, too. I think—"

"Stop thinking so much." He kissed her in a way to ensure she thought about nothing at all. "Now, this is your home. You will repay me from the income your sisters receive. Then you will take over the payments to the landlord yourselves in the future."

"Who is the owner of this place?"

"Me, as it happens. Do not object. It was the easiest way. My solicitor said as much, and in the future you will deal with him, not me." He took her hand. "Actually, I bought two houses."

"How many do you need?"

"One for me, one for you and your sisters, and one for us. I can hardly make love to you here. You will not be comfortable arriving in Belgrave Square for assignations, so I bought a cottage to the west on a little land. We can meet there."

He had been good to his word. He had arranged for discretion, as she had requested.

Gaelic leaked down the stairs. Mary was arguing with Joan about the choice of bedrooms.

"You do realize that they all have guessed about us," Lyndale said. "I can see it in their eyes when they look at me. Or do not look at me, to be more accurate."

Bride had noticed the signs. She was sure Jilly had not told them, but they knew. None of her sisters had said anything, but then, they had never said a word about Walter, either. Everyone had pretended ignorance about the way Walter climbed in her bedroom window. One night the wind had tumbled the ladder, stranding him, but she woke to find it back in place.

"If they have guessed, it could be credited to your change in behavior," she scolded.

"My behavior toward you has been above reproach. When others can see us, at least." His devilish smile had her blushing at the things that happened when no one saw them.

"You were at every dinner the last week. You never went out at night. You even spoke to Mary as if she were other than a nuisance, and invited us all to tour the colosseum at Regent's Park. They would have to be living in the clouds not to notice."

"Which leaves only Anne in ignorance, I suppose. I want you to tell them I offered marriage. I do not like their thinking I am misusing you."

"I cannot tell them of your offer. If Mary knew that I refused, she would do me grave harm."

The sister in question could be heard coming down the stairs, calling for Bride to decide who got which room.

Lyndale pressed a small paper into her hand. "Your trunks will arrive this afternoon. I expect you will want some time to settle in. Here is the address of the other house. Promise that you will meet me there soon."

She tucked the paper away, and saw him out. She would need at least a day or two to settle in. She also needed the time to address a few other matters that had been neglected during her week of pleasure.

He paused in the portico. "Perhaps now that you can thoroughly unpack, you will let me take another look at those Caraglios."

Her heart twisted at this reminder of the deceptions between them. For a week she had pretended those lies did not exist, but she could no longer.

"I will be sure to dig them out of their trunk as soon as possible."

"It is here," Mary called up the stairs. Her voice cracked with excitement. "The press is here."

Bride listened to the confusion pouring in from the street. Although she was glad their press had finally arrived, she cursed under her breath.

She had intended to go out today, and now that would be delayed.

She set down the burin, rolled her stiff shoulders, and stretched her sore hand. If it took long to set up the press, she would have to finish this plate for Mr. Murray tonight. She had begged off meeting Lyndale today so that she could visit Mr. Twickenham, the papermaker whose name might have been given to Walter.

She rose, and looked down with distaste at her work. She hated engraving on steel plates. It was much harder material than copper. She did not care for the brittle lines and tonalities it produced when printed, either. Book publishers favored them, however, because many more impressions could be printed off steel than off copper.

She went to Joan's chamber across the landing. "I suspect that you also will be glad for the excuse to forgo this work for a while."

Joan kneaded her hands together. "It is fairly tedious. Mr. Murray has very precise ideas of how he wants these drawings reproduced, doesn't he? He does not favor creative burin work. He wants clear, bland illustrations in his books."

"At least that means we have not had to pull proofs to check our work." The presses at Albermarle Street had been available to them. These images were the sort they could do when half asleep, however.

Release from the burin did not appear to lift Joan's spirits.

"You are melancholy. What is amiss?" Bride asked as they walked down the stairs.

Joan shrugged. "I wrote to Michael and invited him to visit for dinner. His return letter arrived this morning."

"When will he come?"

"Never, I think. He explained that the addresses his lord is paying to you means he cannot. It appears it is not permitted for a valet to have a friendship with a family if his lord has a friendship with them as well."

"I am sorry, Joan. I did not intend for my friendship to interfere with yours."

"It is not important. My friendship was only that, and nothing more. It was pleasant to have at least one familiar face in this city, however. I also find it comical that suddenly I am above him."

Bride and Joan arrived in the reception hall to find Mary in the midst of a long, endless description of all the fine ensembles they had bought and all the interesting things they had seen.

The two men who listened appeared skeptical and suspicious. Their lidded gazes shifted from Mary to Bride.

"Took some time finding ye," Roger MacKay said. "Sought out Lyndale as ye said tae. His man told us ye wus here." His jaw twitched. "Said you'd just taken this big house and wus living with the earl 'fore that."

"Sounds like ye had a fine time since coming to London." Jamie's gaze raked Mary's pretty yellow dress.

"Fine enough," Bride said. "We are badly in need of the press, however. I am grateful you have brought it."

"No need fur gratitude. Ye paid the way. Took a bit longer than it should, but the dreich got us stuck a few times." Roger set his hat back on his head. "Ye be telling us whaur ye want it now, and we'll be on our way."

It took an hour to move the wagon to the back of the house and hoist the press onto the sturdy table waiting for it in the carriage house's extra room. The MacKays had also transported books from the library, and everyone helped move those boxes into the chamber, too, to be dealt with later. Finally, Roger and Jamie wiped their hands and necks.

"Are you returning at once to Scotland?" Anne asked. She petted the press's rollers like the machine was an animal.

"Nae." Jamie's grin reflected the rogue in his heart. "Since we cam all this way, we intend to see the toun."

"I can show you the city," Mary said. "I know where everything is now, and all the best diversions and entertainments."

Jamie laughed. "We'll be seeking diversions ye canna help wi', and going places a fine lady like ye canna gae."

"You'd best watch your pockets," Bride warned. "Those diversions could leave you fleeced. This is no little town in a glen."

That made Roger frown. He reached into his coat and turned to Anne. "Maybe ye will hold this money for us. It is what we've set aside to get us home. We dinna want tae be spending or losing this part of it."

Anne accepted the charge. "Where will you be staying?"

"We've a place. We'll come for that 'fore we gae."

Jamie nudged his brother. "Let's be moving. There's *diversions* tae be found." He chuckled at his own joke.

"I think what you seek can be found at a place called Covent Garden." Anne spoke as if they sought directions to the opera house. "You should be careful about disease, of course."

Roger turned red. Jamie looked at Anne as if she were mad to speak so frankly.

Anne smiled placidly, pleased that she had been able to offer practical help.

The MacKay sons left, excited about the trouble they would find.

Bride regarded the press. It seemed strange to see it here. It felt like a year since she had used it in Scotland. It had been a world away. A lifetime ago.

Her world and her life, however. This press, and all it had seen, dictated her past and her future. She was living a wonderful dream with Lyndale, exploring small eternities when they met in that cottage west of the city. This press was a nudge, urging her to wake.

Sadness ached in her heart. She was not sure what she mourned.

"You should have asked them to dinner," Mary said. Her pique at Jamie MacKay's impatience to be gone was showing.

"They've no interest in dining with us," Bride said. "Jamie plans to be tasting things we can't offer."

"I think they are just jealous that we have done so well. I think they feel we are above them now."

Mary seemed to take comfort in that notion. Bride did not disabuse her of it. Mary had clearly misunderstood the hooded looks the MacKays had given their new dresses and big house.

Those Scottish eyes had been full of speculation on just which sister had sold herself to the Earl of Lyndale.

She did not care what they thought. Right now her worry was with this press, and the way Anne kept stroking it.

She could see her sister's mind working. They

had a press, and the plates, and the paper, and the skill.

Anne was going to be trouble.

Sooner than Bride expected.

"We could pass the notes here in London, then Roger could bring the money back to Scotland, Bride. He would do it for us, I'm sure."

"I am not going to put our lives or that money in the hands of a MacKay, Anne. We will be printing no notes, so turn your mind away from that idea."

It took Bride a good while to find Mr. Twickenham's place of business. The hackney cab brought her to the City, and she had to make her way through the narrow streets on foot, asking for directions.

Finally a bookseller sent her to a lane off Fleet Street. She spied the sign announcing Twickenham's papermaking business.

As soon as she entered, her hope died. This was not the kind of papermaker she sought. It was a factory.

Right now it was a deserted factory.

The machine with its big roller and long ribbon of screen stood silently inside the cavernous chamber. A huge screw press in one corner showed a thick stack of paper being squeezed dry, however. Perhaps the day's work was finished.

She strolled around, noting the big vats where pulp would be readied for the process. They were empty.

As she examined the works, a shadow intruded in the corner of her sight.

The room was not deserted, as she had thought. A well-dressed man loitered near the wall that had been blocked from view by the machinery when she entered. At the sound of her step, he turned.

"Bride, what are you doing here?"

"What are *you* doing here?"

Lyndale walked over to her. "Awaiting the return of the proprietor." His expression invited her explanation in turn.

"Our press arrived today. I had heard Mr. Twickenham makes the kind of handmade paper we like to use."

Lyndale gestured to the machine. "He has joined industry, it appears. However, his days of laying down pulp on screens by hand are not over. I was told he might accept commissions for private stock."

Her eyes took in the deep shelves on this wall, stacked with reams of paper.

Lyndale gestured to the door where he had been standing when she entered. "I think there is another chamber behind that door. Maybe he makes the hand-laid paper in there. Should we peek?"

She wanted badly to peek. Desperately. She just did not want Lyndale peeking with her.

To her consternation, he strolled back to the door. "I am sure he won't mind, and it will spare us both another visit, should he not return soon. I was convincing myself to poke my nose in, when you arrived."

She hurried to catch up to him. "We really shouldn't . . ."

"Since we each may offer a commission, I am sure he would want us to."

He turned the latch and pushed the door ajar. She looked around him to see the room's interior.

It was indeed a room used to make paper. A stack of framed screens on the floor stood as high as her head. In a far corner she spied a table holding newly laid paper drying between felt layers.

A man stood with his back to them, framed by the light of a window. He was intent on lifting a screen from a vat. He was dressed in shirt, waistcoat and trousers, and his steely hair hung to his thick shoulders. As the screen rose, the window's light showed the top lines of the screen, ghostly in the sodden pulp.

Bride glimpsed the wire pattern of the screen in the brief instant before Mr. Twickenham leveled it and began the motions to even the pulp into a consistent layer. Her breath caught.

Mr. Twickenham heard her. He dropped the screen back into the pulp and turned with alarm.

"Our apologies," Lyndale said. "We did not intend to startle you. I fear we have ruined that sheet, and perhaps the whole vat."

Mr. Twickenham composed himself. He gestured dismissively at the vat. "No matter."

"If you would like to finish with it—"

"I said no matter." He wiped his pulpy hands on

his waistcoat. "There's a bell on the table in the outer room. If you had rung I'd have heard."

"Is there? We did not see it." Lyndale stepped into the room. "You work alone?"

"My apprentices are sick. They are needed for the machine, so I do a bit of screening in here on such days. Is there a reason you have visited, sir?" A skeptical scan of their garments accompanied the question. Neither one of them looked like a publisher or stationer.

Lyndale strolled toward Twickenham, exuding the affable confidence that only privilege can breed. "I was told that you still make hand-laid paper, and might accept a commission."

Bride strolled, too, but inconspicuously along the wall. She aimed for the stack of felts, itching to see what kind of paper they dried. She silently urged Lyndale to keep Twickenham's attention occupied.

"I do not take direct commissions. You will have to speak with a stationer. They don't care for us cutting them out, you see."

"Of course." Lyndale gazed around with admiration. "I have always found this fascinating. Rags one day, paper the next." He peered into the vat. "Is that one of your commissions?"

"It is. One that is past due, so if you will excuse me . . ."

"We do not want to interfere with your industry. However, just so I do not waste yours or a stationer's time, do you make thin white wove paper?"

Startled by the question, Bride almost bumped into a case.

Twickenham began fussing with the stack of screens. "I have been known to. Now, good day to you both."

Dismissed without ceremony, Lyndale headed for the door. Bride almost stomped her foot. She was within arm's length of the felts, but she would not be able to sneak a look at Mr. Twickenham's new paper.

"You could have distracted him longer," she said once they emerged from the building.

"Why would I?"

"I wanted to see the quality of his paper. You had your question answered, but I did not have mine satisfied." Her pique caused her to walk with some speed toward Fleet Street.

"You only need to visit a shop and choose the paper you want, Bride. If you require something special, it will be arranged for you."

"And for you, sir. Your private stationery can also be so arranged."

"I confess I pursue more than private stationery. I took the free day to see about the forged *'I Modi.'* I doubt their paper was bought through the normal channels, so I have begun checking the sources."

"You mean the *possibly* forged *'I Modi,'* don't you?"

"As time passes, the more possible the possibility strikes me."

His coach waited on Fleet Street. He handed her in and it rolled toward Portman Square.

"So, your press has arrived. Now you can accept

more ambitious commissions besides Mr. Murray's illustrations. Perhaps you should compose your own images. There are collectors who still prefer the work of *peintre-graveurs* over reproductive prints."

She knew that. She had seen the landscapes and city views in the print shops. She had never considered herself an artist, but she thought she could do as well as many who called themselves such. Some of those prints had been hand-colored, and Mary and Anne would be good at such enhancements.

"It is less secure," she said. "A reproductive plate can be sold outright to a publisher. An original work is only worth the prints that actually sell."

"Soon your family will not need to earn its keep. If you want to try something different with that press, you will be able to." He closed the coach curtains and lifted her onto his lap. "If you do, I promise to purchase an impression of every plate you make."

"So that you can patronize me?"

"Because I do not doubt they will be beautiful."

She expected him to kiss her and grab the opportunity for intimacy, as he normally did. Instead he only held her as the coach worked its way through the town.

The dark interior of the carriage seemed full of words unspoken. He appeared as deep in thought as she found herself.

Only her mind did not dwell on forged plates and paper. She contemplated how right it felt to be held by him, even now in this silence so heavy with deceptions. She knew true joy when they were together. It went beyond the pleasure they shared, although it was tied to that. Her spirit soared whether they made love or merely talked. Even the silences enlivened her.

She had worried his attention would be intrusive and dangerous. Instead, he made her feel free and safe. And happy.

That would end soon, one way or the other. She could not erase a foreboding that it was starting to end right now, in this carriage.

When the coach stopped at her house, he kissed her cheek. "Will I see you tomorrow?"

"I will be there by midafternoon."

"Since you are finally settled, I would like you to bring the Caraglio prints. I am impatient to examine them."

Her heart had been heavy since their meeting with Mr. Twickenham, and now it sank like lead. It was one thing to anticipate the end of the dream, and another to know the exact hour of its demise.

"I will be sure to remember to bring them this time."

She looked at his shadowy profile, unable to fathom his expression. Did he know? Had he guessed? And if so, how much?

The footman opened the coach door and handed her down. From her doorstep, she looked down the street as the Lyndale insignia moved away and turned a corner.

The outing had unsettled her badly. The weight in her heart burst, showering her with sorrow.

They had both been lying at Twickenham's, and she suspected that they both knew it. She had not been there to find paper for her press, and he had not been there to see if Twickenham had made the paper for the forged *"I Modi."*

For one thing, Lyndale's *"I Modi"* were not printed on thin white wove paper, but heavy laid cream.

Thin white wove paper was what Twickenham had been making when they intruded, however. Lyndale must have noticed that, just as she did.

It was also the kind of paper used in banknotes.

CHAPTER TWENTY-TWO

Bride entered the house, eager to seek the privacy of her bedroom so she could rebuild her composure after the unsettling visit to Mr. Twickenham's factory.

It was not to be.

As soon as she opened the door, she knew something was amiss. The house was too quiet, as if no one moved in it.

Suddenly Joan was standing atop the stairs leading to the basement kitchen. Joan's eyes held the misty sympathy that Bride so often glimpsed in them, only now the mist threatened to turn to rain.

"What is it?" Bride asked.

"You had best come down, Bride. It is Anne."

"Is she ill?"

Joan shook her head. She turned and walked back down to the kitchen. Bride hurried after her.

Jilly stirred a pot at the kitchen fire and Mary sat

near the door. The mood in the room made the silence of the carriage seem benign in comparison.

"Anne left," Mary blurted as soon as she saw Bride. "Can you believe it? She just left. She had them carry down her trunks right in front of us. Then she was gone." Mary's awed tone implied the entire drama had impressed her as much as dismayed her.

"I told her she could not go, but she paid me no mind," Jilly said with a shake of her head.

Bride felt as stunned as her sisters and Jilly looked. "Where has she gone?"

"Back to Scotland," Mary said, rolling her eyes. " 'Back home,' she said. She is mad."

"She is *not* mad," Joan said. "She went back with the MacKays, Bride. Roger promised me he would watch out for her, and see that she found a home. He will not allow her to come to harm, so you are not to worry too much."

Bride sank onto a stool near the worktable. If she had not left today— She doubted it would have made a difference. In her quiet way, Anne could be very stubborn.

"She is a grown woman," Bride said. "If she wants to leave, we cannot hold her."

"She must have been planning it for days, maybe weeks," Mary said. "She knew Roger would have to come here to get the money he left with her. She was all packed when he did. It was something to behold, Bride. I think he tried to dissuade her, but to no avail. So they left with her in one of their wagons."

"Mary offered to go with her," Jilly said. "Anne would not hear of it."

Bride looked over at Mary. "I thought you never intended to leave London."

Mary shrugged. "It did not seem right that she should go alone, and I am not much use to you the way Joan is. London will always be here. I could have always come back."

It was the most mature thing Mary had ever said or done, and it left Bride speechless. She sensed that she was glimpsing the future, when her little sister would shed her childhood.

Joan forced a small smile. "I have never seen Anne so determined. She had made up her mind, that was clear. She said—she said to give you her love. Also this." Joan put a folded paper on the table in front of Bride.

Bride opened it. Anne had written a parting letter.

Dearest sister,

I mourn that you are not here as I leave, but perhaps it is for the best. Do not be distressed on my behalf. The MacKays will see to my safety on the journey, and their mother will help me once we arrive home. I have a long friendship with Roger, deeper than you know, and he will take care of me.

I do not blame you for the decision to leave Scotland. It was necessary. However, we are not all needed in London. I know that you want us to remain together, but it is time for me to go home.

I have taken some of Father's journals. I hope you do not mind my desire to have these tokens in my possession. I sold most of my new dresses yesterday, so I have some money. I ask that you arrange for my income to be sent to me once the funds pay. I will use it wisely, I promise.

Please find it in your heart to forgive me for abandoning you. I believe that you will do fine without me, however. Joan is here for you, and Mary will not always be a spoiled child.

I think that you belong in London, Bride, but I know that I do not.

We will see each other again. I believe that in my heart.

Your loving sister,
Anne

Bride read the letter several times. Then she ran up the stairs to her bedroom. She unlocked and threw open the trunk that held her father's plates and papers, dreading what she would see.

Her racing heart calmed. Nothing looked amiss. She lifted the larger plates and glanced beneath them. The banknote plates and paper still nestled in their neat stacks.

"I dared not look." Joan's voice broke the silence of the room. She stood in the doorway.

"She did not take them. Of course, she would not

have a press, and there is no way to pass them, so it would have been foolish—"

"No doubt she intends to use her income."

"No doubt."

Joan walked over and embraced Bride. "You appear shocked. And very concerned."

"She is so vague, Joan. It is as if she sees a different world and breathes different air. She may only be my junior by two years, but she is childlike. If it had been you—but *Anne*? How will she take care of herself?"

"She did not appear childlike today, I promise you. She was a knight starting a crusade. Roger was very sincere when he promised to look after her. He is the best of the MacKay sons."

"That is not a high reference, considering the rest of them."

Joan laughed. Bride did, too, but she felt her face folding into another emotion. Her vision blurred.

"She will make a terrible faerie, too," she said, sniffing to hold in the tears. Picturing that made her laugh despite the streams snaking down her cheeks. "She will get lost in the glens at night."

"She will probably try to give some of the money to Sutherland's factors, or lecture them on their bad behavior," Joan said, biting her lower lip.

"And the clothes. The faerie is thought to be a man. Did she take the clothes and hat?"

"I will check. I am guessing she did. Or maybe she is counting on a real faerie helping her."

They both laughed again. Then they both cried.

Bride wiped her face and took a deep breath. "I am glad she left. If we are caught, I do not know if she could survive what will happen. Maybe now she will be safe. I will write to her and say if anyone comes asking about us, she is to be as vague as she ever has been. She is to let them think it was me alone."

"You had better write to Roger and tell him to put her someplace safe, and tell her to take a different name, too. It would be best if it is thought we all left the glens for good."

They stood in silence for a long spell. Bride looked down at the letter in her hand. Her heart was breaking. "I will badly miss her."

"We all will. Although it is as if she is still here, in an odd way. I can feel her in the house. I do not sense the hole such a departure normally leaves."

Joan gave her a consoling kiss, then left to help Jilly finish the supper. Bride opened her sister's letter and again read the carefully controlled script that hinted at Anne's skills in forgery.

Dear, sweet, dreamy Anne.

She pictured her sister in doublet and pantaloons and hat, riding through the night to bring coin to the displaced families. Their father had done so for years, then Bride had taken his place. Now Anne would continue the legend.

Perhaps their father had been right. Maybe Anne did have faerie blood, and the myth would be made truth this time.

Bride would have liked to put off meeting Lyndale the next day. She could have used some time to accommodate her emotions to Anne's departure before facing a further loss.

Sick at heart, she set out in the afternoon for the little cottage west of the city.

They had met there twice already, and she relived those hours as she rode in the hackney cab. Lyndale always made her smile. His good humor brought out her own. Future duties and responsibilities seemed bearable when she was laughing with him.

She did not expect there to be much laughter today.

She looked down at the flat package resting on her lap. She had brought the Caraglio prints. It was time to be honest with this man, at least about this part of her father's legacy.

When Lyndale learned of it, he would probably be very angry. He would also be relieved at his narrow escape from the marriage he had impulsively offered.

The cottage was deserted when she arrived. Lyndale's carriage was nowhere to be seen. She entered to see evidence that the woman who came to clean had visited earlier. A cold supper waited in the little kitchen.

She strolled through the sitting room, with its simple furnishings. There was the little writing table and chair, and the comfortable sofa to which Lyndale had immediately pulled her upon her first visit, impatient after the passage of two days apart.

She went upstairs and gazed at the bed they had shared. No mirror hung above this one, nor any luxurious drapes.

She would miss making love with him.

She doubted she would ever know anything like it again. It was not the pleasure she would remember most, however. Rather it would be his aura of both command and caring.

He sensed what pleased her before she realized it herself. More important, he sensed what did not. There had been novelties enough to fill a lifetime, but no demands. He abandoned any game if he perceived she did not want to play.

She gazed out the window at a small kitchen garden in the back. All the plants were dormant. The low sun warmed her skin, but it could not penetrate the chill in her heart.

She wished . . . It did not matter what she wished. Her path had been laid long before Lyndale rode into their Highland glen. She could not undo her past or escape her father's legacy.

Nor was she sure that she would, even if she could.

She heard the carriage approach and a little panic beat in her heart. She glanced around the bedroom.

Not here. Not in this house. She did not want her memories sullied.

She hurried below and arrived just as Lyndale entered the house. His eyes sparked with seductive, joyful lights when he saw her. He removed his hat and gloves and tossed them aside.

She let him kiss her, but stopped him from removing his frock coat. "Let us go to the garden and enjoy the sun while we can."

"Certainly. We should take advantage of the clear air and sunshine of the country."

He followed her through the cottage to the kitchen door. A little stone path sliced the garden in half. A rustic bench waited at its end, and they sat there under the bare branches of a fruit tree.

Lyndale gestured to the package she had carried out with her. "What is that you have there?"

"The Caraglio prints. You asked me to bring them." She carefully broke the seal fastening the paper in which she had packed them.

He displayed none of the enthusiasm she expected. That made it easier. She folded back the paper to reveal the top image.

He lifted it to the sharp scrutiny of an expert. She searched his expression for any indications of suspicion.

She took a deep breath. "I need to tell you something. It is a forgery. You will know as soon as you compare it to your series."

He barely reacted. He merely returned the print to its stack and looked at her. Waiting.

"My father made it. He saw some old, worn impressions of these images in France, and realized they must belong to the Caraglio series. So he created plates based on them."

"An artist's exercise, no doubt."

She grimaced. "Not entirely."

"Are you saying he sold some as Caraglio originals?"

"I do not think so." She was sorely tempted to leave it there, but she had decided to give Lyndale the truth about this, at least. "He expected the extra images to eventually be connected to the series, however. I do not think he sold any impressions, but he made the plates with the intention of doing so and selling them as originals."

There it was, baldly stated. Her father was a forger.

Lyndale remained calm. She would have preferred outrage.

"When did he make the plates?"

"Before I was born. When he was a young man, soon after his travels, I think. To my knowledge, he pulled no impressions from these plates while I was alive. Even these prints on my lap were earlier."

"It appears he saw the error of his ways. I do not think any harm was done."

She hated having to go on. Dreaded it. "He also engraved other plates to re-create images that were lost, but known to history." She swallowed. "Raimondi's *'I Modi,'* for example."

He went very still. She had to look away. She could not bear that silence.

"Did your father print those plates and sell the images, Bride?"

"No."

There was a horrible pause.

"Did you, darling?"

"No. But someone did. The plates were stolen just over a year ago. I am convinced your series was printed from them."

His stillness deepened and spread until it engulfed her. It seemed as if the breeze could not penetrate it. She stared at a dead vegetable vine clinging to a stick, feeling sick.

Finally she snuck a glance at him. His expression astonished her.

His face was firm and serious, but not angry. He looked confident. And oddly contented.

"You *knew.*"

"I suspected."

"How?"

"Something happened long ago that ultimately sent me to that Highland glen. My uncle ruined your father for a reason. At first I thought it involved your father's radical politics, but Uncle Duncan was not very interested in politics. He was very fond of engravings, however."

"That would not mean anything in itself."

"No, but you knew my uncle's name, even though you pretended you did not. You knew what had transpired between Duncan McLean and your father, but did not want me to know. So, I suspected your father either sold Duncan some questionable work, or tried to, and my uncle discovered it and made your father leave the city and the trade on threat of exposure."

"You are right. I did not want you to know my

father had done this, and if I admitted I had heard him speak of your uncle, you would have wanted to know in what way. I hope you can understand why I pretended ignorance."

"Of course I understand." He gestured to the prints. "Possibly it was even those prints that started it all. I inherited my series from Duncan. It was in his collection for a long time. He might have seen your father's newly discovered Caraglios, and realized they were forgeries."

"I do not see how my feigning ignorance of your uncle's name led you to suspect my father had engraved your *'I Modi,'* however."

He stretched out one leg and made patterns in the dirt with his heel. "In asking around for engravers talented enough to forge old masters, the name Thomas Waterfield was offered to me. I ignored it, since I thought you were Waterfield. When I learned your father had also used that name in his latter career, possibly to avoid Uncle Duncan's detection, I realized it could have been him. So I compared my *'I Modi'* against a print by the late Mr. Waterfield. I was sure then."

"You were so certain it was not me?"

"It was a thought I considered and discarded. For one thing, if you *had* engraved them, you would not have had to study the burin work so closely in my salon that night. If the forgeries were yours, you would have known it at once." He gestured to the Caraglio prints on her lap. "Were those plates stolen along with the *'Modi'*?"

"Yes."

"We had better find all of them. There could be printings being made and sold very privately. The erotic subject matter would make many collectors secretive about their purchase and ownership."

She had expected a storm. She had steeled herself for scorn and accusations. Instead he merely recommended continuing the search.

"You are taking it very well."

He clasped her hand in his. "I am honored that you confided in me. Perhaps now that you have revealed your dark secret, you will look more kindly on my proposal."

Gratitude swelled inside her. So did sorrow. Another emotion joined them, shading her pain with its sweet poignancy.

She gazed down at the hand holding hers firmly but gently. The scathing ache in her heart insisted she admit the truth to herself.

She was in love with him.

She squeezed his hand to release the building emotion. She barely managed to keep her composure and hold her tongue.

She had thought admitting to the smaller deception would cause him to leave, and she would thus be spared a decision on making the worst revelations. Now his generosity and her love provoked the urge to go on, to admit to all her father's crimes, and her own as well.

She swallowed the impulse. She could not tell him everything. For her sisters' safety, she could not.

Nor could she allow this affair to continue. Not because she feared his discovering the truth, but because continuing her deception would be a betrayal of her love.

"You made that proposal recklessly. I relieve you of any obligations you may feel."

"I do not asked to be released. In fact, I just proposed again, in case you did not notice."

"If those plates have been used, it will all come out eventually. At best, your countess will be known as the daughter of a criminal. Since I also engraved under the name Waterfield, there will be those who think I was the forger, not my father." She pressed her other hand atop his. "You are kind not to end our association, but you know that you should. Even this affair will taint you."

The first flicker of anger lit his eyes. "Did you come here today thinking to throw me over, Bride? A month, you agreed, and it is barely a fortnight."

"You know our parting is for the best."

"Then let the best be damned. You may be accustomed to sacrificing your life and happiness for the best, but I am not. I'll not let the best make a martyr of either you or me." He rose. "Now, I am done with sunshine and fresh air. Come to bed."

She had to laugh, despite the brimming tears. "Is that your best way of concluding this conversation, Lyndale?"

"If you speak of ending and parting, it is." He held out his hand. "Come with me, Bride. There are no worries where we are going. No fears that cannot be conquered, and no sins that cannot be redeemed."

She knew she should not agree, but she could not refuse him. She could not refuse herself the solace he promised. She could not deny her love the chance to know the joy he gave, at least one more time.

She placed her hand in his, and laid all her sorrow at his feet.

CHAPTER
TWENTY-THREE

$\sim$

He led her down the little stone path, and into the house. Her spirit had lifted, but not as much as he expected. Something still shadowed her. It created a peculiar serenity in her, and a palpable vulnerability.

This was a side of Bride he had not seen. He did not hand a Boudicca up the stairs, but a woman who had laid down her armor and needed shielding. It flattered him beyond words that she trusted him enough to stay, if her admissions had sapped her strength.

He sat on the bed and pulled her in front of him. She made no attempt to help, but allowed him to turn her around and unfasten her dress and petticoats. They fell to her feet, and she stepped out.

"You still seem troubled, Bride."

She picked up the garments and walked over to

a chair. She laid the garments on it, then came back to him.

"Anne left us yesterday. She returned to Scotland with Jamie and Roger MacKay."

He drew her into his arms. "That explains your melancholy. I am sure she will be safe on the journey with them. When you learn where she settles, tell me and I will see that she is protected."

A crooked smile broke on her face. "We continue to create more trouble for you. The responsibilities attached to that deathbed promise keep growing, don't they? Your uncle handed you a devil's bargain."

"I am not fond of responsibilities, promises, or trouble, but I have ceased to think of your family in those terms. If not for that promise, I would never have met you." He pulled the lace to release the knot on her stays. "So, there have been compensations."

She laughed. The sound was lovely, but he still sensed a depth to her mood. It created an intense connection between them. That bond had existed before, overwhelming him during the throes of their passion, but rarely like this, rawly present prior to lovemaking.

He had spent his life retreating from the kind of obligations created by comforting the sadness he felt in her. His instincts wanted to do so again.

He knew how to. He had mastered the looks and words and well-timed jokes that gently said *Do not expect too much. Do not misunderstand.*

He possessed neither the heart nor the will to

force a change in the mood now, however. He sensed that if he did, only he would return to shallow water. Bride would be left alone to fend for herself.

He lifted her leg and propped her foot on the bed. He rolled down a stocking. "You expected me not only to break with you today, but to be angry. I am impressed with myself for having surprised you."

"Perhaps you surprised yourself more than me."

He dealt with the other stocking, thinking such comments were the price of not retreating. He did not mind comforting her as she accommodated whatever confused or saddened her, but that did not mean he welcomed discussions about himself.

She stood between his knees as he finished undressing her. He took his time, enjoying the slow emergence of her body. Finally she was naked, and so lovely in the low sun's light that his breath caught.

He slowly caressed his palm along her hip. "You are very beautiful, Bride. It still astonishes me when I see you." And it did, much more than it should.

"You are quite beautiful yourself. Also most remarkable, and unique. You are also not nearly as bad as people say."

"I am very bad. I am also outrageous and dangerous. If I have a weakness for you, do not make me into a dullard because of it."

"There is nothing dull about being kind and generous. In fact, in a man it is most extraordinary."

"Promise you will not describe me like that to anyone. I will be ruined if you do."

"I promise. I also know that there are limits to

any person's generosity. I will never hold it against you when you reach yours."

He had no idea what she meant by that, and at the moment he did not care. His mind had turned to other things, such as the beautiful warmth in her eyes. He was sure that if he gazed in them long enough, he would see every secret hiding in her heart.

He looked at the rest of her, marveling anew at how he found her body so aesthetic and erotic. He doubted the same body with a different woman inside would fascinate him as much. Nor would he feel as possessive. There was a *rightness* to their lovemaking that he could not explain away.

She was thoroughly feminine, almost voluptuous, but a firm tension in her limbs and shoulders spoke of action instead of indulgence. Her high, full breasts firmed under his gaze, and their dark rose nipples hardened to the protruding tips that were so sensitive to his tongue. The faintest pink rose on her face, and her eyes showed the lights of arousal.

Hands on her waist, he drew her closer and kissed the valley between her breasts. "What do you want, Bride?"

Her fingers stroked through his hair and she held his head nestled to her. She kissed his crown. "Only you. I have no other ambitions today, and no need for novelty. I only want to hold you in joy for an hour before we return to the lives and worlds waiting for us."

Separate lives, her quiet tone said. Different worlds. He suddenly understood her mood.

It was not sorrow over Anne that made her so subdued. He had not won the little argument in the garden the way he had thought.

She would not end this. He would not permit that. Later he would explain again why that was unnecessary. For now he would convince her with other than words.

He kissed her to begin doing so, but his confidence wavered with the passionate connection. It was as if some of her sadness leaked into him during that kiss. His desire became tinged by a fear that he might lose her.

Fury split his head, unaccountable and unexpected in its intensity. He cupped her face in his hands and looked her in the eyes. "You are *mine*."

His vehemence startled her. "In this cottage, in this bed, I am totally yours. I daresay that today I am incapable of keeping even a portion for myself." She loosened his neckwear with sinuous fingers. "Now, get undressed, and take me to that place you promised. I badly need to go there."

He was more interested in branding her with his mouth and hands than in undressing. She loosened his garments while he grasped her bottom and held her body to kisses he pressed on her soft skin. When she had stripped off his shirt and he had cast off the rest, he moved back and lifted her to join him.

She climbed on the bed and straddled his lap, her knees flanking his hips, facing him. Entwined in elegant, caressing embraces, they shared long, savoring kisses.

He swam in a luxurious arousal, one drenched with sentiment. It built slowly, but violent passion waited at its edge.

Bride succumbed first. He sensed the change before she expressed it. Suddenly she kissed him as if she tried to release a desperate need.

She pushed him down. Legs still flanking him, weight propped on her hands and knees, she made love to him and permitted almost no reciprocation. Calmly, then almost savagely, her mouth moved over his neck and chest while she tortured him with a flicking tongue and erotic bites.

It was a stunningly effective seduction. Desire made him burn. He reached between their bodies to caress her breast. His other hand moved lower.

She pressed her hands and weight on his upper arms, stopping him. "Do not. If you touch me it will end too soon. You asked what I wanted and I want to taste and touch you for a while."

Her hair poured over his face as her kisses moved to his ear and neck, then brushed his skin like a cascade of silk as her mouth moved lower. She kept her hands near his elbows, as if holding him down.

He closed his eyes so he would feel every detail of her passionate assault. Every gentle kiss and sinuous lick and provocative nip. His consciousness constricted until only pleasure existed. Her mouth made soundless notes that reverberated in his blood.

She released him and rose up, sitting back on his thighs. She looked down with eyes transformed by passion, glistening with deep lights. Her hair was half undone, and a glorious unruly cascade of curls hung over one shoulder. She looked so astonishing in the gathering shadows, all ivory and bronze and womanly and strong.

Mine. The possessive declaration repeated in his head. He had never been jealous about other women, but if another man dared touch Bride, he would want to kill him.

He reached for her. "Come here."

She subtly shook her head. Her gaze drifted down his body. She looked at him as if her eyes sought to absorb his essence. As if she branded her memory with his form, just as she had done so with his taste. The sadness he had sensed earlier poured out of her.

Her sight came to rest near her knees, on his erection. Deliberately, almost curiously, she ran a single fingertip from its base to its tip.

Hunger ripped in him. Her finger circled, and shards of desire assaulted his body. Her fingers fluttered more completely, then stroked.

She kept watching her hand move. He gritted his teeth so the urges would not defeat him too soon. Her caresses were devastating, however.

Her lips parted slightly. He silently begged. When her head finally dipped, he almost groaned. With the first moist touch of her lips he was dying. He found a place in his passion that offered a slim edge of control and anchored himself there.

She swung her leg and knelt so both knees pressed against his hip. He could touch her now, finally, but not the way he wanted. Not the way his rights demanded. Nor did he want her servicing him like this, no matter why she chose to do so.

He reached out and grabbed pillows and shoved them beneath his head and shoulders. He caressed around her hip. "Turn."

He moved her so that her knees flanked him again, only she faced the other way this time. He settled her so her mouth could reach him, and he could pleasure her as well. A shudder trembled through her when he caressed the soft folds of flesh mere inches from his face, shadowed below the erotic swells of her buttocks. Her back arched down and she opened more.

The warm velvet of her mouth absorbed and caressed him. The scent and taste of her musky sweetness maddened him more. The pleasure became almost unbearable. Edgy and ruthless now, his desire pounded through his whole body. He battled to contain the driving impulse building in him.

She suddenly turned, urgently rearranging herself so she embraced him. He clutched her trembling body to his chest. Her heart beat against his, slowly calming.

She nuzzled into the crook of his neck. "I am sorry I did not . . . It is just I want to hold you and . . ."

He wrapped his arms around her. "Do you mean like this?"

She nodded. The day's intimacy made the silence pulse. Despite their stillness, the passion still crackled between them, like a tempest waiting to break again.

She pushed up. "Like that, and like this." She took him into herself, then leaned forward for a kiss. Her hips rocked and she repeatedly drew him in and released him.

The sensation instantly renewed all the hard needs raking his body. So did her breath on his face and chest, and her body under his hands. He eased her up and forward so he could lick her nipples. Her hips circled seductively in response, and her passage flexed to grasp him.

He sucked gently, then more aggressively. Her soft cries of pleasure floated in the sensual daze engulfing him. His mouth caused shudders that streamed down to where they were joined. Her sounds turned frantic and her moves insistent and demanding.

He finally allowed his hunger free rein. With one arm binding her to his chest and the other pressing her hips to his, he thrust deeply and hard until her screams of completion filled the evening silence.

"I must go to Scotland soon. I would like you to come with me."

Bride did not move when his words flowed into her stupor. She remained atop him, surrounded by his strong arms, pressed to his body in a delicious daze of comfort.

Her heart had opened completely during their passion. The emotion that had poured out had been beautiful and peaceful despite the pain it would eventually bring.

"Why do you need to go to Scotland?"

"Lyndale's seat is there. I have to attend to some matters that I have been delaying. I should have gone long ago, but government affairs preoccupied me. As did you."

A sword of fear pierced her bliss. The world crowded in at once, returning her to earth from the cloud on which she floated. She kissed him, trying to cling to the remnants of perfection as they flowed from her grasp.

"Government affairs? I thought you avoided such things. I was of the impression you do not even attend Parliament's sessions."

"I was caught by duty despite my best efforts to remain useless. I expect the obligations to be over soon, however. A day or two at most remain to resolve the inquiries I am undertaking, I think. We can journey to Scotland next week."

She rose up on her forearms so she could see his face. "Inquiries? Are you engaged in an investigation?"

His expression dismissed the matter as so much intrusive nonsense. "Of a sort. A small investigation for the Treasury. Now, will you come with me? I wish I could lure you with a grand manor dripping with luxury, but I regret to say it is an old castle, drafty and cold. We can keep each other warm, however, so it will be tolerable."

"You are only inviting me so you will have a warm bed."

"Absolutely." He rolled her onto her back, and rose on his arm. His gaze followed his hand as it slowly smoothed down her body. "So you will have one, too. We are a good match in many ways, especially in bed."

"You have known better, I am sure."

He did not respond with a witty retort as she expected. Instead he only continued watching his hand move.

"Perhaps. There is a difference, however. And I find you are my match in other ways. My conviction that you will suit me has not wavered. I now also think that I suit you." He lowered and kissed her. "You do not always have to be strong with me, Bride. What a burden that must be for you, having to be strong all the time."

His words touched her. It *was* a burden. Before she met him, the duties had been taking a toll. It was not the day-to-day living of them that made her stoop, but the vision of the years coming without reprieve.

Now for a few weeks she had known joy again. Even with disaster nipping at her heels, she had enjoyed lighthearted respites.

She laid her palm on his face. "You are so sure we will suit, but in truth you do not know me well."

"I know you very well." His head dipped and he kissed the soft side of her breast, and then its tip. It tightened as the thrill shivered through her. "I know you are passionate, and that you do not dissemble. I know you are proud, and more than a little stubborn." Another kiss accompanied each declaration. "I know you are good-hearted, and that you sacrificed your youth for your family. And I know that beneath the strength you are very, very soft."

His tongue started a wonderful torture, flicking and laving. Seducing.

"I am also of a jealous nature," she said. "In that way at least, I would not suit you at all. There would be scenes that you would find very tedious."

His attention remained on arousing her, but devilish humor glinted in his eyes. "How big would the scenes be?"

"Enormous."

"Thank God. I cannot bear middling sorts of scenes. If you are going to have a scene, let hell fly, is what I say."

She had to laugh. "Oh, hell would fly, sir."

"Then you would suit me in that, as well. After you are done, we will reconcile."

"I may not be amenable."

He gently rubbed her other nipple, and the titillation became maddening. "It will be for me to cajole you. If I have been bad, I will beg your forgiveness as best I can." His teeth gently bit, making her breath catch. He smiled slowly as he kissed the tip again. "The way I see it, you cannot be upbraiding me while you are screaming with pleasure."

She accepted the pleasure. It was so bound with her love now that she did not know how to refuse.

She stretched her fingers into his hair. "Were you truly certain that I had not printed my father's forged plates?"

"Mostly certain."

"Did you never plan to ask me if I had?"

His mouth paused its seduction. He appeared to contemplate the question. "I do not think so. It would be rude to ask my lover if she was a forger, don't you think?"

"What if I had used those plates? What would you have done?"

"I would have told you never to use them again."

"Even if I had printed and sold your 'I Modi'?"

"In that case, I would have spanked you soundly, then told you never to use them again." He tapped her nose. "They are a kind of toy, Bride. A dilettante's hobby. I hope my pride is not so high that I would discard a friend over them."

Her throat burned. She did not deserve the trust he had shown. He had been generous about the Renaissance plates, but when his investigation was concluded, the limits of his kindness would be breached.

Soon. Mere days, he said.

He returned to the slow tantalization of her body. She released her hold on control and let pleasure and love conquer her fears one more time. One last time.

CHAPTER
TWENTY-FOUR

I wish you would let me come with you," Joan said.
Bride tucked the shirt into her breeches, then sat to pull on low boots. "If I am discovered, your presence would not make a difference, except you, too, would get caught. Hopefully I will enter and leave quickly and no one will be the wiser."

"And if someone is wise to you?"

Bride paused with a kerchief in her hands. *Someone will be wise to me soon, anyway. If I am caught tonight, perhaps it is for the best.*

She had thought long and hard since leaving Lyndale this evening. She was very sure that time was running out. There was the smallest chance, however, that she would be able to trace those plates before doom struck.

"If I am caught, you are to pretend ignorance of why I was there. And, Joan—if later the forgeries are discovered, and the plates tracked down, you are to pretend ignorance about them, as well. Let it be thought it was entirely my scheme. Save yourself and the others." She tied the dark blue kerchief around her hair. "There is no reason for all of us to be transported."

Joan's worried expression did not boost Bride's confidence. Her sister reached into the wardrobe. "At least take this."

Bride gazed at the pistol her sister offered. There was a sense to taking it. Eventually she would, but not now. "I could not shoot a constable in order to make an escape, nor would you want me to. I do not anticipate confronting the forgers tonight. I merely hope to discover the means to find them."

She held out her arms for Joan's inspection of her garments. Joan's solemn gaze assessed the dark green doublet and fawn breeches, and the kerchief hiding her tightly bound hair.

"Be quick, Bride. And be careful."

Bride stuck a small candle and a flint into her pocket.

Joan accompanied her down to the garden door. "If you do not return by dawn, I will go and ask Lord Lyndale for help."

Bride turned on her. "No. If I do not return, you are to assume I am gone for good and think only of protecting yourself. Run if you think you must, and do not wait to learn what has become of me. And do not go to Lyndale about me, no matter what happens."

Joan's brow furrowed. "I will obey your wishes on this, but I do not agree with them. Surely he would use his influence to help you, Bride."

Perhaps. Most likely. And that was the danger, because if Lyndale learned where she was going tonight, he might surmise why, and it would provide the link between her and the forgers.

She slipped out the door. She had a long walk ahead of her, and she strode with determination, eager to be done with the night's mission. She tried to keep all her attention on the dark streets and moving shadows, and her thoughts on the hours ahead.

Memories of the afternoon with Lyndale kept intruding. Her aching heart wanted to dwell on the sweet intimacy she had experienced, and the new closeness she had felt. In his arms, in their pleasure, there had been no danger waiting. No deceptions threatening to be revealed, and no duties demanding sacrifice.

But by the time his carriage left her at home, heartrending sorrow had claimed her. The next hour had left her desolate. Away from his warmth, away from that bed, she had been unable to deny the truth.

He knew about the forged banknotes. He was investigating them. She was sure of it. He did not know about the role the Cameron sisters had played yet. He expected to find the forgers soon, however, and then he would know everything.

He had been generous about the plates forging artistic compositions. She did not expect the same understanding if he learned there were banknote plates in her legacy, as well, and that she had actually used them.

She wiped her eyes and walked faster. She had

already decided that she would never see him again. Even if she succeeded in finding those plates first, she would break completely with him. She could not continue with that deception between them, even if he remained ignorant of it.

She hoped she would not be caught tonight. If her suspicions were right, if she succeeded, there was a chance, the smallest chance, that she could save her sisters.

She might also keep Lyndale from learning the whole truth.

The town was not all silence and darkness. Others walked in the shadows, and some carriages rolled down the streets. Lamplight glowed in some districts, casting pools of golden glow into the blackness. As she approached the City, the denizens of the night grew more numerous and she felt less alone.

She made her way to Fleet Street, and down the lanes to Twickenham's factory.

A small window revealed a dark and empty front room, and the door was locked. Satisfied that she was invisible within the cloak of night on this deserted street, she found her way to the back of the building. No candles or lamps showed through the back window, either. No sounds came through its glass.

She tried to pry open the window to the back room. It would not budge. She groped the ground for a loose paving stone. With a sharp tap, she broke a low pane of glass. Its pieces fell to the stones, sounding like a crystalline chime.

She hugged the outside wall and listened, her heart pounding, her legs ready to run. Silence echoed around her. No one raised a cry.

She swallowed the fear threatening to paralyze her. She reached in to release the latch and climbed in. She balanced on the edges of the vat under the window, then jumped down.

She lit her candle, and let her eyes adjust to the faint glow. She saw the stack of felts, but no paper dried between them. Moving the candle for illumination, she finally spied several stacks of paper on the edge of a table.

She dripped some wax near them, and set up her candle in it. Her touch told her which stack was wove paper, not laid. Its smooth surface also announced it had been carefully prepared, and was not very thick. She lifted one sheet and held it to the flame so the lines would be visible when it was backlit.

The patterns of the screen and watermark formed elaborate snaking shadows within the paper. They were the same patterns she had glimpsed as Twickenham raised his screen in front of the window.

Distinctive lines. Dense lines. In eight places that corresponded to the bottoms once the sheet was cut into eight pieces, the lines formed the words "Bank of England."

It wasn't a perfect forgery of the paper used for banknotes thirty years ago, but it was very close.

She had recognized those flowing lines in the fleeting moment before Twickenham dropped the screen back into the vat.

She suspected Lyndale had, as well.

She shook the excitement out of her head, and gazed at the paper. Soon Twickenham would deliver this paper to the forgers. She would have to watch this shop. She would have to follow the paper to the plates.

Her mind raced to assess if she could do that alone, or if she would need help. The temptation to confess all to Lyndale poked into her heart. Perhaps if she did, he would not force her sisters to share the punishment. Maybe his feelings for her would permit him to ignore the evidence that she had not done this alone.

Then again, maybe his sense of duty and betrayal would harden him so completely that there would be no generosity left.

She folded one sheet and tucked it into her doublet. She licked her fingers and reached to snuff the candles.

Sounds suddenly poured through the wall, coming from the front room. Voices hummed toward her. She froze with horror and her heart stopped.

Then she moved in a blur of panic. Blowing out the candle as she grabbed it, she hurried to the window. Her instincts shouted warnings as she heard movements on the other side of the door. Mind blanking to everything but the danger approaching, she climbed on the vat and bent to bolt out the opening.

Suddenly she was flying, twirling, as hands grabbed her legs and waist and threw her back into the room. She landed with a bone-shaking crash on the floor. The darkness spun, trying to absorb her.

A light flickered close to her face, and the dark forms of three heads loomed behind it.

"Damn, it's a *woman*."

Another curse sounded in a low hiss. Hands groped her body.

"What you doing to her there?" Twickenham's voice asked, shocked.

"Looking fur a pistol. This ane's been known to use them."

Dull resignation drained her strength. She knew that voice.

A nostalgic sorrow squeezed her heart, but she felt no shock.

The most honest corner of her soul was not as surprised as it should have been.

"I am only saying that it isn't proper, that is all."

Ewan sighed as the mutter rumbled into his ear. Michael was not going to let the topic drop, that was clear.

He aimed their progress through the dark City. Other steps clicked in the night's silence ten yards behind them, those of Dante Duclairc and Colin and Adrian Burchard.

"I have addressed you as Michael for years now. I am incapable of thinking of you any other way, let alone as Hawthorne."

"You do not address the steward by his given

name. All the others notice that I am not paid the same respect."

"It has nothing to do with respect or lack of it. The steward's given name is Spartacus. Why parents would do that to a son is beyond my comprehension, but if I addressed him as Spartacus, I would laugh every time."

"That isn't why you don't. You don't because it would *not be proper.*"

They turned off Fleet Street and Ewan's hand instinctively felt for the pistol under his coat. "Since when are you so particular about what is proper? We are above such petty concerns, Michael. Our relationship long ago transcended the normal bounds of such things."

"More friendly like, is that what you mean?"

"Exactly. If you were a typical servant, the kind I would call Hawthorne, you would not be with me on this adventure."

"I am only with you because I know how to pick locks."

"And what a useful skill it is. But I am wounded you think I only use you for my convenience in this matter."

They turned onto a narrow lane, one utterly deserted. The dark buildings announced that there were no residences here, but only small shops and factories.

"So we are chums, are we? Lads out looking for trouble together." Michael's voice lowered to a whisper. An annoyingly persistent one.

"Now you have it."

"Then I expect you won't mind my addressing you as Ewan."

Ewan looked at the dark form of the young man at his side.

"Fine, damn it. Hawthorne it is."

Their companions closed in with subdued steps. As a group they approached Twickenham's shop. It appeared deserted.

"I think I will go to the back, just in case," Colin said, turning to bleed into the night.

Ewan did not object, but it was an unnecessary precaution. Their numbers were not needed for this part of the mission. They had only come to procure evidence. Ewan was convinced that Twickenham had been making the banknote paper yesterday when he and Bride intruded. The glimpse of the screen held to the light had revealed the distinctive patterns. So had Ewan's quick glance at the top screen on the stack waiting for the pulp.

There should be no trouble at this stop on the night's adventure, however. Later, when they roused Twickenham from his sleep and forced him to take them to the forgers and the plates, pistols and strategies would more likely be employed.

He stood aside. "Deal with the lock."

Michael removed a steel stylus from his coat and bent to the lock. For several long moments he poked and fussed.

"Sorry, sir, but it isn't catching."

"Well, get it to catch, *Hawthorne*," Ewan said.

"What good is having a manservant with your background if he can't pick a simple lock."

Adrian Burchard held out his hand. "Allow me to try."

Michael's skeptical snort greeted the offer. He handed over the stylus.

Adrian poked, paused, and flicked his wrist. Ewan heard the lock click.

Michael made a low whistle of appreciation. "I don't suppose you could teach me how to do that, sir."

Adrian's head turned to Michael. The moment stretched.

"Just a hobby of mine, of course," Michael said. "Never know when it will come in handy for his lordship, is what I meant."

Ewan gave the door a push. It swung silently. He stepped inside.

And knew at once that they might need the pistols after all.

He threw out his arm to stop the others, and signaled for silence.

Light leaked through the crack beneath the door to the back room and streaked under the paper machine. Voices leaked, too. It sounded like an argument.

"Duclairc, make your way around back and join Colin. There is a window there. We don't want all of them bolting," he said.

"Remember that we need to hold them," Adrian said. "We need to retrieve the plates. That is our first goal."

Dante ran off down the lane. Ewan removed his

pistol from his coat. He sensed one in Adrian's hand, as well.

With Michael beside him and Adrian in his wake, he slowly walked around the machine to the back room's door. The argument continued, a rumble of low, indistinct sounds.

Ewan touched the door latch. He pushed the door slightly ajar and looked in.

His heart jumped.

Michael's head craned so he could see, too, and his sharp intake of breath sounded in Ewan's ear. It was fitting accompaniment to the alarm splitting Ewan's head.

"Jesus." Michael whispered so low it was barely audible. "Sir, what in hell is Bodisha doing here?"

What in hell was Bodisha doing here, indeed.

She sat on a stool in the corner farthest from the window. Two candles barely illuminated the chamber, and on first glance she might even be missed.

Much more compelling occupants stood in a clutch near the worktable along the far window wall. Their stances and tones said something serious was afoot, even if their curses and overlapping, guttural statements were too confusing to follow.

Despite Ewan's shock, the answer to Michael's question loomed. Bride was here because her father had not only forged erotic engravings. He had also turned his skill to more lucrative plates.

He peered at Bride and an unholy anger burst in

his head. Another reaction quickly shoved it aside. A desperate, furious urge to protect her.

He took the scene in through flashes of vision, as his instincts quickly assessed her danger.

Adrian shifted, a reminder that her biggest peril came not from the forgers, but from the man at his back.

Ewan's mind raced. She was dressed as a man. A kerchief hid her hair.

He swung his gaze to the window. It was open. Dante and Colin waited outside it. If she got out and revealed her identity, perhaps . . .

Only a few moments had passed since he edged the door open, but time had altered and slowed. Suddenly it righted itself. He nudged Michael and laid a finger on his lips. He prayed Michael would understand the call was for discretion, not mere silence.

Swallowing hard, Ewan pushed the door. It swung wide and banged, announcing their intrusion.

Twickenham froze in shock, but the others did not. With amazing speed of reaction, a tall blond man swerved, knocked one candle to the floor, and pulled down the stack of screens so they tumbled toward the door.

Confusion reigned. The pistols deterred no one. As Adrian and Michael joined the charge into the room, Ewan rushed to the corner where Bride had bolted to her feet. He kept his back to her while he grappled with Twickenham. His blood pounded with excitement during the ensuing melee, but he managed to speak one word to her.

"Go."

A flurry of fisticuffs swung in the dark. Grunts and curses rang in the air. Then suddenly silence fell and the room's occupants froze in a *tableau vivant*.

Ewan had Twickenham on the floor beneath his boot. Michael held a dark-haired gentleman in a death hold, with one arm around the man's neck. Adrian stood over the tall blond man, with a pistol pointed at his heart.

Bride was nowhere to be seen.

Only heavy breaths could be heard for several moments. Then Michael released his prisoner, swung him to hug the wall, and pressed his weight between the man's shoulder blades. In doing so, he repositioned himself closer to Adrian.

He glanced to the blond forger on the floor, then caught Ewan's eye and gestured.

Ewan gave Twickenham a look of warning. Twickenham stuck his face to the floor in resignation. Keeping the weapon ready, Ewan went over to Michael.

Michael angled his head toward Adrian. *"Look."*

Ewan looked. The features of the blond man took form in the dim light.

He had seen this man's face before. The countenance had been drawn with loving care on a little piece of paper tucked inside a leather holder.

It was Walter, Bride's lover.

CHAPTER
TWENTY-FIVE

Commotion crashed inside Twickenham's back room.

Bride crashed, too, squirming and kicking to break free of the hands holding her.

Strong arms wrapped her from behind and raised her off her feet in a bone-crushing hug. With a curse of surprise, the man released her just as abruptly. Breathless, she began sinking to the ground.

"Hell. It is a *woman*, Burchard."

More gently, but very firmly, he grabbed her under her arms and shoved her away from the window, into the shadows. Grasping her arm, he led her a fair distance, then set her back against the wall of a building.

Two men faced her as she gasped for breath. Her heart pounded in her ears. Silence poured out of the building now. She stared at the window down the lane, dreading the emergence or call of Lord Lyndale.

"Who are you?" her captor asked.

"She is very tall, Duclairc, and I got a glimpse of her face as she bolted out the window. I could be mistaken, but I suspect this is Miss Cameron."

"The Scottish woman he has been talking about? Is that who you are?"

"Yes."

"Did Lyndale recognize you?"

"Yes. He told me to go, so I climbed out once the fighting started."

"This is definitely Miss Cameron, Duclairc. I am Colin Burchard. I was with Lyndale that day you arrived in London. This is Dante Duclairc. I believe you know his sister, Lady Mardenford."

Voices dimly sounded within the building. Mr. Duclairc looked at the window, then at his companion. "If he told her to go, he did not want her found in there with the others."

"No, he did not. Forgive me, Miss Cameron." A hand lightly touched her head and kerchief, then skimmed down her side. "She may have even appeared to be a young man."

"If Adrian saw her, I doubt he was deceived," Dante said. "However, his goal is to find those plates, so this one's escape might not be his main concern right now."

Colin's head tipped toward her, as if trying to scrutinize her in the dark. "Miss Cameron, do you know where those plates are?"

"I do not. I swear it. I came here tonight on my own, hoping to find a way to discover their location.

I was caught in the chamber." She gestured to the broken window. "I did that to get in."

"So you knew about the plates. Since you come from a family of engravers, I am beginning to see the outlines of what transpired with these forgeries," Colin said. "Your situation is very precarious."

It was not precarious. It was hopeless. Nor would it matter if Adrian Burchard had seen her. Right now, in that chamber, Walter was probably pointing his finger at Bride and her father.

Her dread of facing Lyndale's scorn overshadowed her disappointment in Walter, but she still cringed as she admitted the miserable facts. She wanted to believe she had not been a total fool about him. After all, he had been with her in town the day of the theft, so she had never suspected him. He must have had someone else do the actual stealing, however.

She remembered his concern as he held her that night. She heard his vow to track the thieves and retrieve the plates. Lies, all of it.

Dante Duclairc struck a thoughtful pose, hands on hips. "Miss Cameron, Lyndale knew we were outside that window. He wanted you to escape the chamber, but we do not know if he wanted you to escape completely. I must insist that you come with me."

"Come with you where?"

"I am taking you to my house. Colin, join the others and tell them that I have taken chase after the one who got away. Let Ewan know privately what I have done. With any luck, Adrian will believe the story, for the present at least. As for you, Miss Cameron, it appears that your fate is in Lyndale's hands."

Ewan stood in the dark drawing room of the Duchess of Everdon's town house, gazing through a window into the night.

He was alone. In the adjoining library, Adrian Burchard, consort to the duchess and investigator for the government, was preparing to question the forgers.

They had all come here to avoid the waking city learning of the entire affair. Michael and Colin were in with Adrian, but Ewan had peeled away from the troop before the library doors closed.

He opened the window in hopes the crisp air would clear his head, but he barely felt the cold. Nor did his thoughts achieve the slightest clarity. His mind was not really in this drawing room at all, but in another one, looking at Bride.

Colin had whispered that Dante had her safely away, and Ewan had been grateful to hear it. That meant there was some chance he could save her.

Ewan McLean was desperate to find a means to do so. Lord Lyndale, however, was not sure he should.

A war waged inside him, one he never expected to experience.

Duty, duty . . .

Was she in it up to her neck?

His heart recoiled at the idea. His brain lined up

what he knew, about her questions regarding Walter and the forgers working in London.

Her friend, gone over a year now. The bastard must have stolen the plates and run.

She had not forged those plates, but she had used them. Not here, but before, in Scotland. He just knew she had. Walter would not have known they existed if she had not.

That was not the real reason for his certainty, however. Her melancholy at the cottage and her desire for them to part, the poignancy of their love-making today, now made sense. Anticipating she might soon be caught, she had wanted to sever his obligations to her.

Except he still had obligations, in ways nothing she did could change.

The devil of it was, the Earl of Lyndale also had obligations. He wished like hell that he could laugh that notion away, but it sat like a rock in his chest, giving physical pain.

She is a forger.

He closed his eyes and fought a scathing anger that wanted to rip his mind to shreds. Thank God the law had been changed. If she had been discovered a year earlier, she would have been hung.

How dare she be so careless with her life, her future? What had possessed her to take such risks?

And what an appalling conclusion to their affair. The one time in his life when a woman had actually mattered to him, and he now faced handing her over to be transported to the ends of the earth.

The library door opened. Colin slipped out and walked across the carpet toward the window.

He paused at the fireplace to light two cigars, and handed one to Ewan upon joining him. "Your man and Adrian are enough to handle them now. With two pistols at the ready, I am not needed."

"Is Adrian contented?"

"Not at all. They are not talking. It is clear they decided how to do it if they were caught. The dark-haired gentleman is the leader and he is sly enough to keep them quiet."

Thank God.

"Aside from Twickenham, we do not even know their names at this point," Colin said.

I do.

Would they maintain their silence? Once separated from the influence of his leader, would that bastard Walter keep his mouth shut?

Ewan pictured the cocky grin on the face gazing up into Adrian's lethal pistol.

Probably not.

Hell.

Colin puffed placidly on his cigar while Ewan chewed his own. The night breeze blew the smoke away.

"Do you know what Miss Cameron was doing there, McLean?"

Ewan glanced over at the silhouette of Colin's profile. The distant flame in the fireplace made little golden spots on his friend's blond hair.

"I think I know, yes. Do not ask me to explain."

"I did not intend to. Nor will Duclairc, I am sure. We will both respect your decision, whatever it is. If you prefer that the man who bolted from that room is never found, that is how it will be."

Ewan's throat burned. His friends' faith touched him all the more because he did not feel the least worthy of it right now.

He turned his attention to the night again and collected himself. "If it were you, Colin, what would you do?"

Colin thought during several long puffs on his cigar. "I envy you the dilemma, McLean. I envy that you care enough to be torn. If I felt like that about a woman, I think I would do whatever I could to protect her. And I would try to satisfy the government, as well, and give them what they want."

"I can at best offer them half a loaf. Will your brother be satisfied with that?"

"Adrian is very good at this, very experienced. I doubt he missed much about the escaped forger and how she got away. If he has not pressed me about it, that means he is awaiting developments."

Ewan absorbed the implications of what Colin said. "I will owe him her life. Which means I will owe him mine."

Colin laughed quietly. "One more obligation. Having that title is hell, isn't it?"

Ewan looked down at the glowing tip of his cigar. *Give them what they want.* He could do that. After all, they did not really want Bride Cameron.

Ewan entered the library during an obvious impasse.

Michael stood guard with a pistol. Adrian Burchard stood near the fireplace, intimidating the three seated culprits with his height and barely checked anger. His own pistol rested on the mantel, in pointed warning, lest the criminals think of bolting.

Ewan sensed a question had just been asked. It still hung in the air.

He turned his attention on Walter and his hand involuntarily clenched into a fist.

What had Bride seen in this cocky, husky Highlander? Walter wore a smile, as if he did not comprehend his peril.

Only Twickenham appeared distraught at the night's events. The third man, the dark-haired one dressed as a gentleman, projected the most placid of demeanors.

"Your names," Adrian demanded. His tone indicated it was not the first time for the query and that he intended to knock heads if he had to ask again.

Walter said nothing and folded his arms.

The gentleman, who was clearly astute enough to sense danger when it was present, cleared his throat. "Oratio Tomlinson."

"He is lying," Ewan said. "Burchard, this gentleman is Peter Ramsey, a bookseller and print dealer from Newcastle. We met once, years ago, Ramsey, when I visited your establishment."

"And you would be? . . ."

"Ewan McLean."

He used his name for a reason. Lights of comprehension immediately sparked in Ramsey's eyes.

It was not only Ewan McLean's reputation as a collector that provoked that gleam. Ramsey would remember the name of the person who had bought the forged *"I Modi"* that he had put up at auction at Bonham's. Ewan subtly nodded, to let Ramsey know that deception had been discovered, as well.

"At least now I know with whom I am dealing. Mr. Ramsey, where are the plates?" Adrian asked.

Ewan hoped the forgers would stand their ground.

For one thing, and the reason the least honorable among many that lacked honor, he fully expected Adrian Burchard to use his fists if necessary, to get the information.

If so, he would encourage him to start with Walter, who appeared too stupid to recognize how a lethal edge had risen in Adrian's demeanor.

"The plates," Adrian said again. "The paper alone is enough to convict you, so have no illusions that you will escape punishment by dissembling."

Ramsey leaned against the back of his chair, almost nonchalant. "If we are going to be transported anyway, why should we give you the plates?"

Sweat was streaming down Twickenham's face. "I'd give 'em to you if I knew where they was, I swear. I never saw them or—"

"Be *quiet*," Ramsey snapped. He looked at Walter. "You, too."

Adrian turned his attention fully on Ramsey. "Who engraved them? You?"

"The man who engraved them is dead. They were found among his belongings. I do not know if he ever used them himself."

"And the forger of the signatures?" Ewan asked. "Badly done, by the way."

"Yes, well, that was an unexpected complication. One of our members went and died of malaria right when all was in place to start. Finding another to take his place was risky and difficult. I have a good hand, so . . ."

"So you did it yourself," Ewan finished. "Careless decision."

Ramsey sighed. "Apparently so."

"A dead engraver and a dead signature forger, a papermaker right here, and no doubt the press was hired with the owner unaware of its use. It appears we have all of them, Burchard," Ewan announced victory with confident authority.

Walter grinned. "Och, noo, Burchard, Ah'm not sure as that is—"

His sentence dissolved into a howl as Michael punched him on the back of his sandy head.

"The gentleman said to be quiet," Michael said. He looked at Adrian and shook his head. "My apologies for losing my temper, sir, but I've just no patience at all with his sort, being so familiar in his addresses and not obeying his betters. It makes all of us look bad."

Adrian ignored Walter's anguished expression.

"It appears all of you will not cooperate and disclose the location of the plates. We will hand you to the police, therefore, and let them deal with you. Perhaps some time in Newgate will make you amenable to answering my questions."

That sounded like an opening for the "further developments" that Colin had suggested Adrian anticipated. Ewan sidled over to Adrian. "A private word, if you will."

After gesturing to Michael to stay alert for trouble, Adrian followed Ewan out to the library. Colin noted their arrival, but remained near the window.

Ewan faced Adrian in front of the fireplace. Adrian's dark, foreign eyes appeared as deep, black pools in this light, and his long wavy hair did little to soften the countenance turned hard by the night's events.

This particular Burchard was more mysterious and deep than Colin, but he was from all accounts an honorable man.

Unfortunately, at the moment it would help immensely if he were not.

"We want the plates, correct?" Ewan said. "If the engraver is dead, and I have reason to believe he is, once the plates are destroyed there will be no further forgery from this lot."

"The plates must be found, yes. What makes you so sure the engraver is dead?"

"My expertise. The same superb eye that dragged me into this investigation. I think I identified the forger's hand and know who he was. Do not ask me for the name. I would never accuse a man who cannot defend himself on account of being underground."

Adrian appeared skeptical, as well he might.

"So, we need the plates," Ewan continued, trying to sound like a responsible lord of the realm. "The longer they refuse to disclose their location, the more chance those plates will be discovered by someone else. I say it is imperative that we get to them at once. By Zeus, man, the future solvency of Britain is at stake. Duty calls, and we mustn't allow our delicate sense of justice to interfere."

Adrian shifted his weight just enough to express subdued amusement. "Your fervor is unexpected, but your points well taken."

"The title has done that to me. Made me serious and zealous about my responsibilities, that is."

"Commendable. However, you are correct, and we should not delay. It looks like we will have to beat it out of them. That blond one is all bluff, and should break quickly enough." He turned toward the door.

"No." Ewan grabbed his arm. "Good heavens, we are civilized, are we not? British gentlemen. We cannot just beat it out of them."

Much as he wanted to see Walter bloodied, in truth he could not allow it. Who knew what Walter would blurt? "Ramsey has intimated he is willing to trade information for freedom. Allow me and your brother to speak with them alone. You will not be responsible for whatever transpires. With luck, the results will be efficient and the matter finished."

Adrian looked at Ewan as directly as any man ever had. His dark eyes reflected a disturbing level of comprehension. "They are not to remain in Britain."

"Of course. I swear that those men in there will be gone on the next packet. Furthermore, if we cannot deliver the plates to you by dawn, you can have them dragged off to Newgate."

Colin strolled over. "I could not help but overhear. It sounds sensible to me, Adrian. It will ensure you have the plates. The plates are the true danger."

"The true danger, but not the only problem. There are notes being used that will someday be identified as forgeries. Whoever holds them will be suspect, or at least out the money," Adrian said.

Ewan cleared his throat and thought fast. "Say, I have been considering some charitable giving now that I am the earl. Good works and all that. Suppose I set aside a sum to cover such eventualities? It is as noble a cause as any."

"How good of you, McLean," Colin said.

Adrian thought it over, then nodded. He moved, but not toward the library. Instead he walked down the length of the drawing room to another set of doors.

"He knows absolutely everything, doesn't he?" Ewan said.

"I may have mentioned during a conversation a

week or so ago that you had a *tendre* for this Scottish woman who was an engraver."

Ewan strode to the library. "Well, *thank you,* Colin. The next time you are drinking brandy with your brother and discussing my affairs, be sure to tell him that she *did not* make those plates."

"You are sure about that, I suppose."

"Yes." And his heart was.

The rest of him wasn't sure about anything anymore.

Within ten minutes of returning to the library, Ewan had the location of the plates. He also had the assurance that Twickenham, Ramsey, and Walter would flee Britain immediately or risk being hunted down like dogs.

Convinced all was in order, he gestured to the library door. "Mr. Colin Burchard here will accompany you to the plates. Once he has them, he will see that you are on a boat soon."

Colin opened the door and left. Twickenham was out in an instant. Ramsey took his time but eventually disappeared, too. Walter brought up the rear.

"Not you," Ewan said. "Not just yet."

Michael stepped between Walter and the door, closed it, and turned the lock. Walter pivoted in surprise.

Ewan shed his frock coat. "You are free to defend yourself, you bastard. No one is going to shoot you or hold you down."

Walter looked around, amused and confused. "Whit ye want wi' me? Ramsey planned it all, him and Bloomfield wha was to do the signatures."

"They planned it, but without you there would be no plan, because there would be no plates. You betrayed a helpless woman to get them, and then went looking for men who would know how to use them."

"*Helpless?* Hell. Clear *ye* hae ne'er met her. Stubborn coo. Had the means to a fortune tucked in her stupid trunk, but did she use it? Only in wee bits, and then she went and *gave the money away.*" Laughing, he shook his head in disbelief. "Stupid co—"

Ewan's fist connected before the insult could be repeated. It smashed into Walter's jaw. The blond head jerked back and Walter staggered.

Ewan swung again, bloodying Walter's nose. "Those are for her sisters, and the danger you put them in. The rest will be for Bride. Hawthorne, be sure to stop me before I kill him."

CHAPTER
TWENTY-SIX

A large fire warmed the drawing room, but Bride was shivering.

The high blaze was for Mr. Duclairc's wife, Fleur. He had built it up when she insisted on sitting with Bride.

Fleur's conversation about commonplace things had relieved the room of its earlier quaking silence, but Bride could not ignore that they all sat here because they were waiting for something terrible to happen.

To her.

She did not know what she dreaded more, gaol and transportation, or facing Lyndale.

Perhaps she would not have to suffer the latter punishment. Maybe he would allow the last sorry chapter in their affair to be written without his presence.

She hoped so.

"It will be dawn soon," Fleur said. "Once the servants have risen, I will see that a breakfast is laid out at once. You must be hungry."

Her hostess was willowy and pale, with a dark head of hair and naturally red lips. Mrs. Duclairc epitomized fragile, feminine grace.

In the best of circumstances Bride would have suffered in comparison. Dressed in boots and breeches, she probably looked comical sitting across from this lady and her equally beautiful husband.

"Please do not inconvenience your household, madame. I am not hungry at all." Worry and fear had made her nauseous. She did not think she could ever eat again. "Although, if a message could be sent to my sisters, Mr. Duclairc, I would be grateful."

"I sent one immediately upon our arrival here, so they would know you had come to no harm. Once McLean arrives, a fuller explanation can be sent."

Bride did not miss his sympathetic, gentle tone. Mr. Duclairc seemed confident what that explanation would be. He did not expect it to contain good news for her sisters.

He made an odd gaoler. He was very handsome, with a charming smile. An effortless elegance marked his movements and dress. Lady Mardenford had said her brother Dante had been part of Lyndale's set until his recent marriage to Fleur, and Bride suspected he had been a very successful bachelor.

No one could mistake that he was thoroughly married now, however. He treated his wife with a warmth that touched Bride's heart. The bulge evident beneath Fleur's undressing gown was not the only reason for his care, either. It was not only the coming child that provoked this man's love.

Fleur's hand instinctively went to her stomach when she saw Bride's attention there.

"Perhaps you would like to rest, madame," Bride said. "I am grateful that you have helped me pass these last hours, but what will transpire next will not be pleasant."

"I do nothing but rest. Dante sees to that. If you expect unpleasantness, that is all the more reason for you to have company as you wait. Whatever the reason for this vigil, I am sure that you distress yourself more than is required. Lord Lyndale does not abandon his friends quickly. Is that not so, Dante?"

Mr. Duclairc nodded, but his agreement was noncommittal. Unlike his wife, he knew just how distressing the current situation was.

Bride's hearing had been stretching for hours, listening for the sounds of Lyndale's arrival. Or that of the police. The effort exhausted her, and her senses had dulled.

Suddenly they sharpened. Amid the vague noises outside that spoke of a city wakening, she thought she heard horses and wheels.

She glanced to Mr. Duclairc. His eyes reflected a new concentration. He had heard the carriage, too.

He rose, and offered his hand to his wife. "It would be best if we left now, Miss Cameron. Come,

Fleur. It is past time you returned to bed for the rest Miss Cameron advised."

Clearly reluctant, Fleur obeyed, but not before she gave Bride a reassuring smile. "Lord Lyndale is really a very nice man, and much kinder than he pretends. If your fate is in his hands, I do not think that is such a bad place to be."

Bride smiled weakly. This gentle, lovely lady had no idea what was at stake. There had been oblique references to the disaster in her presence, but nothing to inform her that the oddly dressed woman in her home had been exposed as a criminal.

Mr. Duclairc's parting offered no reassurance. "If I can be of any assistance, Miss Cameron, please do not hesitate to inform me."

They left. Minutes later Bride heard distant sounds of a door opening and voices speaking. Her heart pounded out every second. She braced herself.

She was able to steel her composure, but not her heart. A fissure of regret and sorrow cleaved it in two.

A figure darkened the doorway. Only one man had come up the stairs. Lyndale was alone.

No doubt he had come to prepare her before bringing her to the police.

Bride wanted to embrace him for that consideration, and for so much else. Instead she stayed in her chair during a long pause while he stood there looking at her.

Finally he crossed the room and sat on the sofa facing her, right where Fleur had just been.

He appeared quite stern. The good humor that usually softened his countenance was gone.

"Have you gotten some rest?" he asked.

"Not really, although Mr. Duclairc did his best to see to my comfort."

He relaxed into the sofa's bulk, as if he intended to stay a while. "Did you fall in love with Dante? All women do. He was the bane of my life before he married. I would pursue women, only to discover half of them were pursuing him. For some reason he seemed safe to them. I never understood that."

She had to smile. It made her face feel strange. "I could never fall in love with a man who so obviously loves his wife."

"Remarkable, isn't it? When it happened, I was skeptical at first, but finally I accepted he was besotted." He looked around the chamber, as if taking an inventory of its holdings. "This is one of the few respectable homes to receive me before I inherited the title. Fleur did not demand Dante end our friendship, and even invited me to their first dinner party. It was a kindness I will never forget."

An honest, boyish expression flickered over his face as he said it. Bride bit her lower lip. It was an odd moment for confidences that revealed one's heart.

Lyndale gazed at the fireplace as if the flames mesmerized him. Bride branded her mind with his appearance, trying to contain the pain in her heart.

He turned his gaze directly on her.

"You really came to London to find those plates, didn't you? And to find your lover."

Her heart cringed at the calm way he referred to Walter. "I became aware the plates were being used. Then I learned one forgery had been passed in London. Of course I had to try and find them. The forging was sure to be discovered."

"Fortunately, they did not print too many notes. A thousand pounds' worth, at most. We caught them just in time. That paper at Twickenham's was going to be used for one massive haul before they absconded to the Continent with a fortune."

"It is fortunate indeed that they were stopped."

He cocked his elbow on the sofa's arm, rested his chin on his fist and regarded her. She tried to fathom what he thought, but his expression remained closed to her.

"Dante just told me that you explained how it started," he said. "How your father had used the money from the notes."

She had told Mr. Duclairc in the hopes he would tell Lyndale, should she be denied the chance to do so.

"When I was a girl, my father would leave for a few days and ride south to Sutherland where the clearances were being enforced. I learned later he was passing out coin to the families, coin obtained by passing the forged notes in towns and cities."

"The faerie. He became a legend. Did you take his place so they would not be disappointed?"

"Not a first. After he died, I stopped it for a while."

"What made you begin again?"

"On one journey to Edinburgh, I saw firsthand what was happening as I passed through Sutherland. I understood my father then, and why he had made the choice he did. Then our county was sold and it began happening right in front of me. People would stop at our house, begging. I saw old and young going hungry, and the weak suffering." Her voice caught. "I know the circumstances do not absolve me. It was a crime, and I knew it."

Furious sparks entered his eyes. "You would have hung if they caught you even two years ago."

"I had the means to help those people. I weighed the risk and the sin, and I discovered that I could not refuse to help. Not a penny was used for ourselves, not ever."

"No judge would accept your excuse, no matter how noble it was."

"I am not making excuses to a judge. I am giving my lover an explanation." She exhaled her weariness. "I expect no mercy. I am telling you, so that maybe you will not hate me too much."

The lightning in his eyes dimmed and deepened until his gaze reflected layers she could not see.

"There are other plates, I assume. Smaller denominations. You would not be so stupid as to pass the large notes."

She nodded, feeling miserable. "I never used the big ones. The plates for five and ten pound notes, the ones I used, were not stolen because they were in the studio drawer and not the trunk."

"We will leave soon and retrieve them from your house. They must be destroyed at once."

"Of course." She realized that was another reason why he had come. He wanted to procure those other plates. "I am prepared to face whatever is coming. I would be grateful if you will spare my sisters. This was all my doing, not theirs. They had no idea—"

"Nonsense." His voice snapped and his eyes blazed. "You were all in it up to your pretty necks. Was that your plan all along? If you were discovered, you would throw yourself into the breach all alone and save them? You did not forge the signatures, Bride. I have seen no indication you have that skill."

"You have no proof I do not. No proof they were involved. I am begging you to spare my sisters. There is no need for their lives to be destroyed. I was the eldest. This was my plan, my decision, and I alone am responsible."

"As usual, you have it all worked out." He rose with exasperation and hovered over her. "This is the resolution you see? I hand you over for trial and you trade yourself for your sisters? That is the help you expect from me?"

Her head instinctively bowed in front of his anger. "I know I have no right to expect it. I know that I have compromised you enough already."

"Hell, *yes,* you have compromised me. Thoroughly. I was left to choose between you and this damned duty that has been thrust on me. Between you and what little honor I ever claimed to possess."

The room shook from his fury. It seemed to rattle the vases and china figurines.

The ensuing silence was horrible. She stared at the carpet beneath her boots, unable to summon one word on her own behalf.

"I had to choose," he said, his voice suddenly calm and mellow. Resigned. Almost gentle. "Only I discovered there was no real choice. The man who betrayed you by stealing those plates will be on his way to France in a few days. So will the others. We have the plates and the paper. As compromises go, it was not too dishonorable."

She looked up. His meaning penetrated her desolation. Tears began blurring her eyes.

He gazed down warmly, but the edge of anger had not receded. "Walter did not name you. Be glad he was under the influence of a man with some intelligence, because on his own he would have sold you for a hot meal in prison."

She pulled off her kerchief, and wiped her eyes with it. "You must think me a great fool. It appears the loneliness of an aging spinster made me blind."

"Yes, you were a great fool with him. Just as you have been with me. I have been grateful for whatever makes you blind to a worthless man's faults, however, so I cannot blame you about him."

"You are not worthless." Her scathing throat barely let the words out. If she tried to speak louder she would sob.

He paced away. "Unfortunately, the night's events mean that you are stuck with my faults for good. I have asked you to marry me before. Now I must insist on it. My actions on your behalf leave me more exposed than I like. There is an honest man who turned a blind eye tonight, but he will not a second time. Should you take up forging again, my complicity will be apparent."

"I would never—"

"You are as good an engraver as your father. Should your sympathies for the poor and oppressed move you again, you have the skill and the intelligence to do it."

"You have my word I would not."

"Forgive me if I demand more assurance. We will marry. I can keep an eye on you and your sisters, then. I am decided on this and will brook no arguments to the contrary." He folded his arms over his chest. "As for the recipients of your largesse, we will find a more suitable way to aid them. I daresay I can replace the income from those forged plates with little pain to my pocket."

He announced her sentence in the most lordly manner. His shield of arrogance declared that the matter was settled.

His proclamation and imperious pose calmed her at once.

Her heart ached with gratitude and love. It was so full she could barely breathe.

"It is an odd prison you condemn me to, my lord. After all, you will be the one in chains."

"I am a peer. It is impossible to chain us. You will be the one under close confinement."

"This is a most peculiar proposal, however. I am convinced you make it without comprehending the dire implications for you if I accept."

"I do not see any dire implications for *me*."

She rose and moved close to him. "They are most dire. You see, if I accept, it will not be because you demand it, nor to save myself, nor even to save my sisters."

He reached out and wiped a line of tears from her cheek. "Do not say it will be out of gratitude, Bride. Of all the possible reasons, that would be the worst."

"No, not gratitude, although I owe you my life. If I accept, it will be because I love you to the depths of my heart. All that you are, faults and all."

His pose cracked. His arms fell to his sides. Warmth entered his eyes, hinting at astonishment and a very masculine, fearful hope.

"And are you inclined to accept, Bride?"

"Most definitely. Because I do love you, very much. A life with you would make me happy even if we dwelled in poverty in a Highland glen. However, if you offer out of practicality or compromise, I cannot accept. If I loved a man within a marriage like that, I would indeed be enchained and imprisoned. The torture would be worse than any misery that occurs when one is transported."

His brow puckered. He looked to the fire, as if debating with himself.

His lips parted, then closed, like something blocked the impulse to speak.

He took a deep breath. "Would it make a difference if I admitted that more moved me than what I have stated thus far?"

She fought to hold in the reckless hope that wanted to explode in her. "It would make all the difference in the world."

His jaw twitched. His eyes blinked. He took another deep breath.

"Then, although I will insist that you marry me because of tonight if necessary, I request that you do so because I love you most dearly."

A surprised, bemused smile broke on his face. He looked like a man who had just jumped off a cliff and discovered to his amazement that the fall did not kill him.

"I would be proud to be your wife, Ewan."

He pulled her into an embrace. "You have stolen my heart, Bride. I cannot deny that in this I am your captive. I love you and there is no other woman for me except you."

He kissed her firmly. Seductively. She was so happy she felt unreal, as if the moment were a dream.

"I am glad your heart is completely mine, Lyndale, and that I am the only woman for you. Because should you think to break that chain and turn to another, there will be hell to pay."

"Big scenes, you warned. I am prepared."

"Are you? Remember, please, that I am very good with a pistol!"

His expression fell just enough to satisfy her.

"You are joking, of course."

"I will not share you. It would break my heart if you took another lover, and there is no telling what I would do then."

"I thought you loved me faults and all."

"I never said I would not expect some small improvements."

The dire implications she had alluded to were now clarified.

It surprised him enough that his embrace loosened. His hands came to rest on her shoulders. His gaze penetrated hers, as if he sought to learn if she really meant it. But his vision also turned inward, and his expression very serious.

She watched him with her heart in her throat as he weighed her demand.

"How odd," he muttered.

"Odd?"

"I am picturing a life of relentless fidelity to you, and the notion does not dismay me. I cannot imagine wanting another woman, nor could I hurt you that way if I ever did. I am very sure I can be faithful." A devilish glint entered his eyes. "Of course, I am also picturing untold rewards for my good behavior, too."

"I promise to make it worth your while, my love."

He wrapped his arms around her. Love poured through her, evoking both heady excitement and a perfect, contented peace. She wanted to weep with happiness and also shout with joy.

Being loved by this man felt so good. Loving him felt even better.

A dramatic little sigh escaped him.

"What is wrong, Lyndale?"

"Nothing really. I am deliriously happy, I promise you. Only it has all turned out just as I feared. Inheriting the title has destroyed the life I knew."

"Do you mind too much?"

His low laugh carried a note of wonder. He gave her a sweet kiss.

"The Earl of Lyndale finds he does not mind at all, my darling Bride. Ewan McLean, however, is stunned beyond words."

ABOUT THE AUTHOR

MADELINE HUNTER'S first novel was published in June 2000. Since then she has seen ten historical romances and one novella published, and her books have been translated into five languages. She is a four-time RITA finalist and won the long historical RITA in 2003. Nine of her books have been on the *USA Today* bestseller list, and she has also had titles on the *New York Times* extended list. Madeline has a Ph.D. in art history, which she teaches at an eastern university. She currently lives in Pennsylvania with her husband and two sons. She can be contacted through her website: www.madelinehunter.com.

And look for

ONE
SCANDALOUS NIGHT

by

Madeline Hunter

Coming from Bantam in March
2006
Read on for a preview . . .

ONE SCANDALOUS NIGHT

On sale March 2006

Nathaniel Knightridge dwelled in a special hell, one where men of action and command are rendered powerless by events beyond their control.

Chained in that underworld of the spirit, he awaited the dreadful result of his impotence. The chill in his body could not be warmed by either the fire he sat beside or the brandy he freely imbibed.

The spirits dulled his mind enough to keep his futile fury contained, but not so much that he did not hear every damned tick of the damned clock. It constantly poked at his soul from its place on a far table in the sitting room of his apartment in The Albany.

He stared at the fire's flames, all too aware that his vigil paled compared to another being endured a few miles away.

"Sir." The address came quietly. Tentatively.

Nathaniel slowly turned his gaze to the doorway. Jacobs, his manservant, stood there. Jacobs' aging, cherubic face wore a caution born of Nathaniel's angry outbursts all day long.

"A lady is here, sir. She went to your chambers and your clerk directed her here. She insists it is most important."

"If she is here, she cannot be too much a lady."

"Oh, but she is." Jacobs proffered a silver salver. "Her card, sir."

"Tell her I am not receiving."

"But it is—"

"Send her away, damn you."

Jacobs left. Nathaniel poured more brandy. He did not need to look at the clock to know the time. A half-hour remained, no more.

He gulped enough of the spirits to send his mind flying for a few blissful moments.

It did not last. Soon he was back in the chair, half-foxed but mercilessly aware. Of the clock. And of voices. Jacobs' and a woman's. Their alternating high and low rumble approached and grew louder until the words became audible.

"I tell you again, my lady, that Mr. Knightridge is not receiving."

"And I tell you that this cannot wait. I do not have the leisure to waste another day looking all over town for him."

Despite the muffling effects of the thick door, that voice sounded familiar. Nathaniel's dulled sense tried to poke around his fogged brain to identify it.

The door opened. Jacobs entered, looking apologetic and helpless. A woman sailed in behind him.

Nathaniel took in the dark hair beneath the crepe

bonnet's cream brim, the middling height of perfect posture, the crimson mantle trimmed in fur. Her hand grasped the ivory handle of a parasol.

As she brazenly intruded on his private misery, she passed one half-draped window. The overcast day's silver light revealed her lovely, determined face.

"Oh, God have mercy," Nathaniel muttered.

"Charlotte, Lady Mardenford," Jacobs announced.

Charlotte waited for Mr. Knightridge to stand and greet her. Instead he propped his elbow on his chair's arm and rested his forehead in his hand. The pose communicated weary resignation. It also obscured his eyes.

Dark eyes. Deep set and compelling. They contrasted dramatically with his golden hair.

Those eyes could mesmerize like an actor's, and he used them to deliberate effect. Mr. Knightridge did not perform in the theater, but he was known to command different kinds of stages. Those in courtrooms and drawing rooms.

Women were especially vulnerable to his magnetic presence. That was one reason why Charlotte had sought him out today despite her determined efforts to avoid him the last month.

The other reason for her visit, the one that had led her to this apartment today and not his chambers tomorrow, involved his seclusion in this shadowed sitting room and his disheveled appearance.

He finally acknowledged her with a sour, exasperated glance. A long strand of his collar-length hair hung over one eye in a lazy, sinuous curve. His waistcoat was unbuttoned and his collar and cuffs loose. He was the kind of man who still looked handsome when he was unkempt. Disarray became him. She could do without the roguish danger he projected in this state, however.

She removed her mantle and handed it to the servant, who retreated. She positioned herself so that she could not be ignored.

Mr. Knightridge remained in his deeply upholstered chair, his tall body slouched and stretched. He looked her over slowly. Annoyance hardened his countenance.

Then it faded, as if other thoughts had claimed his mind.

He turned his face away and gazed into the flames. His hair, swept back from his high brow except for the errant lock, permitted his profile to chisel the space around it. With its high cheekbones and straight nose and full lips, it was a handsome face but not very soft even in the best of situations, which this definitely was not.

The chamber fell silent, except for the ticking of a clock on a far table.

Charlotte had not expected the visit to start this badly. Then again, she had not anticipated joyful welcome either. After all, she and Nathaniel Knightridge did not like each other very much.

"You are being rude," she said.

He sighed. "No, madame, you are being rude. My man told you I am not receiving and I will not humor this inexplicable invasion. I am in no mood for social calls today. Jacobs will see you out."

"This is not a social call. I am here to discuss business."

"In case you did not notice, I am almost drunk and intend to be thoroughly so very soon. I am in no condition to conduct business, so it must wait."

"It cannot wait."

"Then find another man to irritate with it."

They had never rubbed well together, but he was being unusually blunt today. His behavior would be inexcusable if she did not know the reason for it.

She set down her parasol so he would know she did not intend to leave. The action drew his attention back to her.

"This may not be a good day to put aside your weapons, Lady Mardenford."

"I have never needed weapons with you."

"You act as if you do. You carry a parasol like a sword. You have one with you even in winter when the sun does not shine. I keep expecting you to stab me with it."

"I would never stab you. I might hit you with it if you gave me cause, but never stab."

"If you insist on staying, I may give you such cause. Hence my warning."

"You are being deliberately provocative today. While you have never been what I would call gracious, this is extreme."

His gaze sharpened, then warmed as it took her in again. Male calculation reflected in his eyes, and deep predatory sparks in them made her neck prickle.

It was a boldly familiar gaze, and it aroused both caution and concern in her, along with an irritating, sensual stirring. It was not a look that a gentleman should let a lady see. It entered her head that his inebriated state not only freed him from the normal constraints, but also permitted him to perceive and remember more than he did while sober.

"You are a fine one to speak of being provocative. It is no mistake, I think, that you donned that dress for this visit. It shows a lot of shoulder. When I see that much of a woman's skin, I know she wants something." He smiled, not kindly. "What is it you want, Lady M.?"

She felt the skin he observed flushing. Her cross bodice did show a bit of shoulder and neck, but not enough to warrant comment. Nor had she chosen it because of this visit. She had a full day scheduled and could not bear spending hours on the town trussed into the stiff stomachers that had become fashionable again for some malicious reason.

Just like Mr. Knightridge to assume a woman dressed only for his benefit.

She composed a sharp response, only to realize he wasn't waiting for one. His mind had turned elsewhere again. She thought she knew where.

The clock chimed the three-quarter hour. It startled him out of the reverie into which he had drifted. "You really should leave. Your visiting me alone could create a scandal."

"If anyone saw me arrive, which no one did, they would assume I sought your counsel, just as I am doing. Besides, the whole town knows we do not have a warm friendship. My reputation is quite safe with you."

Since he showed no inclination to invite her to

sit, she took it upon herself to do so. She perched on a cane-backed settee that faced him. From her new position she could see a decanter and glass on the rug beside his chair.

"When you hear why I have come, you will not mind the intrusion," she said.

"I promise you that I will since I already do."

"Hear me out, that is all I ask."

"Do I have a choice?"

"As you know, I am hosting a meeting in four days time. The goal is to begin petitions to send to Parliament requesting changes in the laws governing married women. Including, of course, the laws of divorce."

"I received your invitation. You did not need to call."

"I feared you would not accept because of our—well, our occasional disagreements."

"Occasional? Madame, you and I are incapable of forming a right understanding on any subject."

That was not true. Twice they had come to complete agreement. One time they had not even needed words to know the other's mind.

Of course, he was unaware of that. She was the only one who incurred a debt because of it.

She forged ahead. "I have come to explain why you need to be there. Three times now you have served as defense counsel in trials that touched on the misery some wives endure—"

"Four. I have been involved in four such trials. There was one you would not know about. But go on, please." His voice sounded bored, as if she engaged half his attention at best.

"You have seen and heard firsthand how some women suffer. You know better than most the inequities under the law. If you attend the meeting, your mere presence will lend weight to our cause."

"The testimony of lawyers who argue divorces in the ecclesiastical courts will aid you more. My experience only touches on the cases where a bad union leads to tragedy, and those examples will only turn many against you."

"I think you are wrong. There is great sympathy for women who have needed the voice you lend. Also, your fame alone will attract others to the meeting."

He began to respond, but stopped. His eyes glazed. What little attention he gave her flew away.

His hand reached down, found the decanter, and poured liquid into the glass. Lifting the glass, he rose and walked away.

Toward the ticking clock.

"What say you, sir? Will you attend?"

He stood at the other side of the chamber, his back to her. He tilted his head to drink.

"You want me there because I am notorious."

"Not notorious. Famous."

"It is the fame of a circus performer."

"You are much admired. The ladies in particular will appreciate your presence, as you well know."

"You want me because I will attract a crowd? Worse than a circus performer, then. I will be your dancing dog at a village market."

"You will dance to a very pleasant tune. I daresay you will have your pick of the gawkers when all is done, so there will be compensation."

She expected that to recapture his attention. At least she expected a barbed response. Instead he did not move or speak. He just stood there near the clock. Silence fell until only its ticks sounded.

She searched for something else to say, something to disperse the terrible atmosphere gathering. Normally Mr. Knightridge and she ended up arguing when they spoke at all, and a row would be better than this.

Anything would be preferable to the awful expectation that thickened the air.

Time stretched and slowed. The clock's sounds got louder as the silence deepened. They became a beat matching the throb in her chest. From the way his stance grew taut, she knew the hour's chime was imminent.

"My apologies, Lady Mardenford, but I am too drunk to behave civilly. You should leave now."

Yes, she probably should.

She could not. She sensed his turmoil and it twisted her heart. He stood tall, strong and straight, but he looked very alone there. Almost . . . vulnerable.

She owed him much more than he would ever guess, and sharing this terrible vigil was the least of it.

She knew when the moment was almost upon them. He threw back the last of his brandy, then went deathly still. She realized she was gripping the arm of her settee so hard that her fingers hurt.

The clock chimed twice.

The sounds echoed in the chamber for a long time, then left a quaking silence.

Nathaniel abruptly turned. He hurled his glass. It

flew across the chamber into a window, smashing a pane on its path out to the city.

The sudden movement and explosion made her jump.

She could see his face now. Eyes blazing and teeth bared, he wore a mask of fury. Beneath the anger, however, deep in those eyes, something else burned. Raw anguish.

She had not expected such a violent reaction. She had not known it would affect him this deeply.

It had probably been unwise to come.

She should have left when he asked, but she had not. Now she was glimpsing something she had no right to see.

His hard gaze moved from the shattered window to her. His glare made her swallow hard.

She stood and took a few steps toward him. "It was not your fault. You did your best."

His eyes blazed as he realized that she knew what this hour meant. "An innocent man just hanged. Man, *hell*. He was a *boy*. It does not matter that I did my best. It wasn't good enough, damn it."

"You do not know for certain Harry Binchley was innocent. Perhaps—"

"He committed crimes enough in his short life, but not this murder."

"You cannot be sure of that."

"I *know*." He advanced on her. "Do you think I do this for my amusement? For the *fame* you say I have? I know the guilt or innocence of those I defend or I would not speak for them."

He walked right up to her until he was so close she

had the urge to step back. "I look in their eyes and it is all there. No matter how jaded or cold those eyes may be, the soul is visible if you look deeply enough."

He looked in her eyes that way. His gaze pierced until she feared he really could see one's soul.

She fought to hold the invasion at bay. She scrambled to throw up barriers to protect the corners that no one should ever see. Even she did not inspect some of them.

His gaze softened, as if he had perceived more than he expected. To her horror she saw flickers of confusion, even tentative recognition in his eyes.

"Your condition makes you too bold, sir. I remind you that I am not one of your defendants."

In light of his distress, she tried to strike a note of understanding, even kindness, in the reprimand. Instead she only managed to weaken her voice. She heard it shake, like that of a frightened girl.

It checked him, however. And amused him. Like a jouster long experienced in tilting with his current opponent, he saw the gap in her armor.

He did not back away, but held her attention with a very different gaze. Hard, angry, and decidedly male, it alarmed her more than the last.

"You knew about this afternoon," he said.

"I was aware of it, yes."

"Did you come to gloat?"

"Whatever our differences, I hope that you do not think I would take pleasure in a man's death, or your discomfort."

He had not backed away. She still wanted to, but did not care for what that would imply.

His gaze shifted and meandered, over her bonnet and face, down to her shoulders. "Why are you here?"

The manner in which his gaze lingered and slid had her skin warming. "My meeting—"

"That could have waited."

She really wished he would move back and not hover like this, projecting a dominating, raw power. She silently cursed the way she was reacting, and the evidence that she had become susceptible to him. She had found ways to make sure she was never at such a disadvantage in her life, but those strategies now failed her.

She prayed that he did not know why.

"I will admit that I guessed—that I thought that you would be most distressed today. I thought if I made my call now, it would comf—distract you a little. Help the hour to pass."

"How like you to think that talk of political meetings would ease a man's need."

Well, goodness, that was uncalled for, and close to disgracefully ribald. "Forgive me. It was stupid of me to think you might need company when clearly all you required was that decanter."

"It was not stupid. It was very kind. Quite soft, actually. A very warm, womanly gesture. I am touched." He smiled slowly. "However, if you truly want to help, if you truly want to distract me, there are better ways. When I saw that dress, I dared hope you had realized that."

He reached over and slowly skimmed his fingertips along the low, curved edge of her dress's neckline.

She almost jumped out of her skin, except her skin liked that touch too much to allow movement.

She savored the luring stroke and the memories it evoked for a delicious few moments.

Then she backed away. "You are indeed drunk."

He followed, step for step. "As I warned you. I have an excuse. I am sure we can find one for you too."

That flustered her badly. She was against the wall now, and he blocked any gracious retreat.

His fingertips stroked again. A feathery, delicious skimming sensation. He gazed in her eyes with a confident dare. She tightened her jaw and tensed her body to try and contain the lively tremors streaming through her.

"Mr. Knightridge, you are forgetting yourself."

"Indeed I am, and I thank you most kindly. You have succeeded in thoroughly distracting me from the hell of the hour and my dark thoughts. That was your intention, no? To offer solace?" His hand slid up her skin in a trailing, seductive caress of unbearable titillation. It roamed around her neck until it cupped her nape in a gentle hold.

She did not believe he was thoroughly distracted. His manner bore an edge, a danger, that suggested the darkness not only still lived in him but also drove him.

She tried to shrug his hand off, to no avail. She made to move away from the wall, but with one step he blocked her again.

"What a generous woman you are, Lady M. All this time I thought you were an irritating, argumentative, interfering, opinionated female, but I was wrong."

"It was not my intention to distract you like *this*, for heaven's sake. Get hold of yourself, sir."

"I would rather get hold of a woman. That would be very comforting right now. I assure you, nothing else will suffice." He made a display of looking over each of his shoulders. "I'll be damned, it appears you are the only woman here."

His hand pressed against her neck, easing her forward. Panic and shock broke in her.

"Sir, it is ignoble of you to importune me in this manner. Your inebriation does not excuse it. I *insist* that you move and allow me to leave. I will *not* be—"

The next thing she knew he was kissing her.

How outrageous. How *disastrous*.

How . . . wonderful.